Shock Wave

BOOK 5 OF THE AGENT WARD NOVELS

Kate Mathis

www.KateMathis.net

PowWow Publishing
P.O. 31855
Tucson, AZ 85751-1855 U.S.A.

Printed in the United States of America
First Printing February 2016

Library of Congress Control Number: 2016932255
Mathis, Kate.

Shock Wave - Book Five: An Agent Melanie Ward Novel / Kate Mathis - 1st ed.

1. Female Spy – Fiction. 2. Mystery – Fiction. 3. Thriller Romance – Fiction.
4. Romance Suspense – Fiction. 5. Humor – Fiction. 6. Action & Adventure – Fiction.
7. Melanie Ward – Fiction. 8. Suspense – Fiction. 9. Living Lies – Fiction
10. An Agent Melanie Ward Novel – Fiction 11. Sequel to Chase – Fiction.
12. Espionage – Fiction

ISBN-13: 978-0-9859577-6-6
ISBN-10: 0-9859577-6-X

Book design and composition by PowWow Inc.
www.powwowpublishing.com

Dedicated to:

Laura

I love you.

And to all the other mommies because …for everything.

PROLOGUE

"Let's go! Let's go! Let's go!"

Melanie Ward jumped into the fuselage and banged on the back of the pilot's seat. "Now!" she ordered over the pulsing rush of the helicopter's propellers.

The wild wind whipped through the open door as the landing skids separated from the helipad. The fresh air was bitter cold and spiked into her chest, turning the dull ache razor-sharp. *Come on, come on. Faster!* She commanded, her heart racing as her fist thumped a rapid, nervous beat. Even as they gained altitude, her eyes were trained on the shrinking rooftop door as the gunfire erupted and the short blast detached the steel exit from its hinges.

"Move it!" She yelled, watching a handful of uniformed men swarm the roof. Melanie grabbed hold of a secure strap and reached across the opening to slam shut the cabin door – their call to shoot was in German – and the bullets pinged too close to her head.

"Down!" She hollered over the noise as the pilot accelerated too quickly, sending the nose of the chopper downward. Overcorrecting had them launching vertical, she twisted from the swinging strap, grasping the sides until the pilot recovered control.

Out of bullet range; the rescue had been successful and Melanie pressed the heel of her hand to her left eyebrow, letting the moment of dizziness pass.

"Are you okay?" she asked, her eyes sweeping over the other passenger. He was braced against the wall, small and scared, his chest folded into his shoulder blades and he was naked with only a cloth to cover him. *God,* the single thought was wrapped in layers of complicated prayers. "Here," she remembered, reaching into the box of supplies the doctor had thrown together and retrieved the scrubs she'd grabbed on their rush out.

Their fingers brushed as she handed him the clothing. He was cold, colder than the winter outside and the trembling of his hands stole the air from her lungs.

"Thanks," he mouthed through pale, drawn lips.

Heartbreaking sympathy ran along her iced blood and she was powerless to stop her morbid curiosity, he was frail and lost and immersed in the simple task of pulling on a pair of pants. The overwhelming sense of humanity caught her off guard, striking a chord in her heartstrings that squeezed her throat and induced a welling of tears.

Giving him a moment of privacy, she leaned into the cockpit to speak with the pilot and take a glance at the instrument panel. There was no immediate damage from the bullets and they were flying at max speed through a thin cloud layer.

He was dressed when she returned to the seat beside him. Slipping out of her jacket, she draped it over his shoulders and scooted in close to wrap her arms around his chest.

I can fix this, her thought was laced with doubt and fear. Melanie's breaths were ragged as she sat with her eyes closed, holding on. She knew that from the ground nothing would seem unusual just a black spot of composite material passing through the big, white sky.

No one realized that the world had just changed.

CHAPTER 1

Ex-Agent Melanie Ward lifted her face to the sun's rays and breathed in the stench of exhaust and urine. Free from the clutches of Washington D.C. she grinned and turned her eyes to Adam. He was at her side staring down the hill to the overdeveloped city.

"See that?" she pointed her chin toward the first miles of their journey. "That's our future."

"Babe, we can do much better."

Melanie's grin widened. "Think bigger," she said, searching past the congestion of the army of citizens marching to their daily lives, toward the adventure. "It's the unknown," she whispered. "Can't you smell it?"

"Piss?"

She narrowed her eyes at her assassin-turned-chef boyfriend. "Our second start: A life without complications, just you and me and, for the next month and a half … these beauties." Her palms caressed the handlebars of her brand new road bike. "This is freedom."

"How do you even think of this shit? A three-thousand-mile

ride along the goddamned Andes. Mel? Wasn't torture enough?" He cocked his head and his smile sneaked into place while the corners of his eyes creased with concern. "Was that too soon?"

"It was a lifetime ago," she lied, telling herself that her heart palpitations were from the decreased oxygen of the Peruvian air.

Melanie remembered each conscious moment of her kidnapping with clarity. She'd been taken; confined and starved and in what she believed were her last breaths, she'd been graced with the presence of a tranquil spirit.

But Adam had found her, snatched her from death and given her another chance, a chance to be better.

The experience had left her with a question; *How many lives do you think you have, Agent Ward?* Her answer gave her the strength to find a life beyond the Agency. The bike tour was the hardline, separating her from her eleven years of life as a spy.

She blinked to erase the thoughts and let the image of Adam take their place. Adam: tall, broad shouldered, dark hair hidden beneath a baseball cap and a bike helmet. He'd taken a pass on the spandex pants in favor of a pair of padded, gray, nylon, baggy shorts.

"Are you checking me out, Ward?"

"I'm just feeling very lucky," she sucked in a breath and her heart swelled with the overwhelming gratitude of what she had and what she'd nearly lost.

"I'm the lucky one," he answered, solemnly. "I'd do anything for you." His lips curved upward. "I believe my ass on this bike proves that."

With her left foot on the pedal, she placed her full weight on her right and closed the distance between them. His eyes were on her, x-raying their way beneath her clothing.

"Amigo," the call came from outside their universe, "are we going to have to deal with this the whole trip?"

The parting of their lips was painful but she was in high spirits, looking up at him as he grinned over her shoulder.

"Better get used to it." Adam leaned in for a second round amidst the groans of their fellow riders.

The guide gave a 'let's go' signal and the three others whooped and hollered as they began the journey.

Adam turned away from the celebration. "You do realize next week is Thanksgiving. We could be comfortably overstuffed, watching the game and hanging out with family."

"This is better," she said, quashing the suggestion.

His laugh was a harsh bark. "You've clearly never experienced a real Thanksgiving."

"In my house we gave thanks on Friday ... thankful we'd survived salmonella."

The back of his hand caressed her cheek. "Next year we're giving thanks the right way." He winked and his tone changed. "All right, we've got a lot of ground to cover." He pushed off and twisted to see her. "Coming?"

CHAPTER 2

"Another fucking suicide," the director snarled, muting the television but leaving the flicker of the streaming video to give life to the room. "A congressman drove off a bridge. That makes three."

"Dozens have called and petitioned assistance in the wake of the release of The Circle Society membership. They're worried." Garret Gardner answered, content at the low digit.

"Everyone needs to be patient. We're managing the fallout but there are going to be repercussions, keeping them to a minimum isn't going to be easy when we have elected officials dropping off like flies."

Gardner nodded. "We've been lucky."

"No such thing as luck. Two years working under me should've convinced you of that. But I suppose I should be thankful, when you put weak minded people in office..." the director shut his eyes, leaving his thought unspoken. "But what was that woman thinking? Releasing those documents? She should be tried for treason."

"Actually," Gardner swallowed, plucking up his courage, "I think she'd been pushed too far and since there was no one else to deliver justice to Senator Parker … she did it herself."

"You sound like you agree."

"No." He quickly retreated, under the harsh gaze of his superior.

"Well, exposing the Circle Society was not an answer to anyone's problem. I'd always assumed she was smarter than that. What did she think she was going to accomplish? All she did was ruin her career."

"You're aware of Agent Ward's history with the Parker family. After Finn was killed I'm sure she was expecting relief from the harassment."

"Though Finn was such an inconsequential little man, his assassination was unexpected and for whatever irrational reason, Hugh held her culpable. No, Hugh will never be satisfied with her alive. The man clawed his way to the top by way of secrets and lies and he won't stop. I'm sure he's arranged an ironclad contract with the Devil."

The silence in the room stretched and Gardner waited before continuing. "Ward was on the verge of starvation when she was found."

"I wish she'd remained in that box, it would have saved me a great deal of effort. And who the hell found her? Are we any closer to finding out?"

Gardner shook his head. "The few leads we had turned into dead ends. Best I can ascertain is Ben Jackson hired outside sources, independent of the Agency. He must have had concerns that Senator Parker was involved with Agent Ward's abduction."

"Where's Jackson now?"

"Working to contain the damage and struggling with the Board," Gardner said. He knew every move of the Agency's personnel, without ever having spoken to any one of them. "He looks in poor health, exhausted."

The director dismissed the notion and turned to gaze out the window to the early onset of winter. "And the senator? Where is he?"

"Tucked away at his estate."

"Such an arrogant prick." His mumbled was followed with a sigh. "Go ahead and send in the feds. What about Ward?"

"Gone. Disappeared." Gardner had overlooked the possibility that she'd abandon each of her Agency identities.

"How the hell did she come out of that alive?" he asked, shaking his head at the outside world.

"She's good."

The director kept his back to the room. "And Ben is crafty. I want to know where she is, find her."

"Then what?" he asked, responding to the tingle of concern for her safety.

"She's a wild card, I want to keep tabs on her. I don't need another stunt hitting the Washington shit fan. Our nation can't afford it. It's a fucking zoo out there. Three suicides?" He turned. "What kind of asshole does that? Almost screwed up the entire deal … what more admission of guilt do we need? At least there wasn't any confessional suicide notes."

"Yes, Sir."

CHAPTER 3

Melanie sat with her back to the snakes, the dragons and the masked figures carved into the flat façade of the sixteenth-century Iglesia de San Francisco. Under seventy-degree weather, three weeks before Christmas, La Paz, Bolivia was buzzing with tourist traffic. She and Adam had been eagerly awaiting the first of three respite days from the rigorous bike tour. It was market day and the plaza was laden with hundreds of stalls loaded with goods and under the protection of ratty plastic tarps tied together by knots at the frayed corners.

Melanie soaked up the warm winter sun and tasted the smoke from the grilled meats that permeated the air.

"This is the life," she said to Adam who was sitting on the step beside her.

He was casually leaning back on his elbows and Melanie straightened her legs, relaxing into the lull of the day. Entertained by the flurry of shoppers, she cast a wide gaze over the activity. Her eyes stumbled and the familiar instinct of caution lightly grazed over her spine. Moving upright she expelled the last liter of air from her lungs as the prickles skimmed over her arms, igniting the fine hairs to attention.

Okay, she purred through the abrupt rush of excitement that had her pitching forward, narrowing her focus and attempting to pinpoint the source of the pull on her intuition.

"Come out, come out, whoever you are." Her voice was a low hum, luring her mark to show himself.

Probing with her eyes to see beyond the obvious, her gaze locked onto a couple wearing straw hats. *Who are you and what are you doing?* Keeping the marks in view she continued her search.

"What's at the bottom of this cup?" Adam asked, swirling the ring of caramelized residue.

His deep voice suspended her hunt. "Sludge," she answered, distracted, her sights on ... *the target. Edward Brooks.* Her mind raced and her attention slipped back to the couple tracking ... *no*, she noticed a third person ... the *people* tracking Edward Brooks.

"Adam," her voice cracked, "I'm going to need your help." Not looking away from the plaza, she felt his gaze as he agreed without a shred of information. Her heartbeat quickened, loving him just a tiny bit more. "See the man with the round glasses and green turtleneck?" He did. "Edward Brooks. Three summers ago he vanished from his job with the CIA and took hard drives along with him." It wasn't the full story but ... her eyes shifted to the people trailing Brooks. "He's about to be trapped."

"By you?"

Two seconds ticked before she laughed and took the risk of swiveling her eyes toward him. He hadn't adjusted his casual position on the steps and Melanie slid closer to set her shoulder against his.

"No. I want to keep him out of the hands of the man in the red and yellow stripes and the couple with the Panama hats."

"Is there a plan?"

What she had wasn't organized enough to be considered a plan. "I'll create a distraction while you get him out of the plaza. I want to find out who they are before I deal with Brooks."

"We passed a cemetery on our way here," Adam informed, "about 2 kilometers north-west. I'll take him there. The problem," a wisp of his breath tickled her ear, "will be getting him to go with me *willingly*." She glanced up. Adam's brows were knitted and the pleats at the corner of his eyes deepened. "I'll figure it out and meet you within the crypts."

"Thank you." Inhaling expanded her chest and she held the moment to admire him. "Damn, you are handsome." Adam's baritone laugh added to her stimulation. His kiss was quick, an unsatisfying scratch at the edge of her appetite. "How long has it been since I've shown you how much I love you?"

"Awhile," he admitted with a shaky breath. "Not your fault. I blame the nylon walls of the tent and the air mattress. But tonight..." his mischievous grin stretched beneath a layer of rough beard, "we're in a hotel."

Melanie digested a lungful of atmosphere. "I think I'm available."

"I promise," he winked, "it'll be worth the wait."

"You better go before Brooks becomes secondary."

"I'm glad I haven't lost my effect on you," his laugh faded and the intensity in his emerald eyes cooled. "I wish you had a phone."

"This is supposed to be a tech-free experience," she reminded him. "No outside world interference."

"I'll remember that, if you will."

"Good point." She didn't let the kiss linger before she was on her feet, slipping into the lively market.

The booths were tightly packed, brimming with eager sellers bellowing their best lines as Melanie negotiated the aisles. She looped around back to Brooks, who sat at a table with a cup of coffee and a paper just beyond the shelter of the plastic shade. Admiring the canopy of red and blue tarps tethered to aluminum posts in a rudimentary form of a highwayman's hitch, she had an idea.

The folding chair cracked under her weight as she reached for the corner knot that secured the tarp to the post. With one swift yank, the plastic sheet was sent sailing, ripping across two rows of carts before slackening and fluttering to the ground.

Tourists screamed and scattered, rushing out to open sky while the locals kept their heads and aimed to fix the roofing. By the time the dilemma was resolved, Brooks was gone. But she'd also lost the trio tracking him. Circling the market, ignoring the catcalls and the hands that grabbed at her sleeves, she searched.

It was the brim of his hat that she spotted first, disappearing into a stall of handmade leather shoes. Melanie shopped the dyed footwear, maintaining her position at the narrow shaft of an entrance and listened beyond the outer layer of merchandise.

Her mind raced to unscramble the language ... Arabic? She was still holding a huarache when the trio exited the shop. Tempering her speed to avoid triggering suspicion, she trailed them to a hotel. Followed them to their room, paced the pattern of the tile under her feet and calculated the chances of achieving a positive outcome. Limited options and zero support had her heading to the cemetery.

Edward Brooks had lost his round glasses, was sporting a misspelled Yankees ball cap and swimming in Adam's black windbreaker. The deeply etched avenues along his forehead and around his eyes should have been reserved for a much older man.

"I got you a hat, too." Adam smiled and offered her a blue Red Socks cap. "There's an angel headstone," he pointed, "out of the way."

"Who are you?" Brooks asked, lifting his hand in a salute to shade his eyes. "Bounty hunters? What's my going rate?"

Melanie kept moving through the wedged tombstones. "What are you doing in Bolivia?"

"Learning Spanish."

Edward Dean Brooks had been a junior analyst at the CIA when his five-year-old daughter was kidnapped. The ransom was a flash drive of documents.

"How's your daughter?"

"Safe," he replied through gritted teeth. "Still having nightmares."

"I'm sorry."

"What are you going to do with me?"

"Right now there are three Arabs ready to apprehend you." Brooks gave her a once over and started to walk. "Where do you think you're going?"

"I've survived scarier than you." He freed his shoulder from her grasp.

"I'm not trying to scare you, I'm trying to keep you alive."

"Is that what you tell yourself?" The five fingers of his right hand were on her chest, pushing her away.

"Listen, asshole," Melanie stepped into the shove, "you'd be answering questions under a lamplight if we weren't here." She held out her open hand. "I'm going to make a call … I need your phone."

"Are you kidding me?" He tilted his head at her and glared.

Adam's brows raised in a one-syllable question, *Ben?* "Speed dial," he said, smirking and handing her his phone. The call went straight to voicemail. She hung up without leaving a message. "There's an American embassy," Adam started.

"Turn myself in? Now you really are kidding. What kind of loser bounty hunters are you?" Brooks took off his cap, ran his fingers through his hair. "I gave you a shot, you almost sounded sincere but you don't know shit. You have no idea what I'm worth or what I can do. I'm taking off."

"How long can you keep running? If the *Arabs* can find you, others are closing in. *Others* who are more vicious, willing to go to extreme measures to get to you."

"Bullshit." He returned his glasses to the bridge of his nose. "What you think you know isn't the truth. You're a tool, manipulated and used just like all the rest. You don't know jack."

"You had an obligation," Melanie continued, "to maintain secrets. An obligation you took freely when you cashed those CIA payroll checks."

"That's what they want you to believe. What I did is choose to save my daughter, my flesh and blood. And I'd do it again." He said, in a mild tone almost to the point of bored. "You only know what you're told, what they want you to know, what they want you to think. And what do you do? Obediently, you believe." Brooks paused. "Think about where you get your information. Who's controlling you? Who's your master? I did what I had to do. And I have no guilt about it."

"We should keep moving," Adam said, with a pull at her elbow.

The cemetery was a maze; miles of vaults stacked four levels high that held cremated remains behind glass windows. It was the practice; interred bodies exhumed after ten years, cremated and placed within the lengthy towers. Loved ones left flowers and mementos for the departed.

"I just want to go home. I don't have any money." He slowed his step. "I can't pay you much – but maybe a trade?"

"What do you have?" Melanie asked, curious.

"I know you don't care that I'm not a bad guy but I didn't ask for any of this," he said. "I have other flash drives. Insurance. My freedom for one of the drives."

"Edward, I can't let you wander about to be caught." *Especially with flash drives.* "It isn't safe for anyone." She redialed Ben, as she walked with a silent invocation for him to pick up his damn phone. Voicemail. Concentrating was causing her brain to swell, pressing against her skull. "What's on the flash drives?"

"Do we have a deal?"

Melanie caught Brooks by the neck, slamming him against the wall. "Maybe you're smart, maybe you've gotten lucky. Either way," she pushed harder and stepped closer, "you're a danger. What is on the fucking drives?"

"Same kind of stuff, account numbers, really, nothing vital." He squirmed and Melanie released his throat, not believing a word. Lifting the phone to her ear, she waited for a live voice.

"Jack," she spoke, relieved to hear the familiar voice of Agent Jack Scott. "Remember Edward Brooks? Well, he's in Bolivia. La Paz Cemetery. I can't hold him."

"Jesus, Melanie, I don't need this right now."

"Too bad because it's in your lap. Where's Ben?"

"How should I know? Edward Brooks? Great. Thanks."

"Consider it an early Christmas present."

He sighed. "Where?"

"You okay?" she asked, grabbing Brooks' wallet from his back pocket.

"Wonderful. Just give me the address." She read off the information on Brooks' ID. "Sorry we can't catch up but I've got phone calls to make."

"You're welcome," she said into the dead air and looked at Brooks. "Agents are on their way so if you're going to run, you'd better run fast. But Brooks," she sighed, "maybe it's time to turn yourself in."

He nodded and ran ten feet before he turned back. "Don't believe everything you think, Bounty Hunter."

Brooks disappeared. Melanie stood in the middle of the cemetery and tried to breathe. She'd let a wanted man escape. Her internal battle raged and Adam's thumb crossed her forehead, smoothing out the worry lines.

"It's going to be all right."

"I hate this," she said, the feeling of helpless rising up from her toes. "This is not how I do things. I'm here, powerless. And what about Ben? I would understand if he ignored an unknown number, but calls from *you*?" Walking faster didn't alleviate the pinch in her gut. "I feel bad about capturing Brooks, about the conversation with Jack, about Ben." She looked to her side – she was alone. Adam was waiting yards behind.

"Mel," he said, taking a step forward.

"What am I going to do?" she asked, as her legs shook under her personal earthquake. "Who am I? If I'm not an agent, who am I? I just let Edward Brooks walk." Melanie stared up at him, her throat too dry to swallow.

"I'm sorry. I don't know what to say, but you have choices. You can go back or not but whatever you decide, it's going to be okay."

She nodded, exhaling slowly as her eyes never left his. "Okay," she stepped away, inhaling. "Moment of panic is over. I'm better."

"Want to get a drink?"

"There's a three drink minimum for how I'm feeling."

"Not too drunk." His eyes narrowed and she caught the tail end of his smile as it melted into a Grinch Grin.

She shivered under the heat of her blush that scorched the edges of her regret and for the brief moment desire dominated her insides as Adam signaled a cab.

"You did what you could," he said ten minutes into their silent ride to the hotel.

"Just didn't feel right," she answered, the bad vibe returning to infect her core. "I couldn't stop myself from pursuing him and then," she sighed, "when we had him ... I had to let him go!" The driver pulled to the curb of their hotel. Adam paid the man and her anger faded into frustration. "And Jack! What was with him?"

"Baby," they stood on the sidewalk, "I love that you're energetic and dedicated and I can't wait until I'm the focus of all that energy."

It took a moment for her to understand; his hands on her hips helped and his green eyes held promises that only he could deliver. "I'm sorry I'm so scattered. I'm having a bit of an identity crisis but if you're patient" – his lips were masters of distraction – "I can do that, give you my undivided attention."

"They're at it again." The laughing taunts were from their tour mates. "Get a crowbar."

"No, a hose!"

Melanie's body slackened against Adam's. "They're not going to stop hassling us."

"Is there a surgeon in the house?"

"Enough," she laughed. Weeks on the road, dinners at campfires and early mornings of bad coffee had bonded the group.

"We're going for dinner. Come with," the youngest of the riders invited. "We're testing the limits of our stomachs with street food."

"I *am* hungry," Melanie said, "but..." Her teeth tugged on the inside of her cheek in anticipation of Adam's touch. It'd been days since they'd been comfortable enough and awake enough and he looked really good ... Her imagination had him undressed.

She felt him reading her mind.

"We are going to need to keep up our stamina..." *then we've got things to do,* his look finished the sentence.

The group crossed to the vendors and indulged in ispi, a small fried fish and grilled beef hearts served on a skewer. She was still eating when they wandered into a dingy bar with stylishly dressed patrons. The techno music was loud and every twenty minutes the bar hopping crowd rotated.

They were two drinks in, when Adam cocked his eyebrows toward the door and laid out a few bills to cover the tab. "Baby."

"You can't leave now," the young man protested. "We're going to follow the White Hare."

Adam's fingers, already laced with hers, clamped. "No. That's not a good idea."

"What's the White Hare?" Melanie asked, intrigued by his reaction but his lips were sealed and his jaw was tight.

"I met a couple of guys at a smoke shop. They said the white rabbit was the only way to party." The bicyclist grinned, high-fived his friends and jumped to his feet. "Dude, there they are. They said we could hang with them for a night we'll never forget! Come on, it's part of the adventure. Right, Pops?" He slapped Adam on the shoulder and rushed out the door.

"Damn it." Adam blew out an embittered sigh.

"I take it we're following the hare?" Melanie asked, interested.

"Fuck," he growled. "This is *not* how I wanted to spend the evening." His eyes grazed over her, down her blouse. "The White Rabbit leaves clues for drunken idiots. It's a hunt for the ever-changing location of Route 36."

"Cryptic." The wind had turned cold and she pulled her sweater tighter across her chest as they clung to the end of the drunken idiot quest. "What is Route 36?"

"Cocaine bar."

"I see," she said, giving her time to interpret the implications.

"I lived in Bolivia for awhile," Adam answered as they followed the troupe. "South America was my territory."

"Not Mexico?"

"I did time in both."

"You trafficked drugs?"

"Guns. The drugs were a perk." He looked down at her with repentance, "a hobby."

"You don't have to keep confessing this to me. I already know about your past."

Adam angled his head to watch the group as emotion crossed his face. She pretended she couldn't read it but his meaning was clear … *You don't know everything*.

"They are idiots." Melanie said, after six wrong turns that eventually led them to a forgotten part of the city. The area was sordid and empty, with rusted cars curbside, hoods up and parts missing. They'd reached a building with bars on the windows and a steroid-enhanced bouncer in the doorway.

"That's it," Adam sighed. "I had hopes they were too stupid to find it."

"Really?" Melanie questioned, scoping the landscape that didn't look like much. A guard in front of the heavy wooden door, the chipped Coca-Cola ads peeling from the neighboring boarded-up buildings with two-foot high weeds growing from the cracks in the sidewalk.

Adam held her back.

"What's going on?"

"Ghost location ... checking for police. Cocaine is still illegal. They don't want to flaunt the abuse." Though Morales, the president of Bolivia, was the head of the coca growers union. He pushed for the coca leaf to be removed from the list of internationally banned drugs and he had tossed DEA agents from his borders. "So they go through the motions of secrecy."

The boys trekked a half block to another gateway. Adam's index finger and thumb wrapped around her wrist, leading her inside a dark, unembellished corpse of a room. The tables and chairs were foldouts and the only light came from dozens of candles flickering to the pulse of the trance music. The glowing ambiance cast menacing shadows on the cinderblock walls and she counted six different languages as they followed their group to a table.

"So, this is a cocaine bar. It's a first for me."

The escort handed out menus, with costs ranging from high quality to regular. Adam led her to observe from a dark corner.

"Can I help you, friend?" The man appeared at Adam's side.

"Thank you, no. Designated driver," Adam answered coolly with a tilt of his head. "Is Tortuga still running this place?"

The security guard in a sleek suit took a careful look at Adam. "Not for years. Enrique."

"Really?" Adam's response was filled with amazement. "But he's such an asshole."

"I know," the guard mumbled. "Who are you?"

"An acquaintance."

"I'll send the good stuff to your table with a couple of lines, on the house."

"Keep it."

"What about you, Gorgeous?"

"No, thanks," Melanie declined.

"A virgin? I can see it in your eyes. You don't know what you're missing."

"Take a hike." Adam's snarl was a low and potent warning.

"I can't let you linger, I've got a business to run."

Adam slipped bills off the top and dropped them into the man's palm. A quick nod and he disappeared into the back room.

"Hard to admit, and harder to believe, that this was my world." He didn't look at her, but scrutinized the room from the corner of his eyes. "I did this." He looked out over the room, incredulously. "Though," his chest lifted, "I remember it to be much more pleasant."

She watched the strange collection of travelers snort the powder off mirrored trays through cut straws.

Adam looked over at her, his jawline linear as he clenched his teeth. "Being here, this place, brings back memories."

"Are you tempted?" she asked, her eyes holding steadfast to his.

"By the drugs," his face lost its hard marble form, "no."

"Then what?"

"I had power, Mel."

Melanie scooted in, dipped her shoulder under his arm and held his too-warm hand. "We have everything we need."

"You're right," he said, squeezing her until she could feel his heartbeat through their clothing. "All I need is you, Melanie," he swallowed hard but his fingers were gentle on her cheek. He lifted her face until they were inches apart. His eyes were glassy as he stared down at her. “You’re all I’ve ever needed.”

CHAPTER 4

"That didn't go as well as I'd hoped," Agent Ben Jackson grumbled, setting the phone on the cradle and rising to his feet, knuckles pressed on the desk.

"Now what?" Jack asked.

Ben studied Jack, missing Ward. "As soon as I solve one issue another is spawned." He raked his unruly, overgrown hair off his forehead. "The media has been handled and I believe the impact from the Circle Society has cooled. But now the Board is balking at..."

"Maybe you should get some rest," Jack interrupted, his brows pinched so they were nearly touching. "I can handle the Board."

"I'm afraid not. It goes deeper than you're imagining." Agitated, Ben wrenched his glasses off his face. Rubbing his burning eyes only alleviated the pain for a moment. "Damn it!" He fidgeted. "I need to take the edge off, what about you?" he asked, in need of a fair dose of scotch. "Damn." His foul mood encouraged at the sight of the drained crystal decanter, and swelled as he bent to find the spare bottle hadn't yet been replaced. "Judith!" he bellowed. *Now this toothache,* he swore massaging his jaw at the spot that had begun to throb. "Oh, never mind," he barked remembering that the best liquor was only a few doors away. "I'll be right back," he snapped, palming a couple of paperclips and heading to Hugh Parker's forsaken office.

The room had been vacant for months, first with Parker's stroke and then by his arrest for corruption. Yet Ben was greeted by the sharp scent of a spicy cigar. He flicked on the lights, the liquor cabinet was at the back of the room within arm's reach of Hugh's desk.

Hugh's desk. Ben's anger deflated, replaced by nostalgia. His fingers ran shallow trails through the dust on the mahogany. Hugh had commissioned an exact replica of Theodore Roosevelt's presidential desk. He'd spent a small fortune on the piece, which was repaid in bragging rights. Ben walked around the colonial-style pulpit, pulled back the accompanying chair and sat. The rich surface still held Hugh's papers as if he'd simply stepped away and was expected at any moment.

Ben allowed the sensations of regret and disappointment to penetrate. His fingers splayed over the desktop, feeling the unfinished tasks. The scent was distorting his emotions, blinking to clear the cobwebs, Ben sighed and accepted the unfortunate events. He returned from the past with a dry throat and received the calling from the eighteen-year-old scotch behind the cabinet doors.

Pushing to his feet his eyes caught on the paperwork beneath his hands. From under an index finger, Melanie Ward stared up at him. It was her Agency photo with hand-scrawled adjustments; The fangs and the black eye were disturbing, but it was the bullet hole in her forehead that caused sweat to break out along his hairline.

Picking up the phone he dialed.

"Hello Mr. Jackson," Mike answered with trepidation in his voice.

"What can I do for you, Sir?"

"Locate Melanie Ward."

CHAPTER 5

By noon on the forty-third day of riding, sleeping inches off the ground and eating out of tinware, the pink hotel was a symbol of luxury and accomplishment. Their journey's end. The group had made it to the tip of Argentina two days early. Ushuaia was a small town on a big, wide, icy bay and a view not to be forgotten.

Returning her bike was bittersweet. Melanie was going to miss the open road, even the blisters and flat tires didn't seem so bad … she inhaled … but it was the connection with Adam that meant the most. Racing down the long strips of asphalt, reaching out and brushing fingertips, sleeping within the tight confines of the bag, inside his warm embrace and their constant togetherness.

And now she was going to have to share him with the rest of the world. She extended her arm and her let fingertips brush lightly along the grain of his full beard.

"You want me to shave?"

"No." She approved of the look. "I like it. I like you. I may not tell you enough."

"Mel?"

"Let's walk." She pressed their palms together against the cold.

They strolled the picturesque boardwalk, the waves lapping up on the rocky embankment. Bundled in layers and under wool caps they blended with the other tourists visiting the glaciers.

"Hard to believe the trip is over," Melanie said, zipping her fleece jacket under her windbreaker and pulling them both to her chin. "My legs were ready to get off the bike but walking feels strange, like I've got wheel legs."

"I was worried at the start. Your body has gone through so much." He stared deep into her eyes. "I'm so proud of you. And to be here, it's beautiful, but those glaciers aren't a tenth as stunning as you."

"Then you haven't taken a good look, because they are magnificent."

"Want to get closer?" he asked, opening his wallet.

"Always." She grinned.

The ice mountain at the tip of South America had jagged tops and towered 200 feet above the Atlantic. Melanie craned her neck to see the top as they paddled the orange, rented kayak through crystalline blue-green water that reflected a dual image of the majestic glacier.

Dipping her fingers into the smooth water, she broke the glass surface and ignited sparks of golden sunlight that danced across the sea.

"It's like an unsullied Las Vegas," Melanie murmured, mesmerized by the spectacular marquee.

Adam's laugh carried over the calm sea. "That's not exactly what I was thinking."

They glided as close as they dared to the base of the glacier that threatened to release bus-sized chunks into the water, then paddled into a cavity in the side of the mountain. Navigating their kayak through the narrowing ice canal that led them through an opening – into an enormous cavern illuminated blue by light penetrating from under the shallow walls. The sight of the bright world froze the breath in her lungs.

The kayak bobbed in the middle of a deep, glowing pool of color. It was as glorious as any European Cathedral. The sculpted walls and a stalactite ceiling had been divinely carved by weather and the passage of time.

Water dripped, causing ripples. Melanie gazed until the beauty became almost painful. Paddling out, they moored their kayaks on a gravely shore beside the others. With the help of crampons on their boots and a knotted rope, they ascended the sloping side of the glacier.

At the peak, the icy wind whipped, knocking Melanie's hood off her head and pressing her clothing to her body. She opened her arms to the gale and leaned forward letting the force of nature hold her upright.

Every direction was breathtaking.

"Amazing," Adam sighed, surprising her with his presence.

Seeing him at the summit of a mountain built from hundreds of billions of individual snowflakes over two million years was worth every bit of the journey.

Borrowing Adam's phone, she tried to capture snapshots of memories.

"Smile." She lifted the camera and tiptoed to press her cheek to his.

"I'm going to love you forever," he whispered. She sucked in a ragged breath before snapping, preserving the sentiment behind a pair of grins.

Her eyes glistened, her heart hammered and the heat from their kiss left a crater in the ice. In the photo, the sky at the horizon had darkened while directly above was pale gray.

Her forehead constricted as she calculated the cumulating clouds and length of time to reach the kayaks and paddle back to the Jeeps.

"We'd better get out of here." Adam was the first to speak, grabbing her hand and leading them to the base with the other tourists.

Ankle deep in icy water, guides hustled day-trippers into the two-person kayaks. Shouts to move quickly rose above the gusty canyon. Melanie and Adam assisted the naturalists getting everyone safely in their boats, tugging them through the choppy waters of the narrow strip.

They'd just crossed the inlet when the storm hit, fat drops of rain soaking them as they loaded the boats onto a trailer rack. By the last kayak Adam had taken off his jacket, holding it up to shield Melanie from the thrashing sleet that pelted their clothing.

Piling into the dry vehicles, Melanie shivered while tires tore rivets into the mud and the wipers squawked furiously against the windshield. The heater blasted and she gripped the roll bar to keep from banging her head against the side. The roads were deserted as they rolled into town and were discarded at the front doors of the pink hotel.

She was pushing the water from her face and her soggy boots hadn't yet crossed the threshold when she spotted Logan Holland seated comfortably beside the fireplace in the foyer.

"Give me a minute," she whispered to Adam, shuddering from the warmth and draping her coat onto the hook over the rubber mat.

Melanie dragged her fingers through her matted hair and headed toward the agent. Logan's blonde hair was pulled into a thick ponytail. And if Melanie could ignore the etching of concern in her features and her foot beating a rapid rhythm into the area rug, she'd have been happy to see her.

"Boss." Logan's eyes sparkled as she leaped up, her arms encircling Melanie in a tight hug.

"What are you doing way down here?" Melanie asked, her hand pressed to the girl's spine.

"God, it's good to see you, but..." Her chest collapsed in a sigh of relief. "You're freezing. Let's move by the fire."

"We got caught," she said, noticing Logan peering over Melanie's shoulder, "in the storm."

"Is that the boyfriend?" Logan scowled through her curiosity. Melanie was smiling as she ran her eyes over 'the boyfriend', *definitely gorgeous*, rough and rugged and soaking wet. "He's cute, really cute, but cute enough to leave the Agency? Tell me it's only rumors."

"You didn't answer my question. What are you doing here?"

"Ever hear of a man," Logan said in a conspiratorial hush, "who goes by the name of Ben Jackson?" She laughed and Melanie's shoulders dropped. "Well, I've been instructed to hand this to you. Directly."

In Logan's open palm was a cell phone.

"You trekked to the tip of Argentina to give me a phone?" Melanie mused. "Seriously, it's a two-day flight."

"And charger," Logan added, reaching into her pocket.

Melanie took both, knowing Logan would be tormented if she declined. "Tell him I said thank you." *He doesn't answer my calls but he can send a phone?*

"Ha! And they said I was going to have to resort to *measures*." Air quotes wrapped the word.

"I guess he doesn't know me as well as he thinks." Melanie smiled, stripping off another layer of clothing and rubbing her hands near the flames.

"Tell me you *are* coming back." Logan's wide eyes lost their sparkle. Melanie held contact as expectations faded. "That's what the cell phone is about, right?"

"I have no idea what that man has planned."

"Please, Boss." Her words were only air between them. "Is it because of *him*?" she accused, her eyes darting toward Adam. "It sucks. I mean, it really sucks. You're the best. You belong with us. Nothing is the same without you, it's chaotic." Her forehead was creased and her eyes shot lasers at Adam. "Do you even know what's going on?"

"More rumors, Logan?"

"No." She tilted her head left, then right. "Yeah, but I see it for myself. Something big is going on and it's bad."

"Big and bad? Those are always coming. It's the nature of the job."

"Maybe, but don't you miss it?"

Melanie answered with a single nod.

"I can't imagine you anywhere else. You. Are. So. Good. Inspirational. Please."

"Nice try."

"I mean it. Agent Scott is always behind closed doors and when he does come out he looks terrible. There haven't been any new assignments in days and..."

"Don't tell me," Melanie raised her palms.

"Change your mind." Logan was dogged, clinging to Melanie's

arm. “There’re a million cute boys in the world, but only one Agency.” Melanie laughed. “Was it because you were tortured?”

“Logan,” Melanie cut her off. She didn’t want to have this conversation here or anywhere. “Let it go.”

“I, I had to find out for myself.” The corners of her mouth tightened. “Directly from you.”

“When did you see Ben?”

“I didn’t. Judith called and she gave me his instructions. I got the phone from Mike.”

“Mike,” Melanie said wistfully.

“Just, whatever Mr. Jackson offers you,” her hand tightened on Melanie’s forearm, “promise me you’ll consider it.”

Melanie looked at the cell phone in her hand. Troubled, she conceded to the promise. “But don’t get your hopes up. This could mean anything. I doubt he’s asking me back.” Melanie changed the subject. “Want to meet Adam?”

“Not particularly.” Her weight shifted to her right foot.

“Come on. You’ll like him.”

“Doubt it.”

CHAPTER 6

"Please." Ben pleaded, switching from the failed tactic of the dictatorial hammer he'd tried over the last four weeks. Now his face-to-face meeting with the remaining members of the Agency's Board of Executives was pushing him further from his goal of keeping the agency in operation. "You cannot mean that." Ben swallowed to evict the lump that had caught at the base of his throat. His blood rushed and his pupils pulsed as he stared into apathetic eyes of the healthiest member of the Agency's governing body.

"But we do." Richard said, the old man who'd never had much of a voice in the operations of the Agency, was now the spokesman.

Ben looked to the other three members who were well enough to make the journey to the office. *How had this happened so quickly?* He marveled in appalled amazement at their rapid deterioration.

"How can this be?" Ben said, partially to himself. "There are only five of us here ... that's not a majority vote. We have to wait..."

"Wait for what? We are not getting any younger or healthier, the Agency has served its purpose and its time has come to an end. You know that," the man added, sliding a sheet of paper across the table toward Ben. "Your requisition to establish a subdivision. You wanted to enlist Ward as a sort of Agency Special Forces unit. Yes, we know about that."

"Yes, but..." Ben started to object but the man raised his shaky hand to stop the noise.

One of the others spoke. "If you had better control over your agents we may have been able to avoid this conversation. Agent Ward should've been dealt with years ago."

"The spread of information regarding the Circle Society has been managed." Ben clenched his teeth. "The repercussions were kept to a minimum and the fallout that did occur was used to our favor. But we've veered off topic. We cannot close the Agency."

"I never liked her."

"The Agency is a vital organization. We have agents worldwide, imbedded. To forget that is..."

"Throwing the baby out with the bathwater?" responded the spokesman and the most friendly of the wrinkled faces.

"Exactly." Ben breathed and pointed to the sheet of paper. "This adjunct was meant to broaden our spectrum, not replace it!"

"Ben," the droop in his eyes softened, "the Board is an assembly of old men. We were stubborn, egotistical and we thought we were invincible. We've enjoyed a substantial amount of power and now we're unable to function with no one to replace us. One man does not form a Board of Executives. I am sorry. Your agents..."

"Our agents," Ben interrupted to correct.

"*Our agents* will find new homes."

The third man added, "including you."

"But..."

"The Agency as we know it no longer exists."

"But we are still necessary." Ben tried.

The old man motioned for his nurse. "What is done cannot be undone."

"But..." Ben's vision clouded. His heart felt enlarged and he exhaled in heavy bursts. Adjusting his position, sitting farther back to alleviate the tension in his back, helped slightly. He clamped his fingers to the edge of the table, holding on until the pressure inside his chest subsided. Ben watched the Board members with their walkers and wheelchairs be escorted out of the room.

Richard dragged his oxygen tank to the door, then turned to view Ben from the corner of his eye. "You did your best. As for Agent Ward ... this step was inevitable. She just accelerated the process. She was a fine agent and what Hugh did, well ... I suppose we're all guilty in some respects. Goodbye and good luck, Ben."

"I'm not going to stop," he coughed.

Richard's eyes became slivers and he muttered inaudibly before following his colleagues.

Ben heaved himself to the doorway, extinguished the light that was sending skewers through his eyeballs and retook his seat. He sat in despair. The malaise he'd been banning was coming full force in the form of a migraine. He was feeling lightheaded and his breathing was shallow and unsatisfying. Ben rubbed his chest and attempted to calm his state of mind.

In the dark, alone – the sharp, stabbing pain in his chest knocked him out of his seat. His head cracked the side of the table just before his cheek hit the carpeting.

CHAPTER 7

The 'Storm of the Century' had left the southern states under six feet of snow causing an airline nightmare. Hundreds of diverted flights left thousands stranded, including Melanie and Adam. Their connection into Atlanta was redirected to Knoxville, where the airport had seemingly expanded into the hostelry trade. Holiday travelers waited for skies to clear, closed airports to reopen and canceled flights to be reinstated. Camping from carry-on baggage, passengers dozed against the walls and took turns plugging in their phones into the too few electrical outlets.

Adam left Melanie, giving her time to check out Ben's gift. Still no calls, no messages ... nothing. She called home to tell them she wouldn't be home for Christmas and forty minutes later Adam was dropping their backpacks in the back of a silver Prius.

"How'd you get a car?"

"Don't ask," he said.

She didn't. It took a few minutes before she lowered the volume on the radio. "Just so you know, your uncle doesn't like me."

"He doesn't like many people. But why you in particular?"

"Thinks I'm a stalker."

"Were you stalking?"

She drew her lip between her teeth and narrowed her eyes. "What did he tell you?"

Adam's laugh was light and mocking. "Just that a woman had followed me to the farm. He might've called her a falconer. He didn't mention a name but he did say that she was a pretty brunette and Becca had fallen for her. I can't be sure he was talking about you."

"Great." Melanie sighed. "What's a falconer?"

"Has to do with being a huntress."

"God, that's embarrassing." She groaned but continued, "I snooped around at your high school, too." He gave her the slightest of sideways glances. "You may not remember her but your classmate, Gloria, she works in the office now. She let me thumb through your senior yearbook." Melanie dropped her face into her hands and laughed. "*I really am a falconer*."

"I wouldn't have it any other way." He reached over and pulled her hand into his.

"Where are we going?" she asked as he exited the freeway.

"It's Christmas and we're visiting family."

The parking lot of the sprawling mall was swollen with automobiles. Adam cruised the outer rim, waited and finally replaced an exiting family van with the rental.

"Mel," he said, adjusting in the seat to face her. "I don't want you to feel bad."

"I don't," she said, too quickly. "Well, maybe a little bit, I did sort of pursue you in an obsessive manner." Melanie mixed a grimace with a smile.

"Days. I've spent days watching your building," he shrugged. "Hanging onto a possibility that I'd catch a glimpse of you. I saw you a few times and it hurt – to be so close and not be able to talk to you. It was painful knowing that I'd lost you. But the next day, I'd find myself right back on that bench, waiting. I broke into your apartment and laid on your bed just to be closer to you. I could smell your shampoo on the pillowcase. I missed you to the edge of insanity." He angled his head so his eyes were cast down at her legs.

"Adam."

"I'm guilty of stalking, too. I vowed," he lifted his gaze slightly, "that when I got you back I'd never let you go."

"I can't believe you were so sure that I'd..."

"I wasn't." The hint of a smile played on his perfect lips. "But I was hopeful and determined."

"Why are you telling me this?"

"Uncle Rob is rough around the edges but that's only because he's got a huge, gentle heart to protect. He doesn't have a bad feeling about you." His eyes steadied and his grin was gradual, "At least, not anymore."

"Great," she shook her head.

"So, in that yearbook," his smile had settled. "What'd you think?"

"About?"

"Would you have gone out with him?"

His question sounded sincere. "*He* wouldn't have noticed me," Melanie answered, truthfully, knowing Adam had seen her high school pictures.

"Are you kidding?" He stopped, his glinting eyes widening to expose the deep green irises. "Melanie Ward," he began, the lecture softening. "I would've loved you no matter when or where we met."

He held her gaze. "If it had been in the nursery, I'd have shared my bottle. Or on the playground, I would've pushed your swing. You didn't steal my heart and I didn't give it to you ... you were born with it. I loved you before I'd ever laid eyes on you." She didn't move. "I love you. Do you know what that means?" She couldn't think. "It means I belong to you ... forever."

Her body pooled, melted to slush, with only a heartbeat to prove she was still alive. "I," she stammered, freed from the cyclone of his emerald eyes. "I *was* a cute baby," she managed. "But in high school ... not so much. Unremarkably average." The grimace echoed her thoughts.

"Did you not hear anything I said?" he questioned, shaking her arm. "We were meant to be together, through time or space. Mel, you would've been mine. Sweetheart, I love you because you're in me and I'm in you."

"Adam." Her voice vaporized in the encroaching chill. "When did you become a romantic?"

"When I met you. Never before. Now tell me, would you have given me a second glance?"

She tasted the coffee as she sucked her bottom lip. "Yes. I would've loved cocky, handsome, immature high school you."

"I was those things but you would've loved me because..." he held the last syllable in a higher tone expecting her to finish.

"Because," her pent up nerves had transformed to a chuckle, "our love transcends time and space."

His playfulness ended abruptly and a dark cloud passed through his gaze. "It's getting cold. We should get the gifts and head over to Rob's."

"Wait," Melanie said, jumping out of the car to mimic his movements. "What just happened? You shut me out of some thought."

"I didn't shut you out," he said, taking her hand.

"Then tell me." She stopped his progress.

He pulled in a breath. "Okay, I wondered if I'd met you in high school … if you'd have been in that car, if I would have found your body on the road."

She'd seen photos from the newspaper. The accident had killed five teenagers on their way to an after prom party. Adam had been first on the scene, hearing the crash and racing to his friends. Melanie couldn't even imagine the horror. He'd suffered from survivor's guilt and the experience had dismantled his future.

"I wouldn't have been in that car. We would've danced all night and you would've walked me to my door and kissed me goodnight. No hotel. No drinking. Just dancing." She placed a peck on the corner of his mouth. "I was a good girl, remember? *Am*. I *am* a good girl."

His smile returned and his eyes smoldered. "You wouldn't have slept with me?" There was a challenge to his words. "I've always been persuasive." He laced their fingers and kissed the back of her hand, looking a notch above satisfied. "Now," he glanced over her head, "we've got shopping to do. What should we get everyone?"

"I don't know them," Melanie said and was given the rundown as they dodged the distracted drivers outside and the crazed shoppers inside. There were three female cousins, Rob and Becca, and two nephews who were spending the holiday with their father. "How about I get the wine?" she offered.

"Twenty minutes." His lips were firm on her cheek. "Right here."

Disappearing into the crowd, she withdrew the cell … *Ben was still incommunicado*.

"Howdy, Candy Cane." Her best friend Trish sang. "Want to hear

Jingle Bells? I've been practicing."

"Been hitting the eggnog, have you?"

"I hate eggnog. No Jingle Bells? Your loss."

"Later. I only have a few minutes. I'm at the mall…"

"Ooh. You're in town?"

"No. Tennessee. Blizzard. I'll be home in three days but I need your help, I haven't gotten Adam a present. What'd you think I should get him?"

"What? Seriously? Jeez! I've been collecting stuff for Jace for months."

"I'm calling for ideas, not to be scolded. And don't say sexy underwear."

"If you know what I'm gonna say then why do you ask?"

Melanie ignored Trish. "I was thinking cologne or a pen, maybe a watch."

"Jesus, did you just meet this guy? Have you no imagination? Those are lame suggestions."

"That's why I'm calling you."

"You need something more personal." She hummed. "I've got it! Mugs! Coffee mugs. Oh my God. Hold on," Trish said, and then silence.

"What are you doing?" Melanie asked when her friend's rhythmic breathing blew through the speaker.

"Writing this down. Every time I have a genius idea I'm journaling it so I won't forget. You know, when some asshole makes a blonde joke I'll have proof they're full of shit."

"Okay." Melanie didn't bother pressing for details. "Do you need help with spelling?"

"I can spell bitch," Trish snorted.

Melanie laughed. "No offense, but I'm missing the brilliant part of your idea."

"Hello, Madam Thick Skull, it's an *intimate* gift. After a night of hanky-panky you wake up to a cup of joe and it's for your home. Like cherished mornings together."

"Whose home? His? He has mugs … I think. I'm sure."

"No, dumb-dumb. Jeez, and I'm the blonde? Your home."

"My parents have mugs, too."

"What are you talking about? When you move in with him, you can drink from these special Christmas mugs!"

Melanie felt sick and sweaty all at once. "We'll be sipping in different kitchens because I'm not moving in with him."

"What the hell?" Trish hollered and then apologized to someone in the room with her. "Why?"

"For one, Adam hasn't asked and two I can't move into his place."

"Can't?"

"Do you know how many women he's had at that house, that bed, the couch, the counter, floors?"

"No and neither does he or you. He loves you…"

"Yes, but…"

"Shut up and let me speak, will you? It doesn't matter who came before you. It's just a blur to him. He couldn't tell you any specifics of any of those women. They were sex, Mel, nothing more. You can't hold him to your strict, puritanical rules. Don't judge."

"Are we still talking about me and Adam?"

Trish grunted her laugh. "It's funny. You end up with a guy like me and I end up with one like you." She huffed. "Jace gets jealous and then I feel guilty for all the times I had stupid fun. I understand that he gets hurt but seriously each time we have this argument, I want to slap him. Do you want Adam to slap you?"

"I just called for advice with a Christmas present." Melanie sighed and rubbed her temples.

"Fine," Trish hummed. "No mugs. Video games. Viagra?"

"Adam?"

"Tell him you'll move in with him. He'll like that. Tie a bow around your vagina if you don't want sexy underwear."

"I think that's anatomically impossible. You're a lot of help. Thanks. I've got ten minutes and there's a million people here."

"It's Christmas Eve. Good luck." Trish laughed and ended the call.

Melanie closed her eyes. *A bow on my vagina?*

CHAPTER 8

"How can I be out of money?" Hugh roared, his flat fingers thumping impressions into the gold-leafed desk blotter.

"You are not out of money, but we have depleted your surplus funds. I can't explain it any other way, Hugh. Your assets have been frozen. They've subpoenaed your records. I don't want to be dipping into the offshore accounts in case I'm being watched – and that is a distinct possibility. I'm protecting you, Hugh. It's just for the time being."

"How is that possible?" The implication was rooted far deeper than the single question. "There was plenty of money stashed, what have you been doing? Another yacht, Kenneth?"

"You were locked in a federal facility." Frustration had his voice on edge. "Do you think your release was cheap? Getting a high-profile fugitive out of the country is no simple task – and it's sure as hell not cheap. Let's not forget the militants you requested. And what about that mansion you insisted on renting?"

Hugh looked around the room – it wasn't quite a mansion. "You expect me to believe it all went to my benefit?" he scoffed. *Damn, lying, cheating lawyers.*

"You are welcome to fire me."

His acid reflex burned as he reached the proverbial corner at his back. It wasn't a comfortable position. *Bastard. I'll relent. For now.* Suddenly, reality seeped into the equation. "Where shall I live? *How* shall I live?"

"I've got that covered," Kenneth soothed. "A few months back I arranged a job for Marie. It's in Rome, restoring stained glass for the Vatican. She's established an apartment and an identity … no one knows she's your daughter."

"Why. Would. You. Do. That?"

"She's your last option."

My last option. The acid resurged. "Then I am in dire straits. What about you? I've paid for your luxuriant lifestyle, Ken. Don't you have any spare change you can afford your best client?" Hugh sat in the stiff chair. "A room in one of your penthouse suites?"

"Besides the fact that I'm your attorney and that would be unethical, they've got me under surveillance."

"You've got an answer for everything, don't you?"

"What I'm proposing," he continued, "is that you set up residence with Marie until such time that we can access your funds, safely."

"I could do you serious harm," Hugh threatened.

Ken ignored the old man's bluff. "You will be safe with your daughter. She's off the radar and, according to Baylor, another sweep of the estate happened yesterday. Believe it or not Hugh, my only goal is to keep you free."

Hugh considered the decades of alliance. "You've contacted everyone?"

"Hugh," Ken sighed, "there is no one left."

He knew how it worked, but still he was surprised. *No one left? They'll be sorry.*

"Hugh?"

"You feel this is the best course?"

"I do."

"Is there an alternative?"

"No."

He gnawed on the taste of revenge for a moment before conceding. "Very well. Rome."

"I'll organize your travel plans."

"This is a set back, but it will not distract me, *or you*, from my objective," Hugh hissed.

"Understood."

CHAPTER 9

Two and a half days at the farm blurred in a spectacle of red and green decorations, a cacophony of loud opinions all interrupting one another and the rich asphyxiation of cinnamon, nutmeg and pine.

The first five minutes of arriving at the house with its big porch was a swarm of sound and motion. Adam was rammed by a full-body assault from his cousins, who smothered him in hugs and kisses. His arms were outstretched, scooping as many as would fit, and lifting.

Melanie watched with amusement. The cousins, with their long brown hair and brown eyes, two were no more than 5'5" while the third soared an additional six inches.

"Melanie," Adam gestured for her to join, "these trouble makers are Rachel, Rhonda and Robin. And you know my aunt, Becca."

The four stopped talking, stopped moving and stood with their full attention focused on Melanie.

"Hi," Melanie gave a short wave and smiled under the tingling sensation of their body scan.

"So this is the famous *Melanie*?"

"More like infamous."

"We've been restless to meet you," Rachel said, her grin contradicting the scrutinizing angle of her head.

"Be nice." Adam warned. "Where's Rob?"

"Around here someplace," Rhonda, the tall one with the smoker's voice, replied. Her eyes taking a second pass over Melanie. "Go ahead. We want alone time to talk to your lady friend."

"Yeah, well, that's going to have to wait," Adam took Melanie's hand. "We're going to find Rob."

"More testosterone won't help you, little cousin," Rhonda smirked.

His strong grasp was a life preserver in the Arctic Ocean of gawking.

"You know, I've never met anyone's family before." She confided, "I don't think they liked me."

"You met them for forty seconds, Mel," he laughed. "Besides, who couldn't love you? Don't worry, it's just the way they are and unfortunately, that *is* their best behavior." His lips were cold on her cheek.

She walked briskly to keep pace with his long strides, her breath breaking the path before them as they stopped at a split-rail fence. Adam perched on the corner and leant her a hand up as he summarized the 150 acres, the livestock arena and the land cleared for soybeans. Their fingers remained laced as he lifted both of their hands to point out the old barn, the new one, the corrals. He explained that the farm butted against miles of forestry and showed the top of a gable that belonged to the nearest neighbor, across the road.

"You should see it in spring," he said, hopping off the fence. His feet landing in front of her, eye-to-eye, he laid his hands comfortably on her thighs. The wool of his coat was rough as her fists clenched to the lapel to pull him closer. His gaze returned from admiring the landscape, "I like being here," he said, smiling.

She ran her fingers through his hair, the ends curling around her fingers.

"Your nose is pink," he said, eyes softening.

She leaned to kiss him and over his shoulder four sets of eyes peered through lace curtains.

"Show me the goats?" she said, pulling back. He'd mentioned they were penned at the rear field, farthest from the house.

"Away from prying spectators?" His gaze was mischievous and she knew she was in trouble when he reached. His palm caressed her cheek as he drew her hair back from her face. His eyes never left hers, intense, her teeth nipped at her lip as he moistened his.

The kiss was rough – his tongue was not – as her toes crimped inside her boots.

"Adam," she said, leaving a visible breath between them.

"That should give them something to talk about."

Melanie sucked in enough oxygen to dispel the dizziness as Rob rounded into view. His silver/gray hair was tucked beneath a bright yellow baseball cap embroidered with a large letter T. And his hunting jacket was ablaze with bright orange patches on his chest and elbows.

"I see the cat was around," he joked and they both laughed, their hug was a back clap, with shoulders touching for only an instant.

"You remember Melanie," Adam said, as they appraised her with identical grins.

"Good to see you, again." Rob's green eyes twinkled.

"What's going on?" Adam asked, nodding to the rifle slung over Rob's shoulder.

"Foxes. They've been getting into the hen house." He shrugged, taking steps toward the house. "We better get in. Becca called, lunch is ready. Damn, I'm happy to see you."

"When was the last time you cleaned this?" Adam asked, having taken the gun and set his eye to the scope. "Moisture…"

Rob gave Melanie a look of begrudging acceptance and cocked his thumb at his nephew. "Stickler."

"… damages the barrel." Adam wasn't listening. "There's already premature wearing and this is a nice piece..." he stopped and laughed at the colliding of his two lives, letting his assassin show.

Melanie had been watching his smooth, gentle, capable hands handle the weapon. "Teach me," she breathed, riveted. "Teach me to shoot?"

"Always good for a woman to know how," Rob interrupted the moment. "My girls learned to shoot when they were," his hand found his hip, "about that tall. They're all real good with a bow, too."

Becca lightly scolded Rob as they stomped the muck off their shoes to enter the house. The cousins had already claimed their seats for the myriad of questions and sandwiches that were served up for lunch.

The inquisition came fast and fierce and Melanie did her best to answer the personal prodding without hesitation.

Until…

"Are you expecting to live off Adam's money?"

"Um…"

"What kind of question is that?" Adam broke in.

"Well, you said she quit her job," Rhonda responded. "It's reasonable to assume she's…"

"No. Don't." Adam raised his had to stop her from continuing. "That's none of your business. I knew you'd be nosy, but I didn't think you'd be small and unkind. Why don't you three eat and keep your mouths shut, while I talk myself out of breaking your necks."

"It's okay." Melanie set her grilled cheese triangle on the floral plate and put her hand on his. "They're looking out for you."

"They're being b–"

"Adam!" Becca shouted, "watch your language."

"I have money and I don't expect…"

"You don't have to answer…"

"I want to. It's your family." Melanie adjusted her gaze to the oldest cousin. "I have money and I can honestly guarantee that there are more impressive parts to Adam. His money is the least interesting."

The cousins paused before laughing.

"Okay."

"We like her."

"Oh and you can thank us for Adam's expert kissing ability." Robin said and was immediately hit by her sister.

Her fingers were pinching the greasy bread, she stopped and looked up to understand.

"It's not weird."

Melanie had doubts as each of the girls turned red and Adam groaned.

"We wanted to practice kissing so we gave Adam to our friends and they gave us their brothers. No family lips ever met."

"We have pie." Becca tried to change the subject.

"How old were you?" She asked Adam.

"Ten."

"Oh Lord." Becca stood.

"Trust me, I was a happy participant. I got to kiss teenage girls." He smiled, easily.

"See." Robin shrugged. "I liked that Billy kid, he was cute and I was ten, too so ..."

Rob coughed. "You girls should show Melanie how to shoot a bow."

"Now? It's freezing outside."

"I could use the air." Melanie admitted.

The women grumbled as they pulled off their slippers in exchange for snow boots and trudged their way to the back of the big barn. Faded targets were already pinned to round hay bales. Each woman had a turn, without hesitation, an arrow was released with the precision of "close enough".

"Your turn," Robin handed the bow to Melanie. "And by the way, I've never seen him happier or as talkative. But just because we like you doesn't mean we're going to be nice. Oh, and don't over shoot. Looking for the arrows in the forest is a bitch." Robin called over her shoulder as she jogged to catch up with her sisters.

Melanie notched the arrow, set the anchor point and aimed the tip to the top of the target and released. She glanced at Adam, *I wanted to learn how to be a sniper.*

Space on the pews at midnight service on Christmas Eve was a valuable commodity and parishioners were wedged hip-to-hip. A trio of guitarists performed the hymns and the vocalist, a senior no less than ninety, napped between songs.

After mass, dinner was served and gifts were exchanged. Adam waited until they were alone in their room to give her a hand-painted, tin nativity scene that folded into a box.

"I got it in Argentina," he said, as he watched her set the donkey by the manger. "Remember the little girl with the braids? Her mom does all the work, hammers the tin, cuts out the figures and paints them."

"It's beautiful."

"I thought you'd like it."

"Sorry about the mugs." She cringed, blaming herself for listening to Trish.

"No, they're interesting. We'll use them in the morning." His smile was crooked as he lifted the oversized clay cup. "Baby, you look exhausted."

"I am." She said, falling back onto the pillow, fully dressed but for her shoes.

She closed her eyes for a restless four hours until the pale sunlight shone on the paisley wallpaper and the thumping of heavy footsteps fell down the hall. The plump pillow was no match against the voices that cut right to the center of her headache.

Stuffing her feet into her boots, she bent, kissed Adam on the cheek and slipped out of the house unnoticed. What started as a walk morphed into a jog and then into a run. Her body reveled in the effort, with her lungs expanding and her muscles responding to the quickening pace. The cold, woodsy air infiltrated her bloodstream as her feet pounded out a mindless rhythm.

Tearing a path over fallen trees she raced – then pulled to a hard, gasping stop at the vibration in the side pocket of her cargo pants.

Ben! Her heart leaped. "Hello!" Nothing. "Ben? Hello?" She pulled the phone from her ear and gave the lifeless device a questioning stare.

Jabbing the home button to make sure the thing was working, the generic wallpaper awakened her screen, notifying her she'd missed no calls, no texts, no messages. Disappointment knocked the rest of the air from her lungs. The phantom vibrations were maddening and wearing on her psyche. *Enough*, she growled a mental rant and dialed.

Frustration had her gripping the phone as Ben's voicemail instructed her to leave a message.

Damn it!

She tried Jack.

"Ward?"

"Scott?" she returned his dismal greeting.

"What can I do for you?" He coughed. "I thought you retired."

She ignored his comment. "I'm still trying to reach Ben, he hasn't been picking up my calls."

"He's a busy man."

"I know but," she stuttered.

"I'll let him know you called when I see him. Okay? Good enough?"

"No. Not. Okay. Jack, what is going on?" Logan's mention of turmoil at the Agency wormed into her conscious and Jack was igniting her agitation.

"Listen, I'm in the middle of something. I don't have all day."

"Wait, I don't understand. What's with the attitude? Did you get Brooks?"

"Melanie." He bit. "You quit. Go get a life and stop trying to be a goddamned agent. Stop calling me."

The line went dead. Melanie stood, stunned.

"What the hell just happened?" She blinked to clear her vision.

A feeling of isolation and abandonment surged from the solitary woods. She felt vulnerable out in the open, she jogged, long strides, getting her nowhere faster. The soles of her boots smashed the moldy, soggy leaves into the earth. The questions were piling faster than her feet could move. Digging deeper into the woods she tried to outrun her thoughts, seeking solutions to unanswerable questions.

The river's ragged edge halted her progress.

"Damn it, Ben!" she screamed, with full force, she pitched the phone. Watching it skip across the surface of the water – regret came on the heels of the splash.

Shit. Smart move, Ward. Melanie reprimanded as she looked out from her station on a boulder at the rocky bank. The cascading motion of the river was the only life in the soundless, leafless woods. She eyed the barren sentinels of the austere, silent forest and felt their condemnation.

One foot in, one foot out, she argued with her subconscious. "No," her voice broke the hush. "You made your choice months ago." *Both feet are beside Adam's.*

Melanie oxygenated her blood, opened her eyes and began to retrace her tracks. Swiping at her runny nose, her fingers were stiff and sore from the cold and her esophagus burned from panting the frigid air.

Slowing to a jog, she replayed her conversation with Jack and flipped through memories of him. The conclusions stung.

"We were never friends. He used me to get ahead. How lonely had I been to be so blind?" Her step had slowed to a walk as she reached the farm. Her eyes welled with the harsh reality that the friendship she'd lost was never real. "Bastard."

At the open field, Adam squatted on a corner of the fence that gave him access to the wide span of landscape.

"Did you have a good run?"

"Not really." She took the empty fence rail to his left.

"Something I can do?"

"No. Thanks."

"They're starting the games."

"Games? Do we have to?"

"No," he said, his gaze sharpened and he misunderstood. "I know they can be overbearing but they can also be fun."

The games were an adequate distraction.

As the credits of Home Alone II rolled, Melanie counted her bank and ignored the violent dismantling of the game board.

"You don't have to count. We already know you've won."

It was their third game and it had promptly ended with a very lucky roll of the die.

"We'd better get out of here." Adam whispered.

The door shut behind them as the FBI warning on the third installment of the Home Alone trilogy disappeared from the screen.

"You doing okay?" he asked, kissing the back of her neck. "You were sort of brutal in there."

"The word is competitive." She smiled, liking the way he used his shoulder to slide open the door to the old barn.

Stepping into the shelter, the warmth was loaded with the scent of hay. The horses whinnied at their approach and Adam rubbed the muzzle of the closest equine. His gaze swept over the barn and she watched his eyes sparkled with mischief as he recalled the past.

"Had a lot of good times in here." He grinned, holding the ladder while she climbed to the loft. "I hope you're not allergic."

The atmosphere became heavier as she reached the platform to the maze of golden bales that were stacked chest high with a single path that led to the back wall. Adam snapped the binding cords and spread the crisp straw over the wooden deck. He'd grabbed a blanket from somewhere, and draped it over the padding in a swift, easy, well-rehearsed maneuver.

"Why do I have the feeling I'm not the first girl you've brought here?" The hay yielded to her weight. She bumped her shoulder against his as he settled in beside her.

"This farm was my safe place. I loved coming here … even after." He shook his head. "This is where I came to clean up, to start over." He laughed. "Every time."

"Who're Lucy and Ace?" She felt him bristle and pointed to the words, 'Lucy + Ace = Forever' carved into the wood right at eye level from where she lay.

"Lucy was a local girl," he answered, his smile awry.

"And…"

"And nothing."

"Who's Ace?"

"Me," he said with enough humility to be adorable. "My initials, A.C. When I was about seven I realized if I added the e … I became Ace." His grin warbled. "I was young, arrogant and it was elementary school – I had to be cool for the third-grade girls."

"Ace and Lucy, huh?"

He shrugged. "There were a *lot* of local girls."

"That doesn't help your case." Her chuckle was formed from discomfort, "and there's only one name etched with yours. She must have been special."

"Lucy was … I liked Lucy." He turned swiftly with one languid movement, her back was pressed into the hay and his hands were on her shoulders. "But not nearly as much as I like you."

"That's reassuring," she said, playfully.

He ran the tip of his cold finger along her cheek and dragged the strand of hair from her eyelashes. His lips were firm with their gentle thievery as he rearranged the pace of her heart, stealing every third beat.

"One second. Don't move," he said, jumping to his feet and disappearing. He returned with a crow bar, scraping the plank until the sentiment of Lucy plus Ace became shavings on the floor and leaving a white scar in the wood.

"I'm not asking you to erase your past."

"I couldn't. Believe me, I've tried. This," he leaned back against the straw, "this is easy." His arm found its way over her shoulders. "I'll be glad to get home tomorrow."

"Me, too." The thought of moving into her old room, across the hall from her parents, wasn't appealing, but ...

"We're going to need a vehicle." He was thinking out loud. "We've only got the motorcycle there. Any suggestions?"

"What if we don't?" She crinkled her nose. "I was thinking about breaking from technology."

"I was talking about a car, not a spaceship."

"I was thinking about riding a bike."

"No way, your mom would kill both of us."

"Not motorcycle, bicycle. Ten-speed. No phone or TV. I might be able to be talked into a radio."

"You're kidding."

"Not really." She yawned deeply. "Think about how free we were in South America. It could be like that all the time."

"Bicycle." He laughed. "Funny. How about a Range Rover? We can use it to haul your things to the house."

"My things?" she scooted to the edge of the padding to look at him. "What things?"

"I don't know but you're going to need your stuff."

"One, I don't have any stuff. And two, why?"

"Because," he tilted his head, "I guess we can get you a new toothbrush and clothes..." The groove between his eyes deepened. "Mel, what are we talking about?"

"Are you asking me to move in with you?"

"I'm sorry." He shifted backward. "We're together, you can't get any more together than we are." They stared into each other's eyes. "I assumed it was implied but okay." His chest lifted, his brows furrowed with concentration. "Mel, will you move in with me?"

"No." She felt bad as his guard dropped and his hurt showed.

"No?"

"No," She repeated. "I can't." She remembered her conversation with Trish and tried to avoid accusations. "That house is your place. Your belongings, your memories. I'd always feel like a guest there. I'd be more comfortable at my home, in my room."

"Your room? At your parents'?" he shifted back further, his eyes filled with disbelief, "You'd rather move back in with your parents than live with me?"

"It's not that," she tried, spooked by his deep, full lung breathing.

His gaze moved across her face as if he were reading a book. "Okay," he nodded, his vision clearing. "I get it. Sweetheart." He reached into his jacket pocket and pulled out his cell phone.

"It's Christmas, who are you calling?"

Adam lifted his finger vertical across his lips. "Hey Mark, it's Adam. Call me after the holidays. I want to list the house. Take care." His green eyes drilled into hers. "You're not comfortable in my house, so, I'll get rid of it." He shrugged. "It's just a house, I have no attachment to it. But you," his face lifted, "you I'm highly attached to you."

"But..." it was an automatic word in a moment of speechlessness.

He cracked of his knuckles, his face lighting up. "This is good. I feel like solving problems. What else?"

"That's a big decision."

"Babe, I know why you don't like the place and I understand." His hand found her thigh. He closed in, his index finger hooking the collar of her turtleneck sweater. "The problem with winter is, too many clothes."

CHAPTER 10

The phone rattled in Jack's palm. *Not another fucking call.* He fought an overwhelming desire to throw the thing against the wall.

"Jane," he called, tucking his shirttail into his pants and shutting down his computer. "Let's go home," he said, walking swiftly past her desk. "Are you coming?" he asked, looking at her for the first time in days.

"I need you to listen to me."

"Something wrong?"

"I've been wanting to talk to you," she started. Her face was bloated and pink as if she'd been crying. "Jack, I'm pregnant."

He snapped to attention, his spine jolted ramrod straight and seconds passed before he mouthed the word, *pregnant?* "How? I mean," his breath tasted foul, "we've been careful."

"I don't know." Her childish voice trembled. "I'm sorry."

"I can't deal with this right now. Great timing, Jane!" The door slammed harder than he'd expected as he stormed out of the room.

The family/sports bar/restaurant was on the ground floor of a hotel five blocks from the White House. Jack warmed a stool at the counter, ordered a draft and didn't watch the game.

Raking his fingers through his hair, he swore under his breath. *The Agency is in the shithole, Ben is in the hospital and … Jane's pregnant. What more could possibly go wrong?*

Two beers later, the game had ended and he realized, "I'm going to be a father." Dropping his head under the weight of the guilt and fatigue he murmured, "God, I am such a dick." Dreading his apology to Jane had him ordering two shots – before heading home to beg forgiveness.

His head was throbbing and the ring of his phone pierced like an ice pick. *Fucking calls,* he growled and sucked in the cloud from the smokers on the sidewalk.

"Ward." He rubbed his fingers over his forehead, "what can I do for you?" he motioned to a woman and bummed a smoke. Lighting up he sucked in the nicotine, "I thought you'd retired." Jack closed his eyes, *she wants Ben … don't we all?* "He's a busy man. I'll let him know you called. Good enough?' He wrapped the scarf around his neck … *Jesus Christ*. "Go get a life. And stop calling me."

He gripped the phone and shoved it deep into his pant pocket and wished he could get Melanie Ward's face and voice out of his head.

At the apartment he shared with Jane, he crushed his cigarette butt on the sidewalk and unlocked the door.

"Hi," she said, nervously wiping away the fallen tears. "I'm sorry. I blurted it out. I didn't give you any warning and you've been under so much stress."

"I'm failing," he said, his head in his hands and bending in half until his knuckles pressed into his knees. "Failing as a director, failing as an agent. I'm failing you."

"No." Jane was at his side, rubbing his back. "You're not failing. Ben has been absent and …"

Jack straightened. "I've done everything I can think of and I can't fix any of it." He was feeling the panic strike, "and then Melanie called … and I…"

"Wait. Melanie called? Why?" Jane edged him to the couch and pulled the coffee table close for a seat in front of him. "What did she want?"

"She's looking for Ben," he told her, looking up and hating the glimmer of hope in her eyes.

"Call her back. Tell her what's going on. She'll help." Jane said, and what was left of his ego vanished. "I didn't mean it that way, Jack. You know I think you're amazing, but Melanie is a fighter. She sees things differently."

"I don't need Ward." Jack felt the rekindling of his personal storm.

"Why are you so angry with her?" Jane gave him a suspicious snarl. "She's your friend."

"Stay out of it." He stood, frustrated.

"Are you still in love with her?"

"I was never in love with her. We've been through this." He sifted through the fridge searching for a beer.

"Then what is it? That she quit? She went through a lot and I don't blame her for wanting out. Good for her." Jane stood to check the ham in the oven.

"I am not asking Ward for help."

CHAPTER 11

"Are you sure?" Adam asked, standing at the stoop of her parents' La Jolla home.

It hadn't changed in as long as she could remember. Two stories with a porch swing, a patch of lawn, shrubs and eyelet curtains covering her second-floor bedroom window.

"I'm not sure of anything," she admitted, "but this doesn't have to be a forever decision." Melanie turned to look at the confusion that occupied his expression and lowered her voice. "Don't be mad."

"I'm not," he said, setting his fiery gaze on hers. "But I *am* going to make sure you miss me," he pulled her into his arms, set her lips on fire and walked away before the sting was gone.

"Bye," she sighed into the thin air. Melanie opened the front door with the roar of his motorcycle at her back. "Mom? Dad?" she called, dropping her bag on the floor by the stairs. "Anyone? I'm home." Giggling from the backyard had her at the sliding glass door. "Mom?" She stopped. *When did they buy a Jacuzzi?* Unable to blink or retreat she watched at the threshold between innocence and – her mom splashing her dad, wine glass in hand and ... *Topless!*

Melanie gasped and darted with insanely fast reflexes to the safety of the living room.

"Seriously, could this day get any worse?" she asked no one as she entered the kitchen. The landline was bolted to the wall and Melanie lifted the receiver and hit speed dial number seven.

"I'm sorry, do I know you?"

The urge to smile couldn't clear the grit from her mind. "I thought we could go for drinks. Lots and lots of them."

"It's kind of early, Mel. Besides, you ignore me for months and with a single call you expect me to drop everything and get wasted with you?"

"I called you three days ago," Melanie answered.

"Whatever. Did you buy the mugs?"

"Yes. And it was one of the most embarrassing moments of my life."

"You made a memory."

That wasn't her take but ... "okay, but Trish, strong, alcoholic drinks. Now."

"Usually I'd say yes," she stalled, "but I have to work and I'm running low on sick days. And I've got a dinner party tonight."

"Next time, then," Melanie said, bummed.

"Hey, do you know how to play Hearts?"

"The card game? Why would I? I'm not in my seventies."

"Ha-ha. Shows how much you know, Hearts is making a come back. Everybody is playing."

"Everyone?"

"It's a thing, Mel. Never mind, you're no help."

"Get rid of your clubs and play high-level cards first. Well, that's what my grandma used to say. Good luck."

"I'm screwed. I have no idea what you just said."

"YouTube it or wear something revealing. The men won't notice your cards and the women will hate you. Are you free to get drunk tomorrow?"

"I'm starting now. Call me."

Disappointed, she ended the call while her eyes skimmed the organized clutter on the bulletin board above the phone. She grinned at pictures, read the notes, 'save the date' cards and a yellow Post-It with Penny's number and address.

"When did you move to La Jolla?" she asked the black ink of the Sharpie and dialed, leaving a quick message before heading upstairs to lace her feet into a pair of running shoes. The giggles were ascending the stairs when she climbed out her bedroom window to the porch roof and jumped onto the soft grass. Her plan was to run hard and fast, feel pain from her toes to her lungs and forget.

"Melanie?" Her name came from the passing red minivan.

"Cheryl," she grinned through her groan and stopped.

"Oh my God. I didn't know you were coming home today." She braked in the middle of the street. "Olivia, look, it's your auntie."

This time Melanie's smile was genuine. "Hey, Olive."

"Maui!" the toddler called from the middle row, arms reaching for her from her car seat.

"Are you going someplace? Want a ride?"

"I was … but, hey, am I Maui?" she asked, laughing. "What are you doing?"

"We're going to the zoo. We have a date with the pandas." Cheryl was in mom mode and her voice sang the information. "You should come with – I just need to pick up Olivia's lunch box from Mom's and then we're off."

"Pandas!" Olivia screeched.

"Yeah," Melanie decided. "I'd love to go, but how about I buy her a new lunch box?"

"You know about the spa." Cheryl gave an understanding nod.

They sang all the way to pulling the emergency brake in the zoo parking lot. School buses and minivans filled the spots while inside the sidewalks were lined with strollers. Olivia's walk turned into a wobbly jog that tumbled into a face plant every few yards. Melanie gave Cheryl a break by keeping up with her niece, catching her before each impact.

By the time they reached the panda encounter Olivia had squirmed out of Melanie's arms, ran, tripped and retreated to the comforts of her king carrier to gobble down handfuls of Goldfish.

"We have a 'behind the scenes' pass," Cheryl said, as she pushed the buggy and Melanie fell into step. "We've watched those cubs grow up and they are the sweetest things."

They entered one of the short buildings with an 'employees only' sign and lined up with the other pass holders. The zookeeper and two perky volunteers greeted them with the gift of a bamboo shoot.

Melanie was schooled in both the detriment and advancement of the panda population. "We are working closely with our counterparts in China," the zookeeper spoke as she walked them between buildings, through the staff parking lot and delivery zone to where the pandas were evaluated.

"What are they delivering?" Melanie asked, unable to overlook the parked big rig being unloaded.

"Panda food," the zoologist answered casually. "Because of the low nutritional value of bamboo, pandas can eat up to 90 pounds a day. Plus we receive supplements, medications and fertility treatments to keep them healthy and help increase their numbers."

Melanie listened, gauging the size of the tractor-trailer. Pallets were stacked on the platform beside the door and a second stack was at the base of the ramp.

"That's a lot of supplements. How often do you get shipments?" Melanie wondered, interrupting a four-year-old asking the more typical question of 'why are pandas black and white?'

"Weekly," the woman answered, closing the conversation and leading them through a set of double doors. "Some say pandas are black and white because one day a girl..."

"Cheryl, I'll catch up," Melanie said, turning toward the emptied truck.

She wasn't interested in the three pallets by the roll-up garage doors to be delivered to the panda enclosure. Melanie jogged to the bundles ready to be loaded into the back of a service vehicle. The side of the van had the silhouettes of a dog, cat and parrot with a slogan of 'our pets, our family' painted on the side.

The area was deserted. The lights on the security cameras were cold. Breaking through the layers of plastic wrap, Melanie removed one of the 2.5-pound buckets and slit the protective seal. Removing the lid, she dug her fingers two inches beneath the top coating of a meal substance and found packets of a neon colored powder. She pressed her fingers against the granules and searched her memory. They'd been having issues controlling the drug trade from China, where they were making designer drugs aimed at the teenage market. She looked over the pallet ... hundreds of pounds of synthetic drugs ready for distribution.

"Hey!" A man's shout from behind had Melanie pocketing a packet and returning the lid to the container. "What are you doing there?"

"I was curious about what you feed the bears," she answered, noticing his eyes were directed behind her to the displaced bucket.

"I don't think so," the guy was in his twenties, thin within baggy, blue coveralls. 'Andy' was embroidered over his left breast pocket.

"It's true," she lied, smiling while analyzing the change in his eyes. "90 pounds a day, huh? I'd be the size of a house."

"You're going to have to come with me," he said, looking troubled.

"No, I'm going to catch up with my group," Melanie answered, but the path back to the pandas was around the semi and the only way to get there was to pass by Andy.

"I can't let you," he said, reaching.

Melanie dodged his grasp, ducked his blow and kicked his feet out from under him. Her running shoe was on his spine when she froze at the sound … "Maui! Maui!" Olivia's little voice reached her from behind the big truck. "Pandas!"

The shot of adrenaline caught her off guard, she paused to breathe and regulate her voice to sound normal. "I'll be there in a minute," she called, stomping compassionately harder between Andy's shoulder blades. "Go on ahead without me."

"Are you sure?" Cheryl asked.

"Yeah," Melanie closed her eyes and swore silently.

"Are you okay?" Cheryl questioned as Olivia yelled for pandas.

"I'm fine. Go. Thanks."

"Okay, we'll see you at the front."

"Great."

"Maui!"

The squeal caught her off guard and Andy twisted in a breakdancing move. Melanie hit the ground. Her back struck the asphalt first and then her head cracked on the pavement. She saw stars right before the blow to her ear knocked her unconscious.

She woke in a muddled, foggy awareness, cramped, in a tight, dark space that smelled of old socks. The voices were muffled and it took a moment for her bearings to adjust. She was crumpled in the narrow gap between the front and back seat of a compact car. Removing the blanket that'd covered her head she could hear…

"And you brought her here?"

Pinned in the small space, Melanie lifted her head high enough to rest against the frame of the car door and scolded herself. *You couldn't just look at the fucking pandas?*

"The Triad will not accept this," the man's reproach held traces of an accent. Asian.

Oh. Shit. He brought me to the Chinese mob. The natural urge to flee gripped her conscious and braided the lining of her stomach but experience had her considering other alternatives.

"What else was I supposed to do?" She recognized the nasal quality of Andy's voice. "She *saw* the K and she totally lied about it and … she attacked me."

"She knew about the shipment?"

"I was moving the cases and when I came back to the truck she was nosing around. So I knocked her out and chloroformed her to keep her quiet. I figured you'd know what to do."

"Did anyone see you take her?"

"No. I unplug the cameras on shipment days."

"Take her to the Tailor."

Tailor? Such a common word sent a round of goose bumps over her skin. Even Andy sounded uncertain as he agreed to her punishment. Melanie eased the door open, squeezed out, took cover behind the back tire and peeked around the corner.

They were on the top floor of a parking structure. The sun was beating down as she shuffled, keeping low to the ground. Melanie rounded to the back of the vehicle and craned her neck, looking for a viable way out. Cars were scattered in a mostly empty concrete field.

From her vantage point she couldn't see above the retaining wall and there were no buildings that matched the height of the lot. Angling to get a view of the men, the Asian man was dressed in a metallic gray suit, his face red with anger. And she was sure she didn't want to wait around for the Tailor.

I am alone, her thought was followed by the memory of Olive's squawk, *"Maui". Shit, I've got to get out of here!*

Squatting, she raced to the next car, then the next, trying the handles of the locked vehicles until she was out of hiding spots. *Here goes*, she took a deep breath and sprinted as fast and hard as her lungs and legs would allow. She was running down the incline when the shouts began and the footsteps pounded behind her.

Shortcutting, she leaped over rails when she could and made her way to the street. Not slowing as she left the shade of the structure – she was at the industrial periphery of the county, close to the international border. Not looking back and, without a dollar in her pocket, she raced another mile before putting her thumb to use and hitched to La Jolla. The pouch of Ketamine still in her pocket.

It was late afternoon when she walked through the front door, dusty and sweaty.

"Where have you been?" Cheryl plodded toward her. Her mom hugged her hard while Bruce and her dad kept to the sidelines. They'd taken up vigil in the living room, waiting for her safe return home.

"We've been so worried."

"Sorry. I got lost."

"We are getting you a cell phone." Her mom commanded under a heavy sigh of relief.

CHAPTER 12

"Good morning. Would you like some carrot juice? It's fresh," Rita offered as Melanie entered the kitchen. "Wasn't that nice of Adam to make dinner last night? You wouldn't think a man that attractive would be so sweet or so handy with a knife." Her mom chattered as Melanie poured herself a glass of juice, her eyes dropping to the picture on the front page.

Andy. "Are you done with the paper?" She reached for the article.

"Isn't that terrible?" Rita said, casting her eyes toward the paper. "Strange that he worked at the zoo and was last seen yesterday, when you girls were there. I called Cheryl but she didn't remember seeing him."

His body, found on a bike path by early-morning joggers, was scheduled for autopsy but preliminary reports indicated he'd died from multiple gunshot wounds.

"He was so young and handsome," Rita mused. "Who would do such a thing?"

The Chinese mob. An involuntary shiver flowed over her skin.

"You said I had some things delivered?"

"Your father put them in the garage."

Jane had forwarded her possessions from D.C. – eleven years amounted to three boxes. Melanie sliced the packing tape, hunting for her laptop. She found bank statements, clothes, pictures, but no computer. The Walther PPK felt good in her hand, unclipping the empty magazine, she popped it back in and tucked it into her pants. Borrowing the iPad her mom used to play poker on, Melanie absently rubbed the packet of chunky powder as she scoured the web for clues to identify the man she'd seen with the zoo employee.

Pages and pages of images. She zoomed in on every possible suspect until her eyes watered and blurred. With three potential candidates, she purchased a facial recognition app and attempted to duplicate Mike's ability. Taking a snapshot of the men, she waited as the technology scanned social media, criminal databases and the Associated Press for matches. When it was finished, the highest percentage of probability, based on location and bone structure, was Yong Li.

With the name she began her research. And thanks to the lack of privacy on the Internet she'd found Li's house on satellite, complete with floor plans and photos from when it was on the market. Zeroing in on Google Earth provided the name of the alarm company that handled his security and the dark web helped with the rest.

From there she moved on to instructional videos.

"Are you almost done with my iPad?" Rita's voice penetrated Melanie's concentration. "I have my word game at seven." Melanie didn't have to see her mom to know her fist was pressed to her hip, irritated. "You really are going to have to buy your own."

"Seven?" Checking her watch, she was surprised to see she'd lost the entire day.

"What are you doing in here?" Rita took two steps into the garage to stare at Melanie's project. Slipping her glasses over her eyes, she leaned in. "Are you building something or breaking something?"

"Ha! Funny," Melanie said, replacing the tools to their pegboard spots. "I can't believe it's so late." She deleted the YouTube site before returning the tablet to her mom. "Go kick those church ladies' butts."

Sauntering into the house, she spoke over her shoulder. "That's not nice. But you know what they say about great minds."

Melanie checked over her work. Using her dad's tools, a dozen different video sources and some scattered parts, she had assembled a bypass to Li's security. Grabbing her notes, she headed to the electronic store and, for a hundred bucks, invested in a software-defined radio system. The geek team gave her a quick rundown of how to operate it and she was in bed by ten.

Rehearsing her plan, playing out every move in her mind, she imagined each step. At midnight she dressed in black, retrieved a ski mask from the sports closet and borrowed her neighbor's motorcycle.

Li lived in the hills. His compound was tucked in a valley surrounded by rocky slopes.

The bike was loud and echoed throughout the canyon … she needed the cover of darkness and silence. Killing the engine, she hiked two miles up the residential pass. Hiding behind the ski mask Melanie jogged to the security box by the east wing of the house and set up her rogue base cellular system. She used the software to confuse the system and allow her to connect, controlling the station and disabling the alarm. Traveling along the perimeter of the house she found the tree she'd seen on the satellite images, the one that scratched Li's bedroom window, she climbed.

The glasscutter was noiseless as it dissected a five-inch diameter from the window. Reaching inside, Melanie unhitched the lock and crawled into the room.

Her foot set lightly on carpeting and she inched to the sleeping figure. He was softly snoring. Melanie took hold of the bedding, grabbing and dragging it, and him, onto the floor.

"This is how it's going to go," she whispered in his ear as she pressed his face to the ground. "You ... stop struggling or this will hurt." She added force until Li stopped moving. Melanie secured his hands and feet with plastic bindings. "You are going to make a video confession of your involvement in Andy's murder, the drugs and your connection with the mob."

"Why would I do that?" His voice was muffled in the carpeting.

"Because I'm telling you to," she said, grasping handfuls of his slippery, silk pajamas. She yanked him to the nearest chair and tied him down with the belt of his robe. On the nightstand were his cell phone and a glass of water. Working quickly she scanned the contacts and slid the camera to video mode. From her messenger bag she pulled out her old Sony camcorder and pressed the record button. "Go ahead. Confess what you did to Andy. Explain how you transport the drugs," she ordered.

"Why would I?"

"Why'd you kill Andy?" she questioned, setting the recorder on a stack of books, freeing her right hand to grip the PPK while her left seized the packet of K from her pocket. Melanie took a seat and waited. "Why would you kill him?" She talked, seeking to unravel the puzzle without Li's help. An hour ticked by…

"Will you ever stop?"

"Why won't you talk? Who are you afraid of?"

"No one."

"Why were you afraid of Andy? That's why you killed him, isn't it?"

"Afraid of him? I didn't even know his name." He rolled his dead eyes as if bored. "*Andy*," he mocked, "was a manageable worthless piece of shit until he made a mistake. Do you think anyone cares that he's dead?" He shrugged and smiled then laughed.

"I care." She said, palming the baggie of neon pink powder. "This is what you distribute, right?" His shrug raised her blood pressure. "How about we see what happens when it is orally ingested?"

He narrowed his eyes in a glare, daring her to try. Leaving an inch of water in the glass, she dumped in the entire contents and swirled the substance. His face turned stoic and he clamped his teeth together as she took her place to stand behind him. Holding him in a choke-hold, with his head pulled back, she used her fingers to dig into his cheeks, prying open a small gap between his lips.

His struggle made it difficult, Melanie released him long enough to leave a mark and curb his fight. She poured the drug into his mouth and with her hands, clamped shut his jaw. Some drooled out the sides but he was mad, tossing his head from side to side.

"You want to know that I had Andy killed, okay." He snarled. "I run a drug empire. You are in over your head. You have no idea who you are fucking with. Whoever you are, I promise you will be dead by sunrise."

"Maybe. We'll see."

"No one will care that I killed you, either. Another statistic. Know how many die from overdoses? Nobody cares. Everyone gets their cut and everyone looks the other way."

Asshole, she growled the thought, using the landline to place a call. "I am a federal agent and you're going to want to hear this," she said, setting the receiver next to Li's phone. She pressed the play arrow even as Li continued yelling obscenities and threats.

With the camcorder in her messenger bag she jumped out the window. Falling from limb to limb until she reached the gravel, landing sideways, she raced. She was winded by the time she had the motorcycle revved.

Melanie hadn't called the police.

CHAPTER 13

"Sir," Gardner said, having been summoned to the below ground bunker.

"Have you seen the information about LI? He was murdered last night. In his bed." The man cocked his head. "I thought you had a handle on her."

"I," he stammered, assuming he was talking about Agent Ward. "I don't know if anyone can handle her. But she retired, moved back in with her parents and …"

"And was involved in a mob killing."

"Are you sure?" he questioned having just read the report on Li and trying to link the pieces together. "I don't know how she'd have … I mean, she's only been in San Diego for 24 hours. She's not a murderer."

"And yet Li is dead."

"Li was a drug lord, entangled with a dangerous entourage," Gardner surmised. "Couldn't he have been assassinated for other reasons? We don't know Ward was involved and no reason to suspect she was."

“I have been analyzing data since before you were born,” the director said. “It’s my job to know and I don’t believe in coincidence and Ward…” he was nodding his head, “her proximity to Li and the clandestine details surrounding his assassination point to a professional.” The director changed directions of his headshake and his cadence was slow and deliberate. “We’ve had him under surveillance. We were controlling the information. Years of work...”

Gardner was confused. “I don’t understand.”

“How did she eliminate a high-ranking member of the Chinese mob on her own?” There was an edge of admiration in his question. “I’m going to need you to get me her file.”

“You’re saying,” Gardner dissected the meaning, hesitantly. “You want her on our side. You want her back?”

“Or I want her out of the way.”

“But,” Gardner cleared his throat, “we don’t know that Ward was involved in Li’s death.”

“I am waiting confirmation.”

CHAPTER 14

Two weeks under the California sun and she had landed a job, Adam had an offer on the house and they'd had their first fight … then the second and third.

Melanie stared out the scratched-up windows of the city bus and reclined into the trance she used to shut down her thought process. Reviving slightly with the flash of the Pacific between buildings as she and a handful of strangers headed north on Mission Blvd.

Her heart groaned under the glaring sun and she rested her forehead on the hot plastic window. Regret, sadness, embarrassment. Her insides felt bruised. Unable to stave off her blistering thoughts she exited the bus three stops early to head west to the cliffs in La Jolla.

It was a winter morning and tourists had gathered to gawk at the shamelessly bold sea lions. Elbowing to the protection of the guardrail, she let the iron bar hold her weight as she leaned over and breathed.

Lacy, red underwear behind the dresser had been a surprise. The Polaroids she found on the top shelf of the closet had been educational. The gold hoop earring had stabbed her thumb as she reached to unplug a lamp behind the nightstand. But her breaking point was on the bed: The softest sheets she'd ever felt had been a gift from Courtney, the supermodel ex-girlfriend.

Preventing an outburst she'd walked out of his house. And he hadn't followed. Stranded, this time with money, she'd boarded the bus.

Melanie let her legs dangle over the edge and propped her arms on the steel post, covering her eyes with the cold tips of her fingers and lamented over her life. She was unrecognizable to herself, ranting and carrying on like a lunatic. She groaned over her situation, mid-thirties and living with her wanton parents, working as a receptionist at her father's practice. And now her jealousy was dismantling her relationship.

"What are you doing?" Voicing her thought as the chipped paint on the metal rod was embedding into her forehead.

She kicked up the memory of her conversation with Trish, when her friend had exhibited a moment of unusual insight. They'd chosen the bar over the restaurant and the chatter of the crowd drowned out the overhead music.

"My problem is," Melanie had said that evening, "is that I came home without a decisive plan. My skill set is limited and ..."

"You moved in with your parents."

"True." She lifted her index finger to further her point. "But..."

"No buts, Mel, that was your first *dumb* mistake."

"Maybe," Melanie relented and lowered the level of her tequila sunrise. "I was good for the first few days. Got up early, ran, checked job listings, transported my neighbor Mr. Federico to his girlfriend's assisted-living apartment, and then..."

"Your mom." Trish squished her face into a ball and signaled the waitress for another round. "Rita is a tiny dictator, like Napoleon. And now you're further down the rabbit hole ... Seriously, Mel? Working with your dad? You. Are. Becoming. A. Loser."

She let the comment sink in before responding, "I know." With a frown she finished her drink and resolved to liberate her conscious. "Adam and I are fighting. I found a thong. And not the kind we used to wear on our feet." She glanced at Trish with her platinum blonde do. "It was red and I went mental. I don't know why the color matters as much as it does but..." Her head shook automatically, attempting to dislodge the image.

"What did I tell you?" Trish scolded.

"That the other women didn't matter." Her voice tired as she mimicked Trish's shrill tone. "I know but I found them and I flew into pure instinct mode, my self-control vanished." Melanie sipped her replenished multi-colored beverage.

"You're a super jealous person." Trish stirred her drink with her finger and then sucked it to her second knuckle. "You think sex is love and love is sex. You went ballistic because you're confused."

"Or maybe I'm just a loser." Melanie, infused with self-pity continued, "I work for minimum wage as a receptionist and am tethered to my desk with a cord that stretches three feet. I live with my parents and carpool with my dad, who gets to the office an hour early."

"Nepotism has a price," Trish offered, slipping the umbrella out of her drink.

"This drink," Melanie said, hoisting up her glass, "is an hours worth of wages. That means," she felt the need to further explain the atrocity, "I have to work *one hour* to pay for it."

"I'm buying."

"So, not the point."

"You have a hot boyfriend."

"True. And he's sweet." She tipped her head back and forth.

"I thought you had a great New Years."

Melanie smiled. "We did."

"Are you getting enough sex? Because that could be part of your slump."

"No." She sighed, deciding it was easier to go along than to argue. "Definitely not enough."

"You're welcome."

"For what?"

"Fixing your life. You need more sex," Trish proclaimed loudly enough for the neighboring drinkers to hear. "Wear the red panties."

"Gross." Melanie grimaced. But she did take to heart Trish's suggestion to rekindle their romance.

Three days after the tequila and orange juice had left her system she was still asking … *How am I going to do that?* "I could go back to his place, say I'm sorry and leap into those super soft sheets," relenting to reality, "… and get pissed off all over again."

She searched the wide, empty horizon, which was beautiful but didn't solve any of her problems. Her butt was cold and the concrete hard, so she pulled herself to her feet and turned her back on the sea.

Across the street were a half-dozen identical, beige cottages with orange tiled roofs and red walkways weaving through the grassy hill to blue front doors. She'd always been drawn to the little homes, which were kept neatly landscaped with trimmed hedges and flowering plants.

It's a sign, she thought, noticing the tin flag flapping from a pole spiked into the lawn.

For Rent.

The palm fronds rustled overhead and the lush green grass squished underfoot as Melanie hopped the two-foot wall and mounted the hill. The earth beneath her treads was soft and she shaded her eyes to peek through the windows. Furnished, clean, fresh paint ... perfect.

"Excuse me," a woman's voice said, "why are you attacking my hydrangea bushes?"

Melanie lifted her foot, which was crushing nothing but mud. "I saw the sign and..."

"Melanie Ward?"

"Yeah." She squinted at the figure in the blue business suit as she hiked out from behind the brush.

"Oh my God! It's me!" the woman jabbed her fingers into her chest. "Sylvia Michaels!"

Melanie knew the name instantly. It was the woman she didn't recognize. *Botox*. Sylvia Michaels was her high school prom queen and every schoolboy's dream. "Sylvia! Wow, I can't believe you remembered me."

"You? Are you kidding, you look the same. It's me ... I've changed."

"You look great."

"Oh, a few extra pounds here and there, but it all seems to have landed in the right spots. How are you? I see your parents around from time to time." She chatted, guiding Melanie away from the foliage and onto the walkway.

"Yeah, they're still in the neighborhood. Are you managing these?"

"You interested?"

"Very." She eyed the trellis.

"You're lucky, I put the sign up like ten minutes ago. Want to take a looksee?"

"I do." The conversation continued as they walked.

"I'm divorced. Still live down the street." She hymned, "my kids go to the same schools as we did. Strange. You?" she asked, with her key in the lock, "I ask because this is a bungalow, cottage and every other cute terminology you can think of for itty-bitty."

"Boyfriend."

"My tip, don't let him move in. You'd be over in a month." Sylvia let the door fly from her fingertips and stepped aside for Melanie to pass. "Seen it a million times."

Ten steps and she stood in the middle of the bright living space. The galley kitchen was more than sufficient and the one door led to the bedroom/bathroom combo.

"Nice," Melanie admired.

"The bath has a clawfoot tub."

"I like it." She nodded, admiring the ceiling molding and the soft blue walls. "How does this work?"

"Usually I pull a credit check, background check and a bunch of other stuff to make sure you can afford it and that you're not a wanted criminal … You aren't, are you?"

"No."

"When did you want to move in?"

"Today."

Sylvia reclined on her high heels and gave Melanie a scrutinizing once over. "I'll tell you what … you're a runner?"

"I guess," she said cautiously.

"Will you be my workout partner like three times a week?"

"Yeah."

"Then," she pulled two keys from her jacket pocket, "move in.

I'll get the paperwork started and … you haven't asked how much."

"How much?"

"I'll give you the Michaels' family discount." She rattled off a number that was a digit too many.

"Is that in pesos?"

"Afraid not. That's monthly, with a year lease. Charm and location aren't cheap."

"A year?" Melanie cringed. "Do you have anything less … lengthy?"

"Month-to-month," Sylvia suggested. "Commitment phobic? I've seen that before, too. It's a hundred bucks more a month, but I guess since we're going to be friends…"

I'm friends with Sylvia Michaels?

"… This doesn't mean you can be late with the rent."

"Never," Melanie assured.

"Then we'll get along. I've got the papers in the car." Sylvia was still grinning when she returned with the contract and a bottle of wine. "Thought we'd celebrate and catch up on fifteen years. Glasses are in the cupboard." The cackle was exactly as Melanie remembered echoing off the tiled hallways. "Never too early, right?" She unscrewed the top. "Guess who I'm seeing," She smirked, filling two wine glasses to the brim.

"No idea," Melanie said, hating this game and wondering why so many enjoyed playing.

"That's not a guess."

"Gandhi."

"I don't remember you being a jokester. Either way, you're wrong." She snorted. "Kevin." Melanie took a second to run through her mental list of contacts. "Yup, Kevin Kincade."

"Wow." Melanie's brows shot up like it was high school gossip. "Prom king and queen, the perfect couple. Reunited."

"We weren't perfect."

"Everyone thought so."

"That's sweet. Now we have a second chance. It's not a romantic story..." she settled onto the sofa, "we met online. One of those dating websites. Ever been on them?"

"Nope." Melanie admitted and sat across from Sylvia. The wine was cold and went down easy.

"You *are* lucky." Sylvia continued, "anyway Kevin and I reconnected and the rest as they say is history. We've been together for almost a year. Shoot." She adjusted her watch. "I've got another appointment and kids to pick-up. I love them, a ton, but life was much easier before they came along. I'm crossing my fingers for an old-age payoff." She finished off her wine, waved and was out the door.

Melanie looked around. She was alone. In a place of her own. *Best decision I've made in a long time,* she thought, kicking off her shoes to set her heels on the coffee table and enjoy the sunny west coast from her picture window. *I just bought myself 800 square feet of freedom.*

CHAPTER 15

It was late afternoon when Melanie headed to her parents', skipping as she considered how to break the news about the cottage to her parental roommates. But the house was unusually vacant. Packing a duffle bag of necessities, she took the city route back to the beach house. It was only a few blocks out of the way but a part of town she hadn't explored since her days of braces and Jane Austen.

The businesses were an eclectic assortment of restaurants, antique stores and beauty and coffee shops. As Melanie began a collection of take-out menus, the red light at the corner gave her time to appreciate a boldly painted window display: 'Amazing New Year Specials'. Looking beyond the offers painted on the glass of the corner building were bright lights over punching bags, speed bags, racks of medicine balls and, in the center, a boxing ring.

"Welcome to Boxing World." The upbeat greeting was accompanied by the fresh scent of cleaning solution that no urban gym should have.

"Thanks," she said, glancing over the colorful mitts.

"We've got it all." The man was in his thirties, with a well-defined torso beneath his logo polo shirt. "Personal trainers and matches three evenings a week. There's also an all-purpose training room in the back. Mirrors, you know? Would you like a tour?"

"Of a gym? I'm good." She glanced at the bags.

"You can go in, first session is on us. Use these," he said, reaching under the counter for a pair of gloves. "Lockers are in the restroom." He pointed.

"Great." She accepted the offer and her energy sparked.

She jabbed, testing the feel of the bag against her fists. Cushioned behind the thick padding, the impact was negligible. Time moved faster than it had in weeks as bottled aggressions surfaced and the bag took the brunt of her temper. Winded, she dropped back a step, remembering where she was. Over an hour had passed and sweat had darkened patches of her cotton shirt. She returned the mitts and the borrowed lock, exiting the gym with jelly arms, eight ruby-red knuckles and a membership.

Hungry, she picked up two meatball subs, a side of coleslaw and potato salad, plus a six pack from the drugstore concealed in a reusable insulated bag, she hoofed Coast Boulevard toward her new apartment. And was fully prepared to call Adam to make nice, she was pondering her dilemma of how to accomplish her task without a cell phone when her dad's voice broke through her thoughts.

"Annie."

"Dad?" She glanced at the road behind his rear bumper. "You can't park there."

"I'm not. Get in. Your mother and I are taking you out to dinner."

"I got dinner." She shook her arms, rattling the bottles.

"Get in."

"Dad. I got food."

"You can put it in the fridge. Honey, you're holding up traffic." Melanie's breath came out in a growl, irritated by his fatherly bullying. "Your mother won't be happy with that outfit."

As he drove she unzipped her duffle bag of essentials, pulled out a pair of jeans and tugged them over her running tights while a sweater covered her T-shirt.

"Better?" she asked, her grin forming at the sight of her cousin Penny waving madly from the curb beside a scowling Rita. "Why is Mom mad?"

"You made us late." He parked, grumbled to his unhappy spouse and hurried inside to put Melanie's food in the fridge.

Ignoring her mother's glower, she climbed over the seats to sit in the back beside Penny. Like magnets they huddled, talking and laughing.

Penny squealed, "I am so sorry I haven't been around sooner but I've been insanely busy!"

"When did you move to town?" Melanie asked, feeling like a teenager with her best friend and catching up in her parents' car.

"Almost two months ago. I stayed in Bruce's room for two weeks – still stinks like feet in there but it's so much better than the crappy apartment I found. What a dump and I'm … Hey!" Penny jumped in her seatbelt. "Why don't we move in together? Do you want to? Oh my God, Mel … it'd be so much fun. Like we planned when we were kids, remember?"

"Too late," Melanie said, feeling guilty. "I got a place."

"No." Penny said, sitting back in disappointment. "Where?"

"One of the little beach cottages on Coast." She winced, breaking the news to her parents.

"When did this happen?" Rita piped in.

"Can you afford that?" Roger asked.

"Today. And, yeah, I think so," she answered, knowing the grilling had only just begun. "You remember Sylvia Michaels?"

"Sylvia Michaels," her mother cooed. "She was an adorable child. Had golden hair like Shirley Temple."

"She still does. Gave me the family discount."

"Oh, that family is part of the mob," Rita added, curtly.

"You don't know that," Roger accused.

"I do." Rita twisted to give Melanie the knowing eye. "Just go through the halls of that casino in Vegas … you know the Italian one downtown. The Michaels name is everywhere."

"Don't listen to her." Roger cleared his throat.

"They were close friends with Sinatra."

"Well, she gave me the keys." Melanie dangled her new treasures from her index finger.

"We should have Sylvia over for dinner," Rita voiced her thoughts.

"No." The harmony in the car was pitch perfect.

Hurt, Rita straightened her back and stared out the windshield. "I made that roast the other night and you both said it was delicious."

Adam had cooked dinner that night.

"Why, Annie? Why would you rent there, at those prices!?" Roger asked, taking an exit on the current conversation of mobsters. "It's highway robbery."

"I could move in with you, split the rent," Penny interrupted.

"Those places aren't big enough for one," her dad chimed in. "They were built in the twenties; Old plumbing, old electrical and no insulation whatsoever. I'm not even sure it's safe to live there."

"I'm sure she keeps it up to code." Melanie sighed.

"Well, after dinner I'll go over, have a look around, you know, kick the tires."

"Okay, but it looks good."

"You never know, could be mold or termite damage."

Dinner was at *the* Mexican restaurant. Her parents had five go-to spots and to suggest a place off the list was punishable by a tirade of complaints and inevitably ending up at one of the five, making the endeavor useless.

Penny was a perfect distraction. Talking through her enchilada and by the end of the meal Melanie was ready to put some Long Island in her iced tea. Roger drove 'senior citizen' style to the cottage and mumbled complaints about everything from the window casings to the lack of water pressure.

"Bye, Dad." She kissed each of her parents on the cheek and held the door open for their easy departure.

"I'll be in the parking lot … 6 a.m. sharp," Roger stated.

"I'll be ready, bright eyed and bushy tailed," Melanie replied.

"Your parents are the Flintstones," Penny said quietly as she followed them out to the car.

"Want to grab a drink?" It was eight-thirty.

"Always. Where?"

"The bar on the corner?" Melanie suggested.

"Are you talking about the Sand Piper?"

"I guess."

"That's closed. Now it's The Garage."

"Then I mean The Garage."

"I have to go home and change first. Roger," Penny hollered from the doorway.

"Why? You look fine." Melanie stood, watching her cousin's

shadow.

"Order me a beer. I'll be there before it's poured," Penny promised over her shoulder, racing after her ride. "I'll be there in a jiff, I swear."

Melanie squinted, knowing better than to trust Penny's swear. She showered off the top layer of salt from her skin, slipped into a pair of tight jeans, strapped on a pair of heels and walked the few blocks, wishing she'd worn a heavier jacket.

CHAPTER 16

His heart rang with the sound of the doorbell. She'd come back and he was ready to apologize for both of their parts of the argument.

He opened the door to 6'3" of disappointment. Having forgotten he'd asked to borrow Jace's truck to move boxes to the storage unit.

"Don't look so happy to see me," Jace said, brushing past Adam.

"Sorry." He shook the troubled thoughts from his head. "Thanks for coming."

"Look at this place," Jace admired from the entry hall that opened to the kitchen and living room. "I can't believe you're selling, it's depressing." He said with his arm folded across his chest. Adam looked over the rooms without the same sentiment. "I feel like I grew up in this house," Jace continued. "So many good times, remember?" He clapped Adam's back.

"I remember." Adam chuckled at the wild spark in his friend's eyes.

"God, the Cirque girls," Jace shivered to his toes.

"Yeah, they could bend, couldn't they?"

The two stood and marveled at the past that was replaying before their eyes.

"Flexible." Jace inhaled. "What about the poker games, the laser tag … so many good times. I hate that you're getting rid of this place."

"Time to move on."

"I guess." Jace didn't sound convinced. "Where's Angel? I thought she'd be here."

Angel. Adam's heart lurched a bit with Jace's nickname for Mel. "She was here," he said, walking into the room they'd just been appreciating. "Water?"

"No, thanks. She makes you sell and then she bounces? Women."

"It's not like that." Adam said, the tape gun in hand. "She's having trouble with…" he looked around, "the past."

"Oh," Jace's nod was complete with understanding. "Is she pissed?"

"A little bit." He lied.

"She'll get over it." Jace's grin was slow in forming, "but you can't deny that it was worth it."

"Melanie hurt? Not worth it."

"You must not remember what I remember," Jace took in a big breath. "Man, I wish I had taken part in more of those opportunities. What was I thinking? The cheerleaders? Why? Why did you let me walk?"

"I admired your commitment to your values."

"You admired all the way to the bedroom. Four to one. Jesus, Adam, I can tell you that I'm regretting my decisions. I should've had more fun, I should've taken every one of those women to bed. I should've…"

"Well, I did and now *I'm* regretting *it*."

"Don't say that!" Jace protested. "You're my hero. I aspire to be you."

"No." Adam shook his head and both saw remorse in each other's eyes. "Come on." Adam slapped Jace on the arm. "Let's load some boxes."

The work went fast. They filled the bed of the truck, hauled it to the self-storage building and unloaded.

"Can I ask," Jace said when they were seated at the bar with their beer, "why her? She's great and all, but you could have anyone."

"She's beautiful," he said, the familiar rustling of warm anxiety spreading through his chest. "What?"

"That isn't enough to put up with her..." Jace grunted. "They're all beautiful."

Adam looked at Jace, his wide, guiltless blue eyes asking for clarification. "Because when I first saw her it was like," his heart fluttered up to the base of his throat, "I was struck by a bolt of lightning." Adam set his gaze and sipped his beer to conceal the emotion that had infused his blood. "I can't explain it any other way. Everything inside me ignited and I knew it was her I'd been looking for. Maybe it sounds like bullshit but," the spark of that moment flared and the flutter revved, "even now she makes my pulse raises." He let the cold beer cool the heat in his chest. "I've made mistakes," he said, his lips pressed together.

"Wow," Jace bobbed his head, "I had no idea it was like that. Well, then I think you need to give her space. That's what I do when Trish is pissed at me. When it seems as if I cannot do anything right and she's up in my face ... I give her room and..." he shrugged, "it works. Give Angel a couple days to settle down and she'll realize she's blown everything out of proportion. She'll come back begging for you to forgive her. Time doesn't heal all wounds but distance will, Bro. Trust me."

"She found the stash of condoms I used to keep in the cushions of the couch."

"Ooh," Jace winced. "At least you were being safe."

"She found a book of sexual positions some woman had given me – the pages had been circled. Ones we'd done in green and the ones she wanted to try in red."

"Why'd you keep that?"

"I'd forgotten about it," Adam groaned. "She found other…"

"The tapes?"

"No. I got rid of those a long time ago."

"That blows."

"Those were just trouble. Never watched them anyway."

"Man, I have to ask," Jace swigged his beer. "You met Trish before she and I got together…"

"Yeah," Adam didn't like the worried tone.

"Did you and she ever…?"

"No." Adam said, bluntly.

"Because I know Trish…"

"No."

"Okay." The apple in his throat jogged up an inch and then settled back down.

"Mel was in my life by then … she introduced me to Trish and," he smiled as he shook his head. "She'd already taken over my head. And heart. Nothing ever happened between me and your wife." Adam slapped Jace's back.

"Thanks. I knew it but…" Jace coughed and drained the bottle. "Angel is tough, but she'll come around."

Adam felt sick. "Why do you call her Angel?"

"She hooked me up with Trish, she was my angel – and she saved my life."

Adam cocked his brow at Jace.

"Didn't she tell you?"

"I don't know what you're talking about."

"Remember she and I went out on a blind date?"

"Yeah…"

"I'd just gotten the Porsche and I thought I'd show off and take her out for a spin." He grimaced. "We spun all right. I lost control and we were carving donuts at 90 miles per hour."

"Jesus Christ."

"Yeah, right." His eyes were wide, "crazy shit. Like I said, we were spiraling when the next thing I know, she's jumping into my lap. Her tiny feet on mine, shifting gears… hell, I don't even know how she did it, but she stopped the momentum. We were literally two inches from a mother fucking tree." Jace was grinning while shaking his head. "I nearly pissed my pants, but not her. Angel was cool. Suave. Like it was no big deal to drive NASCAR style, to walk away from deadly shit, to save our lives. Seriously, she saved my life, she was my guardian angel."

CHAPTER 17

The Garage was on the second floor, with an outside escalator that carried patrons to the revolving retail space. Her fingers were curled around the wrench door handles as she tried to read the colorful, illegible gangster font of the sandwich board. Inside, the repair shop motif continued: workbench tables with tin flood light lampshades suspended from the ceiling, concrete floors, chrome Cadillac grills busting out from the spray-painted walls.

"At least you kept the stage," Melanie mentioned to the grungy tender behind the bar.

"We have a house band for the weekends," he answered with a shrug. "It's called The Garage Band."

"Clever." She ordered a draft and a tequila shot. "Kind of dead in here, isn't it?" she asked, swiveling on her bar stool to consider the lonely room. Outside, on the short balcony heaters warmed the empty space.

"Still early. Livens up after ten." He slid her drinks beside her hand and reached around to add a bowl of pretzels. "Anything else?"

"Another one of these," she said, throwing down the shot. *Whew,* she blew out a burning breath and blinked away the excess moisture that pooled at the rims. "It's been a long time." She conceded, already feeling the effects rush to her head as she picked up her beer.

Snacking and drinking, she added coins to the jukebox. The bartender had been right about the crowd ballooning after ten.

"I don't think he's coming."

"Not a he." Melanie answered, finishing off the pretzels. "And I swear I'm getting a stiff neck from glancing at the door ever other second," she said, checking the time on the big wall clock. *Yup, Penny is still late,* she thought. "But I'm feeling pretty good, anyway." The alcohol made the annoyance more tolerable.

She'd been nursing two beers for an hour when Melanie heard the familiar cackle of her least favorite cousin. Apologies flowed into excuses ... Penny ordered three shots and a beer to catch up. Gulping the tequila, she lifted two fingers to the bartender and started on the beer.

"Why are you wearing a prom dress?" Melanie asked, shielding her eyes from the hundreds of sequins on dark blue satin.

"Shut up," Penny laughed. "That dude at the end of the bar is totally checking you out."

"He's looking at you." She said, not bothering to look over. "He can't believe a grown woman would wear that outfit."

She tilted across Melanie. "Nope. Definitely you."

"Doesn't matter."

"Ooh, really?" she sang, gazing at Melanie from over the rim of her drink. "Still hooked on tall, dark and brooding. Never thought that was your type."

"Gorgeous and talented is everyone's type." Melanie swigged.

"I didn't want to bring it up with your mom there, but you really should think of ditching him..."

"There's nothing wrong with Adam."

"... And give him to me. I'm totally jealous. Do you know how long it's been since I've gotten laid?"

"How's Nate?" Melanie interrupted.

"I wouldn't know." Penny frowned and reduced her beer by half. She continued without prompting. "It's a mystery what happened. I mean, we weren't in love but we were having fun, you know? And then all of a sudden, he pulls the plug. It's over." She snapped her fingers. "Out of nowhere."

"Sucks." Melanie lifted her glass.

"So where is Prince Charming?" Penny cocked her head, searching the crowd.

"Home." More drinks arrived. "Don't look at me like that."

"He's cheating. I have enough experience with men to know."

"He's not. It turns out," Melanie flinched, "I have a deep-seated resentment against his past. And without any other problems to take up my time, it's all I can think or talk about. I seriously need to do something about my life."

"Just admit you're jealous for a reason." Penny was quick to find fault that wasn't there.

"I knew he had dated lots of women before we met, but I can't seem to stop throwing it in his face." Her exhale was eighty proof. "But as of today, I've got my own place and things are going to get better. Trish says we need more sex."

"I do not know how you can stand that chick." Penny scrunched her face.

"She doesn't know how I can stand you," Melanie laughed, her head spinning a little bit. "And I agree with both of you."

"Well, I think you've got pretty good instincts. If you feel there's something slippery about the guy … he's using a manipulation tactic. Trust me, I know all about abusive relationships." She drank and drew a cigarette out of a pack. "Are you sure he's alone right now? A man is gone for months – maybe there was someone he'd been missing." She poked her elbow to Melanie's bicep. "Ever think of that? You gave him opportunity. I bet he's out there boinking some hoe as we speak."

Melanie shook her head. "When did you start smoking?"

"Years ago. But I quit. I carry them around for security – besides, the nicotine police make it illegal to light up anywhere anymore. You didn't answer." Narrowing her gaze, she pointed her index finger while holding a cigarette and a shot glass. "Let's call him, you know, see if the bastard's lying."

"I don't have a phone."

"Did you leave it at home?"

"I don't have one."

"How is that possible?"

"I chucked it."

"Damn, I wish I was that brave, but I've got a job." Her lips stretched and sloped. "Oops, sorry!"

"I have a job." Their eyes met and after a held breath they both laughed.

"Aunt Rita is a beast," Penny said, when they could speak again. "God knows. How is it working with Uncle Roger?"

"It pays the rent … almost."

"Good. I actually love my job." Her face broke in half with a wide, toothy grin. "My love-life is in the crapper but my career –

yeah, an actual career – has taken off. Have you heard of the store called La Bourse?" Melanie shook her head. "It's for tweens. I'm the accessories buyer."

"Well, that explains the dress." Melanie snorted out a chuckle.

Penny's glare was a half-effort. "In the two months since I've already started they've sent me to L.A. and Tijuana. Okay, so those aren't so glamorous but they promised Milan and New York this summer."

"You are talking way too fast."

"I never understood you and your loyalty to that shitty company of yours. But, Mel, I get it now." Penny exclaimed, aggressively grabbing Melanie's forearm and shaking it. "It's fantastic to be doing something you love! I love buying." Her palm covered her heart and she bent way back. "And I am sooo good at it. Hey, we need another round over here." She waved the universal sign over their empty glasses. "Let's call him."

"What are you talking about?"

"Tall, dark and brooding. TBD."

"TDB," Melanie corrected. "You are making my eyes cross." She felt the beginning of a hangover. "I can't."

"You can." Penny shoved her cell into Melanie's palm.

"Between you and me," the bartender leaned across the bar, "calling is a bad idea."

"See?" Melanie pointed.

"You ever had a girlfriend, Chump?" Penny snarled and the bartender waved his white rag in surrender. "Thought not. Douche," she whispered and then ordered Melanie. "Dial. Prove he's not a lying bastard."

"I *do* need to tell him about the cottage and it would show that you're wrong," Melanie gave a curt, decisive nod and stared blankly at the phone. Her first three attempts were wrong numbers.

"Christ, Melanie. Don't you know your boyfriend's number?"

"Shhh, I can't concentrate with your voice in my head." She thought hard and tried again. "Shit."

"We should go there … catch him in the act."

"In the act of sleeping?"

"Come on, Mel, aren't you curious?"

"There isn't anything to be curious about," Melanie hiccupped.

"How can you be so sure?"

"Please, stop talking so much."

"I'm calling." Penny grabbed her phone.

"Need a number for that," Melanie grunted smugly.

"Your BFF, Trish, knows him, right? I bet *she* has his number." Penny was giggling. "I have her number … your mother had me call her a few times. Be quiet." She held her index finger to her lips. "Hi, Trish." She paused to listen. "It's Penny you know, Smelly Melly's cousin." She ended the sentence with a sputter of drunken laughter. "I'm looking for her boyfriend's number." There was hesitation and Melanie sat glued to Penny's expression. "Really? Well, she told me that she didn't know how she could stand you. If you hang up, I'm gonna call back. Look, I don't like you either but Mel and I are here at a bar and … did you know she doesn't own a cell phone?" Melanie waited through the pause. "I know, right. No." Penny's eyes cut to Melanie, "she didn't tell me. Hmmm. Did you know she doesn't even know his number? Seriously. You want to speak to her?" Her smile spread and she reached over, nabbing the ballpoint off the waitress' drink tray. "I knew we could work together. Thank you." She waved the napkin and ended the call as the bartender snagged the pen out of her hand. "Call him."

Melanie took the phone and the napkin. By the fourth ring she slid her eyes to Penny who had her face pressed against the back of the phone.

"Hello?" His voice was thick from sleep. Her heart pounded with the sound and her insides rolled in a tide of longing while Penny covered her mouth to stifle the giggle.

"Hi," Melanie forced out the word.

"Who is this?"

"Don't you recognize me?" Penny coughed out a terrible Melanie imitation.

"Stop." Melanie pushed her cousin off the stool.

"Melanie?"

"Oh, shit!" Penny yelped and pressed the red button.

"What?" Melanie glared at her cousin. "Why'd you do that?"

"I thought we didn't want him to know it was us." She was laughing as she got back up on the chair. "Another round, handsome."

"Now I'm handsome?" He sneered. "I'm calling you a cab."

"I'll call *you* a fucking cab," Penny slurred. "You're a Fucking Cab."

Melanie extracted herself from the brew as Penny's phone vibrated in her hand.

"Do you want to explain that to me?" Adam asked.

"Not really." She turned her back to the ruckus and stuck her index finger in her open ear.

"Who are you with?"

"My cousin, Penny."

"Have you called the bowling alley to ask how big are their balls?"

"Or KFC about their breasts." She laughed. "We sort of regress when we're together."

"Do you need a ride home?"

"I'm okay, we're at the bar by the house. Where are you?"

"Home. Feeling like shit."

"Really?" Her heart melted even as her attention was divided, watching Penny argue with the bartender. "Ah, Adam, I've got to go. I don't want to but, shit. I, I have to." The phone was nestled in her back pocket when she caught the flying bottle of tequila.

The chaos around her had erupted and Penny's shrieking voice cut through the riot. "Run Mel, run!"

She was a dozen steps closer to the exit when she stalled to consider the questions that had made their way to the forefront. Turning, she saw the bartender, a half body higher than the crowd, pointing at her. "Security!" he yelled. "Stop that woman!"

From behind, harsh hands grabbed and lifted her from her shoulders. The bruising fingers dug into her muscle … but only for a second.

CHAPTER 18

The cold sidewalk cut through the seat of her pants as six of them were handcuffed and lined up against the outside wall of The Garage. Melanie was squeezed between Penny and a man with a blood-stained T-shirt, who kept muttering about the abusive power of the law.

She rubbed out the itch on her nose with her shoulder, while the officer looked them over – his heavy boots stomping inches from the soles of their shoes. The man in uniform was mouthing something but Melanie's attention rested exclusively on the bulk of humanity residing on the bumper of the ambulance.

I barely touched him, she thought, though his knees had hit hard when she put him in a headlock. There were no regrets, not even as the paramedic strapped an oxygen tank to the bouncer's face.

Penny's body shuttered against her arm.

"You all right?" Melanie asked.

"I can't get arrested again," she mumbled, sniffling. She'd been silently crying, her clumped mascara was causing her lashes to resemble plump spiders. "The last time, I was fired and…"

"The last time? When? Why were you arrested?"

"Domestic dispute." She whimpered. "I was working at a dentist's office and she didn't like me so I slept with her husband."

"You can't get arrested for that."

"She came home, found us in her bed and took a swing at me but hit the bastard instead. Broke the lamp. After that it just got ugly and the neighbors called the police."

There was nothing to say.

"Excuse me," the middle-aged officer growled. "Am I interrupting?" Both heads swiveled in a resounding no. "Which one of you wants to start?" His horseshoe hairline was silver and his wide girth spilled over the top of his pants covering the belt. "Who started this mess?" he asked, his eyes shifting left-right-left-right as the yelling began. "Stop!"

Melanie leaned forward to see Penny and the bartender glaring at each other.

Penny was the first to break the silence. "He was serving water out of a tequila bottle and charging full price. He's a cheater and a liar and should be put in jail!"

"Well?" The officer placed his hands on his ample hips, listening to the bartender's stammering protest.

"The bottle is right there," Penny interrupted, shifting to point her chin to the young officer who had been first on scene. "He seized the evidence," she continued with the verve that came from too many hours in front of the TV.

"You were drunk. I should've stopped serving you an hour ago."

"Okay," the cop grumbled and nearly rolled his eyes. "Who took out the guard?" His eyes focused on the man with the bloody T-shirt.

"Not me, Man, it was her."

Melanie felt the heat of his blazing stare.

"Be serious." The officer stepped closer, his eyes still zeroed in on her sidewalk-neighbor.

Two car lengths away, the wind waltzed shadows over the lone figure under the historic streetlamp. The butterflies in her stomach went crazy at the sight of him; even from the distance she could see the glint in his eyes that was lit from within. She would have waved but her hands were cuffed behind her back, instead she smiled.

Her left-side companion continued declaring his innocence. "It wasn't me. This is male profiling!"

The cop's face tightened. "How about it?" he asked Melanie with less commitment to his original hunch.

"Self-defense."

"Don't get smart with me young lady. You assaulted…"

"Excuse me, Sir," the junior officer coughed and handed the older man his phone. "You're going to want to take this."

The excess flesh of his face rolled into peaks and valleys as he rammed the phone to his ear and snapped. "Yes?" His pensive tone was short as he listened. "I understand." Tossing the cell back to the younger cop. "Which one of you is Melanie Ward?"

"I am."

"Get her up."

"Not without her," Melanie answered, gesturing toward Penny as she was pulled to her feet.

"You're hardly in the position to make demands."

"I think that phone call says otherwise." She held the stare.

The man's face shuffled through a deck of emotions. "Get 'em both out of here."

"I won't go unless this man is persecuted!" Penny twisted in the hands of the officer as he helped her to a vertical position. Melanie turned toward at her idiot cousin. "Well?" Penny glared at the cop, who glared back. For a moment he caressed the Taser on his belt.

"Pen," Melanie scolded, sounding more like her mother than she'd liked.

"What?" Penny scowled.

"Let him take the cuffs off," Melanie ordered, rubbing her wrists. "And let's get out of here."

"Fine. Nice doing business with you, Convict," Penny spat at the bartender and stepped over his outstretched legs. "He's lucky I didn't kick him."

Melanie followed the blue prom dress into the shadows and away from the strobe lights of the unnecessary ambulance. Adam was inclining against a parking meter, the smug expression broadening, breaking her heart, as he kicked himself out of the lean.

"You hurt?" he asked, the amusement playing across his face.

She liked the weight of his hand gently caressing her wrist while his other lifted her face for inspection.

"How'd you do that?" Penny asked. "How'd you get us out of trouble?"

"I know a guy," he answered coolly.

"I don't trust him," she mouthed to Melanie who punched her cousin's arm. "Owie!" Penny frowned, rubbing the spot on her bicep.

"First a bar brawl and now you're hitting women. Mel?" He lifted her right hand and ran his thumb over her bruised knuckles.

"Brawl?" she tugged her hand away. "Hardly. And Penny deserves it."

"Do not," she humphed. "Tall, dark and brooding. You wouldn't happen to have a fun-loving cousin, would you?"

"I do but they're all girls."

"I don't swing that way."

"You okay to drive?" Melanie asked.

"I was drinking water, remember? Where are my keys?" she asked, absently giving her dress a pat down and reaching into her limited cleavage to conjurer a car key. "There it is. See, I'm fine. Getting shackled on the sidewalk is sort of a buzz kill." She unlocked the door and slipped into the driver's seat. "Oh, Mel, FYI, if you hear sounds coming from the backyard … ignore them." With the blow of a kiss she turned the ignition. "Trust me."

"I could've used that info a couple of weeks ago."

"What was that about?" he asked, stepping in close.

"The hot tub. My parents. They don't believe in swimsuits or Google Earth."

"It's kind of nice."

"Don't tell me it's *nice*. You haven't seen my mom's pink, naked body splashing around. They walk around like they're the only people who live there." She'd missed him. "Adam," she started, "it seems like I'm either apologizing for something or screaming about that same something. I am so sorry."

"No, Baby." His hands moved to cradle her head. "I'm sorry." Releasing one hand to run his fingers through his hair. "Mel," this time he closed his eyes, "I, uh…"

"It's okay." She said, taking his hands in hers.

His expression was etched with grief. "I don't want to fight. And those things you found, scraps of the old life…" – he held eye contact – "that's not who I am anymore. Sweetheart, don't go to your parents'. Please, can we get a hotel for the night and just be together?"

"About that…" She said, her revelation interrupted as he leaned in, his lips brushing across hers. Her mind became still but her body caught fire. She hung on to keep from buckling. *Adam*, her heartbeat pounded out the syllables in a rapid two-beat rhythm.

His breath rushed past her ear. "Jesus, I've missed you."

"I want to take you…" She blew out a deep breath.

"You want to take me?" He raised his brows and humor eased his passion.

"You didn't let me finish. I have something to show you." She extracted herself from his arms and reached for her helmet on the back of his bike.

"I like the way this is going." He said, playfully.

"Let's get out of here," she said, climbing onto the motorcycle and giving directions to parking spot #3.

"Where are we?" The cluster of houses was dark when they parked.

"Come on." She said, leading him down the windy path to her new place. "This is home. I guess," she said uncomfortably, slipping her key into the lock. "I rented it." She filled her lungs with the air of freedom and switched on the lamplight.

"You did?" His surprise carried a grin as his eyes took in the space. "Really, Mel?" he turned to her, his brows pinched and she nodded, bracing for his reaction. "You're brilliant."

"Yeah?"

He poked his head around the counter to the kitchen and she locked the front door before entering the bedroom.

"Are you sure you rented all of it?"

There it was. "I know it's small." Her anxiety thwarted the smile that tried to form. Melanie bit her bottom lip as she stood with her hands gripping the back of a chair. She'd never rented before, never owned a car – or anything that wasn't supplied by the Agency. It was a new experience. "Is it okay? You like it?"

"It's perfect." His green eyes glistened. "When did you do this?"

"Today." She cleared her throat, caught in his emerald web. "I thought since you were going to be homeless in a few days that we were going to need a place. Unless you want to move into my room with me, but then you'd have to have a depraved fondness for living with my parents and their bohemian ways."

"So," his smile spread, "are you asking me to move in with you?"

She blew out a stream of nerves in a single breath. "What do you say?"

"Yes."

"Yes? Really?" She blinked back the moisture that threatened as the wave of emotion bulldozed her defenses.

"God, I love you," he breathed, his eyes glazing over.

There was no time to react, her back was pinned against the wall, her wrists were restrained above her head and Adam's mouth was on hers. Pleasure and pain merged as she squirmed and endured his lips down her neck.

She felt weightless in his arms. Adam set her down gently, kneeled at the edge of the bed, his hands skimmed from her calf to her ankle, while his eyes never wavered from hers. Slowly, carefully, he unbuckled her shoe, his fingers gently massaging the bottom of her foot … and kissed each toe before moving to the right foot.

CHAPTER 19

Moonlight streamed in through the wooden shutters as she lay in the crook of his arm, reveling in the slow, gentle rhythm of his breathing. He'd been intense, focused, and he'd swept her away with him. Her internal engine revved with the memory, still feeling the touch of his lips, his hands – *God, his hands* – she shivered and closed her eyes.

Adam stirred, pulling her closer. "You awake?" he asked drowsily.

"Thinking."

"Want to tell me about what?" he was mostly asleep, running his hands across his face and through his hair.

"About us. About…" The butterflies in her abdomen were charged. "I feel so good about renting this place. As soon as I saw it, I knew it was a game changer. I mean," she smiled at him only inches from her, "if I didn't have money saved up, I could never make the rent on what my father pays."

"I know we've been over this," he smiled gently. "But money

isn't an issue."

"I was thinking that I'd stick it out with my dad through summer, use that time to come up with a strategy that I can sell my parents. I can't leave until I've got another job lined up." She stopped, letting her head lay heavily on the pillow. Melanie stared into his eyes that had been stripped of color from the moonlight. "Have I told you that I'm really glad you're here?"

"There isn't any other place I'd rather be."

"Good." She smiled and relaxed.

"But," he started, his voice dropping. "I have to go to Phoenix in the morning." He paused before explaining. "A guy I know is franchising his restaurant and I wanted to check out how he's doing things."

"Oh." Her word was carried out on a breath disappointed. "How long will you be gone?"

"Two nights." His hand ran down her arm. "When I called him, I thought you needed time away from me." His gaze softened. "Believe me, I'm regretting every second I'll be gone."

"It's only two nights," she said, trying to convince herself.

"Why don't you come with me?" His voice lifted with the possibility.

Her dad would never go for it. "I have to work and you're going to be busy."

"Our timing sucks," he said, brushing the hair from her forehead.

"It does."

"I'll cancel." His decision was crisp. "I'll postpone until you and I have made up … sufficiently." He was grinning as he rolled on top of her, his hips weighing down on hers while he supported his torso with his forearms. "However long that may take."

"No." She giggled as she squirmed. "Go see your friend. I'll be here when you get back." She nodded her consent, her fingers tracing the tattoo on his chest. "Tonight was better."

"Better?" he asked, his brows shooting upwards. "That's my rating? Better? Better is forgettable." His expression turned menacing. "Baby, I am never forgettable."

She wasn't sure, but she might have yelped.

Melanie's picture window had a view of tall palm trees, waving briskly in the constant breeze with the big blue in the background.

"This *is* nice," she said, smiling as she filled her cup. "But the best decision was asking you to move in."

"Is it the coffee?" he smirked, standing in the gateway that separated the kitchen/dining area from the living room.

"Partially. It was either you or Penny." She tasted the black, hot liquid, "good," she nodded.

"I know you're joking," he cocked an eyebrow. "But your cousin…" He shook his head while his gaze traveled from her black slacks to her blue blouse. "I thought your dad required scrubs."

"He does." She grabbed a slice of toast. "But I sit in the front office. I feel stupid wearing a doctor costume when I'm just answering phones. What's he going to do, fire me?"

"Your mom would never allow it." He laughed.

"I know that, you know that and soon my dad will too."

"Mel," the awkwardness in his voice caught her attention. "Before you go," her gaze traveled from his face to his hands. "My number is programmed. Just while I'm gone."

"You bought me a phone."

"You walked out on me yesterday." His chest lifted and fell. "I couldn't reach you. I was stupid to let you go and I won't be here…" he stopped and bore his eyes into hers. "You'll keep it with you? Right?"

"I will."

"That easy?" he asked, peering at her through slits.

"Yeah." She nodded, giving into a small smile. "I might've been rash in my intolerance toward technology."

"And you'll use the Range Rover? I left the keys on the sideboard."

"You're riding the bike to Phoenix?"

"I've been missing the open road. The Phoenix address and number are in the notes." He set the thin phone in her palm. "Two nights."

"Okay."

"And is it too much to ask that you stay away from Penny?"

Melanie laughed and muttered "maybe" as he pulled her to his chest and traced his warm fingers over the erratic pulse at her throat.

"We only have a few minutes, huh?" Adam's kisses were light on her skin. "I'll be back Wednesday."

"Don't forget to call," she said, in a low, breathy tone as her hand closed around her new phone. "You have my number."

Two horn honks were followed by three rushed angry blasts. Her dad was in the parking lot.

"Duty calls." Melanie frowned and took in oxygen to settle her system. "Thank you for saving me from the clink last night."

"You'd have figured a way out, but I am glad you called … even if it started as a prank call."

"I wanted to tell you about the cottage."

Two longer honks certainly woke the neighbors.

"You better go."

"I wish I didn't have to." She hesitated.

"You really don't, you know? We'll strategize when I get back." He smiled before dusting her lips with soft, coffee flavored kisses.

Dragging her lips into her mouth, torn about leaving, he caught her chin with the tips of his fingers and held her gaze for a second.

Her dad's horn bellowed.

"Wednesday." They agreed and she rushed out into the moist and windy costal winter.

Melanie jogged around the corner to her father's sedan. He was behind the wheel, palms raised up above his head in a posture of praise, but his expression was flush with frustration. And reprimand.

"What are you wearing?" he asked before her ass hit the seat.

"Girl clothes." She eyed the little cottage longingly as he pulled away from the curb.

"That is not the uniform," he reminded her on their routine path to the coffee shop. "The others will think you're getting preferential treatment and then I'll have to let everyone…"

"I'm a receptionist. This is a receptionist costume."

"I wish you'd stop calling it a costume. It's not Halloween."

"Exactly," she sighed. "I don't belong in scrubs." She paused while he ordered coffee and muffins from the drive thru. "A year ago you were drinking the home brew."

"I can never go back." Five minutes later they were on the freeway heading toward Roger's practice. "Don't think we've finished the conversation about your wardrobe."

"I'm not wearing the costume and I hate Sponge Bob," Melanie said, settling back.

"There are a lot of gals who wanted that position."

Trust me, I already know. She'd been pierced by the glares and whispers since Day One. "I know and I'm grateful," she answered dutifully.

"You *are* getting along with the staff?" Her dad gave her a sideways glance.

"Yeah, they're all swell."

"And Bob? He was devastated that you're seeing someone."

"I was thinking about setting him up with Penny."

"That would be a disaster. Besides, she has a beau."

"Nope." She wasn't going to get into the gory details. "She's a free agent."

"Great," Roger groaned as he pulled into his reserved spot. "About the clothes?"

"I'm wearing them."

"It sets a bad precedence."

"You going to fire me?"

His inhale was audible. "You'd make me explain that to your mother?" She nodded. Roger exhaled. "Fine, but only on Wednesdays."

"Every day."

"Annie."

She stared at her dad.

"You are just like your mother."

"In all the good ways, right?"

"You win. Wear what you want, but look like a professional."

"A professional what?" She grinned and was seared by his glare. Prickles of contrition followed. "Sorry."

CHAPTER 20

Having lunch in the break room she took the last empty seat at a full table and still ate alone. The day passed in a half-dream state, answering phones, making appointments and reliving last night. Adam phoned twice and each time she broke regulation to sneak away and take his call.

"Annie, quitting time," Roger said, knocking her out of her thoughts. It was after 5 and for the first time she'd been ambushed by the hour. "I saw you getting along with the staff." Her dad held the car door open for her. "I knew you'd come around. I'm proud of you."

"Dad, I've been thinking..."

"Don't try for a raise." He laughed, his eyes creasing at the corners as he happily tapped the wheel to the beat of the music on the radio. "I told you that rent was too high."

"It's not that."

He raised the volume on The Golden Oldies station and they drove home in the company of crooners that had long since died. Melanie sang along with the doo-wop beat until Roger made a quick pause at her curb.

"See you in the morning." She leaned over to place a kiss on her dad's cheek. "Bye, Pops."

"You sure you're okay there alone?"

"Enjoy the Jacuzzi," Melanie gagged as she closed the door and double tapped the roof of the vehicle.

In her living room, she kicked off her heels and collapsed on the sofa with a sigh and every intention of settling into her new place. She paced the rooms, inspected each drawer and cabinet – fifteen minutes later she was jogging to the corner sports club.

Melanie grinned as the clamor from inside spilt out onto the street, the excitement was contagious and hit as she opened the door. Bright lights flooded the two dozen people who'd gathered, lined single-file along the ropes, to shout catcalls. It was amateur night and the ladies were up. There were two women in the ring, gleaming with sweat, dodging and taking blows when she approached. The women weren't evenly matched, but the thrill of battle had her front row to watch the next two matches.

"Excuse me," she said, working her way to the manager. "How do I get in?"

His eyes dropped, sizing her up in less than a second. "What are you a buck, a buck ten?"

"About that," she told the man, who was her height, with dark black hair, matching eyes and a nose so disfigured she doubted he could breathe out of both sides.

"Okay, I've got one girl waiting … you're after her. You fight the winner." He flicked his head to the back. "David will get you prepped." The manager went back to the fight, announcing the winner and calling out the next contestants.

She pressed to the back of the room. "David?"

"Seriously? Mario is putting you in? We officially have no standards."

"You don't know me."

"But I do know Bianca and she's going to rip the flesh right off your pretty face." His grim expression reached his cagey eyes. "Give me your hands. Christ, you have the smallest fists I've ever wrapped. Like taping a pencil eraser. I hope you've got good insurance."

She was ready for a fight – either David or Bianca, it didn't much matter to her. "I'm going to need you to shut the fuck up."

"Feisty," he snorted, talking as he worked. "I hate Bianca. Egotistical bitch. But she's an animal; never lost a fight. I wish Mario would let me have a crack at her. That's her," he angled his head toward the ring.

Melanie took a few moments to size up her opponent.

"She is big." Melanie watched. Bianca, the demi-giant, was light and quick on her feet and she was no amateur. "Got any tips for me?"

"Yeah. Duck."

"Thanks." She shook her head and took another look at the ring.

"She favors her right side," David said without looking up. "You're pretty so she'll go for your face. She is strong and fast; faster than you'd think. You're short, I'd keep low if I were you." He smiled. "But I'm thanking God I'm not." The cheers were distracting. "How much experience have you got? Any?"

"Not really," she admitted.

"There's time to back out while you've still got a face."

"Funny. But I'm in."

"Okay, if you're still conscious, I'll see you back here in forty seconds."

"I could help straighten that nose of yours," she offered. "Free of charge."

"Why are the beautiful ones so bitchy?"

"Give me forty seconds. Not so beautiful. Right?"

He put the protective headgear on her and held a mouth guard for her bite down.

"Is that clean?"

"Only been used once ... today."

"Gross," she was saying as he shoved the soft plastic between her teeth.

"David!"

"You're up, Sunshine."

"Next up," Mario was announcing from center ring, "what's your name, Sweetheart?"

"She goes by Sunshine," David answered since her mouth was full.

Melanie tried to flip him off but her hands were wrapped inside gloves. She settled for another gesture. David laughed and Mario introduced her as Sunshine.

She bent between the yellow ropes to stand before a formidable soldier. Mario grunted out the rules, made the fighters fist bump and the bell rang. There was no dance. No getting to know your date. No appetizer. Just a swing and a miss. Barely.

The rush of wind blasted past her face. If she hadn't leaned back an inch she'd be on the ground. *Whoa,* Melanie rallied with a bit of cold steel icing her blood and a smile. Bianca was strong and, apparently, liked to jab ... a lot. *This is going to be fun*. Melanie exhaled a satisfied breath – and spent the next minute dodging and figuring out clues to the big woman's next moves.

Bianca was lightning fast and the first punch that landed knocked the air out of Melanie's lungs. *Enough thinking,* she decided as instincts took over … with a vengeance. Months of repressed tension flowed from her shoulders to her fists and pounded until someone interfered. The pressure on her shoulder had her swinging, forgetting she was in a controlled setting. Mario got lucky; she pulled her punch at the very last instant. His lips were moving but the rush of blood had deafened her to everything else.

He pointed and pushed her to the corner.

Bianca's voice rang clear. "I'm going to kill you, Bitch."

The bell rang and Bianca's sprint was expected. Melanie grabbed the opportunity and got a solid hit to the woman's jaw … the favor was returned.

The flashes of light had her dazed, but she had enough insight to remember David's advice and ducked, slamming her eraser fists into Bianca's abdomen. The second round was a blur and by the final bell, Melanie was drenched, drained and revitalized.

"What a treat," Mario called, snapping his fingers to have security escort Bianca out of the ring. "Some of us do enjoy the less-civilized matches," he joked as Bianca swore her vengeance and spat an arch that hit the side of Melanie's face.

Melanie flew, attacking Bianca through the bouncers. Her blow found the tip of the woman's chin before she was grabbed and pushed between the ropes.

"Well done, Sunshine," David laughed, reaching for the mouthpiece.

"Stop calling me that." She growled as he removed her headgear. Melanie straddled the end of the bench, stuck her fists out for him to release her hands and gasped to catch her breath. "Are you positive

Bianca is female? Jesus."

"No personal experience there," he said, tugging off the glove. She wiggled her liberated hand and pressed the tips of her fingers to her face.

"How are you feeling?" he asked, capturing her left hand and rubbing his thumb over her knuckles.

"Fine."

"Adrenaline," he chuckled. "Tomorrow you'll hurt like hell."

She grimaced, knowing his words were true.

"Speaking of which … I noticed you weren't wearing a ring."

"Maybe I left my jewelry at home." She answered, yanking her hand free of his.

"No tan line or indentation marks."

"A real fucking detective." Melanie stretched her neck, her back and her arms while keeping her eyes on him as he worked. "Or just experienced with married women."

"Some." David moved on to her other hand. "I was thinking…"

"No."

"I haven't asked."

"I'm saving you from humiliation."

"I'm just going to pester you again on Saturday."

"What's Saturday?"

"Rematch. The next opportunity for you to make Bianca taste her own blood."

"That'll have to happen without me." She flexed her fingers that had been bound. They were sore and throbbing. "Damn, that hurts." Forcing them open and pulling back on her fingers, stretching them to her wrists.

"Just dinner," he hesitated and gave her a squinty eye. "Or…"

"No."

"You go for the charge, for the circus, don't you? I know your type," he admired, pulsing his eyebrows and stretching out his grin. "What if I have that something you crave? The excitement?" He was whispering and she caught the onion on his breath. "Something you've never experienced and something you'll never forget."

"A movie?"

"*Like* an action/thriller, only this one is for real." Melanie felt the sparks of curiosity, the tingle that pulled at her gut. "Now that I've got your attention, promise you'll have dinner with me and I'll show you the surprise."

"No."

He snorted. "Why do I always fall for your type?" Melanie shrugged. "If I take you, you have to swear to keep it between us."

"Swearing, I can do," she answered.

"Then it has to be tonight." She studied his expression, his tone, his body language and agreed. "I'll pick you up," he offered.

"We'll meet."

"Fine. Burgers beforehand."

"That's dinner."

"I think I divorced you a couple of years ago," he laughed. "It's out in the middle of nowhere. Can you find Poway?"

At a quarter to eleven, Melanie parked the Range Rover in a spot beside the dumpster of a service station forty minutes outside of San Diego. She felt the indention of her Walther pressed into the small of her back as she zipped up her jacket and waved for David to stop honking.

"I see you," she scolded, approaching where he was filling up his convertible, a trashed '98 Mazda Miata.

"I want everyone to know we're together," he laughed, returning the nozzle to the pump.

"How far is this place?" she asked, glancing at the garbage piled onto the passenger seat.

"Let me get that." He hustled to her side of the car, loading his arms with bottles of nutritional supplements, Monster drink cans and clothing and tossed it all into the back seat. "Twenty minutes." He opened his arms with a flourish, inviting her to the newly vacated space. Poway was east, past the lights and fair temperatures of San Diego, and there was nothing twenty minutes in any direction. "You'll see why."

"Better be good or I'll hurt you." She smiled, adding a shoe into the back seat.

"Now you're just teasing me."

"David, what's wrong with you?"

"I like mean women. You turn me on, the way you boss people around and get away with it." He whistled as he inhaled. "Love it."

"That's sick."

"I know."

After a few attempts, he revved the engine and Tejano music rattled the speakers. David chair danced to his favorite song before he lowered the volume to talk boxing. It wasn't until they turned onto a small dirt road that the hackles on the back of her neck stood on end.

"Don't fidget, Sunshine. I'm not a serial killer. No shovel in the trunk."

Rounding the base of a low, rocky hill the landscape opened up to a shallow basin. Beyond the randomly parked cars lights blazed through the moonless night, igniting the desert like a stadium.

"What is this?" she asked, leaning forward.

"You'll see," he answered, weaving his junker through the make-shift lot to park between a Lexus and a creosote bush.

"We're lucky you didn't get stuck in the sand," Melanie said, her boot sinking down an inch.

"You worry too much! Look." He pointed through the dusty atmosphere to the trucks parked side by side, grill to tailgate, forming an oval in a cleared patch of desert. Headlights from the trucks facing center brightened the arena. Cheering spectators poured out of the cabs and the beds of the trucks and even more piled onto the roofs and hoods. The aroma of beer, sweat and weed spun with the dust and somewhere the remote trail of gun powder cut through the crisp desert night.

"What is all of this?" she asked as they approached the mayhem.

"The Coliseum." His voice was filled with awe, his face was laced with excitement and his dark eyes danced. "Gladiators. Come on."

Melanie was engrossed, sorting out the scene she was witnessing as the roar erupted and her nerves stung at the glimpse of a young man. His nearly naked body was bloodied and his face was the color and shape of an eggplant.

"Chill." David's breath fluttered at her ear. "They're only illegals."

"What?" The jeers ramped in a roar of thunderous clapping.

"I said," he shouted, "fighting to the death." He kept walking, pulling on her arm. "We're going to have to push to get a good view." He jumped on a tailgate and turned to yank her up by his side.

The group adjusted to accommodate the extra bodies. Melanie stood at the edge of the truck bed, where the noise of the crowd was drowned out by the rush of her own blood beating in her ears.

Her gaze shifted from the center arena to the men with rifles stationed between every truck, blocking the exits. She was looking for cameras, actors, a director … something to prove this to be impossible. But the mob was pumping fists and all eyes were zeroed in on the two young men on the sandy theater stage.

They were bare-chested and beaten. Limp and gasping, arms hanging loosely at their sides … Melanie watched in horrific fascination.

Holy shit, she thought, distressed at the fact that she was mesmerized. "And they're going to fight to the death?" She saw David nod from the corner of her eye. "Is this a regular event?"

"Every other month or so … depends. Always in a different location." He grinned. "You have to be invited and then … oh." He clenched his gut in empathy pain as one of the riflemen rammed the butt of his gun into the stomach of a fighter. "When the fight slows down the guards do what the can to get things started. This match is almost done, but don't worry, there's more events … usually another four or so."

Gunfire cracked, sending ripples of energy from her core and she fought the instinct to take cover. Her fingers found the smooth pearl grip of her gun, slipping it into her front pocket for easier access. The guards sent a second round of shots into the air, rattling the men who could barely stand.

"Are you okay?" David yelled directly into her ear. Laughing. "God, I love this!"

"Where are the bathrooms?"

"We're in the middle of the desert … pick a bush."

"I'll be right back." Melanie hopped down, her boots hitting the soft dirt and she was off, keeping to the shadows of the periphery.

Racing, she stayed low, traveling unnoticed. She slowed, reaching two guards engrossed with the battering from the hood of a Ford F-150. A short distance behind the sentries, eight wide-eyed men sat cross-legged, chained to each other through metal wrist cuffs. Melanie inched her way forward around the back of the vehicles.

"What do you think you're doing?"

Startled, she turned as the guard advanced. He was alone and he was close enough for her to … she dug the toe of her boot into the sand and kicked. A shower of pebbles and sand pelted his face, his hands went up, protectively, and the butt of her gun slammed against his cheekbone. It cracked and before he could scream Melanie had secured his neck in the crook of her elbow. She squeezed until he passed out.

His heels left track marks to the clump of cacti where she disassembled the rifle, tossing the trigger guard and the assembly rod farther into the desert. Frisking him, she removed a ten-inch fixed blade from his belt, on impulse she stuck it in her boot and headed to the prisoners. Her blood roiled and she had to concentrate to maintain a silent pace. The captives shifted away in mass as she advanced. Fear etched into their faces, Melanie placed a vertical finger across her lips, keeping an eye on the distracted guards.

"Soy aqui para ayudar," she whispered. Trying to calm the young men, whose eyes shifted from her to the guards, their heartbeats could be seen through their skin.

Working fast, she surveyed the situation; they were bound together by a heavy chain that was fastened around the bumper of a truck. Squatting, she positioned herself between two men and buried a section of the chain into the sand.

Okay, she thought, taking a deep, calming breath and opening her ears to absorb individual sounds among the commotion of the crowd. She shoved the barrel of her gun into the sand positioning it against the links, and waited.

Within seconds, the thunder of the horde peaked and Melanie pulled the trigger. The guards were absorbed in the brutality, missing her interference. The captives scrambled, quietly extracting themselves from their bonds.

"Run. Fast. Corelé. Rapido," she whispered as each one was released. "Cualquier direction. Corelé. Any direction. Just run. Now." Melanie followed her own advice, mixing into the pack. Knife in hand, she punctured every tire within reach.

She wound her way back to David just in time to witness the loser's last breaths. One man was left teetering on his bare feet with crazed eyes and blood rushing down his chest.

Her throat tightened and her thought process was limited to *shit, shit, shit*. That she'd freed the other eight, for the moment, was of little consolation.

"What happens now?" she rasped, watching the winner collapse on top of the dead body and scratch at the dirt. "God, David."

"I know. It's fantastic. See, look, they're letting the victor go free. He's cut loose, released into the desert. Now he has to survive the elements covered in blood without water ... so awesome. I put money on the next fight," he said, holding up a ticket. "If you want we can flag the guy over," he said, stretching his neck to see over the crowd. "Great odds."

The rapid popping of bullets ricocheted over their heads and the winner was grabbed, forced to his feet and shoved between the trucks as more rounds were shot over their heads. The fans cheered.

"Gunfire makes them run faster." David laughed. She wrestled with the urge to slam her elbow into his crooked nose. "What's going on?" he asked a neighbor and climbed to balance on the lip of the bed to see the fighters. "Something's wrong."

Melanie set her hearing to listen beyond the upbeat ruckus, to a lower rumble of far-off shouts. The movement came in waves, growing, until a roar broke out as word spread that some of the illegals had escaped.

Melanie looked to David, gauging his reaction. Confusion.

The first of the spectators had already become hunters. The trucks emptied as people ran into the darkness with whatever weapons they had at their disposal.

"Let's get out of here," she said, joining the mass exodus into the desert.

"We can track them." His eyes were crazed and his grin morbid. "I've got knives in the trunk of my car."

"But no shovel," she added absently, jogging with the flow of people heading toward the cars.

David unlocked the trunk, bent to retrieve his stash and Melanie smashed the grip of her gun against the back of his skull. His fall forward made her task of tossing him inside easier. She sifted through the mounds of garbage and removed the canvas roll of knives.

Patting David's pockets she relieved him of his keys and cell phone and moved to the driver's seat. She'd watched him start the vehicle, pumping the gas a couple times before turning the ignition. She tried twice and, not wanting to flood the engine, she stopped. Getting stranded in the desert with a swarm of drunk, untrained, heavily armed militia wasn't an ideal situation.

She turned the key again, pumping the gas and holding it until …

it caught. The vehicle fired to life. Twisting to view the red of the taillights, she reversed the car all the way to the dirt road.

Forty minutes later she pulled into the parking garage of the Agency's San Diego office. David's weight shifted in the trunk and she tested out the brakes. Hard.

"Better be quiet," she shouted, crossing to the security box.

Holding her breath, she punched in her four-digit code. There was a moment of doubt before the red light was extinguished and the green light appeared.

Melanie exhaled and stepped inside. "Hello?" She poked her head into the hall.

"Oh my God," A surprised yelp preceded the actual words. The woman's hands were pressed to her chest. "You startled me. I didn't expect … Can I help you?"

"I'm Agent Ward," she said, using her authoritative tone. "Where is everyone? The night staff?"

"Just two of us now." She said, her brows knitting. "Most were moved in the reorganization, but Agent Campbell is in charge here. Should I get him?"

"Please," she answered. "I'll be outside." *Reorganization?* At the car she pushed the questions aside and banged against the rusted spot above the taillight. "Still breathing?"

"No. Bitch."

"Come on, David. Don't be that way."

"Where are you taking me?" His voice was muffled and hard to make out over the banging of his feet on the inside of the trunk. "Get me out of here!"

"Not if you're going to behave violently."

"Why are you doing this? Those parasites take our jobs, overrun our schools and emergency rooms. And they just keep coming, millions of them."

"This isn't about politics, David. It's a bloodsport." He was silent. She exhaled and unlocked the trunk. David did his best to leap out but his foot caught in the lid of the trunk and she jammed it down on his ankle. Melanie hadn't heard a pitch that high since she'd visited her niece in the nursery.

"Agent Ward?" the woman asked from the open door.

Melanie had never seen the tall man in khaki pants and green polo shirt before. "Campbell?" she asked, he nodded. "Good. Why don't you lead us to an interrogation room?"

"Um," the woman interrupted, "I have Executive Director Scott holding on a line for you."

"Is that what he makes you call him?" Melanie snorted bitterly. "Okay then, Campbell, you're going to have to take over. David this is Campbell." She turned to David, half in the trunk with the other half splayed out over the concrete. "Better behave with him," she said, nudging him with her boot. "He's not as nice as I am."

She was led into a vacated office, sat at the desk and lifted the heavy handset connected to the landline with the blinking light.

"I feel like I've just time-traveled to the 1970's." She picked up the receiver and pushed the button. "Hey."

"It's me."

Melanie watched the woman's tail end sashay out of sight. "Mike?"

"What are you doing? You're supposed to be retired or something."

"I am." She smiled, basking in the worried sound of his voice.

"I forced through your security code. I didn't want to tell Jack before finding out what you were up to."

"Trouble has a way of finding me, even in retirement." She closed her eyes to enjoy the moment. "How've you been?"

"They're eliminating the Agency ... How do you think I've been?"

Reorganization. "Downsizing isn't exactly elimination."

Mike was quiet for a full three seconds. "You haven't been here, Mel. They've *reassigned* over sixty percent of the agents and staff. It's bad. More is expected tomorrow. This time I'm not overreacting," he added, reading her thoughts.

"Get Jack on the line."

"It's five a.m. here."

"If things are as bad as you say, then he should be at work." She chuckled at Mike's exasperated sigh. "I miss you."

"I've missed you, too. Good luck with Jack."

The line went silent...

"This had better be important." Jack griped.

"Good morning," she said.

He groaned. "What's happened?"

"Illegal boarder crossers are being used for sport killing."

"Christ. Of course, what else would it be?"

"I freed eight men and brought a witness to the San Diego office – which, by the way, has the feeling of a morgue. I left two hundred armed drunks out in the desert hunting humans..."

"Great." He was definitely more awake. "I'll call Martinez."

"Martinez, the deputy director of the FBI? Okay. Interesting. You tight with him these days?"

"Shit has gone down while you've been vacationing, Ward. The world doesn't stand still because you decide you don't want to play anymore."

"Are we doing this again?"

"Doing what?"

"Forget it. Does this have to do with the Agency closing?"

"Who told you that?"

"Rumors."

"Well, I guess it doesn't matter … not a rumor. Fact."

"I thought we were being streamlined for efficiency."

"Let me guess, Ben told you that after you'd given your resignation." Melanie didn't like where this was going. "That was bullshit. The Board is dropping dead and they're taking the Agency with them."

The lump built in her throat, clogging the passage. "They can't do that. Can they?"

"You didn't know. I thought that's why you bailed."

"I guess we never really knew each other at all," she said, saddened. "I thought we were friends."

"We were. Right now the satellite branches are being integrated with other offices. That's their word, *integrated*. Actually, that's still the official terminology. The Agency hasn't shut down, yet. But I give it a few weeks."

"Then there is still a chance to save it."

"Jesus, Ward! Give it a break." He didn't raise his voice, but the growl through gritted teeth was more intimidating. "Don't you think we've tried everything?"

"I'm sorry." She was beginning to feel sick. "Did I do this?"

"Damn you've got an ego," he snorted. "No, Ward. This isn't your fault. The Board did it."

"Thanks." She looked beyond the white walls. "I'll text you the coordinates and you can let the FBI deal with the rampage." Setting the heavy plastic receiver into its cradle, she planted her soles on the carpeting and headed to Campbell. He was at the window of the interrogation room. "How'd that happen?" she asked, looking at the welt growing above David's cheekbone.

"It was like that when he came in," Campbell answered. "What's the word?"

"FBI is taking over."

Campbell nodded as they watched David teeter on the hind legs of his aluminum chair.

"I want a lawyer. You can't just beat me up and get away with it," he yelled, shaking his fist. The motion set him off balance and his chair plunged backwards.

Surprised, Melanie looked at Campbell and back at David. He'd knocked himself out. A small amount of his blood trickled, staining the white linoleum next to his head.

"I suppose we should call an ambulance."

CHAPTER 21

"Ben?"

The voice cut through the hum and beeping of the machines, Ben opened his eyes.

"Richard, come in," he invited, shifting in bed and cringing from the dull ache in his chest. Two weeks after his heart surgery the soreness was still keeping him in bed.

"How are you holding up?" Richard asked, hunched to an impossibly bowed position as he wheeled his oxygen tank.

"I've had better days," Ben said, holding on to skepticism about his colleague's visit. "And you?"

"I wanted to talk with you about the fate of the Agency." The feet of the plastic chair scraped a path to the bedside. "I wanted to break the news to you first." Richard's saggy eyelids lifted. "We voted to disband."

"I was under the impression that had already taken place." Ben felt on the outside of exhausted, closer to comatose. "I haven't given up the fight." *Such a weak threat; Even if he were able to stand or walk, who was left to fight?*

"I figured as much." His voice was cloaked with the air of secrecy. "I have to admit that I am uncomfortable with the decision."

Ben had to rely on the words and their ring of truth; the old man's eyelids drooped, shielding his soul. "Then why would you vote for it? Together we could make a difference."

Richard took in an extra hit of pure oxygen. "Politics. Everyone has a master." He raised his bony shoulders. "I've had eighty-six years of rich living and now I'm paying for it. Doctors gave me six months."

"I'm sorry."

"I may have lost my body, but I've still got my mind. I've got some ideas, information … I don't know if it will help you but … if you are dead set on plodding forward..."

The button under Ben's thumb had him adjusting the bed to an upright position, forgetting his pain. "I'm listening."

CHAPTER 22

Through swollen knuckles and makeup to cover the evidence of Bianca's assault, Melanie fought through the aches and pains to endure another day of answering calls, transferring patients, rearranging the supply drawer and taking appointments. She'd waited for the EMT and the FBI to take David into custody and then Campbell had driven her back to Poway. But it was Jack's words she couldn't unhear.

They're closing the Agency?

Her day was surreal, filing files felt pointless when there was real work to be done.

"Pretty wonderful getting a paycheck again, huh?" her dad asked handing her an envelope. "Ready to go home?"

Following him out to the car, she chewed on the inside of her cheek, considering … "Dad," she said, sliding into her seat and swiveling to view his profile. "I don't think I'm cut out to be an office clerk."

"What? Everyone loves you. You're organized and you're friendly with the patients. You're doing a terrific job, Annie. You answer the phone like no one else." His nod of confirmation was swift as he reversed out of the parking lot. "You know how I hate hearing it ring and ring. You're fast. Nope, I can't remember a better worker. I don't know how we got along before you."

"Overkill, Dad."

"I'm serious. I like having you here." His smile touched her heart. "Hey, we're having salmon patties for dinner."

"Can't. Sorry, I'm meeting Trish."

"Get the sweet BBQ chicken. It's the best." Trish said the same to the waitress, adding two Bloody Marys and a spinach salad. "I've been dying to talk with you."

Melanie braced for the tornado that came with those words.

"You know that Court has been in town," Trish started wide-eyed with excitement.

"Court as in runway model Courtney?" Melanie felt her temperature rise. "As in Adam's ex-girlfriend Courtney? As in super soft sheets Courtney?"

"Anyway," Trish huffed. "Last night, Cee and I went out and…"

"Cee? Court? Who are you?"

"They're nicknames. Like code so people don't know who we're talking about," she shook her head. "Jeez, you are so outside of the cool kid's circle."

"This is what you wanted to tell me?"

Trish acknowledged the arrival of their drinks with a grin. "*Cee* and I had an *enlightening* little chat." Melanie's heart skipped in dread rather than excitement. "She took me to this party in L.A. It was totally Hollywood. Everyone was there. Amazing." She sang and sipped. "She knows everyone and though she has all that … I thought you might enjoy knowing that she's crazy jealous of *you*."

"Why?" Melanie's reaction was a confused groan.

"Adam."

"Adam," Melanie scoffed. "She's jealous of me and I went psycho on him about other women … All of that emotion over a man. That's a lot of wasted energy."

Trish's brow arched to a frighteningly high level and held for a moment before her smile broke. "Oh, is this the high ground?" her voice sang with sarcasm. "I didn't recognize it for a minute. So, is this how we're going to play it? Cool?"

"I'm just not interested." Melanie shrugged as goose bumps of curiosity covered her skin.

"You are the sorriest liar I've ever known. *Cee* was totally curious about you. And Adam. We were rocking with M.K and Sheila and you were all Cee wanted to talk about. She tried pumping me for info. But since you're not interested…" She sipped and hummed.

"I don't care." But she was caught. Interested. And horrified with the prospects of what Trish might have spilled. "What did you tell her?"

"Not much." The corners of her lips curled into a spiral smile. "Mostly she wanted to talk and I am a really good listener."

"Right."

"I am. Sure I can talk, but I also know when to stop. I'm balanced. Unlike you, who keeps everything bottled up. Go ahead and continue to percolate, one day it's going to come back at you and … BANG. You'll die from a heart attack. I've seen it happen."

"Do you even listen to yourself?"

Trish's pause held for two seconds before she broke out laughing. Melanie smiled involuntarily. The waitress was using hot pads when she placed the steaming plates on the table.

"What is this?" Melanie asked, knife in hand, dissecting her meal. The hoagie she recognized: it was the heap of white chunks coated in a caramel-colored glaze that were unfamiliar.

"BBQ chicken."

"I've had chicken, and this is not that," she said, puncturing the white cube.

"At a vegan restaurant it is. Imitation chicken."

Melanie took account of her surroundings – the décor, the patrons, the signage. A *vegan restaurant. Shit, how'd I miss this?*

"You're so funny, Mel. Just eat. Anyways," she stretched the syllables, "like I was saying. Cee was doubting Adam's feelings for you. When I told her they were genuine, she thought you must be rich or a dynamo in bed." Trish snorted. "Seriously had a good laugh over that."

I don't want to know, Melanie thought, giving her attention to her sandwich until it squirted at her and she was done.

"She likes him in a whole different way than he liked her," Trish shrugged and took a giant bite. Her mouth was still partially full when she continued. "She thought their relationship was more than sex. But she said the sex was unforgettable, in the best way possible."

"Why would I want to know this?" Melanie finished off her Bloody Mary.

"Thought it'd make you feel better. Adam gave up a swimsuit model with money and connections to be with you."

Melanie squinted at Trish, trying to unwind the compliment,

watching as Trish strained to chew and swallow. "You know we're not vegan."

"It's healthy." Trish nearly gagged.

"Aren't you still smoking?"

"Only sometimes. This is the thing to be, so we'll live longer. Cee eats this way."

"Maybe she's jealous of my bacon cheeseburgers. And stop calling her by an initial."

"You have a very narrow mind. God, you should've heard *Court* go on and on, it was all Adam this and Bitch that."

"Am I Bitch?"

"Yeah, who else? Apparently, she needs –" Trish's voice changed to a Mae West impersonation – "extra stimulation to get a rise."

No! It was too late to cover her ears.

"Get this: Among other things, she likes to have her hair pulled during climax and he wouldn't do it."

"Like hair on her head?"

"She doesn't have any other kind." Duh. "From what I gathered Adam didn't go for her freaky-freaks. He never remembered how she took her coffee or let her stay the night or made a sex tape or whispered sweet nothings in her ear … Do you get what I'm saying?"

"I'm still a couple of images back," Melanie admitted.

"You're dimwitted. They had sex, but he didn't love her. Does he still talk during? Groan out your name?" Trish laughed and groaned, "Melanie, I love you so much."

"Shut up." Melanie held the chuckle until her air ran out. "Why do I tell you anything?"

"Because you love me."

"True. But can we please get out of here?"

"Cranky," Trish huffed but stood and dropped a couple of bills on the table. "Okay, we can go but you're stuck with me all evening." Her blue eyes turned sharp. "Let's have fun, like we used to. Remember the good ole days, Baby Doll?" Trish grabbed Melanie's sleeve, bent her knees to reach Melanie's eye level and batting her extended lashes. "Just a girls' night out!"

Girls' night out was drinking, dancing and bar hopping. It had been unspoken that connecting with a collection of Trish's rowdy friends was part of the plan. The quality of humans partying at after-hours clubs had diminished to men desperate to get laid and woman who hadn't accepted they were past their prime.

"I'm going home," Melanie said, holding her face between her palms. "Does my head look swollen?"

"Yes," Trish giggled. "Front door is in the other direction."

"Why did you let me drink so much? I have to work in the morning."

"It was fun, though, right?"

"Eh," Melanie grunted, too pukish to expend the energy to answer.

Her brain was soaking in tequila. Concentrating to keep down her stomach contents, she rolled down the window as the cabbie drove her home. Melanie waged war with her wallet to pay the driver, stumble over a hedge on her way up the walkway and championed the key and lock battle before finally crash landing into the bed.

Rebounding to her feet, she was throwing fists before she understood … "Jesus, Adam," she panted, her heart racing. He laughed, ducking and rolling to the opposite side of the bed. "I think I'm going to throw up."

"Was it something I did?"

"No!" Melanie swallowed the after taste of too many shots. "I didn't expect you back until tomorrow."

"I left as soon as I could." He leaped across the bed in too much motion, his arms reaching for her…

"You shouldn't kiss me," she warned. "My breath is 80 proof and … wow, now I'm really glad I didn't eat the fake chicken."

"I don't know what a fake chicken is but I'm willing to risk it." He said, smiling and encircling his strong arms around her. "I missed you."

"I missed you, too." Her pulse reaccelerated. "Did you have a good trip?"

"I did."

"That's good." She said. He was lowering her to the bed as she lost control of consciousness. "Goodnight, Adam."

His voice was delicious in her ear. "Sweetheart, your alarm is beeping."

"Can't be." She winced and strained to move her muscles. "I just laid down."

"No, Baby, it's morning."

"Ugh." Through her eyelashes light splashed through the window and she rolled out of bed, feeling her way to the bathroom.

"You're still drunk. Did you go out with Penny?"

"Trish." She slept standing, naked in the chill of the water.

"Thought you might be needing this." He said, waking her and opening the shower curtain, holding two aspirin and a cup of coffee.

"Thank you," she said, swallowing down all three.

"I'm going to make breakfast," he sighed, pulling the curtain back further and sliding his eyes over her. "Nice."

"Today is early release Wednesday," she said, coming alive and shutting off the water. "We could spend the afternoon together."

"We'll talk when you have clothes on."

"Too chivalrous to take advantage of your girlfriend?" Melanie stepped onto the bath mat, dripping until he handed her a towel.

His thumb traced her cheekbone, down her jaw and to her neck. His hands skimmed over her shoulders, her biceps, elbows, forearms, to her hands. His eyes adhered to hers and she flinched as he caressed her knuckles. "Want to tell me about the bruises?"

"I joined a gym." She liked the soreness of her arms better than the throbbing of her head.

He lifted her hands and his eyes dropped for a closer examination. "This is from a bag? What about the mark on your jaw?"

"Um..." She strained to come up with an explanation and decided on the truth. "There was an amateur night."

"You boxed?" His smile could've been condescending but his eyes were appraising.

"It's been a long couple of days," she answered, drying off. "Is something burning?"

"Shit."

"It's okay," she called after him, "I don't have time for breakfast." On cue, her dad's horn honked. "Damn it."

CHAPTER 23

Noon.

Lunch was a broccoli cheese soup served in a sourdough bread bowl at a small restaurant that bragged 'Since 1983' on logoed T-shirts. Fifteen minutes on the 52, toward the landfill, Adam veered onto a two-lane highway and parked beside the flagpole at the American Plus rifle range.

"We're going to start inside. I want to see what you can do," he said, holding open the door before paying the membership fee for use of the grounds.

He'd brought her Walther while he used an M&P 9mm. They stood together in one stall; She put on her protective ear and eye gear and tried to ignore the distracting energy that flowed between them.

"Am I bothering you?" he asked, his warm breath on her neck electrifying the spot just below her abdomen.

"No." She set her stance.

"You don't need me to step back, then?" he asked, full of amusement and passion.

Rejecting the disturbance, she raised her pistol and aimed at the paper target, taking two shots.

He pressed the button and the sheet moved to the very back of the room. She repeated.

His turn.

"I was sort of hoping to learn something new." She complained.

"Are you ready?"

"I just killed a paper man."

Outside they occupied one of fifteen open, long-range shacks with two short sidewalls and a pitched roof. The flags started at 25 yards and increased to the end of a 1,000-yard field.

"That's about a half mile," Adam said, as he lay face down, setting his rifle on a bipod and his eye to the scope. "Come on," he waved her down and reposition to give her access.

Beside him, the grassy ground was cold and hard and the twigs poked into her ribs.

"You're going to need to find a position that's comfortable." His voice had transitioned to instructional. "Use your elbows to hold you up: Less strain on your muscles will help ward off fatigue." He sat beside her, giving suggestions to improve her form. "You have a beautiful slope to your spine," he murmured, gliding his hand from between her shoulder blades to lay flat on her ass. He shook his head. "Sorry, I got distracted. Remember to breathe, but know that every movement will affect the shot, even shallow breathing. Inhale slowly. Exhale." He waited. "Right there. That moment between exhaling and needing another breath … That's the moment you shoot."

His lesson bridged from body position to sight alignments, trigger squeeze and bullet drag.

"Let's see what you can do." He pointed to a mark at the 100-yard line. "Never take your eye off the target."

Melanie set her eye to the sight, found the target and pulled the trigger. The recoil was less than she was anticipating yet she still missed.

Mentally, she chastised her effort.

"Too much to the right. Feel how you're positioned and adjust slightly. Remember this spot, and try again." He lay beside her. "Watch the lateral pressure you're putting on the trigger."

Melanie peered through the scope and shot. Over and over she visualized the target, breathed correctly, held her position, accounted for bullet flight and even the beat of her heart that would cause shakes or flinches to alter her alignment. One after another the bullet rang success until …

"Damn it!" she growled, frustrated and unable to reach the 300-yard target.

"Mel, it's not an easy shot. You're shooting as a purist without the use of technology," he said, trying to ease her frustration.

"There's technology that would help?" she asked, angered. "And you're torturing me with this purist crap?"

"It's not crap," he said calmly. "The gadgets are great, but you need to master the principles first."

"Who are you? The Kung Fu guy of sniping?" She was sick of taking deep breaths. "I need a moment. And I need you to prove it can be done."

He settled on the ground, took a second to adjust the scope and within the next second the clang of metal against metal rang out.

"Wow." Her grumble was pure awe. "Okay, that could be luck. Prove you can do it again?"

His eye pressed to the glass, his finger twitched and a second ring echoed. Then he showed off further – 750 yards and then the next mark rang clear.

"Jesus. Was that 1,000 yards?"

Retaking her spot, she closed one eye, cleared her mind of clutter and focused on the 300-yard line. She breathed in and out, hearing nothing, forgetting the cold ground underneath. Feeling only her finger on the trigger, she tightened.

Nothing.

Fuck the 300, she thought, setting her eye on the 500 mark, she tried again.

The ring had her exhaling and dropping her forehead to the hard ground in relief.

"You did it!"

"One more time." She let the tingles warm the frozen spots inside her jacket. Three more hits were enough to satiate her need to prove it wasn't just luck. "We can't go. I haven't hit the 1,000."

"Another time, Love. We're losing daylight." Adam zipped the rifle in the case and loaded it into the back of the car.

"How far can you shoot?"

"Depends," he said, recalling Jessica Brennan off the coast of Australia.

"But if you had to guess."

"I don't have to guess. With the right circumstances I can hit a target over a mile, maybe mile and a half."

"That's not possible."

"It is." Melanie stopped brushing the dust off her pants to look into his eyes. "You can believe me or you can Google it." He laughed. "I showed you my tricks, I practiced. A lot. And," he shrugged, igniting the engine, "I had incentive. These skills kept me alive. And paid the bills."

CHAPTER 24

"Mel, Sweetie, I'm going to have to cancel our run," Sylvia left the message pinned to Melanie's door. "But how about happy hour on Friday?"

Happy hour turned to dinner at the cottage with Sylvia and Kevin, Trish and Jace and – with great hesitation – a blind date between Penny and Bob. Adam made fish tacos with cabbage and salsa verde under a spattering of crumbly goat cheese; Beans and rice were on the side.

"This one is yours," Trish announced as she and Jace made a fashionably late appearance carrying a margarita machine. "As a house-warming gift."

The wine was re-corked, the ice was crushed and the alcohol flowed with a shot of lime. Penny and Bob found a quiet corner on the patch of porch while Trish and Sylvia got along as if they'd known each other for years – until the triple sec ran out. The party broke at eleven with kisses, hugs and promises of jogs on the beach. Penny gave two thumbs up and said she'd pick her car up in the morning.

"God, they're loud," Melanie said, closing the door and locking it behind the last couple.

"What is our obligation to those two?" Adam asked.

"Sylvia and Kevin or Penny and Bob? I work with Bob and Penny will be my cousin forever ... family get-togethers, holidays, funerals."

"I've resigned myself to the fact that Penny will be around. I was talking about Sylvia and, specifically, Kevin."

"You have no idea how funny this is," Melanie laughed, loading plates into the dishwasher. "I've known Sylvia since kindergarten but she didn't speak one word to me throughout high school and now we're jogging buddies. Hey, this was my first dinner party, it went well, didn't it? I mean, I know I didn't do much – you made dinner and Trish fixed the drinks – but I invited everyone."

"You enjoyed that?" Adam sounded annoyed. "The guy chased you around the room all night."

"Kevin?" Melanie asked, startled. "Really? Well, that's sort of flattering."

"Flattering?" he repeated, alarmed as his eyes traveled to the cabinets above her head. "He was the best your class had to offer? You must have gone to a *very small* school."

Melanie had remembered Kevin differently, but since Adam was jealous ... "He was All-Star baseball," she said, considering how he'd changed physically. "And I think he was on the soccer and track teams." His neck had absorbed his jawline, his waistline had rounded and his hairline had retreated. But he was still Kevin Kincade. "I think he was on the basketball team, too."

"Too short."

"Wrestling and debate."

"Now you're *trying* to make me mad."

She lifted her left shoulder and dropped the last spoon in the rack. "Kevin was the Adam of our school. Everyone either liked him or wanted to be him."

"What about you? Did you swoon?"

"I did watch him walk the halls. He had a nice walk," she chuckled and yelped.

The next moment she was seated at the edge of the counter with his hips pushing her legs apart.

"You watched him walk?" he asked, his hands firmly holding her wrists to her sides. "You think it's flattering to be trapped in a corner by a guy who hasn't seen his toes in years?"

Melanie smiled. "He still has really pretty eyes."

"Now," he said, leaning in close, "you are in trouble." His hands cupped her face and his lips were soft on the corner of her mouth, kissing her before moving down her neck and to her clavicle.

"I think I like being in trouble," she said, her skin rippling under his touch.

The doorbell had them separating, "Did Kevin forget to give you his number?"

"No, he put his card on the fridge." She opened the utensil drawer; taped to the underside was her Walther.

"I'll take care of it." Adam's long strides had him cautiously placing his eye to the peephole. He turned toward her without the earlier tension and stepped aside, twisting the knob.

"Ben?" she gasped.

"Ms. Ward, it's good to see you." He winked and his mouth turned upward.

"Come in," Adam invited.

"What are you doing here?" Melanie asked, taking in the differences in just a few months. "Jesus, Ben, are you all right? Sit." She resisted the urge to take his elbow.

"You haven't been answering the phone I sent you," he said, entering the cottage with an appraising glance.

"What's happened?" She backed away, scanning him head to toe and then returning to the yellow tint in his blue eyes. "Are you sick?" She could barely get the question out.

"I've been better, but..." he answered. "Well, there was a bump."

"A bump? You look like hell. Sit," she ordered again, gesturing to the couch. "Can I get you something – and by the look of you, I'm talking aspirin and vitamin C?"

"A screwdriver?" His chuckle was strained. "Out of curiosity, what happened to the phone I had delivered to you? I had Mike attempt to register the GPS."

She sat in a chair opposite her former boss. "It broke," she simplified. "You never called and I got tired of waiting."

"When was the last time you had a decent meal?" Adam broke into the conversation.

"It's been awhile." Adam clasped Ben on his thin shoulder as he passed to the kitchen. "It looks like you're coping with civilian life," Ben said, glancing around the little house.

"Why didn't you call?" Melanie sounded bruised. "I called you. I tried to leave messages. I spoke to Jack – which didn't go well. So, why didn't *you* call?"

"I'm here now." He evaded the question.

"Do you have cancer?"

"No. Nothing so severe, just a case of exhaustion. My doctors say I'm recovering at an alacritous rate."

"Like hell you are," she erupted. "Damn it, Ben! What are you doing here? Where is Jack? What's going on?" She was having trouble catching her breath. "When were you going to let me know? What if..." she swallowed, "something had happened ... Who would've contacted me?"

"I'm okay," he said, more gently than before. "I've been following doctor's orders."

"Jesus, Ben." Her hands were in fists. "The job isn't worth it. There will always be another crisis. Let someone else handle it." She paused as inspiration hit. "You had a heart attack."

"Well, you're going to be next if you don't calm down."

Her lungs expanded, stretching to their limits. Exhaling, she was shaking as her shoulders relaxed.

"You're right." She released the last of the pent-up air.

"Yes, I suffered a heart attack. I had surgery and there were complications, but I'm on the mend and feeling much better. I'm sorry I didn't have Judith return your calls."

"I realize I'm out of the organization ... but this? Someone should've notified me."

"I'm sorry, I hadn't considered..."

Her eyes stung. "You're okay?"

"I am." He grinned. "Or I'm getting there."

"That's fair," she agreed.

"I'll leave notice for Judith to have you on priority alert if I ever become unresponsive."

"Your jokes aren't funny." Her smile was on life support. "And you aren't here to tell me about your health issues ... You need something. Ask."

"I wish the world worked with your directness. Life would be simpler."

Ben lifted his nose with the beeping of the microwave. "That smells wonderful."

Moving to the kitchen counter, she was a surge of emotions that left her feeling confused and unsure of how to behave. She watched Ben's every move, questions building, stacking until she didn't know where to start.

"Thank you," Ben nodded as Adam set down a plate of leftovers.

Adam cocked his head toward the seat across from Ben. *Sit with him,* he instructed silently. She did.

"I was never quite certain if the chef part of your resume was true." Ben said, picking up his fork and leaning over his food. "But this is very nice."

"So, basically, you dropped by for a bite and to say hello?" Melanie asked, her abdomen knotting through the grind of useless prattle. "Hey, Ward, I had a heart attack. Sorry I didn't return any of your calls. Sorry I gave you a phone and then forgot all about you. But the tacos are supreme."

"Still impatient."

"I've been gone two months, hardly enough time to change a core personality trait. I'll let you eat and then I want answers." She drummed her fingers through the scraping of metal tines on the ceramic plate. Her foot tapping nervously under the table and her incisor was piercing the inside of her cheek.

"Tell me what you've been doing with yourself," Ben asked between bites.

"What have I been doing?" *Seriously?* "Well, let's see ... Captured Edward Brooks in La Paz – too bad I had to let him go – tussled with the Chinese mob and broke up a death ring that was killing illegals for sport. But other than that," she tilted her head, "it's been a slow few months. You?"

"Meetings. Lots of meetings. Making unscrupulous deals and trying, desperately, to change angry, closed minds. The Board, media moguls, congressmen, senators, the Pentagon ... presidential aides, CIA, FBI, NSA and a few others that I either can't remember their acronym or I wasn't sure of their affiliation. Went to a few funerals. Then there's been the doctors, tubes, surgeries..."

Melanie closed her jaw, letting his words sit.

"I didn't mean to..." he began his apology.

"I know," she took over. "I shouldn't have disclosed the Circle Society to the media. I was angry and frustrated. I didn't fully consider the consequences of my actions. I was thoughtless and then I left you to clean up the mess I made."

"I understand why you did what you did and I agree that something needed to be done about Hugh."

Melanie tore her eyes away from Ben. She couldn't let him see her reaction to ... *Senator Hugh Parker,* his name did more than just raise the bile to her esophagus. Though it hadn't been his plot to kidnap and torture her ... he'd been involved.

Ben pushed his plate away with a sigh. "That was delicious. Thank you." Folding his napkin he peered at Melanie through his bifocals "Okay," he cleared his throat, "even if you had kept the phone ... I would have delivered this news in person." He paused, "Senator Parker has found his way out of the CIA facility."

"Hugh escaped?" she gaped. "How? When?"

"Escape sounds a tad overdramatic," Ben said. "But yes, he left before his official release date."

"When was that scheduled for?" Adam asked.

"There was an informal inquiry. His crimes are entangled, implicating too many, so for obvious reasons, details were kept sealed. Because of who he is, papers had been filed requesting that Hugh serve out his time under house arrest."

Melanie snorted. "Figures."

"His misconduct could not become common knowledge. Too much was at stake. Favors were exchanged and back door deals were done to keep the nation in balance."

"You buried the facts," Melanie closed her eyes, defeated. Everything she'd done or tried to do had been suppressed behind 'favors'. "I know I was wrong but still ... *nothing* came of it?"

"What happened to Baylor?" Adam asked, focused.

"Hugh's assistant was in custody, but without evidence of his involvement..."

"Where is he now?" Adam pressed and Melanie searched for a pattern to his line of thought.

"I believe he's taking up residence at the Parker Estate."

"If you're looking for Hugh, Baylor would be the place to start. He's the epitome of a loyal assistant," Adam said.

"Good." Ben nodded as if this were the information he was seeking.

"The mansion was searched?" Melanie asked.

"It was."

"And the vault?"

"It was never found."

"Jesus, Ben," Melanie huffed, standing and pacing to the window. "Was that another token in the Keep Hugh Parker From Paying His Dues trade?"

"I have no way of knowing. The Agency wasn't involved. Our

hands were tied and I had other problems to deal with."

"Why didn't anyone contact me?"

"At that time you were safe. You'd vanished and I believed it was best to leave well enough alone."

"You found me in Argentina." Melanie made eye contact with Adam. They'd been frolicking in South America when she should've been pursuing Hugh's demise.

"I realized that Hugh may still have connections and sent Agent Holland with the cell phone. I didn't answer your calls because I was in the hospital."

Melanie wanted to scream.

"Is there anything else you can suggest?" Ben turned back to Adam, who shook his head and Melanie realized: Ben was here to see Adam.

"Thank you for the hospitality and for the leads. I'll keep you updated on our progress ... if you'd like."

"No," she answered. "It was great seeing you, Ben, but I'm out."

"I wasn't asking you back." He grinned easily and winked. "I'm staying at the La Jolla Inn if you think of anything else. Nice place you have here. Take care, Ward." He ran a quick palm across her shoulder. "You, too, Adam."

Adam nodded and put a hand out for his goodbye. Her eyes burned and she closed the door as Ben's heels crossed the threshold.

"You okay?"

She nodded. Unable to speak, an emotional uprising was clogging her air passages. The episode had grated a raw spot in the center of her thoughts.

"He came to talk to you," she said, wounded.

Adam straightened, lengthening his spine until it added an inch to his height. "I wasn't his main agenda. He was testing the waters, Mel." He folded the dishtowel over the oven door handle. "He used me to see you. Go to the inn, talk with him."

"No." She shook her head in disbelief. "You heard him ... he wasn't asking. And," she sighed, "I'll admit I've wondered if leaving the Agency was the wrong decision." She felt the squirm of truthful guilt. "I was feeling disconnected, but these last few days, playing house with you – and then when Hugh's name was brought up ... It made me sick. Shit!" She shook her head, "I forgot to find out about the Agency! Fucking Parker totally blindsided me."

"Melanie, Sweetheart." He remained calm, tugging on a strand of her hair. "Ben is still here, you can ask him. Go talk to him."

Her head pounded. "How do you know he has something to say to me?"

"He traveled all this way, in poor health, and all I told him was to speak with Baylor, not a revelation."

She doubted. "I'm mad at him."

"I know. You feel betrayed." His strong hands were delicate on her cheek. "If you don't see him, you might always wonder."

"I have more enemies than friends. I'm tired of the bullshit. They killed everything we did, swept it under the rug even after I sent it to the media! What chance do I have against someone that powerful?" She buried the urge to cry.

"I don't have an answer for you," he admitted.

"Besides, you and I don't stand a chance with me at the Agency. I was dragging you in, putting you in harm's way. I mean, Jesus, you were palling around with Hugh fucking Parker?! And I did that, I put you there."

"I make my own choices."

"You weren't making your own choices. I was in a box and you were doing whatever was necessary to save my life."

The muscles in his jaw twitched. "That's true, but now that we're here and you're taking a realistic view of your future … maybe you don't like what you see. Civilian life may not be for you."

She fell silent. "I don't regret leaving but I haven't adjusted well. I thought it'd be easier." She looked up into his deep green eyes and the stress melted. "I *want* to jump in with you, Adam, to make a concrete choice. No more living in two worlds."

"I want you safe but, Baby, I also want you happy and I can't tell if you are." He reached for her hands. "I don't know if I'm going to be enough. There's a part of you that needs the action, the danger. I get it."

"I *don't* want to work for my dad." She finally conceded to the truth. "But I don't have much of a skill set I can sell at an interview." Her small grin was angled and she shrugged, Philly style. "Unless the San Diego mob is looking for a thug, to you know, break some fingers." She gave a nod. "Hey, I ain't emotionally involved, Bob. Ya understand?"

Adam's brows remained knitted but his eyes lost their hard edge and his expression turned to confusion. "What was that?"

"It's from Rocky." She laughed and tried again with more attitude. "You wanna dance, you gotta pay the band. You understand? If you wanna borrow, you gotta pay the man."

"How … *why* have you memorized that?"

"Just stuck with me, ya know?"

"That was really bad, Babe."

Melanie laughed. "I suppose I could open a P.I. firm and take pictures of cheating spouses. That would be fun."

"You underestimate yourself."

Maybe. "I don't see what an ex-agent has to offer. Nothing sellable. I could go back to school or maybe become a beach lifeguard, like Baywatch. Do you think I'm too old for that?"

"Is that what you want to do?"

"I don't know. But what other choice do I have? I try to think about the future, but every time I start, at about a minute in … I lose interest."

"Maybe it's too much to think about."

"I tried to quit my job, but my dad just kept praising me and smiling about how nice it was to have me at the office. How can I abandon him?"

"You could lose his files."

"Yikes. Let me rephrase; how can I leave without him hating me or damaging his practice?"

"He loves you." His temper darkened. "Are you going to see Ben?"

"Are you going to hold me?"

Her dead sleep was broken by hushed voices and light streaming in from under the door. The waft of coffee was a bonus. Letting the sheets fall, Melanie pulled on a pair of jeans and dragged a soft cotton hoodie over her head. And drew her hair up into a ponytail before going to investigate.

Ben and Adam were in the living room, enjoying coffee with the sunrise brightening the green of the palms and throwing sparkles on the mellow waves.

"Morning," she said, feeling awkward under Ben's gaze and avoiding the delight in Adam's.

"Ward," Ben said, under hallowed cheekbones. "I was thanking Adam for the tip." She consumed every detail of his pale expression. "We put extra surveillance on Mr. Baylor, making sure he doesn't leave the country."

"Okay," she nodded, lowering herself into the chair closest to him.

"I wish you'd stop analyzing my every angle, crease and splotch on my face."

"I wish you'd tell me what's happening with the Agency. And don't say rumors – Jack gave me a harsh heads up."

He lifted the coffee cup to his colorless lips, sipped and deliberated before setting the cup on the table. "There has been a hiccup with the Agency. It's the Board; only four are physically able to attend meetings and I am included in that number."

"Are you appointing me?"

"I wish, but not even close." His grin was bleak. "Without a majority vote the last three have decided that the Agency has served its purpose." His eyelids lifted as he viewed her over his glasses. "They're moving to dissolve the Agency." He held up his palms. "Before you get loud and petulant..." He reached into the pocket of his gray trousers.

"Dissolve? What does that mean … exactly?"

Ben's mouth tightened into a seamless line but the skin over his bones slackened and weariness invaded his eyes. "The Board is old and weak, mean and bitter as all hell. They'd rather see the organization die than to continue on without them. I suppose I should've seen it coming." He searched the ceiling for answers.

Melanie didn't move, waiting for the follow-up sentence that explained the how they were going to fix it.

"About thirty percent of our assets have already been reallocated to other organizations with plans for the rest to be transitioned over a few weeks. Melanie, they are closing the Agency."

"Completely closing?"

"Disbanding is the current word that's being thrown around. Last week it was integrating."

Gossip from three sources hadn't protected her from the hard reality. "Is that even possible? I mean, isn't there some other way?" A slight lift of his shoulder ignited her fire. "Well, we can't give up. We can't let it happen."

"I've fought." The bags beneath his eyes were filled with failed attempts. "My arguments fell on deaf ears – or lowered hearing aids."

"Shit." Melanie leaned back, stunned. "What do you want me to do?" Whatever it was, she was ready to comply.

"I was given this." He placed a flash drive on the coffee table. "It has everything – our agents, assets, my proposals, the Boards responses … the original bylaws, everything. I was hoping you'd look through it with fresh eyes to find what I must have missed – a way to override the Board. I know it's a lot to ask and you've just began your separation…"

"I'll email what I find. Parameters?"

"You have the information … Your imagination is the limit." He stood. "Thank you, Melanie."

"Is Hugh behind any of this?" She needed to know.

"No, his troubles are much more complex than the demise of our little organization. Adam," he extended his hand, "thank you." Returning to Melanie, "I look forward to seeing what you come up with. We're on a clock, so the sooner the better."

"Unbelievable," she admitted. "I admired them, hated them and watched them age. To think of them as so callous as to murder the Agency is..." She shook her head. "Unthinkable. I can't imagine the world without the Agency. How am I to believe any of it? We were being governed by a Board of greedy SOB's who were never on our side, who were never the good guys."

Ben's lips collapsed inside his mouth. "I suppose they weren't. We learned our lesson too late. But they weren't all bad and we accomplished good things."

She nodded to the flash drive. "Maybe. I'll see what I can find out."

"Like yesterday, Ward."

"Understood." She nodded, wrapping her arms around him with a tight squeeze. His hug was loose, mostly pats to her shoulder but affection reached his eyes when they parted. Adam handed him a bag of carryout breakfast.

Leaning into Adam, she watched Ben disappear into the back of a black sedan.

"He's going to be okay," Adam said, pulling her closer.

"I know." She smiled. "I wasn't forgotten."

His kiss pressed into the side of her head. "You are going to need a computer."

CHAPTER 25

"Breakthrough?"

Adam's question came from behind the couch as he stood in the bedroom doorway. Melanie had pushed the couch and coffee table against the wall, blocking the entrance to the living room. Rearranging the furniture had made more floor space. She sat on the area rug, leaning against the couch cushion, surrounded by stacks of papers that spread out like ripples in a pond. Organized chaos. Lost in the paperwork, the patches of ideas grouped, forming the skeletal of a concept.

"I might have got something," she said, excitedly but blurry-eyed as Adam hopped over the back of the sofa and sat with his knees at her shoulders. "There was never a defined qualification of how many Board members are required." It was technical, complicated and she took a deep breath. "CliffsNotes version is that I found a loophole. I am almost finished with the pitch for Ben to submit. And" – she opened her heavy lids wide for the best part – "I discovered an address. Ben has been going to the individual Board members, trying to persuade *them* to change their minds. But this, this takes us right up to the top. The decision makers. Now we can bypass the old men of the Board and go straight to the source. Whoever that may be." She grinned, tilting her head back to look up at him. "It's just a drop box but I remember using it once when I had to submit information to the White House."

He bent for a kiss. "Good job."

"I got lucky. That address was buried on the sixtieth page of a boring document. I've got to finish up this email, but do you want to grab a coffee afterward?"

"What about sleep?" he asked, standing to follow the narrow path between papers to the kitchen.

"I'm too wired – tired but wired. Actually, I was leaning toward a slow jog to the bakery. Ten more minutes here," she said, falling back into the world of tactics. *This could work*, she thought as she typed. Learning from her mistakes, she'd tried to consider possible rebuttals to her outline and aftermath from its implementation. She knew the Agency wouldn't be the same, so she was going for better. Excitement surged as she pressed the tip of her index finger on the send arrow. "Okay," she said to her screen, *now it's out of my hands*. She stood, stretched her tight muscles and felt an overwhelming need to eat. "Feed me," she laughed, the feeling of liberation that was more powerful than her achy body.

Breakfast was a mile down the beach. The brisk, damp air made her skin sticky and her head filled with the salty atmosphere. Taking last place in the food truck line, her stomach roared with the heavy aroma of a chorizo burrito.

The mewing seagulls chattered and kept a close watch on her breakfast ready at any moment for an opportunity.

"I will never get tired of this view." She made a seat out of the curb, ready to devour.

"Good thing we got here when we did," Adam said, sitting beside her and looking out over the trail of customers that now circled the vehicle.

"They're getting ready for work." Her words were out when the realization struck. "It's Monday." She twisted Adam's wrist to see the time. "Oh my God. I have to go to work." Her dad was ten minutes away from picking her up and she was a six-minute sprint from home. "I'm late. Oh, he's going to be pissed." She was on her feet when Adam captured her arm.

"Mel, wait." He was steady. "Let's call him. You don't have to be there until 8, right?"

"Yeah," she nodded, doing the math. Her dad had to be early, but she didn't. "Dealing with Ben, and all day yesterday … I completely forgot that I was a working woman."

Adam handed her the coffee she'd abandoned at the curb. "With all that we've been through," he said as they started to eat and walk, "that is the most I've seen you react." It was difficult to simultaneously smile and chew. "You've been strapped to a burning barn, fought off pirates, placed as cargo in a plane but it was being late for your dad that sent you over the edge. I find that … comical."

Her phone was to her ear, waiting for him to answer. "You've met my parents, they're scarier than anything else I've encountered. Hey, Dad," she started, pushing through the grunts of disapproval with her last sentence and vowing to be on time.

Adam laughed, hooked her neck in the crook of his arm and tugged her closer. He snatched her tinfoil wrapper, balled it with his and shoved them in his pocket. They were halfway to the cottage when he cleared his throat, squeezing her hand to brace for a stop.

"Mel, there is something we need to talk about…"

She felt another, *Oh, shit* moment. The numbness started in her fingertips, waltzed up her palms and tingled at her elbows.

"It's about Hugh," he began cautiously, carefully watching as she stopped breathing. "I have to find him."

"You do?" She swallowed the 'why you?' question.

"He's going to keep searching for you. For me. I can find him." His gaze solidified on hers, and then she understood.

Her heart was a roller coaster – plummeting to the pit of her stomach and then racing to lodge in her throat.

"Marie is just a means to an end, Baby, nothing more."

Marie: Senator Hugh Parker's secret, illegitimate, curvy daughter – who happened to have a crush on Adam. And Melanie wasn't totally convinced that the feeling wasn't mutual.

Her incessant nodding was making her queasy *– or maybe it was the burrito*? "I'm suddenly not feeling well."

"I know you don't like her, but…"

"You know it's not that I don't *like* her."

"She's a great lead to Parker." He pressed. "I promise you have nothing to worry about."

Melanie's frown originated in her marrow. "I saw how she looked at you and I saw how you looked at her."

"I am not going to be unfaithful."

"Now I understand why you didn't tell Ben about Marie." She ascertained.

"Ben can't know that I'm going after Hugh."

"Why not? He knows about you."

Adam's eyes steeled. "I have to do this on my own, my own way."

"There's a lot of trust being expelled on my part."

"Mel," she listened, wanting to memorize his exact words, "nothing is going to happen between me and Marie."

Lacy underwear appeared in the back of her mind. "Do what you have to do."

"Mel," he scolded. "I'm just going to make a call."

"Can I listen in?"

His head cocked to the side. "Not a good idea. To convince her I have to become…"

"Never mind." She pulled her arm out of his grasp. "I have to get ready for work."

"No, wait," his voice carrying on the breeze. "I have to work her and I couldn't be effective…"

"It's okay." She turned, standing tall. "You're right, I'm sorry I asked. It was unreasonable and I don't mean that in a passive aggressive way. You have to work her."

"Jesus, Mel, don't do that."

"Just so you know…" Melanie's arms collapsed at her sides. "I don't like the entire idea. I am against you going out on your own to find Hugh and I am definitely against you using Marie to find him. Even as innocent as you think or say it is."

"What do you want me to do?"

"Give the lead to Ben. Let them find Hugh; let authorities bring him in. Why does it *have* to be you?"

Adam searched the horizon, his head shake barely noticeable. "I thought that you'd understand."

Guilt was a traitor of an emotion. "I trust you," it had her saying.

Standing with their feet in the sand at the edge of the world, their eyes locked. Everything she felt and everything he felt passed within the inches of space between them. Melanie broke the connection and Adam fell into step beside her.

"Last night I set a GPS tracker on our phones. One touch and we can locate the other."

"Great."

At the cottage she showered and changed into a black skirt and sweater and raced to the office, taking the phones off the answering service with a full minute to spare.

"I hope this isn't going to become a habit," Roger grunted. "Annie, are you okay?"

"Yeah, of course."

"You look tired."

The phone rang. "Sorry, Dad." She shrugged, offered a pleasant greeting and locked the receiver between her ear and her shoulder to book an appointment.

CHAPTER 26

His eyes followed her around the corner to the parking lot before swapping his coffee cup for his cell phone, Adam flicked through the contacts. Conflicted, his thumb hovered over Marie's number, considering the consequences, the alternatives and the repercussions.

"No freakin' way!" Her squeal rattled the speaker. "I've called you like ten dozen times. You jerk!"

That's my girl, he thought, listening to the laugh that struck a chord deep in his chest. Instinctively, he leaned on the counter and let Marie soak under his skin.

"Hey, Gorgeous." He felt different, even as the simple words echoed back at him.

"Asshole." Her tone was mocking. "After months, that's what you say? Hey, Gorgeous," Marie mimicked, her pitch sharpening. "What took you so fucking long to call? Where the hell have you been?"

"I've been around," he answered smoothly.

"Well, not around me."

"I told you I wouldn't be calling."

"Yeah, then what are you doing now?" She laughed. "I'm going to call you an asshole again, because it felt so good the first time." She paused. "Asshole."

"How'd that time feel?"

"Extraordinary."

"Want to do it again?" The conversation took on a sexual tone.

"Definitely, but later. So, why *are* you calling?"

"Checking up."

"I knew you would. I knew you couldn't live without me."

"I wouldn't be so cocky if I were you," he teased, having forgotten how alive Marie was. "How are you?"

"I'm in Hell. Literally, fucking Hell."

"Literally?"

"Yes. Flames, the devil, judgment … You name it, I've got it here."

"Sounds uncomfortable." The smile hadn't left his lips.

"You are a prick. I'm suffering and you're joking."

"I'm sorry." He was. "Where is this particular Hell?"

"Rome."

"Italy?"

"I'm not talking Pennsylvania."

"What are you doing there?"

"My dad," she snipped at his name, "got me a job with the Vatican."

"Nun?"

"Ha! God, wouldn't that be something? No, I restore stained glass."

"Good for you." Adam approved.

"I guess," she mumbled. "But I'm so glad you called. You can't even imagine how good you sound with your hot and sexy American accent. Admit that you missed me and found it impossible stay away."

"You are sweet," he said, his own spirits lifted.

"In all seriousness," Marie said, "I really have missed you."

"You haven't given me a second thought."

"I know you listened to my messages or else you wouldn't have this number. You've thought about me, too. Admit it, Adam. You long to see me naked."

His playfulness was gone. "I still have a girlfriend."

"Is this the same whore as before?"

"I'm with the same woman, yes."

"She's no good for you. You talk about her but you always come back to me."

"You have no idea what you're talking about."

"Woman's intuition."

"The heart wants what the heart wants."

"And the dick wants what the dick wants."

"Marie, are we going to have this conversation?"

"Come to Hell and be with me. Please. Come. Save me, I'm so lonely. You know how social I am and here ... there's nobody. They all speak Italian."

"I can't go to Rome, Marie."

"Yes, you can. I can pay for half your ticket. It's all I can afford right now but I need you, Adam. Jesus. I'm dying here." She pleaded.

"Babe?"

"Please, I'm begging. I'm stuck with only an old man for company. I need you."

There it is. "An old man? Tell me you're not taking advantage of one of the priests."

She laughed too hard, too long, sniffling at the end. "No, Silly. I'm not supposed to say but I can promise you, I am not sleeping with a priest. Gross. That is for sure a one-way ticket to the authentic, legitimate Hell. Believe me, I've been here a month and that's a big no-no. Besides, I haven't found one as cute as you to convert."

"You must be making the sisters crazy."

"No, here, I'm a proper lady; hence the boredom. Seriously, my offer to pay for a one-way ticket is good. If you ever feel the need to go back that cost is on you. But I guarantee one night with me and you'll be hooked. I'm like heroine."

"Then it's best that I stay on this side of the Atlantic."

"No," she blubbered the syllable, dragging it out.

"I am glad you're doing what you wanted, avoiding the family business."

"Yeah." Her voice dropped. "Let's just say the Feds made that decision for me."

"Really?"

"You've heard about the trouble in Washington ... my dad was pretty much fucked."

"Sorry to hear that."

"He needs *me* now ... silver lining and all. But, damn, he's a crotchety SOB. I slipped an extra tranquilizer in his brandy last night. You've got to come save me, Adam. I need to let off steam and if this goes on too much longer, I'm likely to kill the bastard."

"You're not a killer."

"You think I don't have game? Come find out for yourself. I'm trying to keep my head above water, you know? I just might snap. You don't want me to snap, do you?"

"You're getting everything you wanted; working with glass and a relationship with your dad."

She exhaled with a gagging sound. "God, don't remind me. I wanted to be at a cathedral in Germany, not a glue factory in Hell. Ugh, I don't *hate* the job … not really. I'm just so damn … alone."

"Is that a fake cry?"

"Yes." She snorted and sniffled her lie.

"I'm sorry."

"It is your fault. Come, keep me company."

"Can't."

"The girlfriend?"

"Yeah."

"Please."

"Babe, I wish I could…"

"Then do," she begged. "I really could use a friend. I don't know anyone here and I'm stuck with an old man who only wears robes. I can't do it anymore. Can you imagine me in prison? I'm not strong enough to survive. Are you willing to carry that on your conscience? Could you live with yourself knowing my death was on you?"

"No." He smiled.

"Shit, I wasn't supposed to talk about my dad," she whispered, "I could get in huge trouble."

"But you're safe?"

"If I wasn't, would you come rescue me?" Adam didn't answer. "I'm not being raped if that's your question." She chuckled. "My dad's sort of an escaped felon but worse than that, he's a pain in the ass. I really did drop sleeping pills in his whiskey just to get some peace. He refuses to let me out of the apartment … I have to go to work and then come straight home. One of these nights he's not going to wake up and, frankly, at this point I don't give a shit. You wouldn't recognize me. I'm suffering. I hate you."

"No, you don't."

"You're right. You're too damn sexy to hate. I want to, though." She giggled. "This is the best I've felt in months. Promise you'll visit. Promise you'll put me on speed dial. Promise you'll pick up when I call."

"I promise all three."

"Yay!!" she cheered. "You're the best! Ah, shit, there's my warden. I call him Cerberus … gotta get back to the grind. Remember, you swore."

"Later, Baby."

"Later, Asshole." She laughed.

The sound died as she ended the call and Adam's senses rushed to the present; he was sitting on the arm of the couch he shared with Melanie, half a world away.

"Shit," he breathed. *Fuck*. He closed his eyes to the beach cottage. He and Marie had a connection, that he couldn't dispute, "but it isn't love," he reminded himself. His fingertips ran cool streaks over his heated skin.

Elbows on knees, he lowered his face to his palms, knowing his decision would deepen the rift. But ever since Ben mentioned that Hugh was free … the thoughts playing in his head couldn't be tamed. The target on his back had brightened and he could feel the crosshairs.

The spike of fear came from another thought: *Mel is in danger, too*.

There wasn't much to pack for the flight that left in three hours.

The cab waited as he jogged the short walk from the curb to the tinted glass doors. Within the same second that her expression lifted at seeing him … it fell twice as quickly. Her eyes darkened, her breathing changed patterns and Adam agonized over each miniscule detail of her disappointment.

Mel was sitting behind the reception glass, looking half her size.

"Hi," he choked and she looked up with sad, moist eyes. "I have to go." Her head bobbed with a dozen nods. "He'll come after me, after you. We can't let it rest because he won't."

"When?"

"I have a flight at noon," he answered, wanting desperately to touch her but afraid of the rejection. "I'll be back as soon as I've got it under control."

"Why can't we call Ben and have Hugh picked up?"

"Babe," her recoil was minimal but he noticed. "He won't stop. You know that. I have to see him, talk with him, figure out his intentions."

"He's with Marie?"

"Yeah."

"Where?"

"Rome."

"You're going to Rome?" She looked away, and when her eyes returned to him the emotion was gone. "Be safe."

"I will. I get there after midnight, San Diego time. I'll call when I land."

"Okay."

"Baby…"

"Don't. Just go and come back in one piece."

Her teeth dragging over her bottom lip was the only crack in her otherwise stoic behavior.

"I love you," he said.

"I know." The phone rang, once; twice … "I have to get this." She answered, scheduled an appointment and inhaled. "You better go."

"Okay." He didn't know how to span the distance that was suddenly between them. His hands were on the door when…

"I love you, too."

He turned in time to see her blink away the tears. "I'll be back before you realize I'm gone."

"Welcome back," she said, without humor.

CHAPTER 27

I am not drunk, Melanie growled, stubbing her toe on the quarter-inch rise to the front door of the cottage. *Damn Trish*. She struggled to retrieve the key from the front pocket of her jeans that were too tight for fingertips.

"Bitch!" Trish's call echoed loud enough to wake her neighbors.

Melanie waved, flinging her arms above her head and yelling goodbye at the passing cab with Trish hanging halfway out the back window.

"I love you!"

"Love you, too!"

Melanie laughed, forgetting she was pissed at her friend, and rammed her shoulder against the door, pushing it open. Falling into her living room was hilarious, the carpet smelled fresh and using her foot she kicked the door closed.

"I do love her." Her heartfelt mumble came with a sigh as she laid flat on her back.

She'd gone to Trish's for dinner and discovered that alcohol made life better and Trish funnier.

She crawled to the kitchen to guzzle a glass of water. The clock on the microwave blinked, 11:15. Adam would be in Rome soon. She wondered, briefly, if crying tequila from her tear ducts would burn and then the drumming started. At first she thought it was in her head, but the beat was to a song she remembered ... The Walther filled her empty palm and her steps were soundless under the knocking on the door. Sober, she tiptoed to the peephole. *Bob.*

"Boss!" The overgrown child bounced as she opened the door. "Boss, are you drunk?"

"Not anymore. Come inside," Melanie said, tucking the pistol in her waistband. "What are you doing here?"

"If someone would answer their phone or even set up a voicemail, then I wouldn't have had to fly cross country to watch my boss stumble into her shack. I'll get the coffee going. You go get your stuff."

"What stuff?"

"My orders are to get you to D.C. by 9 a.m. So," he checked his watch, "we gotta go."

"I'm not going anywhere." Melanie stared at the tall hacker. "You got a new hairstyle. You look like you belong in a boy band."

"Don't try to change the subject," he protested with hands digging deep into his hip pocket. "You have to come back with me." His forehead creased in peaks and valleys. "Oh, and there is this." He withdrew his hand and produced a wad of paper that he unfolded and handed to Melanie.

She didn't read the six words; she absorbed them.

"I'm going to take a shower. My duffle bag is in the closet; just throw in whatever."

"Wait." Bob shook his ragtop of black hair. "I wouldn't know..."

"I'm taking a shower and then going to my parents' so if you're on a timetable then you should gather my clothes." Heading into the bathroom, she called over her shoulder. "There's food in the kitchen if you're hungry."

Not waiting for the water to heat, she thought about the note.

Ward, I need your help.

—Ben

The words worked their way through her conscience. The cold water helped clear her head and even as she dressed in jeans and heavy boots and pulled a sweater over a T-shirt, she couldn't get the message out of her head.

"I packed your junk. I swear I turned my head when I grabbed your underwear."

Oops, she chuckled. "Whatever, Bob. Grow up." She took the offered cup of coffee. "We've got to take a trip."

"Mind if I stay here?" He nodded to the spinning microwave.

"Twenty minutes."

"Ten." He retreated as her brow raised. "Sorry. Mind lapse. Take your time."

Melanie drove to her childhood home, nervous, sweating Margarita and rehearsing her apologetic defense. The dark house was still and for a guilty moment she wished she could slip away with no more than a note.

"Mom, Dad." Her voice was hushed as she entered their bedroom.

"Annie?"

"What's wrong?" Rita gasped.

Melanie stepped to the foot of their bed and whispered, "I need to take the rest of the week off; I'll be back Monday."

"What? I don't understand." Roger rasped.

"Why?" her mother asked.

"I have to go to D.C. I can't explain but, look, I wouldn't go if it wasn't necessary."

"Annie." Her dad's sentiment was all disappointment and cut her to the quick.

"I'm sorry."

"We count on you over there. If you gave this position as much loyalty as you did that other one..."

"Roger, she's an adult."

"Dad. Please."

His sigh came from deep in his center.

"Promise us you'll be careful," her mom said, already on her feet for a hug with Roger at her heels.

"I will be. I'm so sorry, dad."

"I know," he sighed. "We can cover you for a few days." He patted her shoulder.

"Thanks." She leaned into her dad's arms. "I love you."

"We love you, too."

Rita sniffed. "Have you been drinking?"

CHAPTER 28

Melanie winced, awakening with locked joints on the leather seat of the company jet. The effects of excessive drinking and lack of sleep were reinforced by the change in cabin pressure. The throbbing, fibrous tissues of her brain were thick and painful.

"Here;" Bob said, offering Tylenol and a cup of coffee.

"What's the plan?" she asked, ignoring the nagging thoughts of Adam and swallowing the pills with a caffeine chaser.

"We're meeting Mr. Jackson at an off-sight locale. That's as much as my pay grade affords."

Out the oval window, Melanie watched the nation's monuments take shape. Her eyes followed the grid pattern of the streets and the dormant, snow-covered trees. The sensation of home buzzed under her skin. Her city was beautiful, magical under a dusting of white.

"Good to see you again, Ms. Ward." Marcos, as much a symbol of her job as any, welcomed her into the sedan.

"You, too." She smiled and slipped into the back seat. The leather interior cupped her body like a glove.

"You okay?" Bob asked inches from her face. "You gonna be sick?"

"No. I'm good." Feeling something between elation and nausea.

Marcos hadn't driven far when he killed the engine in an open spot of a used car lot. Melanie knew the place. Her boots crunched on the icy asphalt and she cast her gaze across the street to the turn-of-the-century, run-down factory. The brick building was Agency-owned – in the early years it was used as interrogation center. Since then it had been abandoned, all but forgotten. She'd run into it a few times while investigating the tunnels that snaked beneath the city.

Crossing the street, Bob led them to the office door, cleared security measures that disengaged the bolt and pushed open the steel door. Expecting a rush of stale air, she was surprised by the muted smell of … pizza.

"This place looks like a dump, but come inside." Bob passed through the inner door.

The warehouse was laid out like many sweatshops of the early 1900's. The factory floor was an open plan, above their heads a metal catwalk hugged the outer walls, suspended from ceiling rods and leading to a glass office that oversaw production. Pale, natural light filtered through the soot-stained windows and dimmed into shadows before reaching the cracked concrete floor.

Melanie followed Bob, the hacker, gamer, man-child who lived for his computer/television/audio system, to a corner of the building.

"Would you like a Mountain Dew?" he asked, falling into his chair and rolling a few inches to open the fridge – placed within arms reach of his computers – along with a shelf of Cheetos, Keebler Fudge Stripes and a Costco-sized tub of Double-Yum bubble gum.

"I'm good, thanks. So," she started, carefully, "what's the deal with you and Ben?" Bob's shoulders rolled up to his ears.

"I'm not supposed..." Nervously he swiveled his chair side-to-side. "I guess you can know. Mr. Jackson snuck me through the paperwork cracks. No one knows I'm here. He has me working Special Ops." Bob waggled his big eyebrows. "I really am Special K." Bob Karlwoski's AKA, 'Special K', was self-endorsed. "The rest of the building is rough, but the equipment..." He whistled his admiration as he looked over the big screens.

"How long have you been here?"

"Over a month. But" – he made a sour face – "I think he forgot about me for most of that time."

Melanie eyes dropped to the cheap IKEA desk that was slightly askew, with chipped particleboard where Bob had trouble with the screws. "I've got everything I need right here." His arms were thrown open in a giant hug to his space. "Isn't it excellent?"

It really was.

"Does Mike know about this?" she questioned. Bob and Mike were practically the same person, separated by a generation.

"Hell, no. He'd freak. He thinks I'm vying for his job ... but why should I? I've got my own sweet deal." His gloating ended abruptly. "I'm glad you're here. I've been worried about Mr. Jackson. He's my ride, you know?" Bob tapped his right foot. "I've missed you, Boss."

"I missed you, too."

"Really?"

She laughed and cocked her chin over to his station. "Some set up."

"Check this out..." He went to the computer and opened a web of confusion.

"I don't know what any of that is." Melanie stared at the numbers. "Bank accounts?"

"Yeah." Bob grinned. "Mr. Jackson wanted me to research Senator Parker's assets. He spent over three million dollars in the four months before he was captured. What does an old man like that spend his money on?"

She leaned forward, reading the screen. "Tell me."

Bob rolled his head to his left shoulder, not taking his eyes off the monitor. "He hid those funds so well that even after a month of research I haven't found a thread. But numbers aren't my expertise. I told Mr. Jackson that Mike would be much faster. I'm good with the people aspect of hacking." He grinned. "I mean, researching."

"Copy that for me?" She pointed to the screen. "Ben said that when the Parker Estate was searched the vault wasn't found."

"That's right."

"What about James Baylor? Did you find anything about him?"

Bob clicked the keyboard and Baylor's weasel face popped up followed by pages of information. *Detailed* information.

"Where'd you get that?"

"Hacked into his doctor's data center. See" – his brown eyes lifted – "people. That's what I'm good at. Banks and computer-initiated passwords ... that's what Mike is for."

"I'm going to take your word for it. Did you find his date book?"

"You mean his schedule app? Boss, nineteen-eighty called, they want their Filofax back." Bob cackled until he met her eyes. "I've got it right here."

"I want a list of Hugh's meetings for the six months prior..."

"Okie-dokie." With minimal finger movements the schedule appeared.

She scanned, absently nudged Bob aside and scrolled through the memos. "Jeez, he was busy." Her knees bent and her ass found the seat of the chair. "All of these initials." She shifted to look up at his face. "I need the actual names of these people or organizations, who they are, what they do. You can find that out, right?"

"Ward?" The call came from the entrance.

"Get me *paper* copies of everything. Yeah, old school paper," she ordered and left to devote her attention to Ben. "Hey." Her walk stuttered when she saw both Ben and Jack. Each was decked out in a suit, crisp dress shirt and tie. "Jack."

"Melanie."

She felt Ben's expert eyes calculating. "Let's take a seat. We've got ground to cover and evidently we've got some personal issues to resolve. Whatever your disagreement is, we need it fixed."

"Can we back up?" Melanie asked, dragging a folding chair from the card table. "Pretend I have no idea what's going on. What meeting? With whom?" Her eyes were directly on Ben, who looked healthier than just a few days ago.

"Great job on your proposal, Ward. We got a sit down." Ben said. "In an hour we're meeting with a man named Marshall Roosevelt. I've never met him, but he's our liaison to the top level. He has some questions about the outline and then he'll give his opinion on our submission, so we've got to impress him. This is our chance to supersede the Board. He asked for the three of us, specifically, so we must be in step."

"I didn't realize it was her proposal." Jack cleared his throat.

"If we want to keep the Agency viable, we need help," Ben explained as if Melanie weren't in the room. "We would not have gotten this opportunity without Ward at the table. I don't know what happened between the two of you … but you're going to have to work it out. Fast."

CHAPTER 29

On the train from the airport, Adam left two messages for Melanie. He tried the office and was told she was out sick.

"She's passed-out drunk," Trish snorted. "We had a party at my house since you seem hell-bent on ditching her every week. You need to appreciate her more. I know there's crazy in her genes but she's good, Adam. She loves you and if you screw this up, I'm going to kill you." She threatened. "Where are you?"

"Bye, Trish." He ended the call with a grin – *she's safe* – that quickly vanished as he lifted his eyes to the apartment building.

Old. Shabby. The first jolt of reluctance surfaced. *No way Hugh is in that shithole*. Adam surveyed the entire square block. They were in the heart of Rome, the diseased artery of low-income families and homelessness, with trash piled on the edges of the wide street.

Adam let himself into the apartment, pausing at the threshold to give his eyes a moment to adjust. The stark contrast from the bright day disabled his vision … but he didn't need his sight to know he was in the right house. Behind the smell of mold was the unmistakable aroma of cigars. Cuban cigars.

On first impression the place had the essence of the home of an agoraphobic. Cigarette butts and ashes filled cups, beer cans and take-out boxes. Crusty dishes covered the stained kitchen counters. Adam shuffled the papers that were spread out over the table.

"Who's there?" barked a familiar voice.

From the bottom of the stairs, Adam gazed up and lost control of his jaw. "Holy shit, Hugh." Adam was eye level with a pair of white, bony chicken legs. One of the most powerful men on the planet was feet away with his bathrobe open, exposing his senior citizen body. "Use the belt, Man," he said, shading the view of the raggedy shag that ran nonstop from the old man's ankles to his sideburns.

"Adam?" He narrowed his eyes and leaned forward.

"Yeah." Adam's shock was settling into fascination.

"How did you find me?"

"Go take a shower." The light was dim and sympathy was replacing interest. "Have you eaten?"

"Um..." Hugh searched the air above Adam's head. "I can't seem to remember."

"Hugh, you need a shower." The stench had reached him. "Meet me downstairs after you've cleaned up."

The kitchen was European-limited, meager space and without luxury appliances. Dragging the clutter of dirty dishes into a box, he cleared out the fridge and took a detour at the garbage bin before walking to the corner market.

The sounds of running water had ceased by the time he returned. Frying the bacon, eggs and potatoes in the single skillet, he toasted two slices of bread, conjuring an American breakfast.

Hugh was pale and gaunt in the poorly lit apartment and Adam dreaded seeing the senator out where the light could show his true jaundice. The pink of his scalp showed through the sparse, damp hair that flipped over the collar of his shirt. His skin suit was two sizes too big and draped over his bones.

"What are you doing here? I thought you were one of *them*." His face pinched beneath the flaps of skin.

"I work for no one but me. You look like shit."

"Fucking sweet talker," Hugh groused and sat. "Where did you get this?" he asked, fork in hand.

"Made it."

"Poisoned?"

"You'll see."

Hugh used his utensil like a weapon, jabbing, poking and skewering before he gnawed. "Tastes like raw sewage."

"Fine." Adam took the second seat at the table and pulled the plate toward him. He picked up a fresh fork.

"What are you doing?"

"Eating breakfast." The eggs were perfect.

"Bastard. Give me that back." He spoke with his mouth full, egg catching in the corners of his mouth. "What are you doing here?"

"I was going to ask you that same question. Really, Hugh?" He looked around the dank place. "I know you've fallen, but this?"

"Better than a prison cell."

"Is it? Fucking depressing is what it is. No wonder you're wandering around like a corpse."

Hugh straightened his spine and followed Adam's glance around the rooms. "You're right. But thanks to you, my options are limited. Are your instructions to bring me in alive?"

"I don't take instructions. I take deposits." He smiled. "*My* plan was to check in with you. See how you're holding up."

Hugh's features tightened and distrust surrounded him like a second, loose skin. "Why?"

Adam paused to think. "Felt like it."

"You came to gawk, to gloat?"

"Nope. But I *was* curious."

"And you've made it abundantly clear as to your thoughts on my current situation."

"How could I lie?"

"So," he perked up slightly, "you're going to help me."

"I haven't decided what I'm going to do," he admitted. "You want to make me an offer?"

"You got to Marie, didn't you? She was the only chink in my armor. Bitch. I'm not going to ask how. She's a whore. Just like her mother. Tries to drug me. As if I don't know what she's doing. Stupid."

"Maybe if you weren't such a bad-tempered, mean son-of-a-bitch, your kids would have turned out differently."

"Typical. Blame the parents." He scraped the plate. "Did you fuck my daughter?"

Adam didn't answer.

"Why was I cursed with two fucking dumb children?"

"Jesus, Hugh. Accept a little unsolicited advice. Pay attention to Marie. She might be your last hope."

His scowl was deeper than usual. "So, are you going to assist me or not?"

"Only if what you're doing is interesting."

"Oh, yes. That's a Parker guarantee."

"And can pay."

"Well, that is entirely up to you."

"Care to be less cryptic?"

"Not until you're in one hundred *and* ten percent."

"I can't commit unless I have the facts." He stood.

"Where are you going?"

"Things to do." He turned.

"Damn you, Adam. Get your ass back in that seat."

CHAPTER 30

Ben's office had been freshened, vacuumed, and Melanie's nose twitched at the odor of lemon polish. She and Jack had come to an amiable compromise, but that didn't satisfy her need to understand why he'd been so hostile. She was puzzled by his outright animosity toward her. Sitting in silence, drinks in hand, each was in their own heads when they were cued by the polite knock on the door.

The trio stood to greet Marshall Roosevelt. A quick assessment put him in his mid-thirties, the ripples already etched into his forehead had him serious, a thinker. His skinny, khaki trousers cuffed at the ankles to expose a pair of pointy brown shoes said he considered himself on trend. And his friendly, broad smile said he wanted to be liked.

"Mr. Roosevelt," Ben greeted, inviting the man into the room.

"Marshall," he corrected and offered his hand to Ben. "Wonderful to meet you, Agent Jackson."

"Ben."

"Ben. Excellent." He turned to Jack and Melanie, his eyes holding on to them for a moment. "Melanie Ward," he smiled, "nice to finally meet you."

"You, too." She responded poorly to the unexpected familiarity that caught her off guard.

"Agent Scott." He added with scarcely a flick of the eye.

"Can I get you a drink?" Ben suggested.

"I'm fine. Thank you," he said, taking the seat at the head of the table. "We're here to discuss the fate of the Agency." He cut straight to the point. "I received your proposal and I have a few questions." Removing a tablet and a pair of chunky Andy Warhol glasses from his jacket pocket, he began flipping through screens.

The sensation of being sent to the principal's office had her dipping her gaze, angling to catch Ben's reaction. Roosevelt read, recounting her recommendations.

"All of this is very well thought out." He nodded, reaching the end of her outline, he looked up. "What it doesn't say is what part Agent Ward will play in this organization?" He shook his head and lifted his narrow shoulders as he looked to Melanie for the answer.

"You have the two most qualified people in D.C. right here. Ben and Jack," she said, matter-of-factly.

"And where do you fit in?" he asked, removing the obstruction of his glasses to regard her directly.

"I've retired. But you know that and still you brought me here. So why don't you tell me?"

"Didn't you write this?" He lifted the rectangular tablet.

Melanie didn't hide her scrutiny; examining his rusty-brown hair, his brown eyes with long lashes, clean-shaven face. A sense of rebellion showed in the mark of a closed earring hole.

"I've been through every file in the Agency, and yours ..." he spoke directly to her, "impressed me. I did some asking and it seems you have an equal number of fans as foes. I wanted to meet you and see which way I'd lean."

Crap, she thought, meeting his gaze. "My reputation, or your impression of me, shouldn't have any bearing on your decision about keeping the Agency open. "

"Agent Ward, I am an impartial observer."

Like hell, she thought.

Shifting in his seat, Marshall Roosevelt angled toward Jack. "Agent Scott," Roosevelt began, his crooked grin shrinking, "you've been executive director for a few months now … Tell me, why do you think the Agency is where it is?"

"The deterioration of the Board." Jack's neutral answer on the outside was politically correct but his tone was filled with an ocean of sentiment.

Confusion had her brows pinched and her eyes ping-ponging from one man to the other.

"What you mean is the Board's health issues was accelerated by the dissemination of the Circle Society?" Roosevelt pressed.

"I didn't say that." He paused. "Well," he scooted forward, "before that, we were at the height of achievement."

"Ben?" Roosevelt questioned.

"I think rehashing the past isn't part of the proposal."

"Mr. Roosevelt, are you blaming me for the obliteration of the Agency?"

"Were you involved with exposing the Circle Society?" Melanie and Roosevelt locked gazes and she buried her grin along with her admission. "Okay, then." He ended the standoff with a nod.

Ben trained his stare pointedly at their guest, "you're leading us down a particular road and I would like to know why."

Roosevelt's eyes narrowed and shifted toward Melanie. "Why did you quit?"

Melanie held his gaze, wondering what game this man was playing. "Torture has a way of making a person reevaluate their priorities."

The hum came from the back of his throat. "Maybe. But I've spent considerable time looking over your file and I've been curious, Ms. Ward…" He clicked his tongue and shook his head.

She knew she should blink, break the tie that was binding them together. But the rational part of her mind shut down and she held the gaze of his testing brown eyes.

"I was tired," she admitted, adding an air of honesty to the partial truth and fractured their contact to look at Ben. "Tired of the bullshit."

"Your tenure as Executive Director was short. A week or two? Did you see that as a failure? Is that why you decided to end your career?"

"No, but I am a better agent than a manager."

"Really? How do you know?" He twisted in his chair to face Jack turning his truth serum gaze onto him. "What do you think?"

"Like she said. She's a great agent."

"Yes, but as an Executive Director … How would you rate her performance?"

"I wouldn't," Jack answered curtly. "It's a difficult job."

"With all due respect, what is this all about?" Ben cut in.

"You're asking me to consider giving a green stamp to spend millions or even billions on reviving the Agency. To do that, I need to know that I'm making a sound investment. So I evaluate. You three are key players, character matters and there can't be secrets among us." His tone lightened. "I've been over every file, through every case this agency has laid a finger on for the last five years. I know just about all there is to know about this particular division and everyone working in it."

Melanie felt the lump in her abdomen twist. *It's okay*, she thought, willing to accept the penalties for her many rash decisions, her breaking protocol ... *God, countless missteps*.

"Ward, do you have any inclination as to why your time as director was riddled with such turmoil?" Roosevelt asked.

The memory of the constant complaints and petty grievances from her fellow agents, the drag of pointless meetings, the mountains of paperwork scratched fingernails down her spine.

"Other than the fact that I lack people skills and the red tape came in the form of a noose?"

He froze for a brief moment before his smile broke. "Yes, other than that."

"This is a waste of time," Jack groaned and rubbed his palms along his thighs, ready to stand.

"Agent Scott, would you like to enlighten Ms. Ward?" Roosevelt spoke slowly and clearly. "Tell her about the promises you made to some of the agents. Tell her how you impeded her advancement at every opportunity. And please explain to her why you did it."

His eyes were deadbolted to Jack's and she was about to instruct him to go fuck himself when Jack's response left her speechless.

"It's not true! Whatever you've read ... it's not true." He said, with the slightest shake to his voice.

She didn't need any more of a confession, she knew. "Jack?"

Jack looked at her, his mouth gaped and his gaze held an apology.

Anger tasted like hot vinegar.

"I didn't mean for it to happen," he began. "Someone said that it should've been my promotion and then it was brought up that you weren't well-liked..." He paused long enough to know he was making matters worse. "I didn't know they'd actually rally more agents. One thing led to another and then you were being overwhelmed."

"But you didn't stop it."

"I couldn't. By the time I realized what was happening it had snowballed and then you were abducted and, well, you know the rest."

Silently she looked to Ben, asking if he knew. His glum expression held nothing more than grief.

Roosevelt turned to Melanie. "So you see, Agent Ward, you really don't know what type of director you would have been."

"And your point?" she snipped at the man with too much information.

"I thought you should know why your tenure was a disappointment," he said, "and I want you to come back to work."

She studied his face, his hair that flopped over his right eyebrow and was unsettled by the confidence in his brown eyes.

"Ward, for me to sign off on your proposal, I'm going to need you to commit to accepting the Executive Director position."

"No." Simple.

"Let me finish." It was the first time he had sounded authoritarian. "I want you and Ben to work together for the first six months. After that, he'll oversee the division and you'll run the daily operations."

"Why?" she asked. "You heard Jack. No matter what he did, they don't like me."

"You're a fifty-fifty split." His smiled included his eyes.

"How did you know about Jack?"

Ben answered for him. "They're monitoring our calls."

"While you were listed as missing ... I was assigned to your case."

Roosevelt looked straight into her. "I've spent considerable time since going over your complete record. You're good, Ward. Fearless. You think fast, make tough decisions and are unapologetic. I want to see what you can do when given a chance. So, what will it be? I've got two stamps in my pocket – one green, one red. And it's up to you."

"Sounds like coercion."

"Opportunity. No one else is interested in resurrecting the Agency, no one but me. I'm betting that between you and Ben, you can devise an improved organization. You're going to lose people, nothing I can do about that, but I think you could do amazing things. With you onboard it's not a gamble." Shifting in his seat, he wheeled back. "I'll give you the evening to think it over."

"What about Jack?"

"I'll tell you what," Roosevelt said, rising to his feet. "When you're director you can decide."

She stood to shake his hand and without knowing what else to say, mumbled. "Thank you."

"It was a pleasure to finally meet you, Agent Ward." He turned to nod at Ben and Jack before giving Melanie his card. "My number."

She accepted. He left and the office fell into a vacuum. She didn't feel like dealing with Jack or his empty apologies.

"Did you know?" she asked Ben.

Melanie didn't need the short shake of his head, the grim, tight purse of his mouth and emptiness of his eyes was enough for her.

"I need to speak with Ben," She broke into Jack's soliloquy, tilting her head toward the door.

"Sure. But this hasn't been easy for me, either."

"You'd better go," Ben said in a cold monotone, "before I say something I might regret."

Melanie poured two small glasses of scotch to the rim and handed one to Ben.

"What the Hell was that?" she asked once they were alone.

"Loss of personal privacy?" Ben held onto his glass. "All of our conversations are compromised."

"That's your takeaway? I'm looking for more personal answers." Melanie sighed and swallowed. Apple juice.

Ben shrugged, "Judith doesn't want me drinking."

She drained the glass before setting it on the table. "What am I going to do? And what was that about Jack?"

Ben had no answers.

Shit, she thought, patting herself down. She'd left her phone in her bag that was still with Marcos.

"Ward. You've got a decision to make," Ben reprimanded scowling at her inattention.

"I want everything." She said, easing her back against the chair. "I want the job. I want a regular life. I want Adam. None of it meshes. Nothing is compatible. But I want it all." She looked up at him. "So I haven't any idea."

"You've only got a few hours." He checked his watch.

"I know." Her head hurt. *But how can I trust anyone? Including Ben.*

He leaned over the table. "I think you've already made your decision."

Her gut fluttered, sick and excited. She shook her head. "I haven't."

"Hey," she said, knocking on Mike's door.

His face exclaimed before the 'holy shit' left his lips. "What are you doing here? You can't..."

"But I can." She smiled. "How've you been? You look good." She nodded her approval of his weight loss as she absorbed the intricacies of his features. "I've missed your face."

"I've started using a night cream."

"Not what I meant," she laughed.

"The tension at work was causing premature aging." Mike rubbed his forehead.

"Who's the lucky lady?"

"She works at CVS." He blinked, yanking Melanie by the arm into the security of the control room and poked his head back out into the hallway to make certain she hadn't been seen. "How'd you get in?"

"I need a favor," Melanie said, fixing herself into a chair and smiling up at her friend. "It's been a long time," she commented. "What happened to the Hawaiian shirt?" she asked checking out his V-neck T-shirt.

"Trying something new. What'd you think?"

"Handsome."

"Cool," he grinned. "Jesus, Melanie, it's good to see you. You look tired and ... dehydrated."

"That's only a start to my problems."

"What'd you need?"

"A visual image. I've got a GPS tracker on a phone. Satellite image of the surrounding area ... I'm not sure. Can it be done?" She'd missed Adam's calls, but hesitated on returning them with the fear she could jeopardize his safety ... if he was with Parker.

"You got the phone info?"

She handed Mike her cell.

"I can do just about anything you can think of." He winked at her.

"Save it for the girlfriend," she laughed. "Here's the thing," she said, turning serious. "What you see is confidential, above your clearance level. It never leaves this room, understand?"

His eyes narrowed. "You are back at work?"

"You're the first to know."

"Really?" The wide smile erased the crimp between his brows and lifted his shoulders. Tipping his head he gave a verbal, "Okay."

"If you don't want to be liable for the knowledge; shut your eyes."

Without raising his gaze from the monitor he held up his three fingers, scout's honor. Her laugh was shortened, remembering Jack … *Who* could *she trust?* Her eyes drifted around the control room.

"Where's Ed?"

"He was transferred," Mike said, distracted. "We're looking at Rome?"

"Yeah." She sat up.

There was nothing spectacular about the old, humble section of Rome. White-gray buildings that predated the Forum, where pigeons had staked their claim to every foot of roof space. The image zoomed closer.

"This is the same place, just inside," Mike said, after minutes of ignoring random pedestrians. "Any specific room?"

She squinted, looking at the view. "How do you do this?"

He shrugged. "Every phone has a camera. I just linked with one that was connected … doesn't have to be a phone. I can use whatever technology is around; tablets, cameras, Blue Tooth … As long as it's got Internet service, I can access it." He was talking and typing and the picture on the monitor was changing. "I'm going to get a visual of the situation and if that doesn't work I'll jump to another device … I. Just. Got. To… There!"

"What is that?"

"Looks like a ceiling with a huge, nasty water stain. If you tell me what we're looking for this will go faster. Otherwise it's a crapshoot."

Then she understood and scooted closer. "We really are inside the building. Damn." Melanie scanned the view. "The phone is lying flat on a table or something."

"Let me try…" Mike was focused. "That's better." Melanie's heart skipped with the grainy image of a kitchen. "Must be an old computer. This is the best I can get. Sorry."

"Sound?"

"Sure," he said, and the volume bar was raised while he leaped to another area of the room.

"Hold it." She raised a shaky hand to stop the image. "Is that the best picture?"

"Let me check," he said, concentrating as his fingers flew.

The dingy kitchen came into focus, a yellowish glow reflecting from the mustard walls, curtains and matching tablecloth.

Oh, shit. She leaned forward, tuned-in on the two men sitting at a table. Adam sat, coolly, a cup of coffee playing between his fingers. Hugh Parker was speaking, hunched and tense over the ashtray, a cigar between two fingers, which he used to punctuate his point, tapping on the tabletop.

"I can't hear."

"Holy Christ, Mel, is that…"

"Shh," she said, taking in the full scene and straining to make out the conversation.

Hugh appeared to have aged a decade. The blue veins under his jaundiced skin were more pronounced beneath his outlandish burgundy silk robe.

"How far are you willing to go?" Parker asked, his voice streaming into the room half a world away.

"I'll stop when I get there." Adam said, the mischievous glint in his eyes registering and causing a reaction beneath her skin.

"I need headphones." Melanie snapped her fingers.

"Mel, should we ..."

"No. Headphones?" She looked at Mike. "I'm sorry. Please."

"On the bench next to you. I'll get you connected."

Engrossed by the scene, her chest was heavy, her breathing labored as she watched both fascinated and horrified. *Adam*. He was magnificent. Handsome. His jaw held the early stages of a beard and his eyes were polished crystals. Her heart somersaulted and lurched forward as she turned her eyes toward Parker.

Senator Parker was a pasty, prehistoric skeleton draped in extra skin. His hair had thinned, displaying a splotchy scalp and the sacks under his eyes drooped to rest on his cheekbones. But his damn aristocrat blue eyes were the same, conniving and corrupt.

Both men looked up, seemingly directly at her. A moment later the blonde ponytail fully blocked her view of the kitchen. It was Marie. Melanie watched the sashay of curvy hips plop directly into Adam's lap. Marie's arms wrapped around his neck and she leaned in to whisper in his ear. Melanie burned, her eyes fused on Marie and Adam. Awkwardly, he shifted her weight, setting her back on her feet.

"There," Mike said, motioning her toward the headphones.

Marie rebounded to his lap and leaned into Adam, her body pressed to his, cupping his face and planting a firm kiss on his lips.

"Sure you won't walk me to work? Or I could be late." Marie purred in Melanie's ears while her finger twisted the curl at the end of his hair.

"You need the job, Babe." Adam smiled and printed a kiss on the inside of her wrist.

"Fine. But know I hate you," she pouted, trotting off. "I can't believe you came all the way to Italy for him. I really do hate you."

"Why don't you just give her what she wants? I know you're not a queer." Hugh's ancient, smoke-tarnished voice came through the airwaves.

"Not how I work." His excuse was delivered without challenge.

"Fool," Hugh scoffed.

"Marie." Adam rose and followed the girl. She dove into his arms, giggling at whatever he whispered in her ear. This time he didn't pull away from the kiss.

Marie was beautiful and Melanie resented the prickles that ignited over her skin as she watched Adam press his lips onto the woman's long neck before retaking his seat at the table.

Hugh picked up the conversation. "I wish you'd reconsider my offer; for both of us."

"I can't agree to something I know nothing about." His head angled and Melanie could see the weariness in the creases at the corner of his eyes. She listened to the cryptic dialogue, concentrating on the hidden meanings.

"It's big, that's all I'm willing to give." The old man grinned. "You'll meet with my contacts to go over the finer points. Visit the locations. Give me your estimations." His constant finger tapping was drowning out his words. "When you agree I will give you the rest of the information."

Adam's eyes fell directly on Melanie – half a world away and she felt he was looking right at her. "We're getting nowhere. I came to check on you – and you're fine." Adam stood. "Good luck, man."

"You can see I am not *fine*."

The pressure on her shoulder made her miss the rest of Hugh's statement but Adam was on his feet, placing his phone in his hip pocket and moving past the old man and out of sight.

"Mel, your phone. It's Ben."

"Thanks." She looked up and lowered the headphones around her neck. "Hey," she said, watching Parker struggle to a vertical position.

"I spoke with Jane and your apartment is ready for move-in. She tells me..."

"You didn't call about my apartment," she snorted.

"Well, have you made a decision?"

"Not yet." Her phone buzzed. "Hold on." Adam. "Ben, I've got to go." She ended the call to answer Adam. "Hey." Her teeth nipped on the inside of her cheek while her feet had her venturing out of the room.

"Babe. Tell me it's *you* spying on me." His voice held a ridged edge.

"Guilty," she confessed. "I was worried about you. Please tell me you know what you're doing."

"Jesus, Melanie."

She listened to the rasping sounds of his rough breathing. "Are you walking?" she asked. *Or are you so pissed you can't catch your wind?* "Can you talk?"

"I'm outside. But you know that already."

She could hear the traffic behind him but she restrained the apology that wanted to leak out.

"I don't want him to see me on the phone," Adam explained. "I don't know if you noticed but the man is a bit unbalanced. How much did you hear?"

"Five minutes."

"Christ."

"I hope you know what you're doing." She shoved her misgivings deeper but the foul taste remained on her tongue.

"Sweetheart." His loving tone was restored. "I'm doing what I do best. You're going to have to trust me."

"I saw." She chastised her lack of control. "That's not why I called. I got a job offer in D.C.," she said. "I'm thinking of accepting. It's temporary, do you think you can work with that?"

"I told you, whatever you want, Babe. At least we've got a home in Georgetown. What are you going to tell the folks?"

"Yeah." She winced. "Haven't thought that all the way through."

"They'll get over it. Is this job stationary?"

"It can be." She smiled, feeling her Adam returning.

"Good. I tried calling."

"I know."

"I've missed you."

"I saw how much I was on your mind." She thought of the kiss he gave Marie.

"You're just going to have to forgive me for that one," he answered, laughing. "God, babe, I love you."

"No more kissing anyone."

"You got it. I'll be home when I can. Just" – he paused – "not yet."

"Don't forget *what* you're dealing with."

"I won't."

It was the close of the conversation. "When you can." She

repeated his return date.

"When I can."

The line died and she was infused with joy and dread. "Damn it." Her words shattered her bubble, delivering her back to Mike's control center.

"You sure we shouldn't tell someone where he is?"

"Not yet." Her attention drifted to Parker. Melanie set the headphones over her ears and relaxed in the chair.

The senator sat, scratched and made phone calls that she couldn't hear – but Mike traced.

"I'm taking off," she said, exposing Mike's left ear from beneath the padded headphone. "Keep a trace going on his phone. Thanks. And remember – nobody."

"Hello? I can keep a secret. You'll be here tomorrow?"

She nodded. "But maybe you should keep that I was here under wraps, too."

"Jesus, Melanie!" His eyes popped open and his fingers dug into his scalp. "Seriously? You're not here legally?" His big brown eyes widened like a small, scared child.

"I'm legal," she laughed. "Sort of." She patted his shoulder on her way out, holding Roosevelt's card between her fingers.

"Hello," she said, feeling comfortable with her decision. "We need to talk."

CHAPTER 31

Roosevelt gave her an address. "There's a bar in the lobby."

"One hour." She took the stairs to the garage to find Marcos, her luggage and a ride downtown.

The fourteen-story, glass building had a modern motif with shops, fast food restaurants and a bar. The dress was business formal, men and women carrying satchels or briefcases, their heels clicking on the waxed tile and walking quickly with an air of self-importance. Melanie fought the flow from the elevators to enter the dimly lit bar and found Marshall Roosevelt in a back, corner booth. The fedora was interesting and she snorted as he signaled her with a single nod. It was then that she realized his back was to the wall and he was wearing a trench coat.

"Seen a few too many movies?" she asked, taking the seat opposite him.

"The hat too much?" he asked, lifting it off his head.

"A bit," she laughed.

"Rum and Diet Coke?" He signaled the waitress with a wave.

She squirmed, feeling exposed and uncomfortable with the amount of information he had on her.

"You've made your decision. Well?" His heavy brow arched.

"I should be asking you. I haven't read my file." She said as the rum and Coke arrived.

Marshall laughed, unconcerned that she was studying him. "Your file doesn't predict the future. It just gives clues from past behavior."

Melanie watched him. "Who do you work for?"

"I can't be specific."

"It's not an agency. CIA, FBI, NSA … No," she decided as she sorted the pieces of … "Marshall Roosevelt." She deciphered. "Who picked your code name?"

"We're getting off topic." He ran his fingers through his hair. "Look, you're right, I've never been liaison to a clandestine branch before." His smile turned shy and he blushed. "I sort of had a cloak-and-dagger image of the whole thing – plus, there's you…" He let that hang.

"I'm not agreeing until I know who I'm working for." She set the first rule. He could be anyone and she'd already spent too much time laboring for an unscrupulous party.

Roosevelt slid his jaw left and right, debating. "If I get the vice president on the phone to assure you … would that be sufficient?"

"Yes."

"Ms. Ward, I'm good at what I do." His voice returned with a subtle force that she recognized as confidence.

"And what is it that you do?"

"Predict the future." He smiled. "I think we'd make a good team. What do you say? Are you in?"

"I'll tell you what, after Ben speaks with the vice president," deciding that was best for everyone. "I'll sign on the dotted line." She sipped her drink, stared into his honey brown eyes. "But I'm only agreeing until the Agency is up and running. At that time I reserve the right to step away, without hassle."

He smiled and lifted his glass. "In a way I had hoped you say no so we could spend time getting to know each other as I convinced you to change your mind." He clinked the corner of his glass with hers. "What are we going to do with Agent Scott?"

"Jack co-manages with me under Ben," she said in a resolute tone to cut off his objections. "You said it was my decision."

"Yes, but…" He hesitated, then backed down quickly. "Loyal to a fault," he whispered as if remembering a line in her file. "Okay. You're the boss. Right?"

"Are we working directly under the vice president?"

"No."

"Who then?"

"I can't answer that because we don't exist." He settled his gaze on hers.

"Do we have to worry about elections? Changes in the administration?"

"We're not under that umbrella. The White House is given our reports, but we're not tied to either party."

"There's a payroll that's accountable to nobody?"

"Does that surprise you?"

It didn't. "And we're going to piggyback or use other governmental resources?"

"Just as you laid out in the plan. You'll have 24 agents. The paperwork has them shuffled into various organizations, easy to hide. I have to admit that Jack did a good job shifting assets and keeping the top people. He didn't hesitate to let the ones who assisted him go."

That's interesting, she thought setting the information aside to consider at a later date.

"Speaking of which, I need a list of our assets and I need to go home, tie up loose ends."

"Your old apartment is ready."

"San Diego home."

"Oh," he nodded. "The Manor will be closed. It's in line for renovation and it solidifies the impression of the Agency's permanent closure. In the meantime your offices, personnel, everything will be moved to The Heights."

Melanie let the rum soothe the barbs of reality. The Manor was more than just a base it was a home.

"For all intents and purposes, the Agency is shut down. No Board of Executives, no agents and, therefore, no assignments. We want to keep that pretense … at least for a while. Later we can reconsider our headquarters."

"If there are no assignments…"

"I'm working on a starter pipeline and from there our opportunities will grow. I promise, we'll have work."

Melanie leaned back to evaluate the man. She didn't doubt his sincerity, but his lack of experience worried her.

"I'm dedicated, Ms. Ward." He said, apparently able to read minds. "I'm good at what I do and…" – his features hardened – "I will make this work."

"Okay, Marshall." She had nothing to lose. "We're moving to The Heights? Here?"

"Four days and it'll be up and ready for business." She could feel him concentrating. "I'm meeting Ben in fifteen minutes. You'll stay?"

"I should notify Jack."

"I'm not 100 percent behind this decision..." His distrust was loud and clear. "Ms. Ward, look, Melanie ... may I call you Melanie?"

"Sure."

"Great. I'm sorry I had to be hard on you, I know you've been through a lot."

Scanning his words, tone, reading for a sign of sarcasm, she found none. "I'm okay."

"I think you are brave to return. You'll see that what I'm doing will be good for you – and for the Agency."

"The title of Director doesn't mean that I'm not going to be tied to a desk ... just to be clear."

"I trust you'll find an effective balance."

Ben arrived, declined a drink and the three took the sidewalk to the rear of the building. The Heights office complex was just outside of D.C. and surrounded by large trees.

"One of the Board members had the Agency invest in this property. It was his brother-in-law's failing scheme." Marshall said.

"We bailed them out." Ben took over the story. "Kept the loss off the books. But then the economy improved and now it's turning a profit."

Reaching the service entrance, Marshall pulled the ivy from the security box and punched in his code. Nothing happened. Ben tried with the same results.

Melanie tried the knob ... It was locked. From her messenger bag she fished out her picking tools.

"You'll set off an alarm," Marshall warned.

"There's no electricity to the box," Melanie pointed out. "Lights are off."

"Oh. This will all be up and running by Saturday."

"Shh," she hushed, listening for the mechanism to catch. "Okay. What?" She twisted the knob. "Is this supposed to be a secret entrance?"

"Hiding in plain sight."

She stepped into the dark stairwell, the elevator doors were closed and lifeless.

"I think we're going to have to hoof it," Melanie said, jabbing the inert elevator buttons.

"It's eight floors." Marshall and Melanie both looked at Ben.

"I'll wait here."

The stairs were metal and her boots clanged with each step. "How sure are you that this is soundproof?"

"This part of the building has been sectioned off. You can't get to it from the main building and with the way it's laid out no one realizes it exists. Even the entrance we came through will be outfitted with high tech security. If someone happens to enter without a code they walk into a regular stairwell. But Saturday," he grinned, "the elevator will be operational with screenings that will knock your socks off." Marshall panted as they exited the stairwell.

"Right out of the movies," Melanie understood, passing into the eighth floor.

"It really is an optimal solution for our current situation." He nodded and Melanie took a look around. The center space was an open forum suitable for desks and tables. "There are a few offices, and we have a portion of the ninth floor as well. Upstairs will be dorm rooms for temporary housing, a kitchen and a living area. I'm thinking we'll get a Ping Pong table or a Pac Man machine."

Melanie took a self-guided tour. "Most of the square footage is this pit?"

"Pit," he laughed. "That's a good word. In the back will be an area for Mike. And this building is complete with gym, pool and you saw the market in the lobby."

She thought of the building beyond their thick walls, everyday folk living out their lives. Accountants, lawyers, engineers, marketing firm and lobbyists occupied most of the building, never missing the absent space.

"It'll work. Small, but there's not many of us and we can make due," she told to Ben when she reached the ground floor. "But now, Marshall has a phone call to make and I've got to catch a flight home."

⁂

The red eye had two seats available. She splurged on the one in first class and slept the full flight. When the cab left her at the curb, it was mid-morning and the birds gave life to the branches above.

"What are you doing here?" her mother asked, having been caught off guard in the short hall from the living room to the stairs.

Melanie's eyes shot to the recessed lighting. "Why aren't you wearing any clothes?"

"We're hot tubbing and you were supposed to be away for the week."

"Uh..." Uncomfortable, she followed the cracks that ran across the living room. "Is dad with you?"

"Of course."

"Why isn't he at work?"

"A patient cancelled"

"I have to talk to you guys. I'm going to wait in the kitchen. I brought donuts."

"Okay, Dear. I'll get your father."

Melanie had scarfed two jelly-filled pastries by the time her parents settled onto a pair of stools at the counter. They were giggling and linking arms to feed each other.

"You're not amusing. Stuff like this scars people." It made breaking the news of her leaving easier.

"You're moving back to D.C.," Rita announced. "We already figured that out. Your father has vetted Maya for your job. Don't look so surprised," she continued. "You're not a great mystery."

"Are you all right with this? I mean, I feel like I'm letting you down," she said, mostly to her dad.

"You were a terrific receptionist, but you should do what you want to do." Roger's smile wilted as he pulled her in his arms. "I'm proud of you."

"Thanks." She eased into his hug.

"I only want you to be happy," he said, patting her cheek and pulling away. "What are you going to do about the rental?"

"I'm paid up for two months so I was thinking of letting Penny take it. I'll talk with Sylvia first."

"And Adam?" Rita inquired.

"He's onboard. We're good." Her smile hid the worry that was eating at her stomach lining.

"I really wish you'd become responsible and settle on a path," Rita scoffed. "Honey, you need a shower."

"I'll take one at the cottage when I clear out my stuff," Melanie said, relieved to have the burden of disappointing her parents off her shoulders.

***

The little cottage felt deserted. She'd left in the middle of the night, her clothes were still crumpled on the bathroom floor and Bob's dirty plate was still on the counter. Melanie took inventory of this short segment of her life as she packed her few belongings. A shower and a change of clothes later, she called Sylvia and arranged for her cousin to take over the lease. Penny was thrilled to have two months of rent free lodging. And by the time Trish arrived, leaving tire tread on the side of the curb, she was ready to say goodbye to the beach rental. Trish waved merrily, the top down on her Mini Cooper, while their straight-laced friend, Carla, scowled. Burning holes into Melanie as she hopped into what was considered a back seat and strapped in beside Jenny.

"This is different," Melanie said, delicately weighing the balance of tempers.

"Have you seen a bluer sky?" Trish asked.

"I wish you'd quit admiring it and pay more attention to the road," Carla snipped.

Jenny shrugged. "They're both in a mood."

"We heard that," they said in unison.

"It *is* a beautiful day."

Lunch was the battle that Melanie had learned to enjoy watching.

"Well, I have news," Melanie said after they'd ordered. "I accepted a position at Global..."

"No." Trish's fist thumped the table.

"Drats." Carla's reaction followed and she bent to reach into her purse.

"Pay up, ladies," Jenny laughed, rubbing her palms together.

"A bet?" Melanie's eyes alternated between the three.

"I thought for sure you'd be gone two weeks ago." Trish handed Jenny a five. "Car had more faith in your restraint."

Melanie sat back. "I feel as though I should be angry." She wasn't. "Please don't tell me you have a wager on Adam."

"You want in?" Jenny asked.

Friends. "Hell yeah," she answered.

CHAPTER 32

"Did you get the email?" Bob greeted as she answered his call while fastening her seatbelt.

"I did, thanks." She'd printed out the pages but hadn't had opportunity to look at them. "I'm on the plane now, I'll be home in five hours," she said, rushing to end the call. "I can't talk now. I'm being pierced by lasers and now she's starting to use hand gestures."

"Stewardess?"

"Flight attendant."

"Gotcha. It's all there … 55 pages and six months worth of schedules, plus a lifetime of information. Whatever you're looking for … you got it. Enjoy the boredom."

"Are you kidding? This is porn for me." She ended the call and shuffled the papers that included material on Parker's lawyer, doctor, accountant and his weekly appointments with the woman that ran the brothel.

Bob had put his skills to use scavenging bank statements, investment accounts, emails and records from poorly protected security services. Document after document, Melanie studied, noted and annotated connecting information. Tackling the financials was her first priority. Somewhere over Kentucky, she had a fractured view of Hugh's monetary objectives.

Mostly, she was curious and confused about his investments in start-up technology companies and the small bio lab in Germany that he kept in constant stream of funding.

Forward thinking for a man on his way out, she mused. It was a side of Hugh that didn't jibe with the old money, entitled, racist male she'd grown to hate.

Putting aside his financials she dove into his legal affairs.

Jesus. She breathed her praise for Bob: Hugh Parker's Living Will and Last Will and Testament.

Melanie held her breath, staggered by the opportunity for an intimate glance into his soul – *if he had one*.

The first few pages were standard text, skimming the legal jargon she moved quickly to the last page that knocked her out of complacency. The final decision for Parker's healthcare was left to doctors at the German bio lab.

Who is this company and what the hell do they have over him? Hugh is leaving his body to science. It didn't follow any pattern; altruism was not a Parker family value. None of it made sense.

Melanie's brain was screwed tight as she moved on to his Last Will … *Who will inherit the vast Parker fortune? Marie?* Bypassing the customary garbage she flipped directly to the back of the document.

Strapped into the small seat, at 35,000 feet above the ground, she felt her world fall out from under her. Even as she listened to the pilot's announcement of turbulence and instructions to fasten seatbelts, she knew that her loss of gravity wasn't from outside sources.

Senator Hugh Parker had only one beneficiary.

She stared at the name through blurred vision.

Adam Chase.

The sensations of cold and hot hit and her goose bumps formed under a layer of sweat. Thoughts, accusations and doubts swept in a whirlwind inside her mind but the only question that mattered was – *Why Adam?*

What connection did they have?

She had to know. She took out her phone.

"Bob get me the details, parameters and the mission statement of BioTech Life. And I need you to do a name check." Her heart was filtering the cold in a slow hibernating state. "Run Adam Chase through every aspect of Hugh Parker's digital life."

"You got it boss, but I've got the intel on the lab right in front of me."

"Go."

"It's a cryogenics research laboratory. Opened 12 years ago and is among the world's leading alternate dying exploration. Creepy, right?"

"Cryogenics." She mouthed the word. "I land in D.C. in forty minutes, could you book me on the next flight to Frankfurt?"

"You're not even coming in?" Bob asked, amazed.

"Straight from the airport. Or better yet, have Ben get the jet prepped."

"I'll get right on that," he snorted. "But FYI, he and I don't have that kind of relationship."

"I'll call Judith."

The lab was outside the city, past the small towns, cut off by road construction and German detour 'Umweg' signs. The storms had passed and she drove the plowed streets through a parapet of dirty snow. At the edge of town the white countryside opened up with an unobstructed view of the valley that in spring would be deep green.

She was an hour north of Frankfurt following the curvy lane to a squat, four-story block building inside a semicircle of tall pines, hoping Bob's email had worked. Melanie parked over a rectangle of cleared asphalt and took the trail of footprints to the revolving glass doors.

Confident, she entered the foyer, her eyes taking in the stark surroundings with posters promoting the cycles of human life. As she approached the kiosk, the images of healthy infants degraded to the elderly in feeble positions.

At the end of the corridor she was greeted by a computer requesting her to sign in and give a reason for the visit. Melanie did as instructed and was directed to a waiting room. Three minutes ticked by before a woman burst through the door full of apology and introduced herself as Dr. Oh.

"James?" the woman asked skeptically. "I always assumed Senator Parker's assistant was a man." She offered a clammy palm.

"Common misunderstanding. It's Jaymes, with a Y. My grandfather passed the week before I was born." Her explanation was brief. "I assume you received the Senator's email?"

"Yes." She nodded, gravely. "And all of us here at BioTech Life are horrified at the terrible way he's been treated."

"Thank you. I'll pass that along," Melanie gave a sorrowful nod. "With Mr. Parker's troubles he needs to reprioritizing his financial commitments. To be blunt ... yours is on the chopping block. I'm here to evaluate your progress and determine if this venture is simple fantasy."

"Oh," she gasped, outraged. "Well, I can guarantee there is no fantasy here."

"The Senator is a patrician, selfish man and with his current predicament he's expecting more reassurance, more specific information about *his* personal care."

"Well," the doctor's nervous habit was blinking in rapid motion – sets of three. "We don't … it is highly unusual but … how much of Mr. Parker's funding are we talking?"

"You're looking to lose all of it."

"His email stated…"

"… that I was here on his behalf and you were to give me *full access* to his information. I realize this may seem drastic but Mr. Parker is in a federal holding cell with a long, tedious trial ahead of him. And no one has unlimited resources."

"I don't know," she stammered, the vein in her jugular pulsed rapidly. "We send semi-annual updates." The woman's conflict was shifting the expression lines behind her eyeglasses. "So if he isn't satisfied, he'll pull our funding?" Her body shuddered upwards from her ankles.

"Every last penny."

"We need his support." She blinked three times. "I can show you his personal zone. No problem. Right this way, please." Dr. Oh's sensible heels clicked rapidly along a long hallway and through a set of stainless steel doors. "We're going to have to change. I'm taking you into the clean room. I hope the Senator appreciates…"

"The Senator donated three-point-five million last year alone. I hope you appreciate." Melanie interrupted.

"Don't misunderstand," she backtracked. "He is among our platinum clients. We have taken great care to facilitate his every need. You will iterate that to him?"

"Actually, I've seen your financials and he is your largest individual donor by far. I'm here to make certain that his money is being well-spent."

"I'm confident Mr. Parker will be impressed." Dr. Oh said, holding up the plastic jumpsuit and smiling for the first time.

The white suit fit neatly over her clothes. Booties stretched over her shoes and latex gloves were taped at her wrists.

"Shower cap, goggles, face mask." Dr. Oh handed her each in a folded clump.

Completely wrapped in plastic they entered the vacuum chamber that sucked up any loose debris. Through protective flap doors they entered a stark, bright lab. The room was vast, two stories high, sixty feet long. Melanie counted six stainless steel cylinders reaching ten-feet high and linked by hoses and tubes to panels with a cockpit of gauges. Dr. Oh explained the features in technical terms that Melanie hadn't heard since high school chemistry class.

"I'm going to need you to lose the thousand-dollar words and give it to me in pedestrian speech," Melanie said at the second cylinder.

"This is the chemical process of deep-freezing tissue," Dr. Oh started and pointed, explaining briefly the elements involved and why the skin wasn't singed with the extreme drop in temperature. She guided Melanie through other rooms with vats of chemicals; even through her face guard her eyes watered and her nose itched. "Over here we have our specimens."

Innocent stupidity had her walking through another set of plastic flaps.

Stretched out on the chrome tables were bodies: chimpanzee and baboons. Melanie's breakfast pastry made a hasty reappearance that stuck in a moist lump at the back of her throat. Her disobedient brain was slow to command her to *look away*. Instead her eyes traveled along their lifeless bodies to the trays of instruments at the side of each primate.

"Jesus, do you have to use monkeys?" Melanie's stomach rolled.

"Well, the chimps are technically apes." Dr. Oh snipped. "We use what we can, besides we need a show room for inspections and what not. We can't very well keep the *other* corpses out in the open."

"I'm going to need to see everything," Melanie demanded with trepidation and steeled herself for whatever was behind door number two.

"Follow me. But I'm doing this under duress and only because of extreme circumstances. These rooms contain our most viable research and…" she continued as she led Melanie out of the general area. Up a flight of stairs, into a closet with a false back wall and stepped through a hidden set of doors. Even then, the room was secured with a badge and handprint scan.

They entered, taking the center path between rows of two dozen steel slabs. Each held a human body in various stages of the cryogenic process and state of decay. Along the far wall were cylinders, some holding full human corpses, while others contained only heads or arms or brains or hearts. It was a Dr. Frankenstein lab.

"Who were these people?" Melanie asked, peering at the dead.

Dr. Oh looked surprised as she shrugged. "No idea. From war torn countries, I imagine. We haven't qualified for bodies left to science, so we get what we can. Hence the need to be discrete."

Melanie walked the aisle feeling disconnected and numb. "None of these look anything like the Senator. Have you considered genetics or age factors? You're experimenting on people of different nationalities. What about inconsistencies?"

"Obviously we've looked into it but it's our belief that all human..."

"Isn't there an expiration time on the tissue?"

"When I spoke about this to Mr. Parker he was in agreement. He understood we are doing the best we can until he can help push along our certification approval," she balked. "We do need specifically preserved bodies. In the meantime, we do not use corpses that just fell off a truck. We have standards and we abide by them." Dr. Oh was showing frustration over Melanie's belligerent ignorance. "Let me assure you, Senator Parker will receive the best care possible; a stand-by and transportation team are on 24-hour alert. He has been our advocate in steering laws and has been financially generous as well. This tumbler" – she pointed to the big one – "is specially designed for Mr. Parker."

Melanie listened, drawn to ... "What's that?" She pointed to the smaller cylinder beside Hugh's luxury modular.

"Oh," the doctor said casually, "that's Mr. Parker's son."

"Finn?" she asked, horrified. *Finn is marinating in a bath of liquid nitrogen,* the understanding formed slowly. "But there wasn't a cryo-team and he was..." She neared the container, calculating the moment he died – picturing his blood covering her hands and arms from where she'd tried to seal the wound in his neck – from the time she'd seen him in the morgue.

"It wasn't optimal timing, that's for certain, but we have no way of knowing future advancements. What appears to us today as dead might be reversible in a decade or two."

"You mean Finn could come back?" She gulped, peering into

the window of the stainless steel coffin filled with a pale blue color. "Christ," she uttered, staring at the murky shadow.

"Actually, it's Ettinger we pray to," Dr. Oh answered with a mocking grin. "Robert Ettinger, the father of cryonics."

"Right." Melanie ripped her eyes away from Finn. "Is his whole body in there?"

"Yes."

"Ettinger."

Dr. Oh sniffled out a laugh. "So true."

"Are the primates really necessary?"

"Monkeys, apes, rats, rabbits, cats, dogs and pigs. They're all necessary. You want to come back to life? You want medication to fix you now? How about safe cosmetics, perfumes, household items? Then it's Auf Wiedersehen to Fluffy."

"Cold."

"I've been called worse. In fact, I like cold, Ms. Baylor. I'm a scientist, not a kindergarten teacher." She expounded. "You've obviously never been on the upside of a discovery. It is..." – she looked up to the ceiling and took an inspired gasp – "it is the most exhilarating thing you can imagine. As a scientist, that's all there is. It's discovery at its most idealistic. You spoke of religion? It's truly speaking with God. Not to God, but *with* him." Dr. Oh raised her arms to the glory of it all, clipboard in tow. "Colleagues in discovery, He and I."

"What is this?" Melanie asked, twisting to stare at the ruffled pages that had flapped open during the doctor's sermon. It was the photo secured to the file that distracted her. Her reach was quick and accurate, snatching the photo from its paper clip.

"Hey..." Dr. Oh's instinct was to grab for it.

"What is that?" She managed to keep the shake out of her voice.

It was the wrong question, she knew what it was … a washed-out picture of Adam. She recognized the background of the front doors to the Parker Estate.

Dr. Oh's brows pinched with obvious confusion. "That's the image Mr. Parker furnished us with," she answered restoring the picture to the file. "He wants us to transplant his brain into this man's body … or a body like this man's."

They locked gazes while Melanie struggled to remain vertical.

"This is just a little too much science fiction for me," Melanie choked, yearning to strip off the plastic suit and run away screaming. "It's crazy. Can you really do that?"

"Not crazy. Not with science, I assure you. A few more years with the continued support of patrons like Mr. Parker, this is our future." She smiled. "That's the tour. Are there other concerns you have that I can set at ease?"

"I'm good." Melanie lied. She was anything but good.

"Very well. I'll show you out. I really think Mr. Parker will be comfortable here. We are the best and are continually advancing. I can assure you there is no better use of his money and no better place than BioTech Life."

Melanie breathed in the refrigerated air. "You really believe all of this is possible."

"I am in this building 20 hours a day, seven days a week. I wouldn't be here if I didn't believe, if I didn't *know* that someday, within my lifetime, people will never have to die. My goal isn't cryogenics. It's the annihilation of death."

"Holy shit." *That would put me out of a job,* Melanie thought. They were back in the dressing room when her thoughts solidified. "Not everyone is going to like the idea of life without death. Wars are fought to solve problems, to make money, and the product of that is death. Religion controls society with the prospect of good and evil, they use God and an afterlife to wield there power. You're going up against money and religion." She shook her head. "There are people willing to kill in order to stop your progress, your ambition."

"That's ridiculous," Dr. Oh said without a shred of concern in her voice. "Everyone will gain from my research."

"Okay," Melanie relented. "Just as a word of caution, be discriminating about who you speak so frankly with. That's all I'm suggesting." They were tossing their bunny suits into the bin when Melanie spoke again. "That man in the photograph…"

"Mr. Va Va Voom?"

"Okay." She tried to erase the words. "Is he an actual prospect or are you looking to find an equivalent, a facsimile?"

"When the time comes to reanimate we'll, or whoever is in charge then, will find a suitable donor. With Mr. Parker's approval, of course …"

"But the photo?"

"Mr. Parker *wanted* this man, but of course that wouldn't be prudent."

"No, it wouldn't." Suddenly her irrational fear for Adam's safety became rational. "I will be giving Senator Parker the results from my observations. Thank you, Doctor. You've been very helpful." Melanie shook the doctor's hand and the phone was to her ear as the engine of the rental car revved. She didn't leave a message.

She was at the turnoff when her phone buzzed.

"Hey," she breathed, answering the call without checking the ID.

CHAPTER 33

The Frankfurt airport was bustling. Melanie hiked the strap of her bag high on her shoulder and searched the crowd. People were rushing toward and away, crossing and dissecting her path.

Their eyes had met for a fraction of a second. He was there. Her chest relaxed, her feet stopped and she waited for him to find her.

"Hi." She dragged her teeth over her bottom lip as the mob that was blocking their view thinned. And all that was left was him, five feet away … head to toe, a sight for sore eyes.

"Baby?" His voice was soft and gentle and the sound hugged her before his arms. His hands were on her back, fingers stretching scapula to scapula and pressing her against him. His face was bent low to the crook between her neck and shoulder. He placed a single, delicate kiss on the skin above her shirt collar.

Her nose was pressed into his chest as he held her and she held onto the tears that threatened to spill after an unthinkable day.

"Are you all right? Your hands are so cold." He stepped back, his eyes scouring hers while stroking the hair from her forehead.

"Better. But you didn't have to come all this way..."

"It's a two-hour flight," he said gently taking her hand as they walked through the airport toward where she'd parked the rental. "Do we know where we're going?"

"I checked us into a room," she said, thinking about the business suit she'd trashed and the chemical smell that took three washings to remove from her hair.

"You're quiet," he said as she drove.

The sick feeling in her stomach was growing and she was building up the nerve to explain what she'd seen to Adam.

"How was your flight?" she asked, while the nagging, dark part of her mind was wondering how much Adam knew. How close was he with Hugh? Why had he flown to Rome and wasn't inclined on bringing the man down?

"Baby, you look shaken and you're beginning to scare me," he said when they reached the room.

She cracked the seal on the whiskey from the minibar and tipped her head back.

"We should eat."

"I'm not hungry." Her stomach rolled and she opened another bottle.

"Are we going to need more of that?" He eyed the tiny bottle in her hand.

"Definitely." She swallowed and dropped to the sofa.

Adam adjusted a chair so they were knee to knee. "You look a little green." The back of his hand found her forehead. "You feel clammy. You're going to have to talk to me."

Adam was patient, giving her time as they sat in silence. She explored his emerald eyes and didn't know where to start. *How do you explain the unexplainable?* It was too graphic, too implausible. Though it felt like ages since she traipsed after Dr. Oh it had only been a few hours – and yet she was having trouble trusting her memory.

"I don't think you're going to believe what ..."

"I'm going to believe you." He stared naively into her eyes.

"Adam." She breathed in a lungful of courage. "Are you ready to hear?"

"Only if you're ready to tell."

"I'm not." She cleared her throat. "But" – she stopped him from letting her off the hook – "I have to. You have to know. You have to hear this."

His hands were soft around hers. But she saw the signs of strain in the clenched muscles of his neck and his perfectly curved lips that had disappeared into a thin line.

She spoke slowly, recounting the events, trying to keep from visualizing the images as she analyzed his reaction. He released her hands, raked his fingers through his hair, paced and returned to the seat facing hers.

"Attached to her clipboard..." The pressure in her chest was crushing as she reached into the back pocket of her jeans. "Was this picture," she handed him the grainy, creased photo she'd stolen twice. "Of you."

"This is at Hugh's estate." He inhaled, gazing at his own image.

"I know. Outside his front doors."

Shrouded in silence they sought solace in each other's eyes.

"I'm going to need you to tell me more about that lab."

"I'm not finished." She held onto his green eyes. "I haven't told you why I went to the lab."

"Christ, there's more?"

She remained steady. "He has a will." Her eyes bored into his. "With only one beneficiary."

"And?"

"And it's you." She watched his face go through a medley of emotions.

Adam leaned back not hiding his surprise. "Jesus. Are you sure?"

"I wondered why it would be you." Melanie said, remaining calm and silencing the badgering voice that had doubted Adam's motives. "And now I think I was better off not knowing." Adam gestured for her to explain. "He wants to be you."

"What? No." Adam was on his feet again. "You're saying he put his assets in my name because he intends to take over my body?" He released a deep sigh and dropped his head into his hands. "I can't even go there, Mel." He looked up at her with a wild gaze. "Do you really believe this? I mean,.." He shook his head in disbelief.

"Yesterday I'd have said impossible, but those scientists are eager, motivated, passionate. And he's funding them." Her voice was sullen, distant. "It didn't sound like they were anywhere near that ability, but the doctor, she was energetic." Melanie read the obscenities that crossed his dark green eyes. His brows dipped in the center and knitted.

"Damn, Baby, this is…" He looked as sick as she felt.

"There's more," she added, worn to the nub, "If you can stand it." Adam retrieved two mini bottles from the mini fridge. He handed her one and swallowed down the other. "There's a room, in the lab." Her bottle was vodka. "The Parker Suite." She winced, stalling, unsure if he'd reached his threshold. "Sure you want to know? Because this next part isn't essential."

"I'm needing some air." Adam stood and laced their fingers.

"Let's walk."

Outside, the skies drizzled and the stagnant air burrowed spikes of cold straight to her bone. Slipping into the Palmengarten, Adam and Melanie coveted the heat from the tropicarium, weaving through the garden paths. They found their way to the café, occupied a bench, drank coffee and listened to the sounds of the rainforest in peace.

"This is nice," Melanie breathed, soothed by the tranquility.

"Like the world is whole again."

She paused to look over the greenhouse and drained two mini bottles of alcohol into her coffee. "There are three cylinders in the Parker Suite," she continued, reaching into her pocket. "You want the rum?"

"I don't mean to push you, but … Mel, you're killing me," he said, ignoring the offer.

"It's difficult for me, okay? I've had a really shitty day." She looked up, bloated with disgust. "The two cylinders that are empty are for you and Hugh. Or a facsimile of you." She forced a smile. "The other one isn't empty." She cleared her throat with a hot swig. "They have Finn."

She waited.

"What are you saying … exactly?"

"Finn's body is pickling inside a near-absolute zero thermodynamic solution. Though I could've gotten that wrong … I was busy trying not to throw up." She was still fighting that war. "Apparently, what's considered dead now may not be the same dead in a decade."

"They were serious about this?"

"As a heart attack. Which, by the way, is what they wait for … then they inject the preservative and …"

"Finn was nearly decapitated," Adam recalled.

"I guess the old bastard loved his son more than I thought."

"He just didn't want to be him."

"You *are* a very handsome specimen. I'd rather be you than Finn."

"That's not funny."

"A little bit. My understanding is that we have some time for technology to catch up with Parker's goals."

"But Hugh is crazy."

"There's that. And old. And rich … rich plus crazy equals a bad combination." She looked at him. "He doesn't trust you?"

"Not yet."

"Really, how could he? I have to be one of his least favorite people and we were together in Las Vegas. You were there when he was handed over to the FBI. There isn't a shot in hell he's going to let you into his plan."

"He's alone and out of options. Hugh is going to have to put his confidence in someone. I'm going to be that someone."

"He already has a man crush." She smiled. "Your rugged good looks and all."

"Stop." He raised his brow. "It's not ideal but it's possible and he's working on something big, Mel. I don't know what, but it's worth a few days of me trying to find out."

"I don't like it," Melanie said, feeling a bit more lifelike. "By law they need for you to have a cardiac arrest before they can administer the cryopreserve that will keep your cells from frostbite. The doctor suggested that Hugh wait until right before reanimation but if he is adamant about wanting you … he'll get his way. I don't care what he's up to." She gritted her teeth. "You have to butcher his brain, not behead but mutilate every piece of brain tissue. Nothing good can come from keeping him alive. Whatever he's got going, Adam, we'll deal with it later. At home, where we're safe."

"He's starting a war and he's been hinting at having a weapon."

"What kind of weapon?"

"He was hinting that it was nuclear."

The muscles in her shoulders slackened. "Shit. Where would he have gotten one of those?"

"That's what I'm going to find out."

"Why can't you just be a regular assassin?" she asked, heartbroken.

"Because you aren't a woman working at a communication company," he said, taking hold of her wrist and pulling her closer. "We're going to be fine."

"I'm worried about you. Not because I don't think you're capable but because I know how slippery and evil Parker is. And that lab." She shivered. "Know when to cut him loose. We can bring him in. Sever his connections. There are other ways. Be careful with him."

"I will."

"And if you find yourself surrounded by a team of men in white coats, shoot the bastard in the fucking head." Her mind was overflowing. She was done, drained. "Maybe we can go back to the hotel and clear out the minibar. Do you think there's anything good on TV?"

"Probably not."

"Adam," she said as they headed back. "I'm going to have Mike search for an unaccounted for nuclear weapon and if Hugh has one … the Agency is taking over."

The moon cast a blue hue into the room. They lay face to face, their bodies entangled.

"Aren't you tired?" he asked.

"Unnaturally tired. Too exhausted to even fall asleep," she admitted, feeling the pressure building behind her eyes.

His gaze fell into a slow blink and then remained closed.

Melanie watched the shadows crawl over the walls until sunrise chased them to the corners.

She was dozing when pleasant kisses cascaded between her breasts down to her abdomen. Adam took his time, slow and deliberate with soft, maddening caresses. The previous day's atrocities were forgotten for a few hours. And then she enjoyed the vanilla sugar scented bath soap and a hot water massage as the world outside the small sanctuary spun out of control.

"I have to go," he said, easily fastening the button fly on his jeans.

"You'll remember to be cautious?" she asked, feeling sick.

"Mel, there's one more thing." His voice dropped to a low rumble. "I've been holding onto this for over a year." Between his left index and thumb was a ring. Her gaze lifted to his. "I've been wanting to ask you something."

"Adam?" her voice was weak.

"But now isn't the right time." His eyes sparkled as he laughed.

"So, you're *not* asking me anything?"

"Well," he started, "I don't want to carry it around. It's an explanation I'd rather avoid." He kept hold of her right hand. "Melanie will you take this complication for me? Say yes."

Her smile disrupted her evil glare. "I will" – her eyes dropped to the diamond – "keep it safe for you."

"Thanks. My future bride and I appreciate the effort." He slipped it on her right hand ring finger. "It belonged to my mom." His tone softened and gently he ran his thumb over her fingers.

"She and I are the same size."

"I had it sized," he said, "and I added the side diamonds."

"How could you know?"

"I've had plenty of time to think about holding your hand, how our fingers intertwined." He laced his hand with hers. "Or just an educated guess."

"It's beautiful. Any girl would be lucky to get you *and* this ring." She smiled at her hand as he disappeared into his shirt.

"Baby," he said, adjusting his collar and taking her wrists. "I'll call when I can but if you don't hear from me, don't worry. I'll be safe. I swear, nothing is going to keep me away from you. You have to promise to do the same." He ran the back of his hand over her cheek. "I love you. And this ring … it belongs on the other hand." His dark green eyes searched hers, drilling until he reached her soul. "We'll deal with everything else later, okay?"

"Exactly what I was thinking." She tiptoed into his lips. And then he was gone. "I love you, too," she said, watching the door close behind him.

Melanie stood at the door feeling a sense of foreboding. She let the agony burn, giving it a moment before pulling the damper to rein it in. She leaped for her cell as it rung.

"Hi," she smiled.

"Ward." Ben's voice dissolved her mood. "Are you in Europe?"

"Last time I checked." She answered, disappointed.

"Great," he said. From beyond his muffled receiver she could hear him tell someone her location. "I'm putting you on speaker phone.

I am here with CIA Director Hill."

"Hello, Agent Ward." The director cleared his throat. "We have an agent assigned to Moscow. I would like you to verify her whereabouts."

Not being in the room put her at a disadvantage. Being able to read expressions, body language, attitudes would have helped answer her questions.

"As soon as possible, Ward."

"Sir, don't you have people for this?"

"I'm asking you."

She nodded to no one. "Of course."

CHAPTER 34

The exchange happened at the airport, her empty suitcase for one with documents, a passport and her assignment. The ticket had her flying into Moscow under an alias on a flight that was already boarding.

Agent Cassie Lowe had disappeared. Melanie's assignment was to make contact and wait for further instructions. "I'm asking you." Hill had said, and each time she heard his words in her head, it was followed by just one of hers. "Why?"

In Moscow she deleted the Russian language app she'd been using as a refresher. Stepping out of the airport she was colder than she'd been in as long as she could remember. Her marrow ran icy and she shivered inside the layers of clothing as the cab left her at Cassie Lowe's apartment building.

The woman lived in an older section of Moscow's city center, seven kilometers from the Kremlin and two from the Literary Museum that provided her cover story.

Melanie climbed the walk-up, used the key that was part of her

CIA kit and entered Cassie's apartment. It had been tossed. All of her possessions were on the floor, either broken or torn. Carefully Melanie stepped over the mess, picking up individual slips of paper as she tried to make sense of the jumble.

Moving quickly, she ventured through the rooms inspecting the pieces of Cassie's life. In the bedroom she lifted a gold ring and necklace from the crushed tufts of carpeting when the thought hit hard. *This could've been me*. Swallowing down the anxiety, she pocketed the jewelry with the vow to either give it to Cassie or her family.

Melanie sifted through what was left of the mail. On the floor beside her was a metal bucket with charred remains of papers. She dug out a slip ... nothing.

The room had been wiped of Cassie's personality. Melanie was closing the door behind her when the neighbor opened his ... they stopped and stared, startling each other for a moment. Melanie was the first to speak, explaining that Cassie was her friend and she was concerned because she hadn't heard from her in a week.

The man fidgeted and admitted to having the same concern.

"Did she seem different the last time you saw her?" Melanie risked.

"Inside," he said, peering down the hall and pulling her inside to close the door behind them. "She's a sweet girl. I didn't notice anything strange – I don't ask too many questions."

"I'm sorry to bother you," she said, catching a glimpse into the interior of his apartment.

"One moment." He ducked into a room and returned with a short stack of envelopes. "Sometimes we get each other's mail. Now go. Hurry. Tell no one."

"Okay. Thank you," Melanie said, taking the mail.

"I hope she's all right," were the neighbor's parting words as his hand pushed her shoulder gently but firmly out the door.

Melanie stuffed the papers in her coat and walked briskly into the winter, looking over her shoulder as she headed to her hotel. The mail was burning a hole in her pocket but she waited until she'd locked the door to her room and checked for surveillance.

Her hotel was modest: two single beds, a sink and a tall wardrobe. She sat on the corner of the rock-firm mattress and read the address labels. It was the white envelope directed to Cassie Lowe, addressed to the neighbor's apartment, with no return address that spiked her interest.

Her index finger ran under the flap, breaking the seal, to remove a single sheet of blank copy paper. Taped to the center page was a flimsy, aluminum key. Carefully, detaching it she held it up to the light, ran her thumb along the head but there was no identifying marks to where it belonged.

Turning her attention to the 8x11, she flipped the page of the seemingly useless piece of paper. Her fingertips hit the first raised bumps in the texture of the weave. Excited, she inspected the sheet and found the indents appeared at the corners. She closed her eyes and considered the placement of the bumps. Numbers. She recalled her brief instruction on Braille a decade ago. 926.

926? September 26th? A.M or P.M.? She added, subtracted and multiplied the numbers and came up with nonsense.

Damn it, Cassie, she scolded. Her brain was on a track of twists and turns, going round-and-round. She wanted to sleep on it, but instead she paced.

The morning came with an overcast sky and Melanie sat up, stiff and sore. She'd fallen asleep at the table, thinking about Cassie, the key and the braille. Swearing a string of mental profanities, she tested the lukewarm shower, stuck the page to the mirror and leaned against the wall to stare. It was obvious once she took a step back.

The page had a watermark. The Literary Museum. Cassie's employer.

Melanie pulled on jeans and fit a thick cable sweater over her button-down cotton blouse. Taking precautions, she tucked her few belongings into her bandolier bag and went in search of 926.

At the museum, she paid the entrance fee and with a map of the building, she negotiated the exhibits. Maneuvering, unnoticed, into the 'employee only' area she found what she was seeking as she passed the first locker.

Locker 926 was on the end of a bank and the cheap lock yielded to the will of the key. Melanie carefully rummaged through the scatterings of Cassie's life, checked the pockets of the sweater hooked to the side, examined the photos stuck to the door with museum magnets. Leafing through the pages of a new copy of War and Peace, she found it. Inside the dust jacket, a dongle and a quarter-sized, push-button remote control. She examined the dongle, a piece of hardware designed to fit into a USB port. Its purpose was to wirelessly secure a connection to specific software. Palming the devices, she caught her reflection in the mirror and paused a moment to examine the lines and the pale plum crescents beneath her eyes. *Jesus, Mel, you look like shit,* she told herself, slamming the locker door.

Slipping out of the restricted area, she merged with a tour and boarded a luxury bus. Taking the first available seat, she ignored the grumbling ruckus from disruption to the seating chart. At a shopping complex she stopped the driver, apologized for having caught the wrong tour and jumped off.

On the surface the mall appeared like any in America but the differences were noticeable once the thin veneer was scratched. Melanie kept her head down and blended in with the shoppers, entering an Apple equivalent store.

"Ya prosto smotryu," *I'm just looking,* she said to a teenager with his name pinned to his shirt. "Spasibo." *Thank you*. She grinned and wandered to a display computer that faced away from the center and away from the glass windows to the mall.

Casually, she inserted the dongle into a computer and linked the software. For a full minute the encrypted text ran rampant over the screen while she smiled and nodded at employees. The search ended with a map of Moscow, a blue arrow marking her location. She synced the information to her cell, erased the hard drive from the display computer and walked into afternoon traffic.

Sidestepping into the subway, she found an empty corner to hide out. Her back to the wall she examined the map. The blue arrow had moved with her. Reaching into her pocket she grazed her thumb over the ridges of the remote and, holding the two side-by-side – she flicked off the bead of sweat on her forehead – and pressed.

Looking up, her eyes scoured the long underground, instinctively seeking out possible threats, weeding through travelers, considering everyone as dangerous. Glancing back to her cell, a red arrow had appeared, blinking on the map a few blocks away.

"Okay," she breathed, making a final appraisal of her situation. Gathering her bearings, she took the closest exit to street level.

Feeling exposed she walked briskly, alert to her surroundings, tracking the red arrow that led her to the doors of a hospital. She stared up at to the oval-shaped building, six stories high with more windows than concrete block.

Heart pounding, she waited for traffic to distract the woman at the reception counter but as Melanie walked in, eye contact was made. She smiled and played her only card, asking for the maternity ward. Directed to the third floor, she thanked the woman and took the elevator one flight at a time.

There were no guards posted, nothing that seemed unlike any other hospital … white, sanitary and smelling of astringent. On the sixth floor she went into the restroom. She stared at the GPS, pressed the button and exhaled as she watched both the red and blue arrows travel across the cell phone screen.

Whatever Cassie had been hiding, it was here. *Maybe so is she*, Melanie thought, realizing that meant Cassie was hospitalized. Her mind raced through the possibilities as the arrows on her phone converged to purple. The image of the map broadened, shape shifted and zoomed into the building … transforming to 3D view and separating the arrows by seven floors; she was on the sixth and red was in the basement almost directly below.

Of course it's the basement, she breathed. *Great*. Apprehension peaked; she was in Russia without an escape plan. Taking the stairs, the flights fell away, along with the multitude of scenarios as she opened the door to the basement and was awarded with a plaque on the wall … Morgue.

"I'm looking for my friend," Melanie said to the pasty, angular man who was mid-bite into an apple.

"Name?" he asked and chomped, filling out a form. The questions continued, they had two unidentified bodies. He ushered her inside the room with the stainless steel drawers. She braced for another up-close view of death.

"Ready?" he questioned sternly. "I don't want to have to clean up when you get sick."

"I'm ready. Open the drawer." Her only contact with Cassie had been a photo and now the young woman's lifeless gray body was laid out on a metal plate. "That's her." Body identified. "What happened?"

"Overdose."

"I have to get her home."

The shrug was universal. "There's more paperwork."

"Give me a pen, I'll fill out the forms. But..." she needed more time. "Can I have a minute alone?"

He turned without a word.

Instinct had her remove the tracker from her pocket and press. The image tightened, detailing the body of Cassie as the red arrow shrank to a spot at the back of her skull.

Opening a utility drawer, Melanie unwrapped a scalpel and grabbed a towel. Turning Cassie's neck sent a surge of acid up her throat. Her fingers skimmed Cassie's head, feeling a small lump at the back. Her first incision was too shallow. She cut deeper and peeled back a thick layer of flesh, with Cassie's brown hair still attached. The pull made a sticky suction sound. Melanie searched, her fingers finding the edge of a microchip. She tipped the plastic square away from the bone and removed the device.

Damn, Cassie. She folded back the flap of skin, wiped away the drops of ooze that had collected on the headrest and retrieved a suture kit. A few big, loose stitches and everything looked normal. The bloody hand towel went into her bag as the morgue attendant returned to shoo her out.

Melanie filled out the basics of Cassie's background information, paid a fee using the CIA credit card and dealt with the cloud of despair that was invading her soul. *At least Cassie was going home*. Dizzy, she rushed out of the hospital, eager to escape the stink of death. Goose bumps scattered as the cold air hit her steamy body.

Two Moscow city police, dressed in berets and bulletproof vests were holding nightsticks and whispered as they looked at her. Erasing the effects of the morgue from her face, she crossed the street and tried to convince herself that she was overreacting.

Trust your instincts, the voice in her head demanded.

Melanie ditched the CIA phone, descended into the safety of the subway and pulled a cash advance from the credit card. At the airport she pickpocketed a passport, purchased a ticket and exchanged Rubles for Euros. Boarding a short flight to Minsk, her plan was to skip to London and get lost in the mayhem.

In Minsk she caught the tendrils of a tail; A heavyset man in a black leather jacket with a ponytail that reached down his back. Lifting a second passport she deflected the man and boarded a flight for Paris. Her ass was hitting seat cushion as the flight attendant latched the cabin door.

Melanie waited until the plane left the ground before breathing. She was shaking and the cold sweat had dampened her hair. It'd been days since she slept and the exhaustion added pounds to her frame. She rested her eyes but couldn't shut down her mind. The images, the information, tumbled. Mixing, fusing ... Pieces dropping, others adhering ... Questions. And then there were the faces. Cassie's, the nameless men and women being used for research, the animals and finally, Finn.

Jesus. Her eyes popped open and remained.

In Paris she paid cash for a computer and rented a room in a tired hotel with an hourly rate. Her room was above a Chinese restaurant. Carrying three boxes upstairs she got two bites in before unfolding the napkin that held the memory chip. Flaking off the dried blood she plugged it into the laptop. There were pictures of warships, diagrams, faces and a code to decipher the transcript that scrolled across her screen.

Her brain expanded as she absorbed what she was reading. The KGB was back.

CHAPTER 35

Her first objective was to get the chip out of her hands; they'd killed Cassie and ponytail man worked for someone. Melanie addressed a padded envelope to Ben and dropped it into La Poste, but not before encrypting a file that she sent to Mike.

She'd spent days in Europe and had yet to experience a blue sky. The low-hanging clouds unleashed and without an umbrella the drizzle cascaded over her skin, clinging to her eyelashes as her boots splashed on the soggy sidewalk.

Melanie felt safe, shrouded within the streets of Paris. Keeping her head down and ducking from under one black umbrella after another, she moved through the drenched city. She wanted answers – and in Paris there was only one person to see...

Barkov.

Barkov was ex-KGB. They'd met last summer, connected over a shared line of work. He'd given her the name of his assisted-living home and now she stood in the 8th arrondissement at the neatly cared for building with green and red striped awnings. Melanie entered the lavish lobby that smelled of French roast coffee, the big windows let the winter inside while the cheery, yellow walls kept the chill at bay. She smiled at the elderly women conversing over a card game.

"I'm looking for Monsieur Barkov," she said to a woman in a black business suit.

"Is he expecting you?"

"No," Melanie admitted.

"I'll ring. Your name?" she asked, phone to her ear.

"Melanie Ward." She hoped he'd remember.

The woman relayed the information and returned her attention to Melanie. "He's on the third floor, last apartment near the exit. Knock twice and let yourself in. We'll be serving lunch soon, will you be staying?"

"Yes. Thank you."

"We will bring it up with Monsieur Barkov's."

Melanie bypassed the elevator for the stairs. His door was like the others; cream with brass hinges, brass knob. She knocked twice and called, "Bonjour," from the doorway.

"Enter." The word was eager and came from a man smaller than she recalled, shorter, thinner and blanched.

"Hi." She smiled, feeling the punch of sanity strike … *What the hell am I doing here? Ben would kill me*. But Barkov was waving, grinning and struggling to shuffle his feet over the hazardous, plush carpeting.

"Come inside." He invited. "Did you order lunch?"

"I did. Thanks."

"Good. Best Paris has to offer." His face lifted and his blue eyes sparkled from between narrow slits. "Sit. Let's talk." Excitedly, he motioned to his sitting area.

Melanie pulled two chairs to face each other and held one steady for him.

"You are prettier than I remembered," he said.

"I bet you say that to all the women," she laughed. "Nice place."

"I like it. Is this a social visit?"

"We can't speak here." She grinned, sitting opposite him.

"And why not?" His brows tried to reach his non-existent hairline. He laughed an old man's laugh, careful with puffs of labored breathing and searching for oxygen.

"It's not safe," she answered, scanning the room for water and surveillance devices.

"Isn't that wonderful?"

"How about we go for a walk?" Melanie suggested.

"We'll dine first and talk second," Barkov said and then the small talk began. "How is my medal?"

"Safe and respected."

"And ..."

"The rest," she shrugged, picking up on the conversation ... the list he'd given her to shine light on the days of WWII. "You know how those things go. I have no idea."

Barkov laughed. "I recall very well. It is wonderful you came. I had hopes, but being as old as I am, I am also well acquainted with disappointment."

Lunch reached her nose from down the hall and her head swooned. Her hunger was beastly. In her excitement over the data, she'd forgotten to eat; the containers of cashew chicken and veggie lo mein remained full in the hotel room.

Their meal was served on delicate china with crystal water glasses and a vase with fresh flowers. The braised beef was tender under a thick sauce, the asparagus were crisp, the potatoes were au gratin and the roll was warm. Melanie savored the chocolate cheesecake that went down easily. It wasn't until she was pushing Barkov's wheelchair over the bridge that she realized she'd overeaten.

"Jeez, Barkov. Have you gained weight in the last half hour?" She was winded and starting to perspire beneath the layers.

"You stuffed yourself like a pig," he laughed, pointing to his preferred bench that faced the Seine with a view of the carousel and the Eiffel Tower. "Or like an American."

She chuckled and tipped her head in uncomfortable agreement. "You've got quite a life," she said, taking the edge of the bench beside his wheelchair. The sun was trying to break through and the air tasted fresh. "It is so beautiful." she mumbled, "I've never been to Paris."

"What? Of course you have ... we met last year on the Champs."

"No." She looked over at the man and then back at the tower. "Physically I've traveled, but I've never *been* to Paris."

"Ahh."

Peacefully, she watched scores of tourists scuttle around the base, ride the elevator and peer through telescopes at the top. She smiled at her companion, who was enjoying the same view.

"What do you know about the Order of the Red Banner?"

The snort was his first reply. "I thought you were going to ask me something difficult, or at least clandestine. The Order is no secret."

"Tell me about it."

"It was before the establishment of the KGB ... awards were given for heroism. But it's no longer active – you must be thinking about the Order of Lenin. And even then..." He shook his head.

"Could they be back?"

Barkov's eyes held hers and she could see the wheels turning as he plotted the potential. "That would be ... unusual. There would be further implications..."

She waited.

"How sure are you?"

"Two percent."

"Well, that's not at all persuasive."

"Humor me."

"There could be factions that have gained support and have chosen to revive that particular dogma. What are your sources?"

"I can't say ... even if I had a stronger grasp on what the hell was going on."

He nodded, staring out over the landscape. "You are not CIA. Which agency are you with, Agent Ward?"

She smiled. "Is the KGB still in operation?"

"Of course."

"Are you on the payroll?"

"No." the smile awoken. "But I am still worthy of eight surveillance devices. There's another retired agent at the home but he has only five bugs in his room."

She chuckled as she regarded the old man. Talking, they enjoyed the swath of sunshine and she listened happily to his anecdotes. Her elbow was on the armrest and with his shaky hand he set two pats on her forearm before settling it there.

"Thank you, Dear Girl." His boney fingers squeezed and she glanced at his profile. "If I'm ever interrogated ... who shall I say you are?"

"Why would you be interrogated?"

"Why would anyone want to eavesdrop on an old man's apartment ... to listen to my television? Things are changing. Can you not feel it?"

"No," she admitted. "Russia isn't my forte."

"I looked you up on the Internet." They turned to face each other. "You don't exist."

Her eyes narrowed.

"I was curious. So, who shall I say visited me today?" he asked again.

"Do you have any American relatives?"

"I think my brother had a daughter who moved to Chicago. You could be her daughter, my great niece. The further the bloodline, the more difficult it will be to verify. Get into that Magic Box" – his finger waggled above her phone – "and give me an identity I can sell."

From her bag she removed a business card given to her by the CIA. "I'm writing a number on the back … I can be reached…"

"But not traced or tracked?"

"No."

"Very good." He set his gaze to a distant point. "Because I think of you as a friend."

"Did I just convert you into a double agent?" she laughed.

"The most useless double agent in the history of either nation. Since I know nothing."

She grinned and stretched her vision to the top of the Eiffel Tower.

"We should get back." He tapped her arm.

She heaved the chair along the green river, passing couples and children playing on the wide walkway until they were beneath the striped awning.

"Keep yourself safe," he said. "Remember there is no war worth your life. Don't sacrifice yourself on the whims of a madman. Know that I will not give you up."

"I don't like the sound of that goodbye," she hemmed. "Leave it alone, Barkov. Don't start sticking your nose where it doesn't belong ..."

"I'm an old man. I have to die sometime."

"No." She felt clammy from head to toe. "I didn't come here to incite your demise."

He laughed. "I haven't really lived in decades. I couldn't have dreamed of a better way to go."

"If you do this you'll be putting *me* in jeopardy."

"That is why I asked for an alias."

There was not going to be any reasoning with the stubborn man. "Okay, just so you know ... I'll be back here in a month or two to check on you. If you're still around I might have information to share."

"So now have I converted you?"

"You are charming, but there's not a chance ... What I give you, will be something deeper than the nightly news but not by much." She clarified. "But you'll want to stay alive for it."

"Well, whatever I find ... will be exclusively yours." He winked and rolled himself to the door. "Bye-bye Melanie."

"Bye-bye, Old Man." His barking laugh was a howl as the doorman took over pushing the wheelchair.

Melanie watched until the glare from the glass door left her alone with the stranger reflecting back at her. At the curb, she hailed a cab and rode in silence through the glorious streets of Paris to the airport.

Heathrow was a cattle farm of people. Back on the CIA track, she was crossing the gangplank when she clipped the battery back into her cell. Immediately it pinged.

Ben had left several voice messages.

"Call me. Immediately."

Fighting against the current of the gangplank, she hit redial. The airport was swarming as she walked, paced and found a quiet corner to count the rings.

Damn! He wasn't picking up. She'd missed her original flight and the next one to D.C. was in an hour. Melanie picked the center seat of a long row of chairs in the departure lounge and released her grip on her boarding pass when her phone buzzed.

"Ward!" She interpreted Ben's shout as stress ... "Where have you been?"

"Everywhere," she sighed, exhausted and troubled.

"The Director had been expecting you..."

"Hold on," she said, feeling eyes on her back. "Have you sent someone? A tall man favoring his left side?"

"No."

"I have a tail. Someone has been tracking me since Minsk."

"Not me," he answered, his tone changing from irritated to concerned. "Be safe."

"All right." She kept an eye on her admirer. "What did you call to yell at me about?"

"Did you find her?"

"Yeah," she answered, paying little attention to the conversation.

"The CIA wants to question you about why you deactivated your cell, where you were and what you were doing."

"They can give me their best shot," she said, feeling the prickles of a fight.

"Ward, watch your temper."

"What temper?" she asked, moving to a position to get a better view of the man. "I arrive at a quarter to eight ..."

"I'll have Marcos waiting."

"Thanks," she said, ending the call. Recognizing the guy, now dressed in business casual, his ponytail tightened into a two-foot braid down his back.

Crossing his line of sight, she made certain he'd saw her before entering the woman's restroom. Immediately she backtracked out of a second exit, switched around and took the vacant seat directly behind him. She twisted to reach beneath the plastic, sling-back of the chair, her hand clamping on the salt and pepper braid, and pulled.

"Shh," she whispered into his ear, bringing his head closer to her lips. "Who sent you?"

"We're on the same side, Agent Ward," he growled, struggling for air and pitching forward to get way. She yanked harder. "The director sent me."

In one quick move, she snapped his head to meet the metal frame of the seats. His skull actually clanked under the impact. Melanie bent down as if a concerned citizen and hissed into his ear, "Tell Hill to stay the hell away from me."

Tacking back to the gate, her angry thoughts rumbled. By the time she was seated she was fevered with hostility. Through the duration of the flight, she opened her computer and banged out her presentation to Director Hill, mentally rehearsing her account of the trip over and over, leaving out all traces of Paris and Barkov.

She was ready to collapse when the plane touched down.

CHAPTER 36

Melanie missed a step, recognizing Jack, curbside, at the company car. He was in dress slacks and a button-down shirt, his hair freshly cut. He smiled and waved as she adjusted the bag on her shoulder and continued forward.

"Don't tell me Marshall fired Marcos," she said, at his slight bow as he opened the passenger door. "Because I will kick his ass."

"No, I volunteered." He jogged around the vehicle and lowered the volume on the radio. "I wanted to thank you." He gave her a brief but intense stare before easing into traffic.

"It wasn't a favor." Her answer was curt; She still carried the scars from his rancor.

"Whatever it was … I appreciate it. I've felt bad about how things went down and …" His explanation lasted until long after the airport was no longer in sight.

"I don't have many friends," she spoke, pulling her eyes from the passing stream of architecture. "But I had considered you one."

"I'm sorry, Mel."

"I know," she sighed, watching him turn into the parking garage of the Heights. "Straight to work? I don't even get a rest?"

"No rest for the wicked," he offered.

"Jack, it's going to take time before you'll be allowed to insult me."

"I'm going to keep trying."

They stood at the evergreen ivy that scrambled up the side of the building to the third-story windows.

"You are going to like me again," Jack predicted as she pressed her thumbprint to the scanner.

Melanie glanced over at him, his boyish charm was spilling through his imploring blue eyes. "Maybe." She said as the door unlocked. "Marshall?" she asked, entering a compartment.

"He likes his security. You'll see."

The door sealed behind them and each set an eye for a retina authentication lock before being admitted through to the next level.

"I don't like this," Melanie said, turning to verify there was no doorknob.

"Does appear to be an overkill," Jack agreed. "The guy has seen too many movies. Just wait."

The laser began at his shoes, scanning the length of his body and projecting his image, in layers from clothed to nude, on the wall.

"Um..." Melanie had just started to speak when the green light shone on her boots. "Hell, no." She rejected the laser with one shot to the control box. The electricity sparked, popped and fizzled.

"Christ, I cannot believe you just did that!"

Melanie was looking into Jack's grin when there was an instant increase in pressure. His grin flipped and she covered her ears to protect them while at the same time her lungs were being crushed.

"We're losing oxygen," Jack yelled, the heels of his palms ramming into his ears.

The elevator had become a coffin.

Heart racing, she fought her way to the glass panel on the wall and lifted the cover. Lighted numbers glowed in the darkening elevator and she punched in her Agency code. Nothing. She tried again and this time a tray beneath the panel slid open. She pressed her hand on the imprint, matching it to the outline. Sharp needles shot out pricking each of her fingertips. She yanked her hand away as the slot closed, her knees buckled. *Fucking DNA samples!* A second later, the pressure began to ease and she pressed her fingers to her tongue. The next was a rocketing sensation. Melanie wobbled on shaky legs as the elevator stopped.

"Fucking Roosevelt." Jack groaned and regarded her handiwork. "You just shot our new building. Jesus, Mel. I can't wait to see how you get out of this one." His snort boosted into a laugh as he fixed his hair. "Woo, that was something."

"Yeah, well, I saw way too much of your anatomy."

He didn't answer before the walls slid apart and they were delivered to their workplace.

"What happened?" Ben asked, his face drawn into a tight ball. "The siren bellowed for..." Jack thumbed his answer, indicating it was Melanie, and Ben's attention shifted to her. "What did you do?"

"She killed the laser."

"I'm not getting a body scan," she said, looking past Ben to the rooms behind him.

Their space in the Heights had been transformed since her initial tour. The smell of fresh paint was strong, she touched the wall to feel if it was still wet.

"You can't go about…" Ben sighed. "Never mind. That's Roosevelt's job."

"You're looking better," she said, studying his color.

"I'm feeling better, thanks. But don't sidetrack me," he said. "I'm angry with you."

He sounded tired, not angry. So she ignored him. "These are our new digs?" She nodded her approval. "Looks official."

Ben narrowed his gaze, inspecting her and then said, "Come, let me show you around." She looked into the windowless space of the conference room before heading toward the offices. Ben opened a door, "and this is the Control Center."

"Mike is going to freak," she said, stepping inside the tech lair.

"He's already been here. I had to send him away … it was like getting gum off my shoe."

She smiled, knowing the feeling. "And Bob?"

"I've been debating whether to leave him at the warehouse. But he's such a social creature, I don't know if he'll last alone."

"We're going to need both. Plus, this is a lot of equipment for one mastermind." The halls were empty as they moved to another room. "I didn't think I was going to like this but…"

"Your office."

She entered, drawn to the sunlight shining onto the antique desk with the leather blotter, her old desk. "Thanks," she said, looking at the artwork and the sofa from the Manor.

"Mike mentioned that you were attached to these items."

Outside her window the Federal-style building occupied most of the block. If horns were honking down below the noise didn't reach her ears. Rapping her knuckles on the window created only a thumping sound.

"Reinforced and bulletproof. It's also impossible to see inside, not from the building across the street or satellite and it's protected against listening devices. No eavesdropping here."

Her eyes drifted to the corners as if she could see a break in security and she thought of Jack. "Doesn't Marshall know the enemy isn't always on the outside?"

Ben's office was like hers, overlooking the same stretch of street. He, too, had brought personal items. "Would you like a club soda?"

"No, thanks."

"Roosevelt insisted that Agent Scott earn his way into an office. He put him in a cubicle near the elevator." Ben leaned on the corner of his desk. "I suppose he deserves it."

Melanie shrugged. "I'm not interested in holding a grudge. I'm not going to be trusting him, either."

Their eyes met as the bellowing from down the hall started. "What?" Marshall's voice carried. "Who?"

Ben slid a sideways glance at her, scolding as they moved out to the hall toward their crazed liaison.

"What happened to my elevator?" he yelled. Behind his wood-framed glasses his eyes glowed fire-engine red.

"I'm not okay with a body scan. They're obscene," she explained.

"Damn." He threw his fists as far down as his arms would allow, then took a breath. "You. Could've. Just. Used. Your. Words. You had to kill it? Are there any other tactics you're vehemently opposed to?" Marshall's growl was winding down.

"Strip searches aren't appealing, either."

"Noted." He gnashed his teeth, lifting the phone to his ear.

As he placed an order to the security maintenance team, Melanie and Ben moved into the conference room.

"Jack." She motioned for him to join.

"You can't..." Marshall paused to grunt, "I mean..." Another pause. "I shouldn't have to tell you not to fire a weapon within the building – at our equipment!" He looked over at Ben. "Who does that?"

"I apologize," Melanie said. "It's not an excuse but I haven't been back an hour when I'm being exploited by technology."

"We're going to have to talk about that, too." His gaze softened behind the warning. "Later."

"Why?"

"Melanie, you took two extra days to get back. The CIA wants to know where you were. You can't simply fall off the grid like that."

"I'm going to save my argument for Hill," Melanie said, lifting her bag onto her shoulder. "But right now, I need a shower and about twelve hours of uninterrupted REM time. I'm going home."

"Wait. How do you like the new Manor?" Marshall grinned.

"It's really more of a condo than a manor. But it'll do once you get the elevator repaired." She was feeling better as she passed her office and stopped. There was a strange woman sitting at Jane's desk.

"Um, hello? Ma'am?"

Squinting sideways she examined the woman. "Can I help you?"

"Yeah." The girl stood. "I'm Rosie." She bobbed her head and waited expectantly.

"Great. What are you doing at that desk?"

"I'm your secretary, personal assistant."

"Where's Jane?" she asked, too tired to curb her irritation.

"I don't know. I just got the call that I was going to be your PA." The girl stammered and paled.

The last she'd heard Jane was still actively employed. "I'll be right back." Leaving her bag, she went on a hunt. Ben was in the pit with Jack. "Where's Jane?"

"Oh, so you've met Ms.... Ms...." Ben's blue eyes narrowed and rolled to the side. "I can't remember her name but, yes, she's your new assistant."

"Melanie," Jack started bravely. "Jane was reassigned to Marshall."

"What?" The good will from earlier faded and she wondered why she hadn't fired Jack's ass. "That's not going to work." She said, to Ben. "Jane is important to me and ..."

"Your office has too much stimulation…" Jack wouldn't stop.

Stimulation? "What does that mean?"

"She's pregnant."

Melanie read into his eyes, searching for more. *He knocked up my Goddamned assistant*. "So? This is the 21st Century…" She began her protest and stopped. "Is there a reason for the extra precaution?" she asked, controlling her concern. "Is she okay?"

"Her morning sickness has been fierce and the doctor wants to make sure she keeps hydrated and she needs to keep her feet up. I'm worried that at your desk she'll forget to take it easy."

She looked from Jack to Ben and relented. "Fine. But I want her back."

"Jane has already made that clear."

Melanie nodded. "Congratulations."

"Thanks."

"Ward," Ben said, "we need to talk."

Melanie exhaled, deeply. "Probably giving me an award."

In her office the plump woman with dull brown hair waited, hands crossed in her lap, looking completely bewildered. Melanie was drained and training an assistant wasn't fun – nor was it something she was good at.

"Rosie, huh?"

"Yes, ma'am."

"How old are you?" Melanie leaned on the edge of her desk, her gaze lingering on the pink flower pinned into Rosie's bushy hair.

"Twenty-six," she said, reaching to pat the pink petals.

"How long have you worked for us?"

"A year and a half."

Rosie's blouse was at least one size too small, the fabric pulled at the buttons and left five oval gaps that exposed pale skin. She was short, not a hair over 5' in her Rockport sandals. Her eyes were puffy, either a consequence of being assigned to work for Agent Ward or there was some other tragedy in her life. Neither option appealed to Melanie.

"Tell me something about yourself," she asked the woman. "How'd you get a job with the Agency?"

"Oh, okay, um, I volunteered for the Young Republicans in college and worked on Governor Massey's campaign. When I graduated he took me with him." The thin line of her lip simulated a smile. "I was his campaign manager's assistant. That's a big deal."

"I'm sure."

"He helped me get this job." Melanie caught Rosie's blush right before the girl dropped her head. It was enough of an answer.

"I have a few rules."

"Right," she said, perking up.

"You're going to need a pen."

Ten minutes in, Rosie answered the phone. "It's for you," she said.

Melanie set her gaze on the girl and took the handset. "Hello?"

"Ward, my office."

"But I was going home." She plodded her way to his office and dropped into a chair. "You rang?"

"Damn it, Melanie." His fingers curled inside his palm and he set a deliberate thump on his desk. "I am furious."

"With me?"

"Yes," he barked. "No. That" – he pointed to the phone – "was Hill. Again."

She poured two tall glasses of cranberry juice. "I'm sorry…" But really, she was stumped. Not sure *what* she should be sorry for.

"You unplugged. You took a detour after your assignment and didn't check in. You went against CIA…"

"I'm not CIA."

"Ward, we have to play along."

"Not my strong suit." Her forehead crumpled under the strain of caution. "I'm sorry. I'll play nice. Are you okay?"

Ben's chest expanded, deflated and his eyes settled. "Yes. I've been explaining your actions for two days."

"We don't explain," she said with conviction. "I found the girl." She twitched with the image. "In and out, two days. There's nothing we have to clarify to anyone."

"Tell me." He ordered.

Melanie recounted the events just as she'd rehearsed on the flight. His questions were surface and he bristled at the news that Hill was having her followed.

"And the chip?"

"One is on its way to you and Mike should've received an encrypted file."

"You did do a good job."

"I know." She finished off her juice. "But I don't work well under a thumb."

"We both better become accustomed to a thumbprint." His head tilted. "That job was a recruiting trial. They believe the Agency is dead and were looking to recruit you."

Melanie laughed out loud. "You are kidding, right?"

"A very limited number of people know about the Agency's revival. Your name has been floating around and…"

"Then I'm glad they think I screwed up."

"Not that simple. They're having a hearing."

"Hearing?"

"Prepare your statement. Make sure you've got it down."

"I never asked for this."

"Mr. Jackson, urgent call on line one," Judith said over the speakerphone.

"We're not done here," Ben warned as Melanie made her way out.

"I am." She replied. "I'll answer questions about Cassie, but I will not let my decisions be put under a microscope. And drink your juice."

"I want scotch." He was grimacing as she opened the door.

Melanie looked at Judith. "How is he, really?"

"He's improving," she answered.

"Ward!" Melanie tilted her head back and closed her eyes. "There's a meeting. Marcos is waiting," Ben said, slipping his arms into his suit jacket.

"Now?" Melanie growled. "I just got back."

Ben raised his brows in response. She gave her computer to Rosie and asked for five copies of her report. Five minutes later, she and Marcos were sharing their typical greeting as Melanie slipped into the back seat and scooted to make room for Ben.

"You need to get your testimony right," Ben said.

"Testimony?"

"Tell me again what happened in Moscow."

Melanie recounted the events slowly, ending with the tail that led her to take cover for two days. Ben would interrupt with questions and she bit her tongue to keep the snide remarks under control.

"I don't need to rehearse the truth," she said, knowing that she'd been preparing for hours.

"They are going to ask where you were hiding out?"

"I'm not at liberty – Jeez, Ben, look at this place." Melanie looked out the window at a large and expensive historic farmhouse. "Maybe I *should* transfer to the CIA," she joked, but her fingers were curling around the escape handle.

"Jumping won't help."

"Are you sure?"

Marcos parked on the driveway of gray pavers, under a big tree with newly budding, bright green leaves. The front door opened before they reached the portico and were directed to an elevator that lowered them to the underground office.

Melanie squared her shoulders and set the mental plated armor across her chest, readying herself for battle. She was walking into the lion's den and she needed to be at the top of her game.

"Welcome, Agent Ward. This is your seat."

The preliminaries with three men and one woman were cordial. Hill was friendly, which Melanie took that as a bad sign.

Her first task was to give a detailed account of her actions.

Melanie handed out the reports and began the review, starting with her CIA connection in London and ending with landing at the

D.C. airport.

"Just a few hours ago, I might add."

"Agent Ward," she was interrupted, "please tell us again about your arrival at Agent Lowe's apartment."

"When I arrived the furniture had been overturned. The place had been ransacked. I searched, found nothing of significance. I spoke with a neighbor who gave me a few pieces of misdelivered mail."

"The neighbor? You say he *just* gave you the mail?"

"I said he invited me into his apartment where he remembered that some of Cassie's mail had been delivered to the wrong address."

"And why would he do that? He doesn't know you."

"Ward is a most persuasive agent," Ben interjected.

Hill's scowl didn't ease as his beady gaze shifted from Melanie to Ben and back.

"Are you asking me to decipher what the neighbor was thinking?" The amusement in her voice was enough to cause Hill's face to flush with anger and Ben to send a dirty look her way.

"And none of your persuasiveness involved violence or force?" he asked snidely.

"Now you're asking me if I beat him up?"

"Agent Ward, the neighbor was found dead the day following your visit."

"Shit," she whispered, her mind revolving through the few facts she knew about the man. "When I left him he was alive and kicking. Had his apartment been tossed?"

"That's a need to know."

"Well, I need to know."

"You're claiming no involvement in his death?"

"Jesus, are you fucking kidding me? You came to me, remember?

Now you're accusing me of murdering a man I didn't even know!?" She looked at Ben. "No. I didn't kill him. I actually haven't killed anyone in quite some time."

"You said you found Agent Lowe's body."

"Yes."

"You're sure she was dead?"

Melanie paused to maintain control. "I'm sure. I found her in the morgue."

"In the morgue, then, did you confirm she was dead and not simply drugged or made to appear deceased?"

"She was dead. I signed forms to have her body shipped back to the location on her bio sheet. I also retrieved a flash drive." She looked into Hill's eyes. "It was embedded in her skull."

"How would you have known where…"

"Like I've said … the tracker implanted was connected to the device that she had in her locker. That's what led me to her. I thought she would still be alive…"

"So you charged in? What was your plan?"

"I was there. Right there. I went to inspect the situation. If I could've gotten her out … I would have."

The questions and what-if speculations continued into the place where fantasy took over and reality had her stealing passports and dodging a spook on her tail.

"You give me an email or Dropbox and I will be happy to forward the information that Agent Lowe had stashed in her head."

"We want the chip."

"I won't have that for a few days."

"You wouldn't mind participating in a polygraph."

Melanie looked into the grim faces and sighed. "Why not?" She could pass a lie detector even if she were lying. "But let me tell you, sometime in the future you are going to need me." She tapped her index finger on the teak table. "I know you are all calculating the possibility of that statement and you're coming up with a very low percentage." She looked around, latching onto as many eyes as she could. "Now you're flipping through the images of your best agents and your confidence is rising. You are pretty sure you'll never need me. But I'm telling you" – she felt the coldness in her spine seep out through her glare – "you will find yourself in a unpredictable situation and you'll keep thinking of me. My name, my face and you know what … you'll apologize and then you'll ask for my help. That's what is getting me through this insulting interrogation."

"Agent Jackson?" Hill's glare was a request to control his agent.

"Yes?" He didn't back down. "There is some validity to what she's saying."

"Am I to understand that you believe we will be in a predicament so unusual that we'll have no other option than Melanie Ward?"

"I have no crystal ball. However, when you're down to your last straw and we're in another Third Armament meeting … her name will come up."

"You know this isn't about that," Hill snapped and faced Melanie. "This assignment you were given, it was about collaboration. It was about giving you and your Agency a chance. You are all but dead."

"We're on crutches." Her retort was meant to be humorous.

"Get her out of here."

"Don't worry about it, I'm leaving. Thank you for the opportunity," Melanie said. "If there is anything else … well … you'll know where to find me. Oh." She reached into her pocket. "These belonged to Cassie." She set the jewelry on the table. "Could you please get them to her parents?"

Finding her way out, the cool breeze sliced through her. The sun had disappeared and the moon had taken its place in the dark sky. Under the light from the old-fashioned converted gas lamp she spotted Marcos. He was ready with the door open.

"Thanks," she said, darting inside. Her head was on the rest for half a minute before Ben was beside her. "It's times like this," she said, "that I wish I had a good drug dealer."

"Don't be ridiculous." He dragged a flask out of his breast pocket and handed it to her.

"I am really hoping this isn't grape juice." She spoke over the actual physical pain that was clamping her chest. "That went well."

"I believe it did."

She snorted and studied him from the corner of her eye, "Were you paying any attention? All that was left was to be burned at the stake."

"Over dramatic?"

"Huh," she huffed, looking out the window, "it wasn't you being skinned."

"You handled yourself well enough. Stuck to your story, never wavered and you agreed to a lie detector."

"It's intro to espionage 101." She let the alcohol flow down her throat, draining the flask before handing it back. It singed the back of her throat and by the time she looked up, it'd taken the edge off. "When did you start drinking bourbon? You shouldn't be drinking, anyway."

"Where to?"

"Do you know where Adam lives?"

"No."

"Then the Metro stop by Agency headquarters will be fine."

"Not trusting anyone?"

"Can you blame me?"

Marcos cut through the dark streets, directing them toward the bright lights across the Potomac.

"Tell me you gave them everything."

"I did," she sighed. "But that envelope you're going to receive with the chip that I scrapped out of Cassie's head. It has schematics and information about the KGB. I don't give a shit what you do with it. Russia isn't my thing and neither is the CIA." Their silence widened to envelop the empty streets. "Nothing can touch us because we don't exist."

"Are you certain you want to be left here?" Ben asked as Marcos created a parking spot where one didn't exist.

"I'm sure," she sighed. "Thanks for standing up for me."

"I spoke the truth."

"Yeah, well, thanks." Her eyes burned from the back to the front and her forehead throbbed with a headache that threatened to swallow her head whole. "Do you want to tell me what the Third Armament is?"

"Not tonight."

"I might not see you tomorrow."

He grinned. "I am proud of you, Ward."

She groaned and let her boots hit the asphalt. The city scented air filled her lungs and through the drowsiness she wished she'd worn running shoes. Instead, she averted the surveillance and entered one of the many forgotten tunnels that ran underground. The path descended and the smells of damp earth filtered the exhaust. Dust particles fell from the ceiling of the unfinished passage as the Metro cars roared a few meters above. She emerged to street level a half-mile from Adam's Georgetown home.

CHAPTER 37

The sun blazed as Adam stepped out of the airport and into the yellowish, dusty world. Two of Hugh's men were waiting for him at the curb in a tattered, rusted-out sedan. The extent of the conversation was the nod of acknowledgement from the passenger as Adam situated himself on the torn vinyl of the back seat. He watched the bright, pale city through dirty windows, apprehensive about their destination.

The white cinderblock house was protected by an iron gate that opened when the driver banged three times on the roof of the sedan. Other than six surveillance cameras on the outside of the building, the place was unprotected. Inside the loud, clunking of the a/c circulated static air. Adam was led down a flight of stairs, where the deadbolt was disengaged and a cleaner smelling waft of cool air greeted him.

"Hello. Come in," said a twenty-something wearing head to toe camouflage and combat boots. Adam clasped the chilled fingers of the outstretched arm. "I'm Barney."

Barney was 5'7", 150 pounds, dark-hair and never once looked Adam in the eye.

The two men from the car followed Adam indoors and stood with their backs to the wall, arms crossed at their stout chests.

"Please, have a seat." Barney motioned.

Adam complied, taking the stool beside Barney's. He was weaponless but the two guards were not. "What have you got there?" he asked, gesturing toward the laptop.

"It's your demonstration," Barney said, twisting to place his fingers on the keyboard. "Proof that we mean business. That we can make good on our promises. We want to be his army and this is our audition for Mr. Parker. Watch the screen." He said, lifting the phone to his ear. "Okay, we're on."

The computer screen split into nine equal compartments. Street views of a pedestrian part of the city, businesses, markets, car lots – everyday life.

"What are you showing me?"

"The bombs. Nine placed across the city central. I've had them set up for days, waiting for you. We want his business and we're told you're the one to impress."

"Your plan is to blow up garbage cans?" Adam asked, surveying the sidewalks and walkways.

"We will invoke fear, we will cause pain and death and everyone will know our name." In his seat, Barney grew a few extra inches and he aged a dozen years.

"Okay," Adam breathed, feeling the atmosphere in the room change.

"We have resources and guts and you're going to watch us perform and then," he pointed at Adam, "you are going to report our success back to him." His index finger, still in the accusing position, he pressed the keypad.

The penetrating glares of the guards scalded his back and then a concrete planter on a street corner exploded. People screamed and scattered. The second bomb went off in another part of the city – a bus bench – followed closely by the third. Half a dozen casualties were spread over the streets and then everything accelerated.

Before the fourth explosion could happen, Adam had snapped Barney's sweaty neck. Was lifting the dead weight out of its seat, using it as a shield before throwing the body at the nearest guard. Bending low, he rammed into the last man standing and knocked him off his feet. The guard's gun slipped easily into Adam's palm and both guards fulfilled their duty. Dying for the cause.

The laptop was hot against his back as he shoved it into his pants. In the hall, he smashed the security box and took the stairs two at a time. Pushing the outside door open, the blanched world was quietly moving along undisturbed as he hotwired the sedan. Aggressively, he merged into the congested traffic and was running through a mental list of contacts he had in the area when his phone buzzed.

He ignored the initial set of rings, letting the call go to voicemail.

"Yeah?" he snapped when immediately the vibrating began for a second time.

"You need to listen to me." Melanie's voice was calm but authoritarian as she gave directions that started with an immediate right turn. "His name is Mark. He's waiting now and will take you across the border. You're going to need to destroy your phone. Pick up a new one when you can. Questions?"

"I have to tell you..."

"Already watching the news. Give Mark whatever information you have when you get there. Be safe."

He could hear the shake in her breath. "I will be."

"Get to our last meeting point. There'll be further arrangements."

Not Frankfurt, I'm going to Rome. "I'm heading to *my* last destination." *There's something I have to do.*

"Okay," she said, mentally rearranging. "Hotel. Not the apartment."

"Thanks," he said and she was gone.

East Jerusalem was piled on what had been a low hill. Adam wound the vehicle through the narrow streets along cinderblock buildings and left the car at the bottom of a five-story structure with a long set of steps and topped with a red, clay roof.

The high humidity made breathing difficult and he reached the front door drenched, from adrenaline and the effort of the steep climb. Trusting Melanie completely, he grazed his knuckles over the chipped paint.

"Mark?" he asked the tall, dark-haired man.

"Quickly. Give me your passport." His hand extended for the booklet. Adam stepped inside just enough to close the door as Mark went to a small corner desk, picked up a rubber stamp, inked it and set a brand to his passport. He tucked a slip of paper between the pages and turned. "Let's go." He swept forward, nudging Adam aside and locking the door behind them.

Mark ushered Adam to a 1980's green Honda Civic with the hatchback glass blown out and hopped behind the wheel.

"You have information?" he asked, skirting into a lane that was already occupied and pressed down on the gas.

Adam rolled up his window that was causing a windstorm through the vehicle, blowing everything that wasn't bolted down. He studied Mark's flat profile before making his decision. "That was three of nine bombs placed around the city." He gave the address and a brief description of what would be found inside Barney's room and handed over the laptop.

Mark made his call and Adam gazed out the window. They were on the road to Tel Aviv.

"I hear you are capable with a sailboat," Mark said after an hour of dodging traffic and turning into the Tel Aviv Marina. "I hope that's true."

Mark drove them through the beachfront promenade, passing hotels and miles of sandy beaches, pausing only long enough at the entrance of the marina to give Adam the name and slip number of the escape boat.

Adam stood on the sidewalk, glancing out over the rippling water. Mark leaned out his window. "Hey." He reversed a few feet, "Twenty minutes. I'll create a disturbance that should give you enough time to avoid the authorities. But if you get stopped, your exit permission has already been granted. There's a copy in your passport. Everything else you need is on board."

The *Eye Of The Dawn* was a 25-foot sloop with a white hull, white sails and fully fueled. Even as he heard the raised voices of an argument in the distance, the feel of the wheel in his hands and the soft purr of the engine replaced anxiety with a sense of satisfaction. The storm hit an hour outside of the port.

The unfriendly blue swells of the Mediterranean kept him up all night, tacking and keeping out of the main shipping lines. Adam stood at the helm for eight hours until the high winds died down. Resting for an hour gave him energy for the next five to Marmaris, Turkey, where he refueled. Encapsulated in the endless blues of the sea and sky he headed, with less urgency, to Athens. The ocean spray misting his skin was healing as if he could feel the actual forgiveness of his sins.

Docking in an empty slip at Piraeus, Greece, his feet were stable under a pair of sea legs. He purchased a change of clothes, checked into a hotel for a shower and took a cab to the airport.

He was having an afternoon smoke, waiting with his back to the old stonewall for the congestion of tourists to flow out of Vatican City. The Pope had concluded his weekly mass in St. Peter's Basilica and the faithful were swathed in the afterglow.

He crushed the butt of his cigarette on the sole of his shoe before entering the hotel. The Italian behind the counter greeted him with a smile and Adam's eyes rose to the man's hair, dark and feathery under a slick coating of hairspray.

"Got anything for Chase?" he asked, recognizing the hair from a Travolta movie.

"Yes." He raised his pointer finger, dropped to the ground and popped back up.

"This it?" Adam asked, his fingers pinching the thin envelope.

"Yes. Nothing else."

The sunlight shined on the slip of paper … a phone number. Catching up with the parishioners, he pickpocketed a Catholic and kept pace with the phone donor as he dialed.

CHAPTER 38

Melanie sat at her desk, absently rolling the diamond ring around her finger. Mark had called; Adam had made it out of Tel Aviv. She'd arranged for him to get her secure number. Now all she could do was wait.

"Melanie?"

She heard her name but she was lost in the complication of Adam.

"Meeting?" Marshall was irritated. "Earth to secret agent."

Her gaze snapped to the door as her phone rang, sending her heart racing. "I have to take this."

"Melanie," Marshall tried again.

"I'll be right there." She held her relief until he was gone. "Ah," she breathed into the receiver. "You're safe."

"I am." His voice sounded so distant.

"What do we need to do to get you back?" She was on go mode.

"I'm sticking around here."

"Rome?" She had begun to hate that Eternal City.

"It was a loyalty test."

"I know." She said. "Marie is still in Rome but Hugh's gone. And he left no forwarding address."

"You checked?"

"Sent the coppers to the apartment but he'd already fled," she said in her secret agent voice.

"Babe," Adam bulldozed over her lightness. "I'm going to talk with her. I'll call when I've got a plan. Shit, the man I borrowed this phone from is heading into a restaurant. I've got to return it. Love you, Babe."

"Bye."

He was safe. She breathed for the first time in ... She tried to recollect how long it'd been since she stepped outside. Days. Her eyes scanned the recessed lighting, inside the heart of the Heights the artificial lighting never changed. No weather patterns. No sense of the passage of time.

Ben and Marshall were in the conference room, sitting at the table with their heads together. There was a quiet heat to their conversation.

"Anything I should know?" She asked, pulling back on a chair and staring at Marshall.

"Oh, Melanie, great." Marshall said, leaning out of Ben's space. "We've moved away from paper..." He blinked slowly. "And some are having a more difficult time than others." He handed her an iPad. "This is how we'll communicate."

Melanie shot Ben a sympathetic glance. Ben hated technology and Marshall was pushing.

"We do everything from here. I'll control the flow of assignments..." Marshall started.

"Wait." Both Melanie and Ben coughed in protest.

"My job is to garner work for an agency that doesn't exist. I have to take what I can get and then hand those assignments over to you and Melanie." Marshall said. "I might have overstated the control part. Sorry."

"So," Melanie studied the tablet. "How secure is this? Did Mike approve?"

"Fine, neither of you trust me." Marshall had lost patience. He rolled back his chair and Melanie and Ben exchanged a worried smile as he left the room. Returning with Mike, he said, "please, tell them it's safe and please take over their training."

Mike grimaced, his brows at his hairline and his eyes wide. "It's as safe as the next big hack."

"Thank you," Marshall said. "I'm trying real hard here, people."

"Marshall, before you go, " she followed him into the hall. "I'm going to need twelve light assignments, continental U.S. only. I'll need them for the meeting tomorrow. Can you do it?"

"Of course."

"And give Ben a break."

"He's incredibly frustrating." Marshall looked like he was ready to pull his floppy, rust-colored hair out.

"I know." She patted his shoulder. "But he's worth it – just keep technology out of his hands. Give him paper. Make him happy."

"But..." his objection stalled. "I can do that."

"Twelve light cases," she reminded as she went back to prepare for the meeting.

Melanie had scrutinized over the list of agents a dozen times, read each file and laid out the game plan. She poked her head back into the office ... Mike was teaching Ben to access the Agency database. Backing out, she considered losing time in the lobby bar.

Taking a table for two, she ordered a beer and a bowl of soup and watched the useless bustle of the Washington hotshots.

"Excuse me," she looked up at the man in the expensive suit.

"Yes?"

"I'm sorry, but you owe me a drink." Melanie gave him a questioning stare. "Because when I looked at you, I dropped mine."

Scooting her chair back, she opened her wallet. "Here's ten-bucks, knock yourself out."

After the third man approached she headed out. The moon was overhead, cascading the city in a silvery glow. She walked. Chill seeping under her coat as she enjoyed the transition from Tuesday to Wednesday. Adam was safe and the Agency was back in business, even if they'd lost the Manor and 90 percent of the agents and were answering to a damn idiot who hadn't a clue about espionage.

Melanie sighed, finding herself at her old apartment. Standing at the sidewalk in front of the short, wrought iron gate, she gazed at the darkened windows and ignored the flashing light of her neighbors' televisions. *How was this the only residence left on the Agency's asset list?* She wondered, reaching for the key in her pocket.

The lock had been changed ... the door, too. Melanie pushed, no squeak. She flicked on the light and took a giant step back. The place had been gutted; painted, carpeted, tiled and refurnished.

Melanie walked through, turning on all the lights. The kitchen was a drastic apple green with stainless steel appliances. The flat panel television was secured above the fireplace, the couch was brown but comfortable, the table was perfect boot height and the blanket was electric.

Upstairs, her bed had a headboard and a footboard, comforter and decorative pillows. The bathroom had been painted beige and a glass door had replaced the shower curtain.

"Okay," she told herself, peeking into the empty fridge, *"this'll work."* Her cell rattled in her pocket. "Hi," she sighed. "How are you?"

"I've had better days."

"How can I help?" She asked, exhaling at the sound of his voice.

"You already have." Adam cleared his throat. "I'm sorry I couldn't talk earlier. But, Mel," he continued in a low voice, "I need to know how you accomplished that."

"I'm really good at my job." Her lie sounded better than the truth, *I was completely fucking lucky*. "How's Marie? Beautiful?"

He snorted. "Upset. Hugh's a bastard."

"That's no surprise," she said, holding her tongue regarding Marie's slow learning curve. "Come home."

"Not yet. Soon. It's late, shouldn't you be in bed?"

"I am. But I don't want you to go. Can you talk?"

There was only a brief pause before he said, "anything specific you want to talk about?"

"I just want to hear your voice."

"I saw a woman today and I could've sworn it was you. I followed her for two blocks..."

CHAPTER 39

Adam wasn't expecting to find Hugh at Marie's apartment, just a clue to his next location. But all that was left were Marie's scattered possessions.

"Marie Sewell," he said to the receptionist at Marie's office building. She smiled, met his eyes and immediately picked up the phone. Her rapid speech had the Italian words blending into a long string of sounds before she flapped her eyelashes at him and said Marie would be down in a moment.

"You can wait in the chair," she smiled. "Would you like a cup of coffee?"

"No, grazie."

Marie's expressionless face turned to a grinning pout as her eyes fell on Adam. "Hey, Handsome." She put her hands on his chest, tip-toeing in for a kiss.

"Outside," Adam ordered.

"Yes, Sir." Marie traded her frown for a scowl. In the piazza she pulled out a smoke and offered one to Adam. "I don't know where he is and I don't care." She took a long drag. "No filters, it's the only thing I love about the Italians."

Adam lit up, watching Marie. "You really are beautiful."

"You only like me when you want to get to him. That hurts my feelings."

"That's not true." He couldn't help but be lured by her childish, feminine playfulness.

"Well, you're evil."

"You keep saying that but you never mean it," he smirked and ran his index finger down the V of her uniform polo shirt.

"Why are you so goddamned gorgeous?" She expanded her lungs while he played the silent card and she continued. "Adam," Her voice turned creamy, "please tell me you like me … at least a little."

In one move he had his arms around her, his hands flat on her back and pressing her hard against him. Her mouth was full and eager as he kissed her. She dragged her teeth over his lips, biting down on his tongue. There was a wild spontaneity behind her beauty. The softness of her body was a bonus.

He pushed away, running his palm across the side of her breast. Marie's groan in his ear cooled the heat.

"Don't go," she whispered in a husky voice, clutching on tighter, her nails digging into his back. "Take me. You know you want to."

"I do." He held her shoulders to stop the attack.

"I want you."

"Marie," he warned, self-control returning.

"She'll never know."

"I'll know."

"You don't love her. She's never around and you want me, you know it. Let's just see where it takes us."

"Marie," he cautioned. "If I fucked you that's all it would be, but it'd be over with her. And I wouldn't be me without her, she's my equilibrium." He reached into his pocket to retrieve a wad of cash. Stripping three bills off the bottom he put the rest into her hand. "It's about 5 thousand Euros. Should be enough to pay off a few bills..."

"I can go home," she squealed.

"No." His hand on her shoulder stopped her bounce. "You can't. Your dad is wanted and ..." He shook his head. "You have a good job here. Independence. And with that" – he nodded to the cash – "you can upgrade your apartment. Make a life. Understand?"

Marie rubbed her red lips together as she considered, staring at the money. "Okay, you're right. Doesn't matter, because I've got nothing back home." Looking up at him, her big blues had warmed.

His eyes searched her sad expression. "You're going to be fine." He smiled and ran his hand from her shoulder to her hand. "I want you to stay safe."

She shifted her weight. "He's in Turkey. Princess Islands or something like that." She shoved the cash into her pocket. "I guess he was able to liquidate one of his Cayman accounts. He skipped out and left me in that shithole without a dime."

Fucking Parker.

"Please tell me you know he's yanking your chain. That whole thing, the wild goose chase, that was to prove a point; either you were with him or you'd get killed." Her blue eyes darkened and lost their playfulness. "Christ, Adam, that man is a bastard. He's a depressed manic. You cannot assume his next move. Bottom line," she peered up at him, "he's fucking nuts. I overheard his whole revenge strategy. He plans to fuck over everyone who did him wrong and you're on the shit list. In the middle of the night he'd pace in his room, mumbling about how the world had screwed him over and grumbling about retribution."

"Why didn't you tell me this earlier?"

"I wanted to and some of it I overheard once you'd gone. But you used me." The hurt in her eyes penetrated through the first layer of his tough exterior and then they began to water.

Oh crap. He pulled her into his arms. "I'm sorry, Baby." he whispered, kissing the top of her head and taking in the scent of varnish on her clothes. "Sweetheart, we met because of him but I went out with you because I like you. Obviously." The rush of warm breath down her neck was followed by a kiss. "It wasn't all about him."

She wiggled, sniffed and leaned back a few inches to wipe away the tears with the palm of her hand. "I'm sorry I didn't tell you he was a lunatic."

"I already knew." He caressed her back.

"He left this for you," she handed him a flash drive.

"What is it?"

"I don't know. He told me not to open it and he was very persuasive." She held up her forearm that had purple, fingerprint bruises from unkind hands.

I am going to kill him. "Marie," he placed kisses on each mark, "I am so sorry."

She rested her cheek on his chest and his body responded as her hand slipped below his waist.

"Not that sorry," he smiled, knowing she was okay. "You are gorgeous, Marie. Maybe one of these days I won't be able to say no."

"Stringing me along," she sighed. "And I'm such a hopeless sucker for your lies. But, we could go to the apartment and you could see if the old man left any clues."

"When do you get off work?"

"For you … I'd quit. I don't even know what the hell I'm doing in this fucking country."

"You're restoring stained glass."

"I guess."

Again, her lips were on his, but this time her kiss was more aggressive.

"You know I have a soft spot for you."

"I *don't* know but I'd like to search for that spot." She offered, "I'll be gentle. Or not."

Tugging on her ponytail he kissed her forehead. "Take care."

Turkey. He considered the possibilities as he walked away.

CHAPTER 40

Melanie rode the elevator to the eighth floor of the Heights. Happily the body scan had been modified; Taking weights and measurements without the intrusion of the projected image. However, the DNA confirmation plate was still ready to prick a finger.

Melanie could smell Ben's office from the hall. Coffee.

"Hi, Judith."

She smiled warmly. "Mr. Jackson is on the phone if you'd like to wait. I'll let him know you're here." Judith had a nice smile and kind eyes despite the trove of secrets they held.

"Great. How've you been?"

Judith let the weariness in her eyes speak as Ben's voice boomed from behind the wall.

"Ward?"

"Jeez," she mouthed to Judith and entered his office.

"He's sick of cranberry juice." Judith whispered.

Melanie took refuge in the doorway, observing. "Why are you so grumpy?"

He growled about not being able to sleep and doctors with their damn rules, their probing and asking too many questions.

"Well, you look like you could use a friend."

"An eighteen-year-old friend." He lifted his glass.

"Be careful," she smiled, "eighteen will get you twenty." She laughed as he struggled to understand. "Come on, there's a meeting to attend." She thumped twice on his office door. "Time to include the kids," she said, excited to finally give the Agency life.

The pit was crowded with agents and staff, chattering. She could feel the electricity in the room fade as she and Ben entered. She nodded to Jack, who was in the front row and Marshall, who was standing, awkwardly, to the side.

It was their first official meeting.

Thirty-eight experienced faces stared back at them as Ben began. Melanie reserved a smile for Logan as Bob muscled in and Mike silently tipped back his eyes. After welcoming the group to their new sleek agency, Ben introduced Marshall.

"We've been taken off the grid," Ben continued, an odd grin of satisfaction pasted over the worry. "If you look around all you'll see is the absolute best of the best and I am proud to be a part of this level of excellence." The campaign champion continued his pep talk, leaving the nitty-gritty for Melanie.

She excused the general staff, technical support, Marcos, the medic, personal assistants and anyone who didn't receive assignments. That left 24 eager agents on the edge of their seats.

"I know you have questions. Some I have the answers to and some I don't." she started, leaning to half-sit on the table. "What I promise is that I'll keep you informed as I get information. Agent Scott did a great job keeping the best agents." She looked over at Jack. "I know each of you and you know how I operate." She said, swiveling her gaze from one face to the next. "It's just us now. We're more than a team, we're a family of twenty-seven." She looked over at Marshall. "Twenty-eight. And with all of your help, I intend on making this particular family excel. No one is going to mess with us again." She felt the heat rising to her ears. "I know there have been rumors, so if you have questions … I'd rather you ask so we can get the facts all out in the open."

They weren't shy, and she and Ben answered truthfully, even the personal questions. When they started asking about future operations, Melanie reintroduced Marshall.

He had learned the technique of evasion, passing out cell phones instead of answering questions. Marshall reviewed the *progressive* means he installed for Agency communications, the lifeline to receiving assignments and dossiers. Melanie listened on the proper use of the return button, her eyes accidently falling into the pool of Max De La Croix's soul and her heart sank. *No, things were never going to be the same*.

"Marshall has given us our first assignments," she said. "You've each been paired up and given three objectives, people who have been yellow-flagged as potential militia recruits. I want you to dig into their personal lives, uncover aspects that can't be observed on a computer. Find out if they're working with an organized terrorist group, as lone wolves or are untethered to any political motivation." She directed them to their new electronic devices. "You're assignments have been geographically clustered. Take a moment to look them over."

All heads dropped to their hands, retrieving their assignments.

"I knew I was right about you," Marshall whispered and bumped her shoulder with his. "They respect you."

She eyed him. *How'd we become so familiar?*

"And I got far more cases than you requested," he nodded, proudly.

"Do you mind if I get back?" She motioned to her people.

"Of course, Agent Ward." His lips parted into a broad smile.

Moving toward Jack, she pulled him aside. "You kept the right crew." There was a moment of hesitation. "Hid the right assets. You did good work. I would like for you to manage this first round of assignments."

"Yeah?" He looked skeptical.

"I want to stick close to the condo and you might have to travel. I hope you're good with that."

He nodded, tightening his lips into a thin smile. "Thanks. I appreciate it."

"I've always had faith in you, Jack. You're the one who stopped believing in you." Her gaze moved to the agents and she retook her spot at the corner of the table. "When you're done with these and until we get a regular flow of assignments, I want each of you to work on a skill – survival technique, a foreign language, hell, I don't care, learn to play a musical instrument. Whatever. Let Jack know. Questions?"

The agents scattered and the building fell into a lull, leaving Melanie with empty hands. She paid a visit to the control center, a dark room filled with screens, computers and the unique smells of Mike and Bob.

"I'm here to learn a skill," she said, sitting in a swivel chair. "I was thinking about that GPS tracking trick you guys do." She twisted to face the counter, her fingers on the keyboard.

"Um, please don't touch anything," Mike groaned. "Here." He rolled her to another computer. "That one is busy."

"Don't ever do that again," she cautioned.

"How about we show you how to do background checks?" he asked. "You could lighten *our* load."

"I could do that." She cracked her knuckles.

"Bob." Mike snapped his fingers.

"Hey, Boss," he started, signing her into the system and demonstrating the basics. Fifteen minutes of training and she was on her own. "Practice on people you know or just make up names."

"Why can't I help with your list?" she asked, thinking of the Agency's hundreds of potential suspects.

Bob's big eyes shifted to Mike.

"You don't know enough. Actually you don't know anything," he laughed. "I mean, you could miss something. You're in my world now, Agent Ward. Here, use this." He slid a magazine across the counter toward her. "It's just for practice."

Forbes. The annual list of billionaires. Head down, she started in the middle and worked her way up to the top twenty.

"Interesting stuff," she commented, having reached number seven. "I am improving ... Look at this. No wait, that's gossip. Never mind. But," she grinned, "it's juicy stuff." She looked over at the pale techies. "Sorry. I'm going to continue ... training."

On the list was Ray Bishop, age 84. Inherited his fortune from his oil tycoon father. A widower of eight months after being married for fifty-five years. Melanie squinted at the screen, his engagement had just been announced in the Times. *My, you're a fast worker,* Melanie thought, bringing up the background of Ms. Bridget Meeks, a 46 year-old pharmaceutical representative who'd aided in keeping his ailing wife medicated. Her reddish-brown hair was shoulder length and her eyes were more golden than brown, but it was most likely her enhanced breasts and tight, supple skin that had lured the billionaire.

From a simple check, Melanie learned that Bridget Meeks was from Michigan, the only child of a steel worker and a Tupperware sales woman. She dug further.

"Mike what does this mean?" She pointed to the data.

"Click on the other file" She did. "And again." He drilled deeper. "It says she died, Mel."

"Which one, the mother or the daughter?" She studied the text.

"Both."

"Then," she flicked to her other open window, "how is she marrying Ray Bishop next month?"

Mike blinked hard before peering into her bright monitor. "Are you sure," he rolled his chair to her and scooted hers out of the way, "that you're doing this right?" His fingers flew over the QWERTY board. Screen after screen he went over the data and finally looked up. "She's not supposed to exist."

"Well, she's about to become heiress to an 8.1 billion dollar oil corporation. It has contracts with the Middle East and connections with Mexican utility companies."

"They were also one of the first to invest in fracking," Mike added.

"Ray Bishop is a powerful man. Does he have kids?"

"You mean people who will contest the marriage and Meek's inheritance?"

"Kids to carry on the Bishop legacy?"

"Two," Mike said after a moment of research.

"Any way to find out who Meeks really is?"

"From here?" Mike sighed, considering. "Image recognition. But if she's not in the system then it's hours of wasted time."

"You need fingerprints?" Melanie asked, thinking. "She's in Dallas, right?" She calculated the three-hour flight, the difficulty to get within reach of the future Mrs. Bishop and how she would get the prints. "She doesn't have anything on file? What about the pharmaceutical company she works for, no background check? No arrests? Nothing?"

"Clean. Most companies don't have this level of information." Mike grinned. "Before you go all flighty and rush off to Dallas, give me a minute."

"I'm not going flighty," she balked.

"I can read you like a cheap brochure, Mel." Mike's eyes disappeared behind round cheeks as his smile lifted his face. "Watch and learn."

"That's about enough of that," she cautioned Mike who'd retreated into the keyboard. "I'm going to get a coffee. You want one?"

"Yeah."

"I love you, Mike."

"Go away, I'm busy."

"Do you love me, Boss?" Bob asked.

"Yeah, Bob, I love you, too."

"I could use a coffee," Bob said. "Something sweet-ish. Caramel or chocolate."

"I'll be back."

"Like the Terminator." Bob laughed and crunched on a Dorito.

Melanie converged with the rest of society at Starbucks. In line she called her mom and caught up on the news. Rita had won eight hundred dollars at the Indian Casino playing Keno, her dad was in the garden and Cheryl was going for a sonogram.

By the time she returned to the eighth floor Mike was at *his* computer and there was a printout on the seat of her chair.

"Thought you'd want to bring it home," he said without looking up.

She felt as giddy as an agent. She was in control and her sights were set on Bridget Meeks. Nothing went further back than six years – jobs, schooling, even the Princeton degree she touted on her resume.

Melanie turned the page. "Where'd you get her prints, anyway?"

"I get to keep some secrets," he whispered, his eyes sliding over to Bob.

Bridget Meeks was Anna Pajari.

Melanie read the pages.

"I have to go." Melanie stood, still glued to the images on the screen. Her mind was already in Dallas. Ben was at NSA. She dialed Marshall.

"Ward."

She filled him in and ended with, "I'm going to Dallas."

"Hold on," he cautioned. "I have to take this up the ranks."

"We're talking a Russian sleeper agent who is marrying the majority share owner of an American oil corporation. An oil corporation that controls pipelines out of Texas and feeds the Southwest. He has arrangements with Saudi Arabia, Iran and communication lines to Mexico. All of this will be in Russian hands? How long do you think Bishop will live after the wedding? A month?"

"How'd you uncover this?"

She's a magnet for trouble, it was how Jack would answer. As much as she hated to admit it, "I'm a magnet for trouble."

"Well, it's not ours."

"What do you mean?"

"There's a hierarchy we have to follow."

"We're supposed to just take the scraps? We're better than that."

"We have to prove it."

"I think I just did."

"Ward, you knew the deal."

"This sucks. You suck, Marshall." *And you have a stupid name.*

CHAPTER 41

"Sir," Gardner said when the Director entered. He'd been sitting in the man's office for nearly an hour.

"Problems so soon?" he snorted, taking liberty with the scotch. "I thought you were going to be able to handle this."

"There's been a development." That got the man's attention. "She's uncovered a Russian sleeper…" he recounted the situation and handing over the printouts.

"Ward found this?"

"Yes. And I think we should give her the case."

"Who knows about this…" he read the page, "Bridget Meeks?"

"Just a few at the Agency and now you." Gardner waited, not wanting to press too hard.

"Okay," he was far away. "This is good. Very good. I knew having her back would be beneficial."

"So, you're giving us the case."

"No."

"No?" Gardner reacted. "But, with all due respect, she deserves to keep this case. It's big and ..."

"Exactly. It's big and we're keeping the Agency on a low profile."

"She's going to be disappointed." Gardner said, more to himself.

"Are you falling for Agent Ward?"

"No." *But I am a little afraid of her.* "It's just I'm going to have a hell of a time convincing her to let it go."

"Time to let them drop, My Boy. Tell Ward to keep up the good work and as good measure, I'll throw her a bone." He gave Gardner a rare smile and moved to his desk. "Was there anything else?"

"No, Sir."

CHAPTER 42

The dark corners of her mind rebelled and to keep from strangling Marshall she laced up her running shoes and joined the building's civilian tenants, at the gym. Miles of her feet pounding rhythmically on the belt helped ease her murderous urges. She was sweaty and out of breath as she rode the elevator, feeling paralyzed, powerless to fight. *I should've kept my big mouth shut about Meeks – I should've just gone and brought the bitch down on my own.*

She needed to vent but Ben's office was deserted and Jack only offered a sympathetic shrug.

Closing the door to her office, she dialed Adam.

"Yeah?"

"Where are you?" she questioned foregoing the pleasantries as his blistery blast chilled her from her toes to her fingertips. She set the GPS into action.

"London."

"I thought I felt the cold."

"I'm just busy, Mel." She gave the wound a moment to heal.

"Sorry. I'm sort of distracted."

"But you're okay?" it was such a broad question.

"I'm at my old flat. I thought it'd be ransacked or seized by now, but it's untouched."

"I wasn't aware there were remnants of your previous life. Or that it was something you coveted."

"Covet, Mel?" he snarled. "It's a familiar place to gather my thoughts. It was late and raining and, I found myself retrieving the spare key. I don't know why I have to explain myself."

She sank into her chair, her body molding to the old leather that had already been formed by another. The lump at her shoulder dug deeper than it had before and her discomfort stemmed from both internal and external sources.

"Is there a plan?" she asked, closing her eyes and measuring the distance between them and the foreign sound of his voice.

"I'm going to fucking kill the bastard and it's not going to be an easy or a pretty death."

Shit, she thought, checking her phone and gaging how much time she needed for his precise location.

"Mel, I've got to go."

Just another second. "Adam?" He was gone. A string of swear words unleashed inside her head as a growl escaped from her chest. She had a fix on his location to a specific block in the heart of London.

Not bothering with reservations, she left a note on Mike's desk asking for an update on the Circle Society players and signed off … See you tomorrow.

It was noon in London, under a cloudy, gray sky she stood at the curb of an old gray, rain-streaked building. The darkness of the low, heavy clouds eroded the feeling of mid-day as she tipped back her umbrella to see the top-floor windows. She didn't know which room was his.

"Hi," she said, holding her breath when he answered on the fourth ring. "What are you doing?"

"Mel, babe, I'm in the middle of something…"

"Have you tried Vintage on Warwick?" She'd passed the restaurant on her way from the airport.

"Nah," he was distracted.

"It's a restaurant."

"More of a market."

"Meet me there?"

"Where?" he asked, his attention on her.

"Vintage on Warwick."

"When?"

"Now."

"Melanie?"

She ended the call and retreated into the back of the cab. From curbside she watched Adam emerge from the rectangular opening.

"Go ahead," she knocked on the partition window between her and the driver. Melanie pulled her buzzing phone from her pocket.

"Ward?" Ben sighed.

"I'll be there in the morning. Afternoon at the latest. Unless there's a reason to…"

"No," Ben said, tired. "Just check in with me."

"I left a note."

"That's not checking in."

"Granted. Lesson learned. But it was either leave or break protocol and Marshall's mighty hierarchy chart and head to Dallas. I picked the lesser of the evils. Will you speak with Mike and Bob? I left instructions."

"I will."

Vintage was a family-style restaurant with long marble tables running the length of the dining room. Strangers were seated shoulder-to-shoulder as if friends. The walls were covered in white subway tile and lined with shelves that were used to store, flour, sugar, rice, pasta and spices. It wasn't what she'd expected from the window.

"Are there any private tables?" she asked, arriving before Adam.

"An end is open but that's as private as we get around here," he said, glancing over his shoulder. "We're sort of intimate."

"That's fine."

"Can I get you something to drink?"

"Tea." She said, pulling back the chair and slipping out of her jacket.

"Lovely." And the shaggy-haired waiter was gone, opening her line of sight to the dark, drenched man blocking the meager light of the doorway.

It was a sinister shadow, his long deliberate strides moving with purpose to the chair opposite her, scraping the legs along the cold tile and dropping down with a heavy thud. She was at the center point of the assassin's stare.

"You look very menacing," she said.

The waiter arrived with her pot of tea.

"Menus?" he asked cautiously, placing a laminated sheet on the table.

"Thanks."

“We won’t be eating.” Adam’s voice rumbled from his chest.

Melanie ignored the low command and pointed to a bowl three seats away. “What’s she having?”

“Pozole. Hominy, pinto beans, beef. Bowl or cup?”

“Bowl.”

“And for you, Sir?”

“He’ll have the same,” Melanie ordered.

He went off toward the open, diner-style kitchen and Adam’s eyes followed him. “I hate this place,” Adam complained, continuing his judgment of the décor, the wait staff and the customers.

“I like it,” she decided.

“What are you doing here?” He let the back of the chair support his weight and extended his leg.

“Having a meal.” She answered, angling to inspect him. Her eyes ran from the scuffed toe of his boot, following the seam of his Levi’s to his thigh and the heavily soaked, blue coat. She remembered the roughness of that wool and up to his white collar peeking out at the top. The corner of his jaw was clenched beneath a bristly layer of stubble. “Hi.” She smiled when she reached his eyes, as green as the image of the Philippines atoll she’d seen in the airline magazine. His jet-black hair was soaked and divided into four even portions where his fingers had dragged through. She filled her lungs with the warm, moist air and absorbed the shivers that his presence caused deep within her.

“What are you doing here?” he tried a second time.

“Why won’t you look at me?”

Time suspended, as if they were hanging in a void. Her full attention devoted to him, willing him to speak.

“Because I’m about to do really terrible things and I can’t …” his head shifted side-to-side and his gaze made it to her shoulders. "He left me a message…"

The waiter arrived, breaking Adam's momentum. But … her stomach growled and the hot soup arrived in large white bowls with slices of avocado, lime and cilantro flakes. A basket of bolillos was set on the table between them. The beef broth warmed her from the inside out and she pulled her sleeves up to her elbows.

"Yum, right?"

"Actually," he prodded through the bowl searching out the specifics, "it's very good."

Melanie tore one of the breads in half and dipped as she watched him morph from assassin to chef. They shared flan for dessert without having exchanged more than two-dozen words before paying the bill. Outside the rain had turned to a drizzle, he turned up his collar and reached for her hand.

"Where are we going?" she asked, checking her watch.

"My place."

His was a top floor, corner apartment and even more barren than hers. Adam hung their wet coats on the back of a chair, letting water drip on the parquet flooring.

"I like it," she said, twisting to look at him from over her shoulder. "It has potential." She walked around, touching the table he was using as a desk. Her eyes reading over the papers, the notes and photos that were taped in a timeline fashion to the wall. "Is this one of the extra keys on the ring you gave me?"

"No." His pursed lips stretched slightly to the right. "I'd left this place."

"Well, I like what you've done with it," she smiled, gazing up at him her heart lifted.

"You're in a cheerful mood." He scanned her like an x-ray machine.

"I'm not." Her body softened, her shoulders sagged and the muscles in her face relaxed. "Tell me about Hugh's message."

He shook his head. "All you need to know is that I am going to carry out this hit."

"I know." Automatically, she pulled her lower lip between her teeth.

"And?"

"I accept it. You do what you have to do." Her windpipes were constricting but otherwise she was at peace. Parker deserved what he got. "How can I help?"

"What?" He bolted back, "No. I don't want you involved."

"About a decade too late for that. I wish you'd let me in, Adam. I wish you'd tell me what Hugh has planned."

"What are you doing here? Jesus, Melanie. Go home." He paced the length of the room.

"You're tracking him and it feels like you're forgetting me. I'm still here, Adam."

He looked at her. Seconds ticked before he rubbed his palms across his face. "I'm sorry. I didn't mean…" He looked up, sorrow filling his expression. Their eyes locked. "You're right, but I've got a task and I can't let it go. I need you to understand." He took a step forward, cradling her face between his hands and looking into her eyes. "Baby." He smiled and in the time it took him to close the distance between them she had a feeling she was being played.

In his kiss was a stranger. But it didn't matter, she was willing to go along with the fantasy if it gave her one more minute with him.

Her hands were in his, his left thumb rubbing the diamonds of his mother's ring. "Getting used to it?" he asked, one brow arched.

"It's not mine," she answered, soothing her sorrow that was carried along by a rush of nerves.

"It looks good on you." She watched the lines around his grin erase as his gaze slowly lifted to hers. "You've been wearing it?"

"Yes."

The lines reappeared, in an alluring manner that would cause millions of knees to weaken. Thankfully there were only her two and the look was meant only for her … this time.

"When do you have to get back?"

"My flight leaves in a couple of hours."

"Let me show you the accommodations."

CHAPTER 43

She was going to miss her flight. But her feet were planted on the wet concrete outside his building, her arms inside his wool coat, holding on tight.

"We're going to have to stop meeting like this," she said when the kiss was broken.

"I'll be home soon."

"Don't say things you don't mean." Melanie watched his demeanor change, he exhaled, shifting his weight from one foot to the other and the creases on his forehead had returned. Her worry heightened. "I don't want to leave but I've got twenty-four eager souls waiting."

"Go," he said.

His sadness was inconsolable. He'd made up his mind and she was determined to accept his choice.

She faked a smile as he hailed a passing cab. "I'll see you soon."

"I love you. Always." He reached down to open the door. The corner of his eyes tilted downward and his expression had her holding back tears. "Heathrow," he said to the driver. "Get her there safely."

The tires pulled away from the curb into the wet city streets and Melanie watched his shadow for a block. Rolling the ring between her index and thumb she was lost in gloomy thoughts. *I'm not losing him to Marie or to Hugh. I'm losing him to his past.*

Needing a friendly voice, she picked up her phone. "Hi, Mom."

"Oh, good I'm glad you called. I wanted to tell you that Aunt Polly is going in for bunion surgery." Rita rambled and Melanie eased back in the seat to listen. "Really a painful procedure."

"I'm sorry to hear that."

"Not half as sorry as I am. She's staying with us for two weeks while she heals. We've rented a roll-away bed but Penny thinks it's too stiff for her mom." Rita sighed. "And did I mention she can't climb the stairs so she'll be in the living room. I just don't know what else we can do."

"What if you put one of those foam pads over the roll-away? Load it up with cushions and stuff."

"Maybe. But what I really wanted was for you to know that I'm here all by myself, wishing my daughter was around."

"I can't come home yet," she said. "What about Penny?"

Rita groaned. "She'll be here. That's why I need you."

"Sorry."

"Great. Anyway," Rita continued relaying family news until her doorbell rang and she had to go.

"Bye, mom."

"Love you, Honey."

"You, too."

Aunt Polly's bunions had actually made her feel better. She snorted out a laugh. At the revolving doors of the airport her phone rang. Ben.

"Two days ago a body washed up in one of the bends of Lake Lucerne. Mutilated, no fingerprints. Most of the teeth had been extracted and the face was badly burned. The International Leaders Summit began yesterday. We're getting our first case and you're already in Europe, so you're up. You'll have to make your own arrangements. The Agency isn't quite running but Marshall pulled through, put his neck out. Trial run, Ward."

"I'm on it."

"Remember to play by the rules."

"I will." She sighed.

"Do I need to know what's going on in London?"

"Nope. I'll call when I land." She was going to Switzerland.

Her first stop was the morgue. It was just like all the others and she'd been to too many lately. The odor was too similar to the cryogenics lab and the muscles in her throat clenched as she concentrated to fight the urge to barf. The body, laid out on the open drawer was mostly intact, but the face had been hacked-up.

Melanie focused on facts. Male. Young. His limbs were long, lean like a long distance runner. And although he had no ID he did have his stomach contents: Chinese swamp eel, crustaceans with a high concentration of soy sauce. She remembered her time in Eastern China. There'd been a series of trade issues, disputes over seaways but ... she pressed the reaches of her memory to recall any relevance to the humanitarian agenda going on a mile north.

"Bob," she said, roughly turning away from the body. "I need a background check on the delegates from Eastern China." Her walk was brisk and the Swiss Alps were magnificent.

"Okay," he said, munching and slurping in her ear. "I'm on it."

She headed for the convention at the Astoria Lucerne. The lobby was swarming with hundreds of delegates mingling at the reception before the speeches. Energy filled the space and the general hum of conversation had the room buzzing.

She filled a cup with hot water, dunked in a tea bag and tipped in a packet of sugar as she noticed the lanyards. Each delegate wore black lanyards with nametags and country flags in the plastic sleeve. Melanie weaved through the superficial laughing, backslapping, drinking and flirting while she searched for her targets.

"What'cha got?" she asked, Bob.

"Three men in the Eastern Chinese delegation," he said. "I'm sending you their files."

"Thanks."

People were mixing throughout the hotel. Melanie found her three, two fitting the photos Bob had sent. She snapped a picture of the third man and sent it to Bob with a text that she needed facial recognition.

Circling the room, she kept the suspect in sight while waiting for Bob's answer. He wasn't Mike. He didn't have the experience and she needed to remember that. Mike was familiar, he was brilliant and capable and experienced. Bob wasn't there yet.

Wrangling a spot next to the men, overhearing them speak Wu Chinese and struggled to understand the conversation. Her ears were untrained, but from what she gathered it was a first meeting. Her intense listening skills were tested and an hour later she had a headache and no information from Bob.

Releasing the top two buttons of her blouse, she went for plan B.

"Hi, don't you hate these things?" She smiled and leaned in, lifting his nametag. "Mr. Chen."

"No," he snapped and walked away.

"Your loss," she mumbled, having filched his key card. "Bob, I need Mr. Chen's room number."

"I'm still working…"

She muffled her scream of frustration. "Please. The room number. Mr. Chen." She was vibrating as she jabbed the up arrow over and over, trying to hurry the return of the elevator.

"503. Room 503."

Upstairs the halls were quiet and she kept her face out of the view of the surveillance cameras. Chen's room was neat: two suitcases and a duffle bag. The luggage tags read David Chen scrawled in two languages. *These belong to the man in the morgue, but this one,* she knew instinctively as she looked at the blank label of the duffle bag.

Melanie bent to explore, being careful with the contents.

Protected within a pair of jeans and an ugly sweater was a loaded 9 mm and a spare magazine. Inspecting each article, she removed everything from the bag. Grazing her fingers over the lining she pulled a thread at the bottom seam and was rewarded with a phone encased in bubble wrap.

Pining for Mike, she tried to download the app that would transfer the information from his cell to hers. Unsuccessful, she removed the chip, returned the phone and did her best to seal the seam before replacing the items in the bag.

"I need a room," she said, slipping into the elevator.

"Why are you calling me?"

"Because. I. Need. A. Room."

"What about the reception desk?"

"They're booked, Bob. I need you and your computer to get me a room. Preferably on the fifth floor."

"I don't know how … if they're booked."

"Find the empty rooms, screw with the reservations, mix it all up and cancel key cards. Then set a room aside and give me that one."

"Wow, Boss, can you make that sound any easier? I'm still working on the facial recognition."

She exhaled and ended the call before the elevator bell dinged. "Ben, we need to talk."

"Can't, Ward. I'm juggling lives and…"

"Agency lives?"

"An agent was in an accident and Jack is on his way to Oregon. Marshall is running the Agency since I've been at the NSA."

"I can't deal with that right now." She was pulled to her maximum and in search of a murderer.

"Hello?" Mike's voice was puckered.

"Stop making that face, you'll get wrinkles." She took a moment to smile as she watched the variety of people strolling the lobby. "I need a favor."

"Of course you do. I'm already trying to help your pipsqueak hacker. Do you know what he did?"

She lost her concentration for a moment. "Later. Right now I need a room at the Astoria Lucerne. Tonight. Think you could help me?"

"Switzerland? What are you doing there?"

"I've taken up skiing. Do I have a room yet?"

"Jeez, Mel," he huffed. "Okay, what kind of view do you want? Lake? City? Mountains?"

"Anything, as long as it's on the fifth floor overlooking the lake."

"Your wish…"

A blast of hot air slammed into her face with a force that kicked her against the wall. Dazed, she regained consciousness, realizing she'd had momentarily blacked out. Melanie clambered out of dust and debris, head spinning. The only thing penetrating the silence was the fierce ringing. The second explosion struck father from where she stood and then there were more still deeper into the hotel. Her blood was pounding from the shock waves – *someone's throwing grenades.* Lifting her hands, the phone was still in her right hand, she plugged her ears against the deafening ring,

"I can't hear you," she yelled through the chaos, people were screaming and the lights had flickered off. "I'm okay. I'll call you back."

The smells of disaster were the last punch. Running against the tide of people, toward the blasts, into the smoke and broken glass, she blinked back the burning in her eyes and saw him ... the imposter Chen.

In the distance emergency sirens echoed among the choir of howls. Fire alarms sounded throughout the hotel and the colored lights reflecting off the rubble in the air added to the nightmare. The Swiss police were quick to arrive and she followed Chen through the madness. Heading for the stairs.

"Mike, I need a facial recognition done, like yesterday." She was still shouting and straining to hear.

"Melanie? There were bombs at the Astoria Lucerne!"

"I know. Hand grenades, I think."

"Was it you?"

"What? Me?" She slowed her pace. Had she heard right? "Did you fall and crack your head?"

"Mel?"

"Mike, I'm not the bomber. Facial recognition. Now. I've sent you a picture."

She held onto the wall, climbing over broken ceiling tiles as she kept the bomber in view.

"Where's my facial recognition?" she scolded, hurrying to follow her suspect. "Call me when you have something. I'm talking two minutes." Racing up the stairs she slowed when she was half a flight below the terrorist.

Her phone vibrated and she received Mike's email. Chen was Matt Irving of Ohio, twenty-eight and a former member of Fair Pay Labor Coalition. He exited on the fifth floor. Closing their distance, her ears were stuffed and she figured his were, too.

At his door he searched his pockets for his key.

"Matt," she called.

"You?" he asked, confused.

"I have your card," she said, lifting it so he could see. "We could go inside and talk." Melanie wanted to take him down and she couldn't do that in the hall. He was silent as she held the door open for him.

Once inside, he whipped his back to the room as the door locked. "I have one more," he said, shaking as he lifted his left hand.

"I'm not here for trouble," she told him, not breaking eye contact. Her hands were in the surrender pose.

"I'll drop it."

"I hope you don't." She gauged the fear in his eyes and continued. "If you really wanted to die for the cause you'd be under a pile of concrete cinders." She took a step closer, her gaze never faltering. "Matt, give me the grenade." She put her hand out. "You don't want to kill us. Neither of us are the problem. We've all been screwed at some point or another. Underpaid and overworked while the rich keep buying yachts and the poor keep reaching for a handout. The middle is supporting each end. That's what you're fighting against, isn't it?" She let the pause hang. "But this isn't the solution. I'm..."

"So many..." His face was filled with hatred. "What's two more?"

"Huge. Two more is huge. Especially when those two are you and me." She tried again. "Give me the grenade."

"Nothing went the way it was supposed to." The cartilage in his throat bobbed and fear left his eyes. *No!* She dove at him just as he lobbed the hand grenade. His elbow planted in her ribs, tossing her, she sailed over the bed. When the explosion hit, her arms automatically covered her head and she was face down in the carpeting beneath the bedframe. Her world shook.

It took a full minute for her to remember how to breathe. Clawing out from under the debris of the torn mattress, the shards of furniture, she wobbled to her feet, holding onto the wall to see the room in shambles. The windows were blown out and Melanie was disoriented.

Scrambling, she found Matt Irving on his back, the right half of his body missing. The door to the hall had been blasted off its hinges and Melanie lumbered over the pile to the topsy-turvy world of the hallway that, from her view, had slanted to a thirty-degree angle. Balance was a challenge. Her shoulder to the wall guided her, keeping her on her feet.

Half a dozen men in uniforms erupted from the stairwell, barreled past her as she hit the down button on the elevator ... If they told her it wasn't safe, she didn't hear, she couldn't hear.

Bracing herself in the corner of the car, she held on as it lowered and her stomach was hoisted to her chest. The doors opened to a war zone.

Melanie swallowed the rush of guilt as she traversed the lobby that had become a strange combination of triage and gossip center.

I could've prevented this, she thought, regaining her equilibrium. *I should've stuck with Irving. Damn it, Mel. Damn it.*

"Ben," she said. "There are so many casualties."

"Has help arrived?"

"Yes, but..."

"The bomber?"

"Dead."

"Accomplices?"

"None. But I'm staying."

"Let the medical staff do their job. No, listen to me," he said, over her interruption. "I know you want to help but you're not qualified..." he was still talking when she slipped the phone in her pocket.

Two hours later and she was covered in sweat and soot but the injured had been accounted for and she'd led half of them outside to the medics. But it didn't end the berating, even as she left the hotel, the streets were still pandemonium and each victim added to her burden. The cold air loosened the cobwebs from her head.

Melanie made her way to the train station, cleaned up in the bathroom. Shrugging out of her coat, she washed her face – the grit had gotten down beneath her collar and up her sleeves and she had to scrape the ash out of her ears.

She boarded a train, took a seat by the window and from behind her eyelids she re-watched the mayhem play out.

"Hi. There's been an accident but I'm..."

"Tell me you're okay," Adam pressed, urgently.

"I'm fine."

"Baby, where are you? What happened?"

It's bad, she thought. His concern was soothing.

"I'm fine. On a train." She looked up to read the destination.

He cleared his throat. “I was thinking about the Georgetown house,” he said, without any more prompting. “If it’s going to be our permanent home, I would like to … get some furniture.”

It was so normal that she smiled. “I thought you were going to say something like you wanted to add a helipad on the roof.”

“Can’t. Pitched roof.” The pause was filled with emotion. “When we parted, I was under the impression that you were heading to D.C.”

“There was a change of plans. I’m on my way now. Adam,” she said softly, “I think I might’ve lost my edge. Don’t say I haven’t because you don’t know…” her confession had her filled with emotion. “I made a mistake,” *And it cost lives.* Her breath stuck in her esophagus and for a moment she suffered a panic that she’d never catch her breath again.

“I’m here for you.”

Here? Where’s here? She silently demanded without the use of her vocal cords and anger swept through her body like wildfire.

“Whatever you need, I’ll drop everything.”

“I know,” she lied, knowing nothing except her exhaustion. “My stop is coming up, I better go.”

CHAPTER 44

It was late and there was no Marcos waiting for her when her flight landed in D.C. A cab left her beneath the vertical stream of elevator lights in the otherwise blackened building. On the eighth level she was greeted with the humming of electronic equipment.

The eerie factor followed her as she walked over the industrial carpeting of the empty, white halls to her office. It wasn't the first time she noticed the Condo lacked the homey feel of the Manor. She tugged on the light from her lamp, six flash drives were set on her computer.

They could wait. The lights had been on in Ben's office and she was debating between a hot shower and company.

"Hey," she said, heading straight for the crystal decanters. "Need a refresher?"

"Undoubtedly. One cube, please." He scooted his glass to the corner of his desk. "You look like hell. Rough flight?"

"Yeah. It was the flight." She snorted, filling their drinks.

"You want to talk about it?"

"What's to say? I screwed up," she admitted. "I let the bomber out of my sight and..." Her eyes closed, fighting the shock that threatened to take over.

"Tell me what happened," he said, leaning on his forearms over the desk.

She sat, sipped and started. "Switzerland is so clean and the people are so pleasant."

"Except when they're throwing bombs?"

"He wasn't Swiss," she said, returning to the scene. "I didn't expect the grenades. He mutilated Chen and dumped the body in a remote spot. He had a plan." Her forehead furrowed with stress, she'd been over and over each minute. "It made no sense to randomly bomb ... why walk into the hotel and fling grenades? Why kill Chen? He caught me off guard." She wiped the sweat from her face. "When I first approached him, he was focused and calm. There was no sign of radicalism. From the time I left him, something must have happened to spook him. Maybe someone knew Chen and confronted him." She exhaled. "I'll probably never know. But I should've stuck with him."

"Why didn't you?"

"I wanted to check his room." She bumped her fist on the tabletop. "I hate these fucking amateurs. They're unpredictable. You know? Oh, I did get this from his phone."

"I'll get it to Mike."

She set the card on the desk and looked up, seeing Ben for the first time. He was tired. "I'm sorry. You should go home." Melanie drained the remaining inch of scotch. "Hey, you shouldn't be drinking this."

He edged his glass away from him. It was still full. "Judith is letting me keep liquor for nostalgia purposes only."

Her fingers drummed a slow beat into her left brow. "I've been thinking about taking a step back from field work." From over his silver frames he gave her a look that needed no words. "These last assignments have been brutal. I'm done until I can work the stench of a morgue out of my system."

"One of Hugh's offshore accounts was drained." Ben cocked his head. "Right from under the FBI's nose. He's got three others that are being watched more closely but the man has a special kind of gumption."

"So many other words to choose from," she said, standing to take her exit.

"You wouldn't have any information on him, would you?"

"Me? No. Why would I?"

"How's Adam?"

"He's hanging in there." She answered, very aware of the ring on her finger. "Ben, how'd you and Lily make it work?"

Ben leaned back, his jowls sagging. "Lily was amazing, so trusting. It was difficult at first … until we fell into a rhythm. Took about a year."

Melanie nodded. "You should go home."

"Soon. He's good for you, Ward. He's strong enough to handle you." Ben laughed. "You know what I mean. He's like us and he knows who you are. That should make it easier. Because, Lily was a saint but you, Ms. Ward, are no saint. You are a … pain in the ass."

Melanie was startled into laughing. "What happened to your eloquence?"

"Too tired."

They looked at each other through the gloom of the Agency's corpse.

"We had a good run." Melanie nodded.

"That we did." Ben's smile was rueful. "But we have our sights on new horizons, right?"

"That's right, Mr. Jackson." The alcohol was working its way into her brain. "New horizons."

"Why don't we enjoy each other's company in silence." A quick turn of a dial had the sound system humming.

She returned to her seat, closed her eyes and listened to the soft instrumental melody. Three minutes into Bach's St. John Passion, she was too antsy and took the stairs down to street level.

Melanie had reviewed Jack's evaluations and read Marshall's list of assignments. Life as an agent was beginning to roll. Aligning assignment with agent, playing to their strengths or giving them freedom to strengthen weaknesses, Melanie did what she'd never done before ... she became involved in her colleagues. She had been invited for after work drinks and was included in on jokes.

Working through dinner, she was sorting out the puzzle in the pit while outside rain pinged silently against the windowpanes. Inside, the multi-cultural scents of take-out filled the office space.

"Save me the noodles." She pointed with a pair of chopsticks as she picked up her phone.

"Hey, Bubblegum Frosting." Trish's voice sang from the speaker.

"Why are you so happy?"

"Can't a girl just be in a good mood?"

"Okay," Melanie said, realizing she knew little about happy, carefree humanity. "It's just strange to hear."

"I'm calling to invite you to a party," Trish said as Melanie moved to the hallway. "Jace's birthday is around the corner and I want to make the party big!"

"Why, is he turning twenty-one?"

"Ha. I'm no cradle robber. He's nearly thirty. If you think about it, he's actually older than I am."

"I never studied that funny math. When's this party?" she asked, her eyes on the activity of the pit.

"Three weeks from Saturday. It'll be at the house, with a band, catered ... fireworks. Do you know if they're legal? Whatever."

"I'll be there."

"What?" Trish annunciated.

"What?" she repeated, having stepped on some hidden landmine.

"*I'll be there*. Is that what you said?"

"Um, I meant, we'll be there."

"I'll rip the skin off your bones if you've screwed up AGAIN."

"Violent. *We'll* be there." Melanie corrected, distracted by the breaking news banner on the five televisions tuned onto five different networks. "Trish. I've got to go, but Adam and I will both be at the party."

"It's going to be a surprise..." Trish continued and Melanie listened, stepping back into the center arena. "I might include monkeys."

"They throw food," Melanie offered, her eyes glued to the televisions. "Maybe their own poop, too."

"Gross. Okay, I'll reevaluate."

Each of the televisions had a slightly different angle but they were all trained on a single man, on stage in a packed auditorium. The panel of six behind him looked frightened but defiant. Melanie set her gaze on the man at the microphone. He was in black, a rifle slung over his shoulder, his belt was loaded with handguns and extra magazines poking out of his pocket. But it was the AK-47 with a 200-round clip on his right arm that got her attention.

"Turn up the volume," she ordered, with her hand over the phone to muffle her words. Trish was still talking.

In surround sound the man's words rang through the speakers. "I don't want to hurt anyone." His monotone voice echoed as he spoke too close to the mouthpiece. "You should know that my vest is rigged. If you shoot me ... it blows. I just want to be heard." *Oh God.* Melanie felt cold. The man turned away from the crowd to speak at the members of the panel who were retreating behind the drapery. "You aren't going anywhere." Ceiling panels crumbled under the gunfire, "not until you've heard what I have to say." The man was sweating. "I only want you" – he used the muzzle as a pointed finger – "to know how my son felt." He paused to reign in his emotion as the six gingerly retook their seats. "He was at school when a man came in with a gun. Not unlike this one." He grimaced at the weapon in his hand, his chin trembling. "Two hundred rounds. That's what you call it, right? Two hundred lives is how I see it. Unnecessary deaths. Who are we? And who needs a gun like this?" He questioned the audience. "My son was one of the seven who died that day. He was shot multiple times, but the coroner said he was killed instantly by the bullet in his head. It was *you* who took his life and with it, you took mine, too." A single tear fell. "His name is Sean and he was only twenty. If you people cared about anyone or anything but your wallets, he would still be here. They all would. Sean didn't have to die."

"Uh-oh," Melanie thought aloud, he's losing it.

"How terrified are you?" he asked the panel. "I'm going to jail and you know what I'll do? Write letters, give interviews with nothing else to take up my time. I am going to reach out to the world. I will never stop working to get these damn *things* banned. I hope you know you all are going to a special kind of hell. What is it? 'Guns don't kill people, people kill people,' 'From my cold dead hands.'" He was still talking but gasps from the crowd made him hesitate.

One of the cameras swiveled while the other four remained on the gunman.

"You forgot 'One good guy with a gun,'" the guy in the crowd shouted, raising his own weapon and firing.

"No!!" Melanie shouted, seven hundred miles from the epicenter.

Lights on the monitors flared and then the screens went out, snow. The broadcasts were cut, leaving the kind of static noise she hadn't seen since she was a kid. She stood with Mike, Bob and Jack, the four of them listening to the crackling of the television.

"Jesus."

From her hand Trish was still talking. Melanie bent her elbow to set the phone to her ear.

"Mel?"

"I'm here." She was numb.

"What do you think?"

Melanie closed her eyes. "I think you should cancel the ice sculpture."

"Maybe. Well, you sound busy. We'll talk later, when I have more details about the party. It is going to be epic! Tootles."

"Tootles." She repeated in a dead voice.

"What the hell just happened?" Jack questioned.

"I think we lost the NRA."

"Fuck."

A TV flickered to life. The reporter was behind the anchor desk, looking as shocked as Melanie felt.

"What do we do?" Mike asked.

"We let the other agencies handle this one," Ben said, walking into the control center. "But someone had better make certain that man was not on our watch list."

The screens flickered, wavered and the second one came to life with a pretty blonde, her microphone shaking, "There has been a terrible tragedy…" she announced from behind her rectangular glasses.

"Is it me" – Mike was the first to gather his bearings – "or does it feel like this shit is happening more and more often?"

CHAPTER 45

Two weeks and she'd been caught in a revolving door of terrorist suspects. Hundreds of threats in every state and her agents were sent to evaluate every one. The event at the NRA had set fire to the urgency and broadened the scope of potential radicals.

"It's important. We don't need another gunman taking out Wall Street or derailing a train or the local farmer's market," Marshall had tried to explain when Melanie confronted him about sending elite agents on entry-level assignments.

"You're going to have to do better, Marshall." She was tired and her temper was short. "Anything?" she asked, walking into the control center. "What am I looking at?" she asked, leaning into Mike's computer. The landscape was a desolate desert ... California, South America, Middle East ... She couldn't ID the location.

"Turkey." He expanded the view. "That crumbling castle, somewhere inside or underneath is Parker." He spoke into the Madonna mic at his mouth.

"You've got photographic proof?"

"Not yet."

"I need to authenticate before making a move." His nod was all she was going to get.

"I've been trying to find a hidden entrance but there's so many rocks and chasms..."

"Boss." Bob beckoned her.

"Find it, Mike," she ordered, moving to Bob's end of the room.

Bob's grin was wide, reducing his line of vision. "Look here. Can't you just feel the fingers of manipulation reaching into your brain?"

"No."

"Well, you're not a bored adolescent with a rebellious side."

"True. What have you got?"

"I was doing what you asked ... looking at these potential terrorists and then – Pow! I started thinking. All of these sites are linked. So, you ask yourself, who would bother?" His eyes sparkled. "A recruiter. That's what you wanted, right? So we don't have to run around chasing individuals – they don't want to do that either. This site lures you to join their cause. It's so clear, right? You get them to flock to you and snap," he snapped his fingers. "You have a willing army from all over the globe. I'm brilliant. Say I'm brilliant, Boss."

"Send me the information," she began, but Bob's excitement was revving and he took direction of the assignment.

"I need two agents. I'll make them from Illinois, a suburb of Chicago." He typed, pulling up images of Logan and Dante. "Make them rich enough to be bored and looking for excitement. Change the IP address, GPS tags on photos..."

"You got this?" He didn't answer, completely absorbed and unable to hear.

She looked over to Mike, who was equally engrossed with his own task. She smiled, confident in her ... *trusted men-children.*

Rosie jumped each time Melanie entered her office. "Please stop doing that."

"Yes, Ma'am."

Measuring the depth of Rosie's skin, she decided it was too thin for a response. "I'm going to..." She hitched her thumb toward her desk.

Fingering the ring, her mind went to Adam. She didn't need his profile picture to conjure his image. She dialed and her call went straight to voicemail. He'd disengaged the GPS signal and hadn't answered her calls. He'd locked her out. Automatically, her next step was to check the cryo-lab, searching through Dr. Oh's emails and texts. Mike had installed trigger words to alert her whenever Hugh Parker's name was mentioned.

Nothing.

Marie was still working in Rome, though she'd changed apartments and paid off bills. Marie's sudden flush of cash had Adam written all over it while her heart flushed with despair.

The activity in the London flat had gone dormant.

She was alone and her brain felt stretched and bruised – there was too much to manipulate.

"Ms. Ward?" Rosie entered. "I'm leaving for the night, would you like anything?"

"No, thank you. I'm going..." – the word *home* lodged in her throat – "to the apartment."

"Would you like me to call Mr. Marcos?"

"I'm walking," Melanie said, forcing herself to her feet.

The sunset ignited Tidal Basin and the cherry blossoms glowed in a shining, golden/pink hue. At the corner deli, she ate a packaged salad, swallowed a beer and dragged herself to the apartment. Her feet were just inside the door when she stripped to her underwear ripped back the blankets and sank into the mattress. Restlessly, the night passed. Staring down the hours, waiting for sunrise. At dawn she took the Metro to Georgetown, raided Adam's weapons cabinet, jumped into the Audi and headed out of town to the gun range. She did as Adam had done – warmed up at the inside lane and worked her way to the open-air shooting gallery.

The smell of dead grass filled her senses while the weight of Adam's rifle satisfied her hands.

Squinting, she recalled Adam's training and set the crosshairs. Her blood ran in a calm, gentle flow as she looked through the scope, calculated for the breeze and caressed the trigger. One after the other, metal on metal, the clang of success reached her ears and she set her sight farther.

From between the clouds, a ray of sunlight fell on a thin branch at the top of a tree and Melanie set her mind, focused and shot. It broke.

She laughed and realized … there was no one to celebrate with … when had she become accustomed to company? She flipped on her back and searched the cloudy sky.

"Ma'am? Are you all right?"

"I'm fine." She sat up, her joints stiff.

She lifted the rifle, dusted off the dried brush from her body. It'd been a good day. The speakers rattled as she cranked up the volume, drowning out thoughts. The rich grass sent clung to her clothing as she spent the evening in her office, working.

"Thought I'd find you here," Ben said at her door.

"I'm leaving for San Diego in the morning. I'll be back Sunday afternoon."

"One day?"

"One party. I'd offer you a drink, but sadly it's a dry office."

CHAPTER 46

As Melanie climbed the portico steps Trish bounded out the door before her finger touched the bell.

"Oh, thank God!" Trish said, reaching out and pulling her inside. "What is that on your hand?" She twisted Melanie's right hand to her face.

"A ring."

"Did he ask?"

"No. It's a placeholder."

"I'm too busy for your weirdo ways. Come on. Seriously, you two should see a shrink." Trish looked beyond Melanie to the driveway. "Where is he?"

"Coming. He's going to be late." Trish was about to give her disapproving hum when Melanie looked through the wide windows to the backyard. "You're having a band?"

Trish blinked her blue eyes and forgot about a world that wasn't hers. "Cool, huh?"

"Very." She admired the decorations, a mix of between keg party and sophistication as Trish tugged her outside. "Hey," Melanie narrowed her eyes, "is that Nate?"

"I hired *his* band." Trish paused to look at the people milling in her backyard.

"He looks good," she said, staring. He was cute, bossing the carpenters around and wearing his straw fedora and faded red Vans.

"Stop ogling him." Trish groaned.

"I can look."

"Please don't tell me you've got googly eyes for Nate. Though actually, I wouldn't blame you," Trish said, tipping her head, full of curlers, to the right for a better angle. "He's got a nice ass."

"Does your mind have a gear other than dirty?"

"Never." She aimed her big smile at Melanie. "Adam asked if you'd slept with Nate, just a little FYI. You wouldn't want him finding you chatting it up like old lovers."

"When was this?" she asked, following Trish outside.

"Fall sometime. Nate has a thing for you, Mel. Men are different than woman – any show of kindness and they're all over it with a sexual meaning." Her smile turned into a kissy face.

"Stop!" Melanie shoved Trish's shoulder and laughed as they watched Nate approach.

"I'm making margaritas," she said, heading inside.

"I'll take two." Melanie called to Trish's back.

"Look who's here," Nate greeted her with a loose hug and an awkward peck on the cheek. "I thought I might run into you at this shindig."

"It's good to see you," Melanie said, suddenly uncomfortable and worried about giving the wrong impression. "How've you been?"

"Great."

Standing two feet apart under a wide, California blue sky, his fingertips dipped into the front pockets of his faded jeans and Melanie uncrossed her arms.

"I see that," she said, looking over at the stage construction. "That's some set up."

"Trish." It was an explanation. "I've been wanting to call, but I wasn't sure."

"You can always call."

"That's not what I meant," he said, his long eyelashes flickering down. "You back with the asshole?"

"Yeah," she laughed without bothering to correct.

"Well, you look ... beautiful." His eyes lingered a half second too long. She wanted to look away, to break the trap his eyes were setting but couldn't.

"Nate," she pleaded.

"Don't worry." His chuckle lightened the mood. "I'm not making a move. Your virtue is safe with me. Hey!" He shouted at the man with a hammer.

"I'll let you go."

"No. Wait." He finished his instruction with the carpenter. "Hang out with me. You could join the band," he smiled, "not the guitar. I remember how bad you are with that."

"I could play the tambourine." She liked Nate, but she needed to clear the flirtatious air between them. "How's Penny?"

"Jesus, she isn't here, is she?"

"No." Melanie felt the rush of disappointment; it would be easier if he like Penny. "I was just asking. Last time I saw you, you two were steaming it up in the back seat of your 1970's boat."

The whites of his eyes disappeared as the shape narrowed. "Yeah, well, that didn't go so well."

Trish was crossing the stone patio with two glasses and a pitcher of margaritas.

"You didn't invite Penny, right?" Nate asked her.

"Hell, no. That girl's a stalker."

"She isn't, she's … fun." Melanie defended her cousin. "Unique. Special."

"Special needs, maybe," Trish snorted.

"Passionate," Melanie reworded, taking the glasses from Trish.

"That kind of passion gets you a prison sentence. Ask Nate if you don't believe your best friend."

"I caught her peeking into my bedroom window," he said in an almost nonjudgmental tone.

"Crazy as a loon." Trish wound her index finger beside her crossed eyes.

"And you've never done something insane in the name of love?"

"Of course I have," Trish admitted. "Difference being, when I was caught they were *happy* to catch me. Nate, say goodbye to Mels … we've got a party to get ready for."

Her gaze locked with Nate's in apology. "No tambourine."

"Next time. We'll talk later."

"Where are we going?" Melanie followed her up the staircase.

"I have a stack of clothes that I bought and will never wear." She opened the doors to her giant walk-in closet with all the clothes color-coded. "Some are too big but most are too small. The same goes for the shoes." Trish poured, filling the glasses and licking her fingers to her wrist before handing Melanie her beverage.

"Why do you buy stuff that doesn't fit?" Melanie asked, sipping as she slid hangars across the rod.

"Because I'm a girl." Her face contorted. "I need to make room for new outfits. Purging the old, you know?"

Melanie pulled out a white sleeveless dress with the tags still on.

"Ooh, that'd look perfect on you." On the heels of her compliment the space between her threaded brows puckered and she swallowed. "You really should invest in bigger boobs. Ready for a refill?"

"Jeez, you should've let me know this was a glass of tequila with a drop of lime juice."

"Good, huh?" Trish's blue eyes sparkled but her voice dropped. "Can I tell you something?"

Melanie stopped her mindless shopping and prepared for bad news. "There's this news woman. She flirts with Jace, which would be fine but she's so aggressive with it and Jace is so stupid." She shook her head. "Seriously, he blushes. Can you believe that big, freckled dope blushes? I know he's crushing on her and all I want is to tear her face off." Her bottom lip jutted out in a pout.

"Have you talked to him?"

"About what?"

"The woman."

"No," Trish sighed. "It's not like he's cheating." Melanie loosened her pursed lips and pretended to be interested in the blouses. Trish stood with her hand on her hip. "Don't try to look busy. I know he's faithful."

"Okay. I don't want to cause problems but *how* do you know?"

"I've got this thing I do." She gave Melanie the sideways glance that always meant trouble. "I do a groin check."

Melanie's mind raced with the possibilities ... "I know I'm going to be sorry I asked, but..."

"After he does an interview or whatever, I check his groin." She arched her right brow. “You know, a little squeeze to see if he’s got a boner.”

“You reach in his pants and feel his…?” The question came out in phases. “Holy shit, Trish.”

“I don’t reach in, I dry squeeze.”

“Eww. Trish. You do boner checks?”

“It’s a good idea. Adam might enjoy it.”

“Or you might be causing your own problem. Don’t you think there’s going to be some Pavlov’s Dog effect? When he sees her he’s going to expect a hand rub and automatically get a …”

Trish’s eyes widened. “Oh,” she gulped, “I hadn’t thought about that. Good point.”

“Something to consider.” Melanie snorted a laugh. “Or here’s a thought, maybe you could just talk to him.”

“We’ll see.”

“Can I take any of these?”

“Put them to the side. You know how grabby Carla can get.” Trish stripped to her underwear and removed a dress from the blue group.

“Am I underdressed?” Melanie asked, looking down at her pleaded skirt and thin blue sweater.

“I like that your top is a little tight, brings out your eyes.” Trish posed. “How about me?”

“You’re always beautiful.”

She made a face. “I want irresistible. Mouthwatering. Alluring. Have you seen Jace? He only gets younger.”

“How can you be insecure?” Melanie asked. “You are all of those adjectives … and you forgot hot.”

“I want his friends to drool over me.”

Music and chatter filtered up from downstairs and the sounds and smells were making Melanie that restless.

"Come on, I smell BBQ. Real BBQ, not that fake meat you eat."

"We have to make an entrance. We can't just run downstairs and shove ribs in our mouths."

"That is exactly what I want to do." Melanie said, crossing the threshold. "I'll be at a party."

"Traitor."

Downstairs, the bustle of a gathering was calling her ... music, laughter, food. The large house and yard were filling up and Nate was preparing on stage as some of Jace's teammates were filling cups at the keg.

"Let's try those little puff-pastry things." Trish giggled, catching up and linking arms as they snatched appetizers off trays. "That bitchy caterer is going to freak," she said, with her palms full and a crumb on her bottom lip.

Melanie laughed and grabbed a handful.

"Hey, Car!" she yelled over the increased volume of the music spilling in through the open sliding glass doors.

"Mel! Trish!"

And as if no time had passed, they fell into conversation, got drinks and moved to the patio.

"Can you believe this place?" Carla observed.

The pool had been covered to create a dance floor and Jace was like a giant planet in the center with a dozen dancers orbiting around him.

"Trish, you should save him," Carla suggested, wincing as he twirled in a stiff, awkward movement.

"No way, I'm going to film it." She was laughing, cell phone in hand, moving to get a better view.

There were no seats, only tall tables scattered throughout the backyard. She and Carla picked one to lean against.

"Don't we know him?" Carla asked, jutting her chin toward the band.

"He was in Mexico with us. Girl's weekend, remember?" Melanie reminded. Nate was on guitar and lead vocals. "Look who's here," Jenny and Ryan had arrived.

"So, this is what too much money will buy you." Jenny said, leaning in and setting her drink and plate on the table. "Isn't that the guy from Mexico?"

Carla picked from the appetizers. Melanie breathed in, tasting the cigarette smoke. Voices mingled into a blur and beyond the twinkling lights she spotted her parents, Bruce and a very pregnant Cheryl. More tables were added. She was amid hugs and laughter as her little group grew. It was perfect – but for the hole in the center of her heart.

"Would you look at her," Carla whistled as she scooted toward Melanie giving Ted room. "She's lovely."

Trish was in a June Cleaver, fifties-style, blue satin dress and four-inch heels. Her blonde hair had been in rollers when Melanie arrived but now spilled out in loose, buoyant curls. And her big grin was outlined in a glossy, cardinal red.

Nate noticed and dedicated his next song, *Beautiful Girl*, to Trish – but he saved his last glance for Melanie. The wink came as he started the slow melody.

Jace and Trish got handsy in a sweet, loving way that made her miss Adam even more. They were obviously in love and even his poor dance skills were forgiven. Others flowed onto the floor and Melanie found herself alone at her nest of tables, riding solo with the empty cups and cleaned plates.

She caught Nate's eye for a brief moment. He looked away and returned with a charming, rueful expression. One eyebrow cocked high on his forehead, still holding the pick he pointed behind her.

She followed his gesture. Adam. The crooked smile reached his eyes and her accelerated heartbeat was the only part of her that was able to move as he approached.

"Hi," he whispered.

"Is it really you?" she blinked. "What are you doing here?"

"Baby." His hands were on her face, angling it upwards, his eyes enveloping, exploring her like it was the first time.

"Adam." She choked back the reservoir of tears. "You're supposed to be somewhere across the planet? What are you doing here?" she asked, lifting to her toes, to reach her arms over his shoulders and held on hard.

"It's Jace's nearly thirty birthday party." His lips were touching her forehead as he spoke and his hands were splayed across her back. "How could I miss it?"

She wanted to ask if he was done, if he was back, but the answer might spoil the moment. Slowly her heartbeat fell into rhythm with his. He stepped back, running his hands over her arms and stopping at the ring on her right hand.

He smiled. "Dance?"

CHAPTER 47

She was secure in his embrace as he led them between the couples.

"Adam," she began.

"Shh," he hushed, "we'll talk later. Right now, this night is for us." They danced as if they were the only two under the stars, swaying with her cheek to his chest and his arms bracing her against him.

She'd lost track of time, when he took her hand and directed them away from the stage. Beneath the giant fig tree, strings of white lights looped around the branches brightening the shadows and kindling his eyes. It felt like ages since she'd seen him. Him this way. Not the dark, menacing man from London or the man with his arms and lips on another woman. But him: relaxed and happy. His dark hair was swept off his face with every breathtaking angle she couldn't tear her eyes away.

"Sweetheart," he said, filling his lungs under an unrecognizable expression.

Fear, raced from the pads of her feet to her scalp, igniting the cells along the way. "I thought we weren't going to talk." She said, suddenly afraid of what he was going to say. That he'd completed the hit, that he hadn't. Or worse … *he's leaving me for Marie*. The images of their kiss had worn through her sheer wall of resilience.

"I don't want to talk but I do have something to say," he said, the corner of his lips tipping upward then drooping as his composure was exchanged with fear. "Melanie," he took her hands in his. Losing feeling in her outer body, her mind freed as she watched him dip to one knee. Unmoving, she stared, captivated, forfeiting all sense of time and distance. "Melanie," he continued, his emerald gaze penetrating through her. "From that first moment I knew that my life would forever be changed … that we belonged together. You are the home that I thought I had lost." His voice was rough but calm and his smile wavered as he rubbed his lips together. His eyes were intense and passionate. "You make me a better man. I'm not me without you and," a small chuckle escaped, "I'm a little nervous … so, Baby, I'm just going to ask. Melanie Ward, will you marry me? Please?"

Her mouth opened, but nothing … the backyard had fallen into a vortex of silence and all she could hear was the rushing of her blood. "Yes." It was a small, powerful word.

"Yes?" He broke into a smile.

"Yes!" Bigger. "Oh my God, yes."

"I'm supposed to give you this." His hands were shaking as he took her left hand and eased the ring – that had just been on her right – into position.

Her own hand was shaking as she realized he'd taken it off her finger, unnoticed. The terror had turned to joy and she laughed as he lifted her in his arms, spinning and disoriented.

"I love you."

The wedding march played and Nate's voice echoed … "Seems

there's more to celebrate than Jace Johnson's nearly thirty birthday. Congratulations, Melanie and Adam. I wish you a long, happy life together."

Her feet were on the ground but she was floating, Adam was staring down at her and the night felt more like a dream.

"Do you have a song?" Nate asked, gave them a second to respond. "Then let me give you your first engagement gift." Nate thought for a second, rocked his head to some inaudible beat and leaned in toward his band. "One. Two. Three." The music started. Nate, on bass, shifted forward to the microphone for, "Maybe I'm amazed at the way you love me all the time..."

Adam had her hand, leading her onto the dance floor. Her arms encircled his neck and he brushed his lips over hers.

"Is this really happening? We're getting married?" she asked.

"You did say yes," he said, his happiness reaching his eyes. "You haven't changed your mind?"

"Never. You're stuck."

His hands caressed her from her spine to the nape of her neck. "All I want is to be stuck with you for the rest of my life." His smile was warm, his hands soft. "We have a song."

"And we're engaged."

"If I'd known you'd be so happy I'd have asked you months ago."

"I wasn't ready months ago."

"You are now?" He tilted his head as if trying to read between her words.

"Definitely."

"Congratulations." Nate called out at the end of the song. "As an aside ... Ladies, I'm officially available." Melanie clapped as he tipped his straw hat to them and went directly into Queen's *Crazy*

Little Thing Called Love.

If he was only moderately serious with his shout-out for a girlfriend, the women didn't notice. Five of the most eager were at the edge of the stage, ready with their numbers.

Voices from beyond her bubble penetrated the thin skin of paradise, crowding her space and ripping her from Adam's embrace.

"Honey!"

"Mom!" Melanie was caught in a bear hug.

"Oh, this is so wonderful!" Rita exclaimed, releasing Melanie to embrace Adam. "Oh, thank you."

Melanie looked from her mom to her dad, who was smiling. "Did she just thank him?"

"I believe so," Roger said. His hug was an arm across Melanie's shoulders. "I'm happy for you."

"Me, too." Carla and Jenny were a fraction of a second behind. Melanie lost sight of Adam and was handed a shot of liquid fire to celebrate.

"I cannot believe you guys are getting married! I am so happy. I am going to be the greatest matron of honor the world has ever seen! I look amazing in any color, but Carla and Jenny, they're going to be a problem … nothing I can't handle." Trish was speed talking.

Nate's band continued with the love theme and went into, *Can't Help Falling In Love* and ended with … "Now we're going to get to the reason we're all here!" Nate shouted. "Mr. Jason Johnson would you come up on stage?" Teammates heckled their approval with good-natured catcalls. The band began the intro to Toby Keith's *As Good As I Once Was*.

The party moved to the dance floor, turned rowdy and loud. Melanie was breathless from dancing, dizzy from tequila and both breathless and dizzy from Adam.

"Do you want to get out of here?" Adam asked after the third time Melanie had to adjust the position of his hands.

"We can't. Trish." Melanie looked over her shoulder.

"We could find a bathroom ... Five minutes. Ten, tops." He laughed. "That'll include a few minutes of foreplay."

"No."

"I just want to be alone with you. I've missed you."

They ducked into the first unlocked room.

A closet.

"This door doesn't lock…" she started as his lips covered hers.

"God, you taste so good," he whispered into her ear.

Her back was against the wall, he dipped his head to press kisses into the tender spots as his tongue ran circles over the pulsing vein.

"Melanie," he breathed as his palm on her flesh sent shivers to her core.

The knock on the door was loud. "You don't have to make out in the closet," Trish called. "We have, like, three spare bedrooms. Are you decent?"

He ran his fingers through his hair, "okay?"

She nodded and he stepped aside to open the door.

"Hi," Trish said, brightly. "Look at you two all sweaty and primal. Premarital sex. I like it."

"Shut up." Melanie tried not to smile.

"Seriously, get a room. Upstairs." She flashed the light on and off. "You gave your tiny place to your crazy cousin, Adam's house is sold … Take the room. Mel, I already put your bag in the blue room at the top of the stairs."

"Thanks, Trish," Adam agreed.

"Have fun." She waggled her fingers, walking away and leaving the door open.

"I take it we're rejoining the party?" Adam asked behind wild eyes.

Nate had the crowd on its feet. Food and drinks were flowing for hours and before the police arrived to break-up the party, Nate had one last song. She and Adam found her parents, Bruce and Cheryl had left, Carla and Jenny were dancing and Trish was somewhere.

"I'd like to slow things down before we say goodnight," he said, taking a drink and pulling a stool from the background to the front. "We've been working on this song and I'd like to debut it tonight. This one's for you." A glint reflected off his bright smile. "You know who you are." The women in the audience went crazy.

The rest of the band fell silent as Nate began strumming on his guitar. His voice was clear as he sang. She stood, her back curved against Adam's chest, his arms around her chest.

"He has a thing for you but, he did all right tonight," Adam said, his eyes on the stage.

"He's a nice guy."

"We're leaving. Thank Trish for inviting all of us," Rita said, pulling Melanie out of the embrace to place a kiss on her cheek. "I can't wait to spread the news. You'll be over tomorrow, right?"

"Goodnight, Annie." Roger jumped in to save her.

"How's Maya's phone answering skills?"

"Not as good as yours." Roger nodded toward Adam, "I like him."

"Me, too."

"Hey," Trish said, linking their arms, taking the spot her parents' had vacated. "He looks so happy." She draped her long arm over Melanie's shoulder and leaned backward. "He has a very nice ass. You are a lucky lady, my friend."

Their palms were pressed together as they took the stairs. Trish's guest room had blue carpeting, an attached bathroom and a four-poster bed.

"I'm going to check for bugs," she said. "Audio and video. You never know with Trish."

"It's been a long day," he groaned, dropping heavily onto the firm mattress. "But it is good to be home."

Melanie watched him. Lying on the bed, eyes closed and she was suddenly out of her dream.

"We need to talk." He squinched open one eye to look at her. "I have to know," she said. "Is it over?"

"No."

Time ticked by.

"You can't do that again, Adam. You can't leave me stranded without any word from you." Melanie sat at the edge of the bed. "You have no idea how hard it is for me to function. Every minute there's a piece of me worrying about you, no matter what I'm doing in the background I'm always wondering if you're safe."

"Mel," he started, sitting up.

"No. Adam. I love you but you shut me out and now we're getting married and I'm scared that this won't change. You know what I thought right before you asked me to marry you?" She waited half a second, "I thought you were breaking up with me to be with Marie."

"Mel."

"No. Adam. That's how you make me feel, insecure and doubting. You kissed her, more than once, and I've been trying not to let it bother me but … Adam, I know you love me but do you love her, too?"

"No. I'm sorry." He was sitting up, grief taking hold of his features. "I got lost and I forgot why I'm there."

"No," she shook her head. "You can't do that. What if I disappeared without a word, without a trace? If we get married…"

"If? You're changing your mind?" His chest expanded and the grief drained from his eyes … "Mel, I'm sorry. Please. Sweetheart," she waited to hear something that was going to make her feel better. "I wouldn't be able to rest if you vanished. Marry me and I swear I will never leave you like that. Please."

"I want to believe you and I haven't changed my mind but…"

"I was in Turkey chasing ghosts and tracking shadows when I got Jace's call and" – Melanie felt choked – "and I realized that I couldn't do it anymore. I needed to be with you. I needed to be home."

He'd answered Jace's call.

Adam pulled back an inch. "You're mad."

"I tried contacting you," she said, cautiously.

"I was looking for Hugh."

"We have coordinates. Mike tracked a call made on Hugh's cell phone."

His gaze shifted, interested. "Who'd he call?"

"We can't be sure it was him. He's sneaky enough to swap phones but the call went to an automated arrival and departure informational line. Whoever it was, searched a flight from St. Petersburg to Istanbul. There was nothing significant about the passenger or crew list. No way I could get approval to stop the plane and if I went in alone…"

"Babe," Adam said, the back of his hand gently easing the lines in her face.

"I just wish you'd answered my calls."

Adam's breath had his chest lifting and his eyes elsewhere. "I couldn't."

"Why?"

"Because."

She wasn't sure if he was going to expound and for a minute figured this was all she was going to get.

"Because," his eyes dropped to hers, "Hugh threatened me, you, your Agency and I wanted to find him and hurt him. I have a darkness that I don't want you to see."

"Marrying me won't change that."

"It'll give me something to hang onto, a home."

"Hugh is still out there." She reminded him.

"You said Mike had coordinates? He's good, right?"

"The best."

"I'm going to let you handle Hugh, I'm done. And once he's out of the way … there'll be nothing else to distract me."

She believed every word, every motive and her soul soared. "Okay."

"All I want is to keep you out of the crosshairs. I know my intentions get trampled and the truth is," he looked guilty, "I like Hugh. We're friends in the only way he and I can be friends. I know that makes no sense but…" he left his thought hanging. The corners of his mouth fell as she stared into his repentant, unblinking eyes.

"Adam." Her heart pulled.

He closed his eyes and covered her hand with his. "Say my name again."

"Adam." She leaned into him and they fell back onto the bed. His arms were around her, pulling her close and his lips finding her forehead.

"You agreed to marry me."

"I remember." She smiled and he scooped away the lock of hair that had fallen over her shoulder. "But we should talk."

"I thought we just did."

"People are supposed to talk before they get married." She blushed. "Like" – she thought for a second – "are you going to ask me to sign a prenup?"

"You want a prenup?"

"*I* don't," she answered, "I don't *have* anything."

"Everything I have is already yours." His breath was laced with tequila. "I want you to have all that you've ever dreamed of."

"Like homes, a boat, cars, motorcycles?"

"If that's what you want," he smiled.

"A storage shed?"

"Everything." His body turned languid and heavy resting on hers. "God, you are so beautiful."

"I don't care about any of that stuff."

"I know. Do you *really* want to talk?"

"No."

CHAPTER 48

"Uhg," Trish groaned, her cheek pressed to the cool granite counter,

"Not feeling so well?" Melanie asked, patting Trish's tangle of loosened curls.

"Hungry?" Adam asked, at the refrigerator.

Trish made a gagging sound.

"Yeah." Melanie checked her phone, leaving the conversation to scan the list of assignments.

"Adam, shhh." Trish lifted her index finger to her lips. "But wasn't that a great party? And you guys are getting married?" Her grin was lopsided when she sat up, her eyes clearing a little. "Better not elope, Bitch."

"Jeez, you're grumping at me for something you think I *might* do," Melanie said, returning her attention.

"We can't elope," Adam answered, mixing ingredients. "Your mom would kill you. Us."

"She would," Trish agreed.

"Besides," Adam said, pouring the perfect circle of batter on the heated skillet. "I want to do it right, Mel."

"Actually," she started, her eyes on him, "I was thinking the end of May is a really nice time of year. The weather is perfect and…"

"Really?" He stared at her.

"Is that too soon? We could push it off to fall or …"

"No!" he said quickly, "I've always liked May." He flipped the pancake. "I'm just … surprised. May is great. I love May." He was still grinning as the bacon smoked and Jace descended the stairs with a groan.

He was holding his head and falling out of the gap in his pajama bottoms.

"Honey, put the snake back in his cage," Trish called, cupping her coffee in both hands. "It's not the locker room and we've got company."

"Oops." Jace wiggled back into his pants. Melanie and Adam shared a grin and he refilled her coffee. "Well, that was some night. Hey" – his brows popped up, exposing a pair of blood shot eyes. "Man, I am going to throw you one hell of a bachelor party."

"Not happening." Adam stacked pancakes on four plates. "We could go out for a meal."

"Served on strippers." Jace chuckled and winced.

Trish slapped his arm. "Seriously, Mel, May is like next month."

"End of May," she pointed out as Adam slid a plate in front of her.

"You could have the wedding here! Look how awesome Jace's party was."

"My mom is going to want a church wedding but" – she looked at Adam – "we'd have to go to classes and meet with the priest."

"Is that what you want?"

"That would take months and I don't want to wait," she admitted.

"Vegas?" Trish suggested.

"What about the house on High Street?" Adam said, sliding over the syrup.

"The haunted mansion?" she and Trish said at the same time.

"Jinx!" Trish pointed.

"Baby, you don't believe in ghosts."

"Says who?" she asked, breaking the jinx.

"It's not haunted. It's perfect – big rooms, high ceilings and a huge grassy yard where we can have the reception. All in one location. And the gardens are incredible."

"Ooh, ooh, ooh! You could get married on Halloween and we could have a themed wedding! With costumes. Ghosts and goblins. I love Halloween."

"No." Melanie cut off her friend.

"I'm going to get our stuff," Adam said, placing a kiss to her head.

"You're leaving?" Trish pouted.

"Things to do," Adam called from the stairs.

"Wedding things?"

"No. Commence your goodbyes, because we're out of here."

"Well, thank me very much for the hospitality," Trish's sarcasm was rich as she yelled up to him.

"Sweets, take it down a notch," Jace moaned. "Some of us are still recovering."

"Thank you very much for the hospitality," Melanie smiled, hugging Trish as Adam reappeared and bounded toward the door. "I won't make plans without you. I swear."

She gave Adam a glare. "Yeah, well it looks like *he's* going to want to be involved. And no bachelor party ... what a snob. I hope he doesn't think he's going to control all of it because we're having a bachelorette party no matter what he says. What guy knows about gardens, anyway?"

"Trish," Melanie started … and gave up. "We're definitely having a bachelorette party. Okay?"

"With *male* strippers."

"You're in charge."

"I am. You know that, right?"

"I just said it."

"So long as we're clear. Ugh, in all this excitement, my stomach has churned up the tequila. I've got to go pass out."

"Need help?"

"That's what he's around for, but thanks." She thumbed toward Jace.

"His snake is out again." Melanie laughed, crossing the foyer to the front door. The fresh air filled her lungs. Adam was at the passenger door of the Range Rover. "Where are we going?"

"Depends. When do you have to get back?"

"I can push it until tomorrow," she said, looking over the assignments and reports.

Adam dropped her off at her parents' house in La Jolla with the promise that he'd return in a few hours. "I'll call every half hour."

"Mom. Dad. Please tell me you are completely dressed," she called from the hallway, peeking into the kitchen.

"Hi, Honey," Rita answered from behind her bifocals.

"Where's Dad?"

"Working."

"Sunday?"

"There was some sort of emergency. But I'm glad he's out…"

Beneath the Sunday paper were magazines, crumpled and tabbed with post-it notes. "Because I have some ideas I thought I'd run past you."

"Okay." Melanie approached the tiger with caution.

"I was thinking…" Rita patted the seat beside her. "You could get married at St. Mary's. St. Mary's is so beautiful and convenient. We can rent the hall."

"Well…" She tried to butt in but her mom was on a roll.

"We'll have to contact Father Tomas today."

"Hold on. We can't have a church wedding."

Rita's glare was accusing and just needed a spark to catch fire.

"We've decided on the house on High Street."

"When did this happen?"

"Earlier."

"Oh, I see." She closed the magazine.

"In May."

"Which May?" she questioned. "Is *everything* planned?"

"No." Melanie smiled. "This May."

"May?" She humphed. "But you are getting married, right?"

"Yeah. End of May. Not in a church. But with a white dress. Adam. Justice of the Peace or something. You and dad. A few friends, family. Simple."

"Do I have any say?"

Melanie thought. "No?"

Rita sighed. "Well, as long as it'll be legal." She nodded. "Okay, that's six weeks. There is so much to do, Melanie," she reprimanded. "You've had thirty-four years to get engaged and then you *spring* a wedding and give me six weeks to plan. But I guess I can relent on St. Mary's as long we agree on grandchildren." Melanie choked on the baby bump that suddenly lodged in her esophagus. Rita continued, lifting her index finger. "I did see some lovely wedding gowns that would be perfect for spring."

Reopening the bridal magazine, she tore through the pages, prattling.

"Your dress should be cream or off white," Melanie suggested.

"I can't wear cream to a wedding."

"Everyone will be in cream."

"Cream isn't a wedding color. You can't choose –"

"I just did." Melanie smiled, feeling bold as she looked up the number for the mansion on High Street. "I was wondering if you had any available dates for the end of May."

"What's the occasion?"

"A wedding."

"Saturday the 6th 8am to noon or Sunday the 21st from 6pm to 10:30?"

She reserved the 21st, gave her credit card number for a deposit and ended the call with a shaky thank you. "I cannot believe I just did that." *Dear God, we have a date and time*. "I'm supposed to drop by to check out the property and their packages."

Rita lifted the handset to the landline and dialed.

The gossip wick was lighted.

Rita drove and Melanie sat quietly as they headed to High Street.

The house was on a hill and as the Buick climbed the driveway images of shower curtains and knives tingled her spine. But inside the venue was bright, open and Adam had been right about the gardens.

Adam's boat was exactly as she remembered, white with bright blue cushions, in the hull there was a small kitchen, bedroom and a head.

From the u-shaped bench seat, Melanie sat watching him work, inspecting the ropes and lines before heading out to sea. The water was covered in a blanket of fog that parted with the bow as he guided them out of the marina. Sailing for an hour he maneuvered into the wind, letting the jib catch the push back, stalling the boat in the only patch of sunlight across the dark blue sea.

"I love how quiet it is out here," he said, lifting the storage box and unfolding a blanket.

"What are you doing on May 21st?" She watched his profile as he hesitated. Taking a deep breath of the salty air she swallowed. "I called the High Street Mansion. I gave my credit card as a deposit and I went for a tour. So, I hope you were serious when you asked."

His shock caused a momentary delay in his response.

"May 21st." She reminded.

"I'll have to check my calendar," he laughed and slipped into the space beside her. "We're moving to D.C.? We'll get settled, figure out a routine and then maybe we'll think about opening a restaurant."

"Being an assassin is a waste of your talent."

"I don't know. I'm a pretty good assassin. Difficult to judge which I'm better at."

It was that same spark of arrogance she could see through the photos in his high school yearbook.

"It's cold out here," Adam said, leading them inside the cabin and filled the coffee pot with water. "I haven't asked about your work. Is it going well?"

"Strange mix of the familiar and the completely new," she stated.

"The people are the same and the work, but the place and the way it's done is totally different."

"Who was that you were talking with earlier?"

"Marshall. He's our assigned liaison to upper management."

"Mel, just so there's no confusion, I still have contacts that are searching for Hugh. If there's a clear shot, they're going to take it otherwise I'll pass the information along to you – I'm out of the dirty work. Are you good with that?"

"Yes."

The boat swayed and Adam began assembling dinner, shredding lettuce and frying fish. After dinner they leaned comfortably on the couch, holding hands, talking about Trish, Jace, the party, a honeymoon, everything – but Hugh Parker.

A predawn phone call was never good news. Melanie broke out of Adam's embrace.

"I've got to take this," she said, knowing the ringtone meant an assignment. "What's up?" she asked Ben.

"Ten minutes ago there was an assassination attempt." Melanie's drowsy brain snapped awake. "Mexico City. We could send our agents but this is big."

"Who are we talking about?"

"Estrada. He's running against President Cordoba. We need this man alive and we can't let the public know of our involvement. He was shot at, one of his men is down and he's holed up in a bunker under his office building."

"Okay." She was deciphering. "You want me to…"

"I called Jack but Jane's in the hospital…"

"Why?"

"I didn't ask."

"I'm on my way."

"I've sent you what I've got. Or at least I tried to forward you the information."

"Have Bob help you. I'll be on the first flight I can catch," Melanie added and ended the call.

Adam was already on his feet, buttoning up a pair of 501's and running his fingers through his hair. "Where are you going?"

"Mexico City." Melanie held her breath. "Do you have your passport?"

His lips twitched. "Yes."

"Are you comfortable going with me?"

"A hundred percent."

From the marina they headed for the airport, in the cab, she answered Marshall's call

"Yeah?"

"How much do you know about Mexican politics?" Marshall inquired.

"Let's say very little."

"I'd expect more from the head of a clandestine agency," he snorted.

"Is that helpful, Marshall?"

"No, but it is fun. Okay." He cleared his throat. "Short version is that we don't work well with the current president so we invested in an opponent. Built him up, put him on the ballet and he's gaining in the polls, he's popular and charismatic, and now he's a target. We need him safe. It would be nice to know who's put the hit on him.

Has to be somebody on the inside. But the main objective is to keep Estrada safe."

"Got it."

"Surveillance on the building has given us nothing. Best intel I've got is that the shooter was on a roof across the street. Get him to the safe house. You have the address and the bunker code?"

"I do. How are my people?"

"Outstanding."

"Jack isn't the complete ass you think he is."

"You forgive too easily."

"Fatal flaw."

"Keep me in the loop."

"Radio silence, Marshall."

"I don't like that. My boss…"

"Too bad."

"Ward."

Melanie slipped her phone into her pocket and the startling warmth of Adam's hand against hers brought her to reality.

"That was Marshall on the phone? He's young?"

"Thirties. I think." She looked up at him. "Why?"

"Just curious." He answered, coolly. "How's Ben handling the transition?"

Melanie grimaced. "Marshall is a fan of technology."

"Enough said."

They caught the only direct flight from San Diego to Mexico City.

Taking the window seat, she leaned against the wall, angling to see him better. The light from the window brightened the left half of his face. Her eyes sketched his profile, tracing from his forehead, the straight pitch of his nose, the swell of his lips. She hung there for a moment before following the hard line of his chin, his jawline, the maze of his ear all framed by his dark hair.

"You're staring."

"Admiring." She smiled.

"Want to tell me what we're doing in Mexico?"

"You can delete after you read," she said, handing him her cell phone.

"This is it," Melanie said, evaluating Estrada's building from the sidewalk. "I need a few things." She kept her head down, taking stock of the area without exposing her face.

"There's a shop a few miles down," he said, picking up the pace.

"How do you know they carry what I'm looking for?"

"Assuming. I was a distributor here in Mexico City." He laced their fingers. "God, I never did get used to the thick, brown air." Adam hailed a cab and twenty minutes later they stopped at a pawnshop. "Tell them you meant to get there at 1:48. They'll take care of you. I'll be waiting." He pressed a roll of cash into her hand.

"You want anything special?"

Adam simply shook his head.

She walked the short parking lot and pushed open the glass security door.

"Can I help you?" The offer came before the sound of the bell finished.

"I meant to get here at 1:48," she said, meeting the man's dark eyes.

"Wow, I haven't heard that one in years. Who are you with?"

"Nobody."

"Have you got ID?"

"No," she scoffed.

He took a second to size her up. "Okay, it's in the back." He nodded toward a rear door, unlocking the security gate. "What is it you need?"

She looked around at the arsenal of weapons on the walls. "Two handguns, ammo, Kevlar vest and how many cartridges do those Tasers hold?"

"Two."

"Got four?"

"Yeah, but you'll pay."

Having negotiated the man down to mildly overpriced armaments, she walked out with a small arsenal inside a satchel. A block away, Adam fell into step.

"I take it they had what you wanted?"

"They did. Thank you."

"I have my uses." His arm draped over her shoulders.

At the building they watched. It was a weekday and people were going in and out freely.

"I'm going inside."

"Then what?"

"Walk him out," she said simply. "I had time to study the blueprints of the building, I know the exits and I've got Kevlar vests and you'll be waiting with that rusted pesero." She pointed to the green and white shuttle van. "It's been there, leaking oil, since we arrived."

"You don't know if it runs."

"If it doesn't … you'll figure something else out."

She scanned the building.

"Marshall said the shooter was on the roof of an adjacent building," she spoke, still charting the possibilities. "If I have to, I'll pull the fire alarm. But I'm not going to stand here all day."

"You need a more precise plan."

"I've got you." She crossed the street to the public building and took the stairs to a lower level. The bunker was two floors underground. At the bottom of the stairs, she surprised a pair of smokers who were sharing a step.

"Pardon," she said, pushing open the stairwell door and taking a left. The door hadn't shut when the pair were on her heels.

Testing the Taser out on the man, he dropped, twitching. The woman's eyes widened and she tried to escape back into the stairwell. Melanie used a second cartridge and seconds later the woman was incapacitated beside her partner on the linoleum squares. Frisking the pair and relieving them of their weapons, she picked the lock to the door marked ELECTRICO. Behind a warning/danger sign was a keypad. Tapping in the code to the inner door, the bunker opened. She was faced with a scared man holding a 9 mm. Estrada.

"I'm here to get you out." She lifted her hands, dropping the Taser and splaying her fingers.

"About time you people got here! Your CIA promised to protect me and I've been in here for hours."

"Or you could just say thank you," Melanie answered, feeling like using that third Taser cartridge. "I have a car waiting to take you to a safe house."

"I must go to my office," he said, passing her and poking his head out the door.

"I can't agree to that," she said, leading him into the hallway. She stopped at the two on the ground to snatch their identification and press their fingers on the plastic and dropped them into the grocery bag from the pawnshop.

"Were they here to kill me?"

"They were waiting. Do you recognize them?" She lifted the man, turning him for Estrada to ID.

"No," he shook his head.

"Put this on," Melanie handed him the vest. Estrada did as instructed and then pushed the up button. "We aren't going to your office. The person who shot you is still out there. Just being here is high risk."

"I have to. Life and death. These two weren't expecting you. I predict if there are others they won't be expecting you either. You can come and protect me or I'll go myself. But I am going."

CHAPTER 49

Melanie said the shooter had been on the roof of a nearby building. Adam's eyes followed the rooflines – towers with bad angles and no way to reach the street. Mentally he placed himself, leaning over the edge … there wasn't a shot. Pacing the sidewalk on the opposite side of the street, he worked the hit over and over.

"Fuck," he growled, entering the building across the street from Estrada's with the phone to his ear. "Babe!" He took two stairs at a time. "Get out of the building. Get away from the windows!" He exited on the sixth floor.

"We're in his office."

She was speaking when the echo of gunfire resounded through the wall and from the speaker of his phone.

"Melanie!" he shouted, jamming the phone in his pocket, tracking the gunfire. Stopping to listen, he rammed his shoulder into a door that didn't budge.

Shooting out the lock, he entered to the back of the rifleman. Long strides. Adam knocked the shooter's feet out from under him. With two punches the rifle exchanged hands. The shooter was grounded and Adam leaned to stare out the window.

Across the street the glass had been shattered. There was no movement from the targeted office. “Are you hurt?” he shouted, when she answered his call. From across the street she lifted bloodied hands.

“Not mine. I’m not hurt, but my friend is.”

“I’m on my way,” he said, finishing the knot to bind the man’s arms and legs. He wiped his prints off the rifle and headed to the street.

CHAPTER 50

"I can't think with you screaming," she scolded Estrada. "Let me see where you're hit." She examined around the vest. "Shoulder. You're going to live."

"It hurts," he groaned.

"Lean on me," she offered.

"I have to get the folders." He grimaced, moving toward the corner behind his desk and groaned as he opened the safe.

Melanie reached for the papers. Estrada balked, with his good arm, he clutched them close to his chest. Letting him have his way she grabbed the sports coat off the rack, draped it over his stained shirt and supported him as they weaved through the building.

Adam was at the curb in a minivan with the sliding door open.

"Where'd you find this?" she asked, loading Estrada onto the middle seat and slamming the door behind her.

"Thought it worked best with an injured passenger." Dodging traffic, he drove like he knew where they were going.

In the back seat, she pressed Estrada's jacket into his shoulder.

"He's losing blood."

"I'm on it." Adam aggressively merged onto the freeway, heading toward the outlying fringe of the city. Estrada moaned over every bump and pothole.

"Adam?" Her hand and jacket were covered in blood.

"We're almost there."

"Where?"

"I know a doctor..."

"Can't..." she started.

"He can be bought. He doesn't talk and he'll fix him up." From the rear view mirror their eyes met. *Trust me.*

The hospital was a plastic tent in the very rear of a grocery store; behind the employee break room and hidden by boxes of excess inventory. The doctor was a pudgy man in his mid-fifties with a handlebar mustache and bloodshot veins running along the side of his bulbous nose.

Melanie watched the doctor help Estrada out of the Kevlar, his expression grim as he inspected the wound. It wasn't until his eyes widened in recognition that he waved his hands and shook his head.

"Oh, no! No," he said, retreating. "I don't want any part of this."

"We have money," Adam mentioned, reaching into his pocket and the man paused at the wad of cash. "A lot of money."

"Dentro," he ordered, scrambling to open the back door, knocking down a set of boxes to reveal a gurney. "Up here."

Estrada was coughing and wheezing, finally passing out as they laid him across the table. The doctor's plump hands were quick and his yell was demanding as he called for supplies. The bullet had gone into Estrada's shoulder sideways and was embedded.

"Okay, not so bad," he said, removing packets of blood from a refrigerator.

Turning her back on the scene, she answered her phone. Marshall. "I got him out but he was hit."

"Hit with what?"

"There was a sniper..."

"I told you to keep him alive!"

"He's alive. The sniper is tied up on the sixth floor in the building across the street."

"Hold on," Marshall said and was gone.

Melanie leaned against the wall. There was blood up to the doctor's elbows and Adam was helping to suture the wound.

"I'm back," Marshall said. "Okay, they've already retrieved the sniper but he hasn't been ID'd and so far he's not talking. Shit, Ward, this was supposed to be undercover. Discreet."

"Objective was to keep him alive. He's alive."

"Good thing. We can spin this against the current president. We'll make it work."

Her eyes hadn't left Adam, his head bent over Estrada, holding the bandage as the doctor taped.

"There were two others," she remembered, "in the bunker. I have their fingerprints." She took the laminated badges from her pocket. "I'm sending a photo, Mike can pull prints from the image." She kept talking as she grabbed a bottle of baby powder from a shelf and dusted the plastic to reveal the latent prints. "Also, Estrada's going to need more than the doctoring I have here."

"All right. Our information has been compromised."

"Check into who gave you that intel, because there's no way the original shot was from the roof."

"Forget the safe house. Where are you?"

Her eyes scanned the dirty walls and the jars of pickled pigs feet. "Doesn't matter. Get me instructions on where to proceed."

"Give me a minute."

Shoving her phone into her back pocket, she approached the medic. "How's he doing?"

"His breathing has steadied," the doctor said, wiping his hands on a towel. "Give him a couple of hours rest, another bag of O negative and he'll be ready for campaigning. You know he can't stay here."

"Where do you suggest we take him?" Melanie asked, gesturing toward the shirtless, unconscious man.

"Not my problem."

"I'll be right back." Adam lifted the loading door and vanished into the bright daylight.

Melanie kept her sights on Estrada as the doctor washed his hands.

"You cannot speak a word of this to anyone, including family." Melanie bore a hole in the bald spot at the back of his head.

"I've been around long enough to know nothing." He said, without emotion but she could read the peso signs in his eyes.

"I can't have you talking."

"What are you going to do, shoot me?"

"No." Her gun was pressed to his temple as she reached behind him and removed his wallet from his back pocket. "Tony, you have a beautiful family. Is this a current address?" She flicked through the pictures. "Three grandchildren? Do I need to make a call?"

"No. I won't say anything. I swear."

"That's better." Melanie nodded, believing him this time. Keeping his identification she tossed the billfold at his feet.

Adam drove the van into the grocery storage area. "Ready?" He looked between the doctor and Melanie.

"Get him out of here." The doctor flung his arms up and pointed toward the door.

They rolled Estrada to the side door and gently lifted him into the van.

Melanie eyed the man. "Adios Tony. Nos vemos."

"Something happen?" Adam asked, backing out.

"He wasn't a fan of my charm."

"Where am I headed?"

"Where are my folders?" Estrada coughed.

Melanie handed him the files. "That must be some important information you've got there. Something to risk your life over."

"It keeps me alive. That and my security detail." Estrada attempted to sit upright. "Take me to them."

"We can't." Melanie twisted. "You were shot under their watch, they gave misinformation. You can't trust..."

"I can," he said, trying to sit. "My man got me to the bunker and then I sent him to protect my family."

Melanie looked at Adam, then picked up her phone. "He wants to connect with his people."

"Under no circumstances..." Marshall started.

"Then give me an alternative that doesn't involve babysitting."

"I'm working on it."

"I don't care what he says," Estrada barked, "take me where I want to go."

"We work for the same people," she said. "We are going to wait and see what they want."

"I don't work for anyone," he spat.

"If that were true, I wouldn't be here," she said, answering her cell. "Yeah?" Marshall gave her an address. "Too bad," she told

Estrada, "other plans." Melanie translated the directions to Adam, who made a wide U-turn.

"I am running for president, you cannot take me against my will."

Ignoring his complaints they traveled the periphery of the metropolis.

"Adam," Melanie cautioned as two black SUV's barreled toward them.

"I see," he said, his eyes on the road. "You buckled?"

Melanie leaned to look over her shoulder, worried about Estrada, but he was already laying face down on the floor of the van ready for impact. *That's odd*, was all she was able to think before...

"Hold on," Adam advised and Melanie braced as the van popped over the curb, barely missing a mailbox.

Tires squealing, he swerved to break free from the attack but the old vehicle was no match. Two SUV's charged, ramming the front driver's side and the back passenger's side.

The crash threw her against the window and back against the seat. Seconds after, she regained her bearings and her heart stopped. *Adam!* The front of the van was crushed and he was bleeding from where his head had struck the wheel, he was leaning forward, unconscious.

Jesus, please. She prayed as the men from the SUVs marched toward them. Melanie leaped to the back seat, set Estrada's neck in the crook of her elbow, the muzzle of her gun pressed to his temple. The men had approached, guns drawn and were reaching for Adam through the broken window.

"Get your hands off him." Her voice came out firm and steady. She was in pain but her finger was ready to pull the trigger. "Do. Not. Test. Me. I will do it." She pressed the muzzle harder, enough to make Estrada cry out. Leaning in close to Estrada. "Tell them to back off."

She ordered, ready, imagining the order of their death. Estrada would be first.

Adam was waking as Estrada gave the command and the men raised their hands.

"Drop your weapons." She called, one eye on Adam.

Blood streamed from his right eyebrow and he blinked slowly, as if it were normal to come out of unconsciousness with two guns in his face.

"Can you drive?" she asked.

"Yeah." He used his sleeve to wipe the wetness from his eye. He turned the key, twice, and the van started.

"Behave." She tightened her elbow, feeling the cartilage in Estrada's throat bob. "I have no problem eliminating all of your problems."

Adam pulled out, the front tire scraping on the bend fender, he weaved between the vehicles and floored the gas pedal. Melanie lifted Estrada's phone from his pocket and hit redial.

"I don't give a shit who you are," she said, removing Estrada's phone from his pocket and hitting redial, "I'll kill you." On the other end of the line was silence. "Try another stunt and your man is dead. Comprende, Asshole?" She removed the battery and Adam pulled to the side.

"I can't."

"I wouldn't suggest you try anything," she told the candidate. "Right now I want you to give me a reason to shoot."

Melanie grabbed his papers and took the wheel.

"You arranged that?" Adam asked and jabbed a quick punch to Estrada's wound. "Why would you do that?"

Using her phone, she located the nearest copy center.

Leaving them in the van, she copied the documents onto a flash drive, uploaded the folders to Mike. Melanie drove an hour out of town, left Estrada standing in the desert and headed to the airport.

"You can't leave him there," Adam said.

"I just did."

Passing customs, she switched on her phone and sent Marshall an alert with Estrada's GPS coordinates.

CHAPTER 51

"Where is Krupin?" Hugh Parker asked, seated at the table with the man in a crisp uniform. "I expected him."

"We're taking this meeting out of respect for your grandfather," the soldier said. "At great risk, I might add."

"More like a great reward." Parker smiled. "I'm not here as a beggar. I have bartering chips." He met the man's gaze. Pressing his will through the air space and into the blue eyes of the soldier.

"What is it that you want?"

"I want peace." Parker laughed. "Let me clarify … I want to be accredited for imparting peace." What he assumed was joy filled his belly. "Get me these five individuals and I will give you what you want." He handed the man the 5X7 black-and-white glossies.

The soldier shifted through the photos, disinterested. "And what is it that you think we want?" He set the pictures aside.

"Control over American oil production."

"And you can promise this?" he snorted, skepticism in his voice but longing in his eyes.

"I can."

"Why should I believe you? You're an old man, wanted by your government with no allies and no resources. What power you once had has been stripped." He settled back in his seat. "There is no reason to believe you can supply what you suggest."

"You have a woman, Anna Pajari, in line to take over a major company but … Yes, I know about that. She's being investigated. I can stop that and Bridget Meeks can continue her wedding plans. You'll see that I still have plenty of influence. You can take that to the bank." The smirk was for the earlier insult. "And you can tell Krupin that, too."

"These men…" the soldier tapped on the photos.

"They're not Russian. They're tools that can be replaced."

"If we hand them over we lose trust with…"

"Trust?" Parker barked out his laugh. "You know what they say about trust among thieves. Get me the locations of the men on that list and your interest in American oil will be preserved. You can *trust* me on that." He laughed and his blood rushed in triumph.

Fuck you, he yelled silently. *Fuck all of you because I'm back!*

CHAPTER 52

Three days separated her from her border crossing and Melanie was beginning a routine. Hit the gym by six, spend the next ten hours in her office, home by eight. Marshall had come through with assignments and all of her agents were in the field.

Ben was splitting his time between the Agency and the NSA. Jane had been placed on bed rest and Jack, to her surprise, was doting. Her mom and Trish were on the wedding warpath, collecting information and emailing her with flower, cake and catering suggestions. She'd planned to go home over the weekend, kill the decisions in two days and get back to D.C.

"Oh, I don't know, Mr. Roosevelt." She heard the timid reverberations of Rosie's voice through the office door.

"It's okay," Melanie said, remembering to be patient. "Come in."

"I'm so sorry, Ms. Ward," Rosie stammered. "I know you said you were busy…"

"Wow, what did you do to her?" Marshall asked, entering her office and closing the door.

"I have no idea. Hey, well done on the assignments," she said, sitting in a chair in front of her desk and angling it to face the other.

"The Port Authority is a big get."

"I was thinking of the CIA post. We're spying on our own people?" She shook her head in disapproval even as much as she disliked Hill.

"Yeah," he cringed. "That one has trouble written all over it."

"How's that?"

His face turned somber. "Hill is going to explode when he finds out. We got stuck with a hot potato. I tried to get out of it."

"I put our most harmless-seeming agent on that task." She thought of Logan and her bouncy, blonde ponytail. "When you get these assignments is there a hoard of Marshalls scampering for the choice missions? Greedy little hands grabbing into the mission pot." She could visualize it.

"More clandestine than that but..." He tipped his head left, then right. "Not too far off."

Settling back she asked, "So, what are you here for this time? Scold me about Mexico, threaten me for not responding, for leaving Estrada in the desert ... Bring it on, Marshall Roosevelt, I can take it."

"Nope. I mean, yeah, officially I'm supposed to reprimand you but unofficially within our organization we felt Estrada was the wrong choice from the beginning. We're going to start over with another candidate and he'll be just as dirty as the last but that's politics. I came by to run through completed assignments."

"What's happening with Meeks?"

"No idea. That has been handed up the chain."

Marshall turned the conversation back to assignments and agents. At eight she was done and shrugging into her jacket.

"See you in the morning," she said, fixing her collar as she passed Rosie.

"Yes, Ma'am."

"It's Melanie or Ms. Ward or Hey You, but not Ma'am, okay?" She was in the hall when she reconsidered. "Rosie, you don't have to be afraid of me. I don't know what you've heard, but I'm not dangerous, you can relax. Just get your job done and we'll get along fine."

Rosie's lips pursed, her head bobbed and she looked terrified. "Good night."

Melanie took a spin around the common area. Her agents were active and Bob was playing a video game.

"Hard at work?"

"Hey, Boss. Slow night."

"Call me if that changes." She dialed Adam from the elevator. "I'm sorry I'm running late..." She pushed open the outer door and stopped. "You're here," she said into her phone, staring across the street at Adam leaning against the Audi's driver's door.

She jogged across the deserted black lanes. Having the door held for her was nice but the kiss was better. "What's this?"

"An energy bar to hold you until dinner."

"How long do I have to wait for dinner?" she asked, opening the container. "Did you *make* these? I had no idea that was even possible."

"Just eat."

"Where are we going?" She sniffed the apricot, coconut, chocolate, pistachios.

"I'm sticking around, we're starting a life and I can't live in a skeletal home. We're going shopping."

"You really aren't leaving?"

"Has Mike found anything more?"

"No. It's strange but he's on it."

"Then there isn't any reason for me..." he exhaled. "My sources have lost him, too."

They rode in silent thought.

"These energy bars are really good." Melanie was licking her fingertips as he parked. "What are we looking for?" she asked, stepping into the showroom with mood lighting and the scent of citrus in the air.

"We have a living room, dining room, kitchen nook, three bedrooms and a basement."

"You want to get it all done tonight?"

"Why not?"

Melanie looked around the twenty-thousand-square-foot showroom and needed another energy bar. Adam's hand was becoming a permanent fixture at the end of hers.

"Well, I like this," she said, having escaped the sticky salesman. The couch was billowy, with wide cushions and the color of warm vanilla. The more she looked, the more she liked it all. The chairs were tinted with cauliflower blue vines and the square table between them combined both function and appeal. "Do you?"

"I do," he said, his eyes measuring.

It was only the beginning. Two hours later they were at the car with a three-foot long receipt and a dent in his wallet.

"I wish you owned one of those old trucks," she said, buckling in. "You know, the ones with the bench seats so I could rest my head in you lap and sleep."

"I never wanted one of those more than I do right now."

"I didn't mean it like that. You have a dirty mind."

"I have a man's mind," he clarified. "You can't say things like putting your head in my lap and not expect a reaction." He reached for her hand, playing with her fingers. "How was work?"

"Work? Um, it was good." The day flashed. "Really good." He kissed the back of her hand and she felt the effects of days with little sleep. "Who would have guessed that shopping was so exhausting."

"Close your eyes, we're almost home." The radio played softly and the rhythm of the orange light from the streetlamps was hypnotic.

Her head felt like dead weight that her neck was obligated to hold.

"I'm too tired for food," she said, passing through the kitchen and heading upstairs. She collapsed on the bed, grabbing the covers from his side of the bed and rolling into them.

Her body bounced as his weight displaced the mattress and he pulled the fabric to expose her face and his chilled finger brushed her hair from her eyes.

"You just bought a house full of furniture."

"We did." His lips were cool on her forehead. "Our home is going to be beautiful."

"Well, I'm glad it's over."

"Before you fall asleep, tomorrow would you like to hit the shooting range?"

"I practiced while you were gone," she said happily.

"I'll pick you up at noon." She felt the kiss on her forehead. "I'm going to be gone by the time you wake up."

"Okay," she said, falling asleep.

The line at the lobby coffee shop was only five deep when she stopped on her way to the eighth floor. She picked up an extra cup for Rosie.

The girl hadn't yet arrived at work when Melanie left the cup on the desk. She greeted Judith and the two assistants she'd assigned Bob and Mike to train. They were in need of more technical support and she wasn't allotted any additional personnel.

An agent had been arrested in St. Louis, Missouri for trespassing and suspicion of aiding in a terrorist act. Her morning was lost untangling the mess.

"Babe, it's noon."

"Oh, I'll be right down."

Exiting the elevator, she migrated with the general population and out the big glass doors, stopping cold when she saw him. He stood at the chrome grill front of a forty-year-old classic, rusted truck with big windows and a blue stripe along the side. She raced across the street to the passenger door that creaked its age as he chivalrously held it open for her.

"Borrowed it from a friend." He answered her expression as she climbed up onto the blue leather seat and he took his place behind the jumbo steering wheel. "The whole bench seat is for you … but you'll only need this spot, right here." He grinned, giving the cushion beside him a firm whack.

"I see," she added, a touch of sultry in her voice and slid over. The engine roared to life, too loud for the clean D.C. streets.

"Hard day?"

"I'm sorry, I can't hear you." She pointed to the hood.

"Are you a snob, Melanie Ward?"

She pressed her left side to his right as her legs straddled the gearshift. “I have to say … I am liking this seat.” Her head rested on his shoulder, his arm over her shoulders.

“I’ll need my arm back to shift,” he said, tugging her another inch closer.

“Did you ever see Urban Cowboy?”

“No. Should I?”

“Just a truck thing.” She settled in.

They rode in comfortable silence to the shooting range, where he pulled out two rifles from behind the seat. Unfolding a blanket for a tailgate lunch, then used the same wool layer to cover the ground where they laid to take aim at the targets.

“I like this,” he said, sitting up beside her as she searched through the scope, his hand running from her shoulder blades, down the small of her back and over her jeans.

“You’re messing with my crosshairs,” she smiled, mentally placing Hugh Parker’s face in the center of each bullseye.

“What are you aiming at?” He resumed his position at his scope. She started at the tip of a mountain in the horizon and brought him all the way back to a tree branch. “Remember what I told you,” he whispered above her right ear.

She missed.

“Damn it.” She twisted to give him a glare. “I would like to blame you and your sexiness but…”

“Focus.” He whispered. “There will always be a distraction. Don’t let it get to you.”

Melanie exhaled and the tingles raced up her spine. Clearing her throat and her mind she asked. “How would you align that shot?”

Softly, he explained his process as he placed his deep, green eye to the lens and pulled the trigger. The thin finger of a twig bent and broke off. "That's how it's done."

"Show off." She grinned and checked her phone.

"Time?"

"Yeah." She didn't want to leave, she wanted to snap her own twig from the tree – but duty called.

"I'll clean these," he said, loading everything into the truck. "You've improved. You could have a future as a sniper."

"Or an assassin?" she asked, resuming her spot in the center seat of the cab and angling her legs away from the stick shift.

"Not funny." His tone was all seriousness.

Marshall was in her office.

"How are you?" he asked, his gaze traveling over her face.

"Hmm, why doesn't this feel like a friendly drop-in?" Melanie asked.

"Your Spidey senses are on fire. I have a Priority One assignment." He waggled his phone at her condescendingly. "I forwarded it to you."

"What's the crisis?"

"The CEO of an online game company, Joe McCann, was kidnapped."

"We've been over this … Call the police."

"It's bigger than that. This game is huge…" His arms were open wide. "It's a spy, espionage, space wars game that has ties in reality."

"Meaning?"

His mouth was grim and his eyes were, conspiratorially, deadlocked on hers. "All that happens in that game isn't just fantasy."

"Like a war in the game is a war in real life?" she asked, doubtingly.

"Sometimes. And over the past month the threatening emails and tweets have escalated to include details. Last week a commercial flight McCann was on had to make an emergency landing. Someone had tweeted threats to his life and mentioned the flight in a hashtag – as the flight was in air."

"Are we dealing with real players or gamers? And how much of this game is real?" she asked his blank stare. "Never mind. I'll talk with Mike."

"Boss," Bob called, grinning with a mouthful of chips.

"Do either of you know of a game called Terra Universe?" Their exchange held for a beat before the irritating laughter erupted.

"Sorry, but what rock have you been living under?" With barely a flick of her lashes, Bob was clearing his throat. "Okay. TU is like the oldest, most awesome online game. Ever. Everybody is either playing or has tried."

"Pretend like my rock has been in the real world, actually accomplishing things. Give me the quick *TU* facts," she said, mocking the use of initials.

Mike began. "It was created in the seventies by a pair of high school students on their modified PC. Remember how Dungeons And Dragons was like gospel for the nerds? That was the same with TU and the industrious, first generation of computer geeks."

"You guys play?"

"I do," Bob admitted.

"Not me," Mike said. "I did for awhile, but it can be complicated and slow. Dull 95 percent of the time."

"Super complicated," Bob concurred. "You have to play for like a year before it starts making sense and you can actually achieve goals. Oh, and it's crazy vicious. When you're new and you screw up there is hell to pay. Gamers will target novice players and destroy accomplishments. Once, when I was..."

"So," Melanie preempted the story, "in people terms, could you explain the premise?"

"It's a world where everyone is hiding something. There's an economy, cities and justice system. Set up like a real world and you never know who you can trust. There's backstabbing and violence. It can be amazing." Bob's smile dropped. "Sometimes nothing happens, seriously *nothing happens*. You have to be dedicated ... then it pays off."

"Who is McCann?"

"He's the rich, lawyer dude who bought the whole thing five years ago." Bob said, "He's not a fan favorite. Uber rich D.C. lobbyist and isn't respected. I mean, McCann hasn't screwed things up but he hasn't proved he's one of us, either."

"Did you know Terra Universe isn't just a game?" She held her phone so they could read part of the assignment.

"It's real?" Bob tipped back, his jaw dropping as his eyes danced along the type. "No way!" He gasped, smacking himself on the forehead.

"There were rumors that TU was based on actual events," Mike said, turning to his computer. "Which I ignored because ... conspiracy theorists. But Mel, this is global. If TU is real then..." 'Jesus' was the word he mouthed. "Pardon my French."

"My mind has just been blown!" Bob grabbed both sides of his face. "I've been working here for a year, I thought I knew everything. Jeez!" He looked to Mike for comfort. "What does this mean? Because everything I've ever known is instantly questionable."

"We should use Bob's avatar," Mike suggested.

"Tell me about the rumors," She leaned toward the monitor. "What am I looking at?"

"TU is played worldwide," Bob said, signing in. "The game is set up like a world – not Earth, but Eden."

"They say that some of the players are actually countries trying out military strategies. Testing war applications to see reactions and possible responses, exchanging money, there's tunnels that dip into the dark web and it is awesome." Bob sang, then regained control. "That's the word on the street. I always thought it was a hoax to get more users."

"I've also heard that the game is used as a drop source – that what looks like regular TU interaction is really double-agents passing secrets. Who knows? But it does make for a more tantalizing experience."

"McCann's been kidnapped."

"No shit!"

"No shit. Could you go through his emails and see if anything unusually suspicious jumps out at you?"

"Mike can do that, " Bob said, headset in place, "I'm going into the game. See what's being said there."

"He loves TU." Mike looked from Bob to Melanie. "I'll look into the threats, but you don't know what you're asking. These are elite gamers. Hackers. I guarantee you they didn't leave clues."

"Elite geeks?" she asked.

"I'll be careful," Mike offered. "You have no idea of the following this game has … It's insanity. They worship this world and they're incredibly talented."

"Great," she scoffed. "Nothing like freaking me out."

"Now you know how I've felt for years."

Melanie laughed. "Hey, how are the two assistants doing as techies?"

"Better than expected. They're working in the other room."

"Any news on Hugh?"

"Still nothing. I thought I found a thread in Istanbul but it unraveled." He shrugged. "I haven't given up."

"Keep on him. Thanks." Melanie retreated to her office to think about McCann's disappearance and the boys' energy over the online game. Her research supplied too many questions and too many acronyms. Returning to the control room, the electricity was palatable.

"You should see the chatter about McCann. His kidnapping has gone viral, everybody is speculating and a few have even taken credit. And it isn't even official yet. But" – Bob was jittery – "I found him. See that building? He's on the third floor."

Melanie shifted her gaze to the world behind him. "You found his avatar? Does that correlate to reality? At all?"

"You mean like, is this building really on 321 Copper Street? No, Boss. It isn't."

"Then, *Bob*, you haven't found him. Oh, shit," she blurted at the sight of a flashing WARNING sign.

"What the hell?" Bob and Mike's voices harmonized.

The blinking stopped and a ransom note took its place. It wasn't only the threat of McCann's death, but also the exposure of TU secrets. Bidding started at ten million U.S. dollars.

"There's a trivia challenge," Bob said, looking up at Melanie. "To weed out the players from the dabblers." He read the first question and retreated into himself.

"He's contemplating," Mike explained. "I lose him when he's researching. Kind of nice, actually."

"What are your thoughts on McCann?"

"Bob's better at this than I am. He'll come through."

Melanie could do nothing but wait.

"Got it! Second question." Bob was making progress, completing a succession of tests. "They're willing to accept the codes for the TU's military Trinity Project as payment. Why would they want that?"

"We need to stop that auction and find McCann." She turned, with the phone to her ear to find Marshall standing in the doorway.

"I need you to give me answers," he said.

"I don't have any."

"Mel." It was Mike. "I triangulated the ransom note to Aspen."

"How accurate is that? Could they have used a..." She shook her head, searching for the word.

"Ninety-eight percent. I've checked all the angles, satellite feeds. There doesn't seem to be malware. I found the back door. We don't have much time, our technology is only a fraction faster than most. But the problem is..." he faced her, confused. "It looks like McCann is in his own home."

"Bob, get your gear together," she said, moving swiftly to her office. "Rosie, I need a box of ammo."

"What size?"

Melanie glared at Marshall. "A Walther PPK." Sighed. "38-caliber. And we need the jet prepped."

"Jack," she hollered. "He's coming, too." She picked up her bag with the change of clothes and dialed Marcos on her way to the elevator. "Marshall," she called as she pushed the down arrow, "call the pilot. Ready, Jack? Bob?"

"Ms. Ward, the bullets!" Rosie ran, jostling the box in hand.

"Thanks."

Marcos rounded the corner and they jumped in before he had a chance to put the car in park. Once in the backseat, she pressed Adam's picture on her contact list.

"I'm leaving town," she said, quickly, like ripping off a Band-Aid.

"Sweetheart." The word grumbled in his deep tone.

"I'll keep my phone on me. I'll be careful."

"Please do." The call ended, taking the wind out of her sails. "Okay." She swallowed down the lump and looked to Bob. "Can you get the schematics for McCann's house?"

"Give me a minute." He awakened his laptop.

"Jack, you okay to do this?"

"The distraction is good. Jane is sick of me, anyway." He nodded, "is it possible for him to be kidnapped inside his own home? Where is he, locked in the wine cellar?"

"Dungeon," Bob corrected, his eyes on his computer. "I'm pulling up the blueprints, and not just any blueprints. These are from the original builder."

The flight was spent strategizing. McCann's house was a stone edifice built in the late nineteenth century by a shopkeeper turned silver miner, Jacob Howard. He made millions mining the Aspen Mountain and had his manor built from rocks that were blasted out to form tunnels. Howard fancied himself an amateur magician and as he grew richer his eccentric side grew, too. The house was full of deception – fake walls, hidden rooms and staircases, peep holes and rooms built on false bottoms, including a dungeon that was linked to the mining shafts.

Melanie traced the ins and outs of the building. She shook her head. "If we take the safer, longer route we could get lost in the maze and then there's that pool … " It had been built as an underground swimming pool, heated by the mine and connected to the house by a labyrinth. They'd found no map and for the maze … "I don't want to get stuck underground in a hundred-and-fifty-year-old tunnel."

"You know it's going to be booby-trapped," Bob said. "I'd put surveillance all over that mother if it were me."

"We have to use the trap door at the side of the house."

"They'll hear us," Jack added.

"Then we'll have to device a distraction."

They brainstormed as the jet landed on a small strip outside of Aspen and from there it was a ten-minute drive to Howard's Fortress. The bright moonlight glistened over the snow but the branches were no longer burdened with the weight. The woods were expecting spring.

"I was thinking," Bob choked from the back seat, "that I should be the distraction."

"No." Melanie dispelled the idea.

"Give it a chance," Jack inserted. "Go ahead, Special K, give us your best sell."

"I go right up to the door, knock, and pretend I'm there to help."

"Then they shoot a bullet in your head. Jack, why are you encouraging him?"

"Because I don't think it's a bad idea. It needs adjustment, but there's potential. I'll go in with him and you take the postern and rescue McCann."

"No way," Bob interrupted. "You're not the type of person that usually plays TU."

"Is McCann?"

"Well, no, but..."

"I'm just like him and you don't go in without me. Okay?"

They had decided and Melanie relented.

"You protect him." Melanie commanded as Jack parked under the cover of the trees. "And you" – she turned to Bob – "No heroics. Understood?"

"No worries," he snickered. "I'm not *that* sort of person."

Jack looked over his shoulder, code for Bob to shut up. "Mel, get out. Giggles and I are going in through the gate."

"I'll ping to your phone when I've got him," she said, disappearing into the shadows.

The rock wall made for a convenient climb, providing finger and toe holds as she scaled the nine-foot barricade. To her left, metallic voices through a box told her that Jack and Bob were at the security gate.

She landed in the soft snow and kept a quick pace as she ran silently along the wall closest to the trapdoor. The snow crunching beneath her boots seemed to echo through the compound. Her boot hit an obstruction and she dropped to her knees. She forced the snow away to reveal basement storm doors. They were locked.

"I need help getting inside."

"Of course you do," Mike answered. "I'm going to use the Wi-Fi signal to connect to the security and...."

"Shh."

"Sorry."

The quiet night carried sound, her back pressed into the uneven rocks of the house and her senses were on full alert. Even the light clicking of Mike disengaging the lock boomed like an earthquake.

"Thanks," she mouthed and pocketed her phone.

Slipping inside, gun in hand, she managed the steep, slim steps and found herself at the end of a narrow path. Somewhere deep within the folds of the stone manor, she heard the sounds of … a television. Stepping gingerly, careful not to disturb the pebbles on the stone flooring she followed the sound. Around a corner flickering lights played on the walls. Slowly, pausing after each step to listen.

The basement was an actual dungeon – dark, drab, damp and filled with torture devices that appeared to be well used.

Her heart sped up as her eyes scanned the equipment. An unconscious McCann was strapped to a rack, while the guard was seated on top of … Melanie tilted her head to figure out what type of torture could be inflicted from an antique construction saw horse. He was sitting on top of it, watching a late-night infomercial; one hand held a slice of pizza, the other was down his pants.

A shot would be easy, but the gunfire would be deafening and she didn't want him dead. Her attention returned to McCann and how was she going to get him off the table and up the vertical stairs. She crouched down and crawled from behind one stained, gruesome gadget of torture to another. Holding her breath, she fought off the stench of urine as she passed McCann.

The guard was finishing up, eyes rolling to the back of his head and releasing an exaggerated moan when she cold-cocked him and loaded him into the stocks. Lifting him so his neck and wrists fit into the cutouts, she locked the top plank. Melanie scanned the room, grabbing a rope from smaller, handheld instruments tacked to the wall and used it to gag the kidnapper.

McCann was splayed spread eagle, his wrists and ankles were rubbed raw. Using a serrated knife she sawed through the thick cords binding him to the turnstiles.

McCann was unresponsive, dead weight; she was going to need help. Setting off through the heavy door she climbed the curved staircase to the swivel panel at the top landing and stepped out into a wood-lined den. Leaving the secret passage open an inch, she sent a text to Mike.

A moment later she received an infrared photo/diagram of the house. There was a cluster of six on the ground floor. Two were seated, the other four poised in a semi-circle around them. Taking a moment to locate her position on the map, she found her way through the house. Remaining out of sight, she eavesdropped on Jack making a convincing argument for how he and Bob came to be a part of history.

She knew Jack, how he worked and his tone told her he was in control, stalling to give her time. Sending a ping to his phone, he changed tactics.

"I'm getting the impression you aren't interested in our abilities. So we're going to be taking off," he said, standing.

Melanie paid close attention to the kidnapper's response – which was the cocking of the hammer. She was in the living room when Jack took a swing at one and dodged the fists of another. Entering the melee, she lunged at the man aiming his gun at Bob.

Two minutes later, she and Jack were hunched over, gasping and the four men were on the floor. Bob was still in his seat, glistening under a layer of sweat.

"Good thing gamers are weak," Jack leaned in for a high-five.

"You know this doesn't solve anything," Bob said. "The ransom clock is still ticking."

"McCann is safe and the kidnappers are down," Melanie countered.

"But if we don't stop the clock, TU will collapse – and that leaves its secrets open to be hacked by anyone with skill."

"That's what you're here for, Special K," Jack said. "Go. Find a computer and be the hero. God knows you're useless in a fight."

"You heard him. Go." Melanie waved him on and Bob jumped to his feet. "Now to find out who these idiots are."

Together they hog-tied the kidnappers and sent their images to Mike. Melanie called Marshall while she guided Jack downstairs.

"He's out cold. We've got four disabled on the main floor and one in the dungeon."

"I'll make the calls."

"What the hell is all of this?" Jack asked, wandering around the chamber, waiting for her to end her conversation with Marshall. "What kind of sick bastard has a collection like this? Do you think he uses these things or are they here for show?"

"No idea. But they look genuine, like they were used at some point." She said, eyeing the spikes, the clamps and the two-sided fork.

"Maybe we should retie him and leave him here," Jack suggested. "What the fuck is wrong with people?"

"Get me out of here!" the kidnapper grumbled.

"Is this a pillory or the stocks?" Jack asked, stepping up to the man and bending to stare into his eyes. "You want to talk?" he asked. "I'll take care of him if you want to check on Special K."

"Mike just texted. Two of the men are ex-employees of K-Data Corp."

Every company on the Internet had a security measure and most used K-Data, the largest anti-cyber terrorist company in the world. It covered more than 300 million computers and phones worldwide. It was the secret eyes behind every click of the keyboard, collecting data under the guise of protection.

"My take," Jack said, "is the three, including this idiot, were kids playing a game that went too far. They didn't know what they were getting into … thought it was a college prank. It was the others who meant business. Am I right?" he asked, shaking the wooden stand that held the kidnapper.

"That doesn't exonerate them from their involvement."

"Just saying, Mel."

"Not up to me, anyway," she said, leaving him in the basement of doom. Tracking through the house, she found Bob in a plush, high-tech computer center. "What is this?" she asked, checking out the round room of theater, surround sound and virtual screens.

"Disneyland," he murmured. "This is the most amazing place I've ever been in!"

"Great, you can ask McCann for a job when we're done here."

"Boss? When we're done here, McCann should be locked away in federal prison. He knew the secrets. He's been hoarding the information, he's the one auctioning it off to the highest bidder."

"Are you sure?"

"Duh."

"Shit," she said, dialing Jack. "Tell me McCann is still on the rack."

"He's waking up but, yeah, he's stretched out."

"Handcuff him."

"Isn't he our victim?"

"Victim and criminal."

"You got it."

"Now what?" she asked Bob.

"I'm working on it," he said, his eyes darting from screen to screen. "This is incredible."

She turned away from Bob to answer a call.

"The cleanup team is on their way," Marshall said in her ear. "You have five minutes to evacuate."

"Bob, you've got four minutes."

"No way, Boss."

"No way, Marshall," she repeated. "We need more time."

"I can't call them off and you can't be there when they arrive. Besides, I was under the impression that McCann had been wounded."

"Later." She ended the call and pulled open the cabinet door; it was lined with devices Melanie had seen behind Mike's desk. "Bob, take what you need. Can you delete the security cameras in flight?"

"I can if he uses an off-site server but..." he rose to unplug a box from within the cabinet. "If he's using iCloud storage then I'll need Internet access."

"It was a rhetorical question."

"Can you grab the black book? It contains passwords."

"Want the computer, too?"

"Yeah." They walked out with armfuls of electronics. "This doesn't feel morally right," Bob said.

Jack was waiting at the front door with the car running.

"We'll return it when we're done. Don't ask," she told Jack and picked up the phone to let the pilot know they'd be ready in ten minutes.

CHAPTER 53

"You don't have to pick me up every day," she said, tiptoeing to accept his kiss and liking the weight of his hands on her hips.

"I want to." His breath rustled the hair at her neck. "I get to see you, kiss you and take you home. This is my best dream."

"Okay, then," she said, feeling him reach around her to open the Audi door. "I miss the truck."

He laughed. "Had to return it. Your trip went well?"

"It did. And I think Jack and I are friends again." The flight home had been comfortable. They'd talked, and by the time they landed it was like old times.

"I didn't know you weren't."

"You were courting a ruthless senator at the time. God, Adam, I feel so good."

Sleep was elusive. She looked at the clock. *It's midnight and I'm starving with, an inappropriate case of jet lag,* she thought. Her stomach grumbling as she pulled on her clothes and made her way to the kitchen.

Unlike her cupboards, Adam's were stocked. She opened each utensil, spice and spatula drawer. All filled. Her next objective was the refrigerator – the light shown brightly on shelves that reminded her of a grocery store.

Choosing the boysenberry jelly, crunchy peanut butter and whole grain bread, she fashioned a sandwich, then poured herself a glass of milk. Roaming while she ate, getting acquainted with the layout of the house wasn't satisfying and finally she returned to her side of the bed.

Her index finger pressed into his shoulder. "Are you sleeping?" She whispered and pressed again when he didn't rouse.

Okay, if you can't hear me maybe you can feel me. She ran her fingers along his jaw. He stirred. She touched his neck, his shoulders, her fingertips fluttered over his tattoo and down to his pajama pants.

"Why do you smell like peanut butter?"

"I'm sorry, I'll brush my teeth," she said, trying to sit up.

"I like peanut butter." He kissed her. "A lot."

Marshall closed the door behind him. "We're secure here, right?"

"I hope so," she laughed, but he was nervous and looked as if he were carrying the weight of the world on his thin shoulders. "Have a seat and tell me what's happened."

"This is top classification," he started.

"What's the mission, Marshall?" Melanie asked, needing him to get to the point. "You're starting to make *me* nervous."

"We got a tip." He was speaking slow, cautiously. "We received the location of five leaders of two different terrorist groups operating in the Middle East. Specifically Lebanon. The SEALs are going in tonight."

Melanie waited for the part that involved her. "What's our objective?"

"No. Melanie." Her forehead pinched as she listened. "It wasn't just a tip, but detailed information … here's the kicker and you have to swear to stay calm."

"I can't do that," she said, her pulse already starting to race. "It'll be easier for you if you tell me what is going on," she said, under a relaxed pretense and spoken through gritted teeth.

"The information was supplied by Senator Parker."

Unflinching, she blinked while every facial muscle was engaged.

"He called the Secretary of Defense this afternoon…"

"Hugh?" she asked, "Hugh is giving us detailed information on five terrorists – in exchange for what?"

"It's my understanding that he's been on a peacekeeping mission…"

"Peacekeeping? Are you shitting me? He's a goddamned felon…"

"Not exactly a felon, he was never convicted."

"Because he escaped from his cell!" She was hot and the air felt too thick to breathe. "Okay…" She swallowed hard. "Peacekeeping, authorized by who?"

"I don't know, but the information was good enough to get the SEALs involved."

"Shit," she sighed. "This is so fucked. Where did he get the information, did he say? Jesus, Marshall."

"I don't have the answers, Melanie. But this is big … these five are on the most wanted list and to take them down…" He whistled. "Not something the administration can ignore."

"He's going to get immunity, isn't he?"

"Probably," Marshall admitted. "Yeah. He's coming back as a hero. But think of it this way…" His voice caught as he lifted his gaze to hers. "We're getting a safer world."

"Seriously!?" She felt trapped. "Where's Ben?"

"NSA."

She picked up her phone and dialed Judith. "I need Ben."

"Certainly, Ms. Ward."

Thank God. Melanie breathed.

"Ward?" Ben's voice encircled her like a blanket. "I'm going out on a ledge here … You heard the news." She nodded and somehow he heard. "My old office is still mine. Meet me there for a drink."

"Five minutes." She looked at Marshall, grabbing her jacket on her way out the door.

"Where are you going?"

"Out."

She jogged. The air had warmed, the snow had melted and all that was left were tiny green buds of life clutching onto barren branches. The familiar activity of entering Agency Headquarters had a comforting effect.

"Hi," she greeted Judith. "What are you doing here?"

"I'm wherever he needs me." She smiled and pointed. "He's waiting for you."

"Thanks." Melanie knocked on the doorframe. "Smells moldy in here."

"Hello to you too, Agent." He grinned, pouring two drinks and handing her one.

"Tell me what's going on," she said, taking her scotch … sniffing. "I don't want apple juice. I'm tired of this game, Ben."

He smiled. "Sit." They took either end of the sofa. "Hugh has surfaced." She nodded. "He's" – Ben's eyes searched the ceiling with light admiration – "he's an ingenious SOB. Arranging a trade; A viable trade. Location on five top terrorist commanders, this is a major blow to their network and a major milestone for the U.S."

"Just like that."

"Think about it. We need this victory…"

"So it's a done deal? I get it." She choked, "I don't mean to be selfish here but he cheats and walks away a free man. Everything I did … It just backfired. I'm more vulnerable now than I ever was, and I was captured and tortured." She stared into her cider. "He's going to kill me. Not right away but eventually."

"I won't let that happen." his fingers curled around her forearm. "I promise."

Her eyes reached his pale ones. "You can't promise that. He's going to be too powerful. The public will fall in love and he'll be invincible. I have to go." Melanie stood. "When is all of this going down? Exactly."

He checked his watch. "There's three teams going in simultaneously to three different locations. Three o'clock, Eastern Time. Two hours from now."

She nodded, the ache pulling at her heart.

"I'm going to be watching on a secure line if you'd like to join me," Ben offered. "Bring Adam, too, if you'd like. It'll just be the three of us. It's going to be okay."

"This isn't right," she said before agreeing to arrive before the scheduled time. At the sidewalk she headed north to her apartment, where she had a pair of running shoes. She was going to need a handle on the situation, on her feelings, before she could begin to explain to Adam. Looping the gravel path from the Capitol to the Lincoln Memorial twice still wasn't enough.

I'm so fucked, she thought, sweat soaked her entire body. Her phone was to her ear as she slowed to a walk.

"Sweetheart," Adam greeted.

"We need to talk. Meet me at the apartment?"

"I'm leaving now."

Ben had upgraded his beverage to actual alcohol and the three of them watched the five-minute live feed in breathless silence. Boots on the ground, rifles, breaking down doors – all through the unearthly quality of infrared. Melanie sat glued. Seemingly surreal as three of the five were shot and killed on the spot. The other two were taken into custody – the event playing out in real time. At the end, the screen went black. It was over.

Melanie sat, numb. Not knowing how to feel or what to think.

Ben shut down the monitor. "Hugh's plane should be landing any minute."

"He's officially a hero." Melanie drained her glass, wincing before painfully swallowing. Adam had remained mute, his gaze set to some distant land while his jaw worked under clenched teeth. His features had turned to stone.

"In ten minutes the president will speak," Ben explained. "Hugh will be at the press conference. Possibly even at the podium."

"I've got to go..." Adam stood.

"Wait." Her hand reached for his forearm. "You can't." She felt alone.

"I should've killed him when I had the chance." He grabbed her shoulders, lifting her to her feet. "I am so sorry. Forgive me." He pulled her into a tight squeeze and quickly let her go.

"Adam," she floundered.

"I'm going to make things right."

"There'll be press, cameras."

"It doesn't matter."

"It does to me. You can't," she said with the last breath in her lungs, feeling hopeless. "Ben," she started and looked around. He was gone. They both were.

CHAPTER 54

"My fellow Americans, today we witnessed great acts of heroism..." The president gave his address from the Briefing Room, his hands gripping the sides of the podium as he stood within the frame of American flags. "But not all of our heroes were wearing uniforms." He opened his right arm and motioned for someone to approach. "None of this could've been accomplished without the leadership and diplomacy of my very good friend, Senator Hugh Parker."

The president began clapping as Parker stepped into view of the cameras, smiling, giving two thumbs up and smacking his palms together before leaning into a presidential embrace. He looked healthier than he had in the drab kitchen in Rome. His suit was tailored and his hair was styled. It even looked as if he were sporting a tan.

"Thank you, Mr. President," he began, taking over the microphone. "The president and I have been working nonstop for months. I am very proud of our feat and the bravery and skill of our SEALs. Today the world has become a safer place. Thank you, Mr. President for allowing me to be apart of this historic moment."

The clapping resumed. Another embrace and the president regained his position at the podium. "I want to applaud Senator Parker, a true American, for his willingness to go so far as to sacrifice his good name for the benefit of this great nation, for our people." He stopped, raising his hands. "Actually, for the benefit of the world's people. Bringing down terrorist in a manor that was above and beyond the call of duty," the president continued his praise using words of bravery, selflessness and courage.

"I. Cannot. Listen. To. Another. Word." Her body trembled with each lie.

Ben broke the connection. "Let him be, Ward. He doesn't know where you are or about the resurgence of the Agency. I'd like to keep it that way."

"How long do you think that will last? He's a genuine hero and the White House is in his debt."

Shifting in his seat, his eyes zeroed on hers, "I'm doing my best."

"I know and so am I," she said, thinking about Adam – he hadn't waited for the press conference – and wondering about that mile target he touted.

"Do I need to worry about Adam?"

"He's going to do what he's going to do."

"Profound."

"This job can turn even the most cynical into a prophet. Thanks for the refreshments but I've got to go." Her inadvertent smile was helped along by the scotch.

She waited up for Adam. The door clicked lightly after four am. "You okay?" she asked.

"I didn't mean to wake you."

"You didn't. Where were you?" she asked, sitting up.

He rested on the edge of the bed, slipping out of his shoes.

"I was watching Parker through a scope." The squeak of dread was 100 percent internal. "I wanted to, but…" He twisted to face her. "I kept thinking about us and at times that brought me closer to pulling the trigger but…" He sighed, his body slumping. "I want you to be proud of me. I want to do the right thing. I'm just not sure what that is anymore."

She scooted closer and wrapped her arms around him.

"He was in my sights and I *really* wanted to." He exhaled with the unfulfilled desire.

She didn't know if she was disappointed or not. "I'm always proud of you. You're in me and I'm in you, remember? Transcending time and space."

He smiled. "God what was I before you? And what would I be without you?" His eyes liquefied as he leaned into her embrace.

For two days, Melanie kept her head down, worked assignments, got in close with the returning agents and made it home each night for dinner. Adam spent his days at The Place with Gordy. The strain had wormed its way between them. She actively tried to put the Hugh Parker parade behind her, but from her peripheral she stayed updated. She couldn't help it, he was everywhere.

"I'll be home in an hour or two," Adam said over the phone.

"The furniture was delivered." She tried, lightening the mood, to reach him but he was far away – distant and unreachable. After unpacking the bulk of the delivery, she removed the plastic from the couch and kicked back with a beer.

"Look at this," Adam said, dropping down next to her and tugging the bottle from her hand. He rotated his arm, swinging it over her shoulders. "What do you think?"

"I like it." She leaned in. "I'm leaving tomorrow ... Trish and my mom ... wedding plans."

"I was planning on going with you." He bent to kiss the side of her head.

"I'd like that." The silence between them encased her soul and finally she'd had enough. "Are we okay?"

"We're survivors. Of course we're okay." He reached behind him, "look what I found." From a bag he removed his Christmas mugs and smiled. "My favorite gift, ever." He pulled her to his lap. "We're in love, we're healthy and I think I smell the hint of vanilla wax coming from upstairs."

She smiled. "I lit some candles, attempting sexy but it didn't take."

He kissed the crook of her neck. "Very sexy." His lips ran beneath the button of her blouse. "What's this?" he asked, hooking his finger on the collar and taking a look. "You went shopping."

His fingers knew their way around a button; she was undressed before her lungs filled with the scented atmosphere. Her back on the soft custard colored material.

"I need you to forgive me for not killing Hugh when I had the chance."

"I forgive you."

CHAPTER 55

Three weeks until the wedding, Melanie thought as she handed over her credit card. "The dress is perfect, isn't it?" she asked her mom.

"Totally not sexy enough," Trish said, sticking her head between Melanie and Rita. "I liked the off-the-shoulder one."

"Don't listen to her." Rita's lips had lost their color and Melanie knew her mom was worn to her last nerve with Trish. "It was like that gown was made for you."

"Thank you both." Melanie smiled nervously. "I could never have gotten this done without your help." The three of them had been to High Street twice in the two days. They'd finalized plans for the flowers, photographers and now the dresses could be checked off the list. Carla's husband Ted had asked a retired judge to officiate, and now it was almost time to catch a flight.

"The only thing we have left is the band." Trish said.

"I thought they had a house band."

"Three old men with banjos and pie tins isn't a band, Mel." Trish huffed as they headed to the car.

"They aren't quite that bad and what about the seating chart?" Rita added.

"I don't care where people sit," Melanie answered.

"It's such a great help that Adam is taking care of the caterers and the cake. He's the sweetest and so handsome."

"He and Jace are getting fitted for their tuxes as we speak," Trish grinned. "We should go and see what they pick. You never know with Jace … he wanted blue for our wedding. Do you remember? Men."

"I also don't care what he wears." Melanie breathed in the California sunshine and was glad to be worried about something other than Hugh Parker. "This wedding is just what I need."

"And it's been fun, shopping with your money." Trish giggled.

CHAPTER 56

D.C. was exactly the same as she left it. Melanie had hoped that her few days of West Coast isolation would have been enough time to extinguish the name Hugh Parker from every media outlet. But it seemed as if the buzz had heightened.

Hugh had returned to his mansion to bask in his celebrity status. He was interviewed by every network and cable station and highlighted on every show from morning to late night.

Mike was relying on technology to keep her safe, monitoring Hugh's calls, texts and emails; Using voice recognition and the government data center. While Melanie focused, doubled down, sharpening her GPS skills until she was ready for more advanced hacker techniques. She practiced, learned to follow patterns to jump from public and private cameras, other cell phones, computers – any device with an Internet connection.

"I was just thinking about you," she said answering the phone and jumping to test her ability and pinpoint Adam's location.

"I got a call…" He was speaking as she typed, narrowing down his whereabouts.

"I'm sorry," she said, suddenly at attention, "what did you say?"

"Marie called. She needs help..."

"In Rome?"

"No, she's in D.C. I'm on my way to her new place now."

"Wait," Melanie said, louder than intended. The snake of fear that usually remained coiled in the pit of her stomach sprung to life. Adam was in the Dupont Park area, three miles south. Her mind scrambled as the image zoomed and she switched to a camera on the corner of an apartment complex.

He was easy to spot, tall and strong and looking fit in the jeans she'd watched him put on that morning. The collar of canvas jacket he'd been wearing was turned-up, brushing his nape and his dark hair was covered by the Washington Nationals cap. He'd been sporting it since Hugh's return, in an effort to be inconspicuous. She'd told him he was too handsome for that.

"What did she say?" Melanie asked, watching him as he stopped walking.

"Not much. She was back in town and needed help securing an apartment ... Something about the landlord being a pervert and she wanted me to be there to give the impression that she wasn't alone."

"Why does she want to rent from a pervert? And she doesn't have any other friends?"

"I didn't ask," he said, shaking his head and she watched as he turned. "I didn't think, I'm sorry. I'll call her back, tell her to find someone else. You're right. I don't know why I feel obligated to help her..."

"I know I'm jealous and that's not fair," she said, "but for now I'd rather she not be in you life. Maybe later ... like in a century or two, but I feel …" She didn't know how to finish.

"I completely understand and you're right. I feel the same way." He took over, the camera capturing his smile.

She smiled. "Make your call and we'll meet for lunch?"

"Deal. I love you, Melanie."

"I love you, too."

His smile deepened and she watched as he ended the call with her to dial Marie. Adam was standing on the outskirts of the camera range. Melanie tore her eyes off him for a second to question the black utility van slowing at the curb. Switching viewpoints, the van was suddenly there, beside him, pulling a hard stop. As the side door flew open Melanie yelled … "No!" it was four men who jumped him, grabbing Adam to jab a needle into his neck. Each man took a limb and together they tossed him into the cargo space of the van.

Less than three seconds and the sidewalk that he had just occupied was vacant. Melanie caught the license plate as the van sped away … jotting it down, she was out the door.

"Mike!" she sprinted, "I need this plate found. Now! And…" Her mind sifted through the memory. *Had he dropped his phone?* She didn't know. "Black van, last seen on the corner of Minnesota and Nelson."

"Where are you going?"

She heard the tail end of his question as she flew down the stairs. The company cars were kept in a separate underground section of the parking lot. She ripped a set of keys from the wall, unlocked and started the engine from the fob and was shifting to drive before the door was slammed.

Through red lights she headed south. "Give me a direction."

"They're going south on the 295," Mike said.

She was watching the streets, thinking about a route. "Where are they headed?" Her foot was solid on the gas as she sped onto the 695.

"I don't know, Mel. There's nothing."

"Does Parker own any land, house … anything?"

"Jesus, you're going over 90."

"Stop tracking me. Keep to the van!"

"They're getting off. South Capitol Street. Shit."

"What?" She read the sign – 2.8 miles from that exit.

"They're going to the base."

"I need access," she said. What, why would they take Adam on base? And then the realization hit … planes. *Oh my God*. "Mike, I need to get on that base." Her voice was steady and firm.

"I…" He stumbled. "I don't … give me a second. I'll call you back."

Melanie let the call end. Two minutes she was stopped at the point of entry … "Melanie Ward," she told the guard at the gate.

"You have to sign in," he was instructing.

"It's an emergency."

"I'm sorry, Ma'am." As he spoke a cargo plane lifted off.

Christ. "Never mind." Melanie backed out, tires squealing as she drove the wrong way down a street. "Judith," she called, "I need the jet prepped. Now. Please."

Swallowing down the sickness, she let the calm of a case seep into her system. By the time she met the pilot on the tarmac, an otherworldly tranquility had taken over.

"Where are we headed?"

"Frankfurt. We're on a deadline." She buckled in.

"Yes."

The flight was long. She called every number listed in the Berlin office but all the Agency agents were scattered. She held her fists tight as she imagined how the rest of the day was going to play out.

A helicopter was waiting at the airport. The pilot had been given the coordinates to the bio lab. He landed on the wide stretch of lawn and Melanie gave him orders to meet her on the roof and raced, barging into the lobby, past the security guard. Their yells fading with the distance she was putting between them and finally silence as the doors closed, silence except for her hammering heartbeat that was echoing off the walls of the stairway.

She took the stairs at blinding speed. Her shoulder throbbed where she rammed it against the door to the fourth floor – into a room where she was afraid to go.

She barged past anyone in her way, pushing past animal test subjects, the specimens laid out across the tables sliced open and pulled apart.

"You can't be here," Dr. Oh said, her face contorted as her fingers tried to grab onto Melanie's sleeve.

Melanie snatched the woman's hand and yanked Dr. Oh to the security box. "Put your code in. Now!"

"No. You..." her face met the door.

"Now." Melanie said not caring about the bloodied nose.

"You're not rational." The blood stained the doctor's white coat, she swiped at the liquid flowing over her mouth before pressing her code leaving bloody fingerprints on the five, the six and the seven. "There." She stepped away.

The moan from Melanie's heart spread to her every fiber robbing the energy from her body. Adam was stretched out, like all the other specimens, on the sterile slab. His eyes were closed and his body was bare. It was the anger that kept her moving, grabbing Dr. Oh.

"Fix. Him."

"I, I don't know if I can," she said, wiping blood from her lip onto the lapel of her white coat.

"What did you do to him?" Melanie asked, moving closer and dragging the doctor along with her. She let go of her grasp to walk the circumference of the table. The blue cloth was draped over his groin. "Please," she begged, looking down into the eyes of the woman on the other side of Adam.

The list of chemicals that the woman rattled off sounded like one incredibly long word without any meaning.

"Stop talking and start working. Bring him back!" She said, wiping off the moisture from her cheek her head felt hot, her body burned and ... she wanted to touch but the fear was debilitating. Her hand hovered over his skin, terrified that he'd be cold. "Adam," she panted, leaning close to his face, "I'm here." Her hand trembled as she placed it on his forehead. Warm! *Oh, thank God*. "Dr. Oh." She looked up as her eyes pooled with tears. "Please. You know this isn't right. You're a scientist wanting to beat death and this is pure, evil. You'll kill him. The exact thing you're working against." Melanie stopped not sure if her rattling had made any impact or any sense. She swallowed, pleading. "This is wrong."

"Okay," the woman rubbed her palms together and checked his vitals while Melanie prayed.

Prayers she'd thought she'd long forgotten rose to her tongue. The doctor collected cylinders filled with liquids, syringes, placing each item on a wheeled tray. Melanie's hand rested on Adam's shoulder as the syringes were filled, she held her breath as the fluids were injected into his arm.

"Will this work?" Her brain had stopped and no information was penetrating.

"I don't know. We wait and see." She pressed an oxygen mask over his face.

"Wake up," she said, panicked. "Adam. It's me, Melanie. Please." How many times had she begged in the last twenty seconds? Begged Dr. Oh, begged God, begged the Universe, begged Adam.

From his lifeless form his hand twitched. She looked to the woman for answers.

"It's a good sign."

"Thank you," she repeated. "Adam."

"Give him a moment," she told Melanie, removing the oxygen as Adam lifted his left arm to swipe at the mask. "Let him breathe."

Melanie groaned in pain, agonizing pain as her wish was being fulfilled. Prayers answered. Her cries were moans as she waited.

"I'm here, Adam. I'm here." She pressed her hands to each side of his face. His coughs were shallow and Melanie put her arm around him, helping him sit upright. "You're okay."

He strained to pull in a breath.

"He should lay down," Dr. Oh suggested. "You should lay down," She said to Adam, her hand on his shoulder.

In the distance, Melanie heard the rumbling of chaos that was getting closer.

"Adam." She tried to sound calm. "We have to go. Can you get to your feet?" His eyes were incoherent, foggy as he looked beyond her into the room. "Sweetheart, we have to go," she said, placing her face directly in his line of sight. His expression was confusion and the creases between his brows pinched tighter as he looked at her blankly. "Adam," she whispered, trying to understand. It was then, the jubilation of his recovery, seconds in the past, that she realized something was desperately wrong. *Keep calm,* she commanded while her body was reacting outside of those parameters. "Adam," she tried again. "It's me."

His murky green eyes were empty as they scanned his surroundings. "Where am I?"

"Baby, we're in Germany." Her chest hammered and palpitated in short pants, "But we, sweetheart, we have to go. People are coming."

"Okay." He took deliberate moves getting off the metal slab. She was there helping him to his feet when he looked directly into her eyes. "Who are you?"

Agent Ward returns in Book 6

ACKNOWLEDGEMENTS

I'd like to thank, first and foremost, Brent. None of this would be possible without his help and support.

Sydney and Samantha are the absolute best teenagers I have ever met.

Frank and Laura, the givers of life. Frank. Ralph. Steve. Because hours of home movies prove that I was born an incredibly fortunate child.

The family I am privileged to spend the most important days of the year with:

Linda. Amy, Jack, Kelly, Ryan, Eric, David & Nick.

Jill Jordan-Spitz, thank you for your insight and always making me push harder and do better.

Joyce Mathis, Jessie Montano, Sharon Schaum, Steve Rosenberg

Your continued support and your kind and generous spirits have been influential and thank you for all that you do.

A special and heartfelt thank you to the readers. Without whom I would be alone in my world. Melanie and Adam, Trish and Jace all appreciate your involvement in their lives.

Your kind words are incredibly motivating. (While Special K, at this moment, is hacking into your email.)

A big thank you to friends I've made because of these books: Lynn, Angie, Mike, Paula, Beckie, Elsa, Dale, Julie, Marissa and Dana – thank you for including me in your daily lives.

And to Carolyn who was a friend long before Melanie. To Bonnie Lewis.

Libby, Jack, Luxa and Tori – you are always happy and harmonize in ways that only you can.

In Loving Memory

Ronald Gallardo

Rudolph Vasquez

Richard Vasquez

Fernando Gallardo Jr.

Kate Mathis

Kate's lively personality shows up in all her books. She enjoys all types of genres, which is evident in the Agent Ward Novels. A Mashup of Action, Adventure, Comedy, Romance and Suspense.

On the Urban Fantasy/Young Adult side, Kate has created another world in *Moon Over Monsters*. "I wanted to write a young adult, something that my twin daughters would enjoy. I think it's important to have good strong female characters."

She graduated from the University of Arizona and lives in Tucson, Arizona with her husband, twin daughters, 3 dogs and all her fictional characters.

Kate Mathis on Facebook
http://www.facebook.com/pages/Living-Lies/228205853872791

Kate Mathis Website
http://www.KateMathis.net